CHASING RIVER

ALSO BY K.A. TUCKER

Ten Tiny Breaths
In Her Wake
One Tiny Lie
Four Seconds to Lose
Five Ways to Fall
Burying Water
Becoming Rain

CHASING RIVER

A Novel

K.A. TUCKER

ATRIA PAPERBACK
NEW YORK LONDON TORONTO SYDNEY NEW DELHI

ATRIA PAPERBACK
An Imprint of Simon & Schuster, Inc.
1230 Avenue of the Americas
New York, NY 10020

This book is a work of fiction. Any references to historical events, real people, or real places are used fictitiously. Other names, characters, places, and events are products of the author's imagination, and any resemblance to actual events or places or persons, living or dead, is entirely coincidental.

First Atria Paperback edition July 2015

ATRIA PAPERBACK and colophon are trademarks of Simon & Schuster, Inc.

For information about special discounts for bulk purchases, please contact Simon & Schuster Special Sales at 1-866-506-1949 or business@simonandschuster.com.

The Simon & Schuster Speakers Bureau can bring authors to your live event. For more information or to book an event, contact the Simon & Schuster Speakers Bureau at 1-866-248-3049 or visit our website at www.simonspeakers.com.

Cover design by Anna Dorfman
Cover photograph © Simon Becchetti/Stocksy

Manufactured in the United States of America

10 9 8 7 6 5 4 3 2

Library of Congress Cataloging-in-Publication Data
Tucker, K. A. (Kathleen A.).
Chasing River : a novel / K.A. Tucker.— First Atria paperback edition.
pages ; cm
I. Title.
PR9199.4.T834C48 2015
813'.6—dc23

2015012106

ISBN 978-1-4767-7423-7
ISBN 978-1-4767-7424-4 (ebook)

To Lia and Sadie, and the adventures that await you.

AUTHOR'S NOTE

Ireland's history is fraught with civil unrest, the desire to protect religious identity and gain political independence stretching back to the seventeenth century, when periods of war against English and Scottish settlers decimated as much as half of the Irish population.

The sectarian division between the Irish Catholic and the English Protestant population deepened greatly during that time, as the British began imposing a series of penal laws intended to punish the Irish for supporting the Catholic Stuart king, James II, who had attempted to take the throne from the Protestant king William of Orange, and lost. The vast majority of Ireland was Catholic; these laws stripped Irish Catholics of their civil rights, including the right to own property, attend school, and practice their religion. By 1778, Protestants owned 95 percent of Ireland's land.

Despite rebellion, in 1800, the British and Irish parliaments passed Acts of Union that merged the Kingdom of Great Britain and the Kingdom of Ireland to form a United Kingdom of Great Britain and Ireland. The economies of Great Britain and the northeast of Ireland grew rapidly through industrialization for much of the nineteenth century, while the rest of Ireland did not. With the population relying heavily on one commodity—potatoes—to survive, a devastating potato blight in the 1840s saw the collapse of much of Ireland. A million lives were lost to starvation and disease, and another million people emigrated. But it was Great Britain's inaction (the adoption of a laissez-faire strategy, valuing market over lives) that exacerbated an already volatile relationship.

The second half of the nineteenth century and into the early twentieth century saw several failed rebellions as the Irish continued their fight to be free of England's grip. On Easter Monday of 1916, two thousand Irish Volunteers staged a rebellion in Dublin, proclaiming Ireland a republic. The rebellion lasted a week. Eventually, the Volunteers were forced to surrender. Their subsequent executions only fueled Irish support for independence.

In the 1918 election, the majority of Irish seats in the British Parliament were won by members of Sinn Féin, the Irish revolutionary party. Refusing to sit in England, these members established their own parliament in Dublin and ratified the Easter Uprising's proclamation that Ireland be a republic. Violence between the British army and the Irish Republican Army (IRA, founded by Michael Collins) erupted. This became known as "Bloody Sunday."

The IRA waged guerilla warfare against the British for months, until a truce was called in 1921. The British and Irish parliaments signed a treaty, identifying twenty-six counties in the south and west of Ireland as the Irish Free State, a member of the British Commonwealth of Nations.

There was a divide in support of this treaty, though, with many IRA members demanding full independence from British rule. The IRA split, and civil war erupted between the two sides.

The violence continued off-and-on until 1937 when, under Éamon de Valera's leadership, the Free State was abolished, a second constitution was enacted, and Ireland formed its own government. The Republic of Ireland was declared in 1949 and all ties to the British Crown were severed.

However, Britain maintained rule over six counties in Northern Ireland, a reality that left republican supporters unsatisfied. The years between 1969 and 1998 are known as The Troubles, when frequent and bloody violence between the newly formed Provisional IRA (PIRA), British loyalist paramilitary groups, and British state security forces (the army and the police force) left thousands dead, including many innocent civilians.

In 1997, the PIRA declared a ceasefire. In 1998, the Good Friday Agreement was voted in by the people of Northern Ireland, instituting various political agreements. The PIRA supported the Good Friday Agreement.

Several dissident republican groups formed after the 1997 ceasefire, all calling themselves IRA. One of these groups, the largest and most active, is known as the Real IRA (RIRA). It mainly targets British security forces, with the aim to cause economic harm. It is responsible for many attacks against the Police Service of Northern Ireland (PSNI) involving bombs, guns, and grenades.

The Republic of Ireland has cited all IRA groups as illegal organizations. The United Kingdom and the United States have long since considered the IRA a terrorist organization. The vast majority of Ireland's citizens do not support today's IRA in its objectives.

The IRA has also been implicated in vigilante acts of justice against organized crime and drug dealers, using extortion and violence to spark feuds that have escalated into assassinations. This is especially the case in Dublin. Many consider this particular IRA organization nothing more than another violent gang.

A river may be diverted, its waters pooled,
its natural course interrupted.

But its current will only ever truly flow one way.

ONE

RIVER

I weave around men and women alike with barely a pardon, struggling not to lose Aengus, nor to let on that I'm tailing him. The slick guy has done his part to make that tricky, his flinty gaze darting side-to-side as he briskly navigates the morning swell of pedestrians. Dressed in tan trousers and a plain white collared shirt, the beige tweed driver's cap tipped low to help hide his face, he could pass for an office clerk or a salesman. Maybe a manager at one of the upscale Grafton Street stores. Someone responsible. Someone respectable.

Someone that he's not.

It's not even so much *him* that is making me suspicious. It's that black leather satchel. The one he holds close to his body as if to protect it from being stolen or knocked by a passerby rushing to catch a bus or a streetlight.

It's the sweat seeping through the back of his shirt, when the air this early June morning is crisp.

It's the way he's checked his watch three times in the span of twenty meters.

My gut churns with explanations, all of them bad.

Nothing good has come from Aengus since Portlaoise Prison spat him out four months ago. Six years inside Dublin's maximum security walls have only fortified his connections, poisoned his convictions. Blackened his soul. They took in an ideological twenty-two-year-old Irish Republican and spat out an inspired criminal.

And here I am, thirty steps back, tracking him through the gates of St. Stephen's Green just moments after security opened passage for the day, as if it were all perfectly timed.

Because, after all, he *is* still my brother.

I glance at my own watch. It's seven thirty a.m. While they tend to open the Green earlier during summer months, this seems too early. And Aengus's single nod toward the guard seems unusually familiar.

I haven't been inside Dublin's prime inner-city park in years. It hasn't changed much. It's still a vast expanse of winding paths and gardens—an escape nestled within a bustling city. Right now it's serene, still waking after a night alone, free of visitors, the air misted, the pale yellow sun not yet high enough to warm the grounds. This quiet won't last long, though.

Aengus glances over his shoulder and I dart behind the nearest bush. If he senses a shadow, he doesn't let on, veering right at a fork ahead and disappearing around the bend. I follow cautiously, until he turns off the path and begins trudging through the open field. In a few hours, this place will be crawling with office workers and other Dubliners, lounging in the sun or reading beneath a canopy of leaves. Anything to escape their dreary day jobs and enjoy the fresh air.

Aengus checks his watch yet again as he marches briskly and purposefully toward an oak that's cordoned off by a stream of blue-and-white tape, as if there's a threat of the tree collapsing. Only, I notice that the perimeter reaches far past its widest branches, taking over half of the green space. Making me think that the tape has nothing to do with a hazardous tree at all.

"What the hell are you about, Aengus . . ." I mutter, touching my jaw where his knuckles landed last night, after he threw open his bedroom door and caught me eavesdropping on his phone call. I heard only bits and pieces of it—I couldn't form even a murky guess as to the gist—but it was enough to make him throw a punch first and ask questions later.

When I shoved him into the wall—because violence is how we seem to communicate best—and reminded him that he just got out of prison, the only explanation he volunteered was that a warning needs to be delivered, no one will get hurt, and I need to keep my fucking mouth shut.

Another time check. Aengus crouches down and unzips the satchel.

I'm too engrossed in what he's doing now to be on guard, so when his head suddenly snaps up, I can't move fast enough. Hard eyes lock on me in an instant, freezing me where I stand.

It's a showdown.

I shake my head, willing him to hear my thoughts. *Walk away, big brother. Don't do whatever it is you're about to do.*

His hand stalls inside the bag. For just a moment, I believe that he's heard me. That he's finally listening. That my presence here has derailed him from shortening that length of rope he seems so eager to slip around his own neck.

Foolish of me, really. Aengus has never been malleable to reason.

I inhale sharply, the air hissing through my gritted teeth. I watch him lay the long cylindrical tube down in the grass with careful movements and dread washes over me.

Jesus, Aengus. You've gone too far this time.

Hopping to his feet, he snatches up the satchel and charges toward me, his cell phone in his palm, his head revolving as he scans the emptiness around us. I square my shoulders and brace myself for a collision with his temper, as swift and nasty as a black adder's bite.

"Are you insane?" I bark when he's within easy earshot.

The glint in his eyes—the color of an overripe avocado, beginning to rot—would suggest exactly that.

"You said no one would get hurt."

"Do you see anyone around to get hurt?" he snarls, continuing past me, punching keys into his phone. "You've got exactly sixty seconds to get the fuck out of here, River." He takes off at a light jog, not waiting to see if I'll follow.

Because I always have.

Oh, fuck me. A current of adrenaline shoots through my core. I glance down at my watch. One minute. Less, now. Fifty-five seconds, give or take. The muscles in my thighs twitch, ready to tear after Aengus because there's nothing else for me to do. But a lot can happen in just sixty seconds. My conscience keeps me grounded, my wild eyes scouring the paths around me for signs of life. A jogger bobs along in the distance, so far away that I can't be sure whether it's male or female. Otherwise, I see no one.

I glance at my watch again, my heartbeat doing double time with each second that passes. Only forty-five remain before I look damn guilty to whoever finds me here. Unless I rat out Aengus—which will never happen—I'm as good as locked up for this.

I need to run.

Except . . . that perimeter set isn't wide enough. If someone should come around the bend, cut across the field . . . But what can I do, really?

Thirty seconds. Beads of sweat trickle down my back. I need to get the hell out of here. Now.

I turn, intent on going back the way I came. But movement catches my eye and my stomach drops as I watch the very thing I just feared unravel before my eyes. A girl runs through the field, her attention alternating between her wrist and the unfolded map within her grip, her brow pulled tight with worry.

She's clearly a tourist.

She's clearly late for something.

And she's heading directly into the blast radius of the pipe bomb that's about to explode.

I'm out of time. I don't have a choice.

I run. As fast as my legs can carry me, I run.

TWO

AMBER

The Fusiliers' Arch is this way . . . I think.

I've always seen myself as someone with a keen sense of direction. But then I embarked on this grand adventure to find myself and, well—I've found myself, alright. Twisted and upside down and heading blocks in the wrong direction enough times to accept that I actually suck at reading maps. If not for the tiny charm on my bracelet that doubles as a handy compass—a gift from the sheriff, ever worried for his twenty-five-year-old daughter's safety—I wouldn't know which way was north half the time.

I doubt that even the compass can help me now. The tour company brochure states a seven thirty-five sharp departure and it's now . . . I glance at my watch and my anxiety spikes. Seven thirty-three. Stupid me for booking a day trip the morning after I arrive in Ireland. Just twenty-four hours ago I was plane-hopping from Charlottetown to Toronto to Amsterdam to Dublin, going back in time one hour before jumping ahead five. Instead of sleeping, I spent the overnight flight feeding my addiction to *Mad Men*. By the time I stepped off the plane at three in the afternoon, I was exhausted.

Of course I figured that two years of flip-flopping between night and day shifts at the hospital would make adjusting to the time change easy for me.

Of course my alarm rang for exactly thirty-two minutes this morning before my brain actually registered the sound.

And now I'm going to miss the freaking tour.

Cutting through this park is supposed to save me a few minutes of travel time. That was one of the few pieces of wisdom my taxi driver from the airport imparted to me yesterday. But he didn't tell me which paved path, of the countless ones that snake among gardens and forested areas, to take. So in complete desperation, I choose an unconventional diagonal route, rushing past an English garden ripe with colorful summer blooms to run across a grassy field. The morning air is crisp, leaving my legs—bare, thanks to the jean shorts I threw on in my rush, not thinking—touched by gooseflesh, even as sweat trickles down my back. It'll be okay later, I remind myself. They're calling for a high of 74 degrees Fahrenheit today. Well, technically, 23 degrees Celsius. Even after traveling across Canada for three and a half weeks, I still can't seem to grasp the metric system.

Seven thirty-four. "Crap!" I scan the city map held out in my hands as I run. So distracted that I don't notice a section of the field ahead taped off until I'm almost tearing through it. There are no construction signs or pieces of equipment lying around. Probably just freshly planted grass seed or something. Whatever the reason, it's smack dab in the middle of my path and I'll lose time trying to avoid it. Time I don't have. Beyond the field, another path winds its way to a fountain and benches and more paths. A round glass dome peeks out over the tree line farther ahead. That's the shopping center I've read about. And to the right of that is where my bus will be waiting.

Or not, if I don't hurry up.

I jump over the tape with a grimace and a silent apology. I check my watch again. Maybe it's a few minutes fast. Maybe the tour bus driver isn't really a stickler for a prompt departure. Maybe—

He comes out of nowhere, from the left.

My only warning is the sound of his feet pounding against the grass. I turn my head just as he plows into my side, sending me sailing through the air. Pain explodes in a dozen different body parts as I hit the hard ground, my lungs grappling for oxygen.

He's on top of me in an instant, crushing me under his weight, his thick arms roping around either side of my head, smothering me. I can't breathe, or scream, let alone fight him off right now.

I manage just one fleeting thought—that this man, with his forehead pressed against mine and his ragged breaths assaulting my face—is about to rape me in broad daylight in a city park.

And then I'm plunged into a strange void that devours all my pain and fear.

A wave of pressure races past a split second before all of my senses are swallowed by a deafening bang that rattles my brain and the ground beneath me. Then . . . nothing at all. Only eerie silence and air.

I know that time has passed, but I can't say whether it's been a split second or ten minutes or an hour when I realize I'm lying on my back, staring up at a plume of white smoke, the familiar sweet metallic scent of expended gunpowder permeating my nostrils, my head stuffed with cotton. That eerie silence has given way to a high-pitched ringing and I cringe as it echoes in my eardrum. Maybe I cry out, too. If I do, I can't hear it. I'm struggling to string together enough thoughts to understand what the hell just happened.

"Are you okay?" The question floats in from somewhere distant. And then suddenly a man hovers over me, a fringe of coppery hair like an untidy halo framing his face, staring down at me through mossy green eyes.

"What happened?" I manage to ask, though my voice sounds far away. At least I'm no longer winded.

"An explosion. A bomb."

A bomb? A chill runs through my limbs as my brain wraps around that word, delivered in a light Irish brogue.

I sense hands slide along my thighs, over my knees, curling to the undersides, but I don't think to deflect them. "You'll be fine," he mutters, a sigh of relief sailing from his lips. He shifts on his knees, making to stand.

And I seize his forearm, surprising myself with a sudden wave of strength as I hold him down. "Stay."

His muscles tense beneath my fingertips. "I can't. But please know that I didn't do this." Honest, pleading eyes implore me silently for a few heartbeats, and then he's gone, running—albeit staggered and off-balance—before I can ask more questions. I roll my head to the side and watch him disappear into a line of trees, a dark stain blooming in the material of his vibrant green T-shirt.

Moments later, a jogger reaches me in a pant, a cell phone pressed against her ear and a panicked look on her face. Shouts sound from somewhere in the park and a chorus of sirens scream in the distance. Another jogger arrives some thirty seconds later. Next a security guard, and then a couple dressed in suits, on their way to work. Within minutes I'm encircled by people.

Despite everyone's insistence that I stay lying down, I manage to sit up. Everything is spinning. The granola bar and orange juice that I stuffed into my mouth on my way out the front door churn and I can't be sure I'll keep them down. But I force myself to focus on my surroundings—the charred grass, the divots gouged in the oak tree trunk nearby, the singed leaves dangling above, their ashes floating like sooty snowflakes.

It begins to sink in.

I could be dead right now.

Had it not been for that guy, I might have been. He wasn't trying to suffocate me. He was shielding me.

"You saved my life," I whisper under my breath, knowing that my words will never find his ear.

Cocooned within a haze, I watch emergency vehicles and the police and bomb squad charge in, herding the spectators away from the crime scene like cattle, their radios buzzing, their notebooks and pens out and ready. Reflective yellow letters that read "Garda" stretch across bulletproof vests everywhere.

Paramedics rush over to me. I'm fine, I tell them. In shock and my hearing is still muffled, but otherwise . . .

I can't believe I'm fine.

They help me onto a stretcher and wheel me over to the ambulance to examine me further. Again, I promise them that I know what I'm talking about. I'm a nurse, after all. The female paramedic nods and smiles, dabbing at my bottom lip with gauze. Only then do I see the blood, do I taste the copper.

I allow them to check my vitals as I watch the police dropping numbered markers all over the grass and beginning to question witnesses. I wonder how my dad would handle something like this. I'm pretty sure he's never dealt with a bombing in Deschutes County, Oregon.

"How is she?" someone asks, pulling my attention to the left, where two police officers stand, watching.

"Only the small laceration on her bottom lip from what we can see, and her vitals are fine. Though it'll take a while for the shock to wear off. She's had quite the scare." That assessment's delivered with a wink, and then she begins packing up her kit.

"She's awfully lucky . . ." To me, the tall, average-looking officer says, "I'm Detective Garda Garret Duffy. This is me partner, Detective Garda Paul O'Brien." The man next to him, a pudgy middle-aged officer with a shiny, bald head, offers a tight smile. "Can we ask ya some questions?"

Despite the situation, I smile. Duffy sounds exactly like the leprechaun in the Lucky Charms cereal commercial. "Sure. Okay."

"And would ya mind terribly if our colleagues examined your bag? This is yours, yeah?" He gestures at a man with white gloves hovering at the side.

I look down at the limp black knapsack that holds my umbrella, a couple of bottles of water, and a bag of grapes, no doubt a mess of pulp and juices now. I don't know why they'd want to, but . . . "Go ahead."

"Thank you," Duffy says, smiling kindly at me, his notepad already open in his hand and waiting to be filled. "Let's start with your name?"

"Amber Welles."

"And you're American, from the sounds of it?"

I nod but then answer, "Yes." My dad taught me to always answer verbally, to avoid misinterpretation.

"Do ya have identification?"

"My passport. It's in my backpack."

"Okay." He nods toward O'Brien. "We'll get that. What are ya doing here in Ireland?"

"Traveling."

"Are ya here alone?"

"Yes."

His forehead wrinkles in surprise. I get that reaction a lot. I guess I can understand it. It is a bit strange for a girl my age to be traveling alone. If he knew that I have thirteen other countries to visit after this, I'm sure he'd have a comment. "Do ya have friends or family, or acquaintances, in Ireland?"

"No."

"And how long have ya been in Dublin?"

"Just landed yesterday."

He scribbles his notes down quickly. "And what were ya doing in the Green this morning, so early?"

"I was late for my tour bus and I was running through here to try to make up some time." I guess it's safe to say that the bus has left without me.

"So . . . ya were running across the grass." His eyes and finger trail through the air, as if trying to get his bearings. "From which direction, exactly?"

I point across the way.

"Right. And then the bomb just exploded?" His impassive eyes remain glued to my face, waiting, as if readying my answer for a scale, to weigh its truth. Just like my dad's eyes weigh on a person whenever he's asking questions, whenever he's digging for information that he thinks the person may be hiding.

My heart pounds in my chest as I begin to see this for what it really is. You don't grow up with a father like Gabe Welles without learning what distrust feels like. And you don't grow up with a brother like Jesse Welles without learning what questioning a person who you think is guilty of something sounds like.

Twenty-five years in the Welles family has taught me the art of suspicion well.

I summon whatever calm I can muster and look at the blast site—cordoned off with a new, bigger square of blue-and-white tape—through new eyes. A marker sits where I was found. Another one indicates where I'm guessing the bomb went off. A man is measuring the distance between the two points. Another man photographs the oak's tree trunk, riddled with gashes, while his partner waits behind him, with plastic gloves and bags and tweezers to collect evidence.

I can see why the police might be suspicious. They're probably wondering how I could have been that close and not earned a single shrapnel wound, when that tree has been brutalized. But what do they seriously think happened . . . that *I* set the bomb and decided to play victim?

My stomach drops.

Maybe that's exactly what they're wondering. When I replay the detective's words about being awfully lucky from a moment ago inside my head, it doesn't sound as sincere anymore. I can't believe this. One day in Ireland and I'm being questioned by the police. This is something that happens to Jesse. Not to me.

"No. A man ran out of nowhere and knocked me down to the ground. *Then* the bomb exploded."

It's so slight that it's almost imperceptible, but Duffy's brow definitely jumps. "What did this man look like?"

"I don't . . ." I frown, trying to picture his face. "He was young . . . Irish . . . I don't know. He ran off right after."

"In which direction?"

I point toward the bushes where I last saw him.

"What else can ya tell us about him?" O'Brien asks. They both stare at me, waiting, their demeanor having softened somewhat now that I've given them reason to suspect that maybe I'm just an American tourist who was in the wrong place at the wrong time.

"I didn't get a good look at him. I was in shock." I'm still in shock.

"Anything at all. Was he tall, short? Twelve stone, fourteen stone . . ."

I frown.

Duffy smirks. "Ye Americans call it 'pounds.'"

"Oh." I shake my head. "I'm . . . not sure. A hundred and eighty pounds, maybe?"

"Think hard, Amber. We need to find him," he pushes. "You said he was Irish. How do ya know that? Did he speak to ya?"

"Yes. He said that he didn't do this," I whisper, hearing his voice as I repeat the words. Remembering that pleading look in his eyes.

Duffy and O'Brien share a glance.

"You think he set it, don't you?" I ask.

"Maybe," Duffy says.

I frown. "That doesn't make sense. Why would he jump in front of it to save me, then?"

O'Brien shrugs. "Change of heart? He saw a pretty bird and didn't want to be responsible for her death."

My cheeks heat with the unwanted compliment, although I really want to roll my eyes. Sometimes people with the best intentions say the most stupid things. I mean, does it all come down to looks? If I were ugly, would the guy have run the other way and let me blow to pieces?

Duffy must see my irritation. "He ran. Innocent people don't run."

My eyes drift to the spot in the trees where I saw him vanish, and I start to question myself. Am I a fool for believing him the second the words came out of his mouth? I didn't even question why he might say something like that. Maybe . . . he knew the bomb was there, lying in quiet wait in the grass. He knew exactly where it was and he must have known when it would go off, the way he ran at me. If he had nothing to do with it, how would he know those kinds of details?

Maybe a bomber's word isn't worth much when he's . . . a bomber.

But he saved my life. He put himself in harm's way to protect me. Maybe innocent people don't run, but bombers don't save lives.

I dismiss the detective's suspicion. After all, five minutes ago, he was ready to accuse me.

"What else did he say?" Duffy pushes.

"He asked if I was alright," I mumble. "And then he ran."

Duffy scribbles it down. "Good, Amber. What else? What about hair color? Eye color?"

"Green eyes." Rich, insistent green eyes. "And I think he was hurt." Because he put himself in harm's way . . . for me. Suddenly, I don't want to tell these two officers anything else. Not until I can wrap my head around this. "That's all I can remember. I'm sorry."

Duffy brings his radio to his mouth and begins spouting off a series of words and numbers that I can't identify beyond knowing it's police code. Buzzing fills the air and several uniforms scatter, directing each other with fingers and shouts. They'll be canvassing the park and the area beyond the walls.

I wonder if they'll find him.

"That's helpful, Amber. We'll check the hospitals." He pulls a business card out of his pocket and hands it to me. "Ya may remember more after a few hours or a few days. Give me a ring if ya do."

"They're going to be wanting to talk to ya." O'Brien nods toward something in the distance. I peek out around the back doors of the ambulance that shield me from prying eyes. News crews have begun to trickle in, their mammoth black cameras sweeping over the area. Fortunately they're held back by a wide perimeter of tape and I'm still hidden.

I can see the headline now: *American Girl Saved by Irish Good Samaritan, Who Then Runs.*

I'm guessing this would be a story that the media would love. It would probably go viral. It would certainly be my way of making sure my thank you reaches him.

But it would also reach my parents, and guarantee that my

dad's first trip out of America would be to Ireland, for the sole purpose of dragging his daughter back in handcuffs if need be, twenty-five years old or not.

I pull the rim of my pink baseball cap down. "Any chance we can avoid them? And keep my name and picture out of the media? My dad won't take this too well."

Duffy eyes the gathering crowd. "They are hounds, aren't they? Maybe we should give ya a lift somewhere."

"That'd be great. I'm staying at a house on Hatch Street, just off Leeson. It's a few blocks away."

"I know the street." He radios for a spare jacket, and I use it to shield my face and upper body as they usher me to their car.

THREE

RIVER

"What's the story, lad?" Eamon stands in his doorway, his robe tied tight around his scrawny waist, his thinning white hair standing on end. One long, shrewd look at me—my teeth gritted to hide the pain, a cold sweat coating my face—and he ushers me inside as quickly as his eighty-six-year-old bones can manage. "Didn't expect to see ya like this, River. Your brother, of course . . . but not you." His slippers scratch across the dated linoleum floor. I've been to Dr. Eamon O'Hare's semidetached house a handful of times in my twenty-four years. It has never changed. The same vinyl flowery tablecloth covers the kitchen table, the same braided rug—a worn shade of sky blue—protects feet from the cool living room floor. The lace curtains that I remember watching his wife—God rest her soul—stitch still hang over the windows, growing more gray and dusty as each year passes.

"What have you gotten yourself into?" He leads me into the dining room—a cramped room with no window, dwarfed by a sturdy wooden table and lit by a gaudy bell-shaped light from above.

"Aengus," is all I say. I don't need to explain any more. Eamon has known us since we were shitting diapers and sucking on our ma's teat. He knew my father when he was shitting diapers and sucking on *his* ma's teat. He's been a friend of the Delaney family for decades, fixing one generation or another up when going to the hospital isn't an option. He doesn't ask too many questions and he doesn't report anything.

"Let's have us a look, then."

With slow, pained movements, I peel off the forest-green football jersey. The few minutes of mass hysteria after the bombing allowed me the opportunity to swipe a hat and shirt from a street vendor just outside the walls of the Green. I used them to help cover my wounds and hide in plain sight.

The pub T-shirt I wear to work—the first thing I grabbed from the floor this morning, in a rush to follow Aengus—comes off next.

Eamon harrumphs.

"How bad is it?" Because it feels bloody awful and the shredded rag in my hand now doesn't look promising.

"Looks superficial, but you never know with these things."

"I was on the ground when it went off, if that helps any."

"It must have. I'd say you were very lucky, from what I've seen before. These two here," he taps two spots on my back, "are protruding slightly. I'll need to remove them. This one, though, I could leave in—"

"No, get it out." I don't want any pieces left in my body. The image of my father's friend Glenden pulling a chunk of metal out of his cheek at our kitchen sink, and the mess of dark lumps still waiting to work their way out, comes to mind. I was five, and the sight still haunts me to this day.

Eamon opens the china cabinet and pulls out his doctor's bag, which I doubt gets much use anymore. He's long since retired. Rifling through it with a low hum, he finally shakes his head. "Do you have anywhere to be today?"

"Just the pub."

"Best you call in sick. I don't see you being in any shape to work." He sets a bottle of cheap whiskey on the table. "I'm out of the good stuff."

No anesthetic. This is going to fucking hurt.

While Eamon heads to the kitchen, I pull out my phone to text Rowen.

I can't cover the bar today. It's because of Aengus . . .

I can't really explain any of this over the phone, but that should be enough for my little brother to understand that this is serious. Still, he's going to curse me. When he enrolled in summer classes, I promised that I'd cover the bar on Wednesdays and Thursdays for him.

Maybe he can get one of our part-time bartenders in.

I crack the lid on the bottle of whiskey and take a long swig, the liquor burning inside my stomach as I prepare myself mentally, relieved that I could come to Eamon. Walking into a hospital with shrapnel wounds on the day of a bombing wouldn't have been wise.

Within a few minutes I hear the whistle of his kettle singing. He returns with a bowl of steaming water, fresh rags, and a handful of surgical instruments swirling in a tall glass container filled with what I assume is antiseptic. Thick-lensed glasses rest on his nose now, and he's exchanged his morning robe for a coat that I'm sure was once pristinely white, but has seen its share of blood that no amount of bleach can completely erase.

"On your stomach," he instructs, patting the lacquered surface with one hand, while his other fusses with a desk lamp.

I take another swig and then comply, stretching out on the cool wood. It feels soothing against my bare chest.

He hands me a short wooden stick, marred by little divots. "I can't have my neighbors calling the gardai on me," he warns.

Fuck. I comply, biting down on it.

Eamon snaps a glove over his wrist.

■ ■ ■

I exhale slowly, watching the tendrils of smoke curl their way out the window and vanish into the night sky. The pack I opened earlier today lies empty on the table and I haven't taken a single puff, content to let the tobacco burn and the red embers glow and then fade into ash while I relish the calm before the coming storm.

Listening for the telltale jangle of keys at the door. Aengus didn't even come home last night, which was probably the first smart move he's made in all this, because I would have taken the agony from my day out on his jaw.

And he'd deserve it.

The front door to our house creaks open. Measured footfalls make their way down the hall, his boot scraping the worn wood floor on every fourth step.

"River . . . ya here?" Aengus's deep voice cuts through the peace. Though we grew up in the same household, in the same city, people have said his accent is thicker, the way Rowen and I speak more refined.

I could answer but I don't, don't get up to greet him. I just sit in my rickety kitchen chair, shrouded in darkness, stewing in rage. And I wonder what kind of "warning" could be worth walking four kilometers with a volatile explosive tucked under your arm. I know my brother's not suicidal, but that . . . only an idiot would do that.

I sense him standing at the kitchen threshold now, his eyes on my shirtless back, no doubt seeing the gauze patches covering the three shrapnel wounds. They weren't too bad, after all. Tiny slivers that cut into my skin, thin enough that Eamon was able to stitch me up. That didn't stop me from passing out from the pain as he dug into my flesh for that last one, though.

"Thought ya quit." A beam of light hits my face as Aengus pulls two cans of Smithwick's out of the fridge. He drops one in front of me, not saying a word about the five empty cans lined up at the table's edge. Normally he'd cuff me for touching his beer.

That's how I know he feels at least some remorse.

"I did." I take a single haul off the smoke burning between my fingers, exhale slowly, and then mash the rest of it into the heap of other butts. "Funny what almost getting blown up does to a person."

He drags out the chair across from me and sits down, straddling it. "Ya weren't supposed to be there."

I finally meet eyes with my brother for the first time since the Green yesterday morning. His face is rosy from drink and covered in strawberry scruff, the jeans and shirt that he traded his disguise for rumpled. He looks like he's been hiding at the bottom of a barrel for the past thirty-six hours.

"You made the front page." I toss the *Times* at him. The *Herald* and the *Mirror* share similar headlines. In fact, I'm guessing that the bombing in St. Stephen's Green made every front page from Cork to Belfast.

His eyes only flicker toward it. "Been in to work yet?"

I shake my head. "Rowen's covering." The youngest of the Delaney boys, and the one I can always count on, had to miss classes both yesterday and today to cover for me. He was mighty pissed yesterday, but after he found me belly-down in bed last night, moaning in pain, he played it off like it was no big deal. Who needs a college degree when you can watch Greta—the tall blonde from Germany that we just hired—bend over tables to hand out pints to customers, he had joked.

That's my younger brother. Day and night from the asshole sitting across from me.

"Did he mention anyone stopping by there?"

Aengus doesn't really mean just "anyone." "Not yet. But they will." Gardai always come sniffing around our pub when there's trouble. It just comes with the territory of being a Delaney.

Aengus nods slowly and then pulls a smoke from his own pack and lights up. The real estate agent who's trying to sell our house warned us about smoking inside, but right now I don't care. We already had to cancel one showing this morning because I wasn't about to leave my bed.

A long, uncomfortable silence settles over us, and it almost unnerves me more than what happened. Normally we collide and combust—yelling, punching, swearing at each other. This is different. This means he's gone too far and he knows it.

Finally he sighs, lifting his cap from his head to run his hand over his scalp. I'm still not used to seeing the copper-top mop gone. It was the trademark of the only Aengus I've ever known. You could see him from a city block away. I think that's why he shaved it off the day he was convicted. It was too recognizable. Witnesses could easily identify him. "What the hell were you thinking, following me there? Ya knew something was going down."

"What was *I* thinking?" I level him with a glare, fighting to keep my voice to a low hiss. Though our house may be detached, the night's quiet and the windows are open. "You almost killed someone yesterday."

"Fucking American," he mutters under his breath, taking another drag. "What was she doin' jumping past the tape anyway?"

"Doesn't matter. Can you imagine the madness that would have stirred up? They'd have all of the gardai on this and you'd be back behind bars within a week, and for a hell of a lot longer than six years. And I'd probably be thrown in there with ya," I add bitterly. "Da already had one heart attack. You want him to have another one?" Doctors say one more would likely kill him.

Aengus ignores the mention of our father and it makes me wonder if he'd care at all. They've been on the outs for years. "Did anyone see ya?"

"Besides the American girl who you almost blew up?" I shake my head. "I used the trees and then I scaled the wall." Not an easy feat, especially with bits of plastic explosive embedded in my body.

He stabs at the newspaper headline. "What can she tell them?"

"Nothing."

"The article says that she told police the man who fled the scene had an Irish accent. So ya talked to her." He pushes. "What'd ya say?"

"I told her help was coming. That's all." It doesn't sound like she told them anything else, but who the hell knows what the gardai didn't tell reporters? Her name isn't mentioned anywhere and I know they have that. "She was in shock. I doubt she remembers any of it." I left her lying in the grass, her pretty light green eyes wild with confusion. I hated doing it, too. She's the only reason I left the house today, to buy every newspaper I could find within a two-block radius.

I needed to know she was okay.

A part of me was hoping for more information, something to tell me who she is and why she's in Ireland. How long she's here for.

Where I could find her, if I just wanted to see her again. Then again, the bomb left me off-balance, struggling to get myself out of there in time. I don't even know if I'd be able to identify her in a lineup now. All I really can remember is a pink cap, lean strong legs, and those beautiful green eyes.

Aengus's heavy gaze levels me. "They're already blaming us, without any proof."

"Not *us*, Aengus. *You*, and rightfully so. You and Jimmy and whoever else he coerced into doing this."

"Jimmy didn't coerce me into doing anything," Aengus snaps and I roll my eyes. I've never seen my big brother bend to anyone else, not even our father. But for Jimmy Conlon . . . he'd polish his bleeding shoes if the man held up a foot and a rag. As his right-hand man, Aengus is wrapped around Jimmy's pinky finger.

And I can't stand the bastard. He had the nerve to come into Delaney's about three years ago, order a Guinness, and tell me that he was proud of my brother. How he had proved he was strong for "the cause."

Jimmy isn't fighting for "the cause."

I thought I was going to crack my teeth that day, wrestling down the urge to label Jimmy for what he really is out loud—a low-life racketeer, twisting what my family—my da, my granddad, and many generations before him—fought for. But I kept my mouth shut because you don't go up against a guy like Jimmy—a convicted felon himself and a snake if I ever saw one—and come out without a bullet in the back of the head.

I suck back the rest of my beer, the alcohol helping to numb my pain. "You could have blown yourself up, Aengus." The walk from our house in Crumlin to the Green is a good forty minutes.

He shakes his head decisively. "It was solid."

I roll my eyes. If my parents were ever asked to put their three sons into boxes based on characteristics, I'd bet my life that Aengus would fit neatly into the one marked "loyal, volatile idiot." He's not smart enough to question what really matters, and Jimmy feeds off of that. He's just using him for his dirty work.

"Just a warning, like I said."

I crush the empty beer can in my hand, hiding my shudder at the thought of how much worse it could have been. "For who, this time?" If it's not one gang, it's another.

He weighs me with a heavy gaze, his beer stalling at his lips for a long moment. "The Gypsy."

Of course. Adrian Beznick, a true Romanian drifter who started out as a petty thief twenty years ago and is now one of Dublin's main crime bosses. The media gifted him with that name—politically correct or not—and that's how he's best known in all circles. I remember Aengus pointing him out to me once, strolling along the sidewalk, a man of small stature and graceful moves. He didn't look like much at all. "Isn't he in jail?"

"One cell block over from where I was. Doesn't stop him from selling heroin to kids. Gardai know and they aren't doin' a fucking thing about it."

I pull a smoke from Aengus's pack and light it up. "What's wrong? Cutting into Jimmy's income?"

"Fuck off!" He swats at the empty cans, scattering them. "You know we don't sell drugs."

And yet they're profiting from it. Extorting the city's drug dealers—threatening their lives and promising their safety through cooperation, all in the name of the IRA. Sure, the official stance is that Jimmy and his rabble of do-gooders relieve these scum of their funds and stop future illicit activities.

But none of them have stopped dealing. They're just required to pay a tithe to Jimmy's guys while they do it.

I don't know how long Aengus is going to deny what we all know Jimmy is involved in. What Aengus, by rights, is involved in. But I may as well be holding a candle in outer space if I'm trying to make Aengus see the light.

"Let me guess—Jimmy tried to take a cut off Beznick and Beznick's having none of that." When the IRA comes knocking on some everyday drug dealer's door with one hand opened, the other clenched around a gun or a hacksaw, there's usually no issue. The dealer hands money to them with a please and thank you. But Beznick's organization probably isn't so easily swayed. They make the papers nearly as often as the IRA nowadays.

He hesitates, which tells me I'm right. "Beznick put a hit out on Jimmy."

"That's serious. And Jimmy can't get to him on the inside?" I find that hard to believe.

"Tried. Beznick has friends protecting him." Aengus breaks eye contact to look out the window. The nasty hooked scar by his left brow glows silver from a neighbor's stray garden light. Two centimeters over and he would have lost his eye. I remember visiting him in prison just after that happened, not even three months before he was released.

"So what does the Green have to do with Beznick?"

"Jimmy wants to remind Beznick who he's saying no to. Remind him of the fear and respect he should have when he's dealing with us."

"And . . ."

That left eye twitches, a sign that I'm not going to like hearing the answer.

"I kept innocent blood off your hands yesterday, Aengus," I remind him, my tone biting. "Why the Green?"

"Because it's where Beznick's sister takes his niece and nephew every day." When he sees my face—the rage about to explode—he quickly adds, "Later in the day, of course!"

My chair topples over as I push to my feet, the back slamming into the linoleum floor. "You're going after kids now? Family? Innocent civilians?"

Aengus is on his feet right away, never one to sit when anyone hovers over him. "Like I said . . . it was just a warning to grab his attention."

Threatening the family of a crime boss. Yeah, I'd say that's going to earn his attention. "Jesus, Aengus! Jimmy *really* thought that would persuade Beznick to lift the hit? How much do they go for these days, anyway?"

"Twenty."

"Twenty thousand euro! The man will pay that much money to be rid of Jimmy—and you, surely—and Jimmy thinks trying to kill his family will make him back down? Is he completely daft?"

"We weren't trying to kill them," Aengus insists. "That's why we took the right precautions and planned it out well. We taped off the area during the night. One of our guys opened the gates extra early, before people would ever expect the Green to be open. We made the pipe small. No glass or nails or anything. Just meant to scare."

"Well, thank heavens for that or I might not be standing here now, would I?" I shake my head at him. "Why wouldn't you just go after his fellas? Why not just wait outside one of their houses and put a bullet in them?"

"How many would we have to pick off before Beznick learns his lesson? How long would that take? Jimmy figured this was quicker, more impactful."

Jimmy's finally gone mad. "And if Beznick doesn't call off the hit? Are you going to fill the next one with glass and nails and leave it on their doorstep for wee, little fingers to wrap around?" He shoves my hands away before I can grab hold of his shirt, standing to face me chest-to-chest. We've been the same height since I hit puberty and sprouted almost overnight. But years behind bars has made Aengus's body stronger, harder.

His fighting dirtier.

I back away, knowing I'll only end up on the ground with my stitches ripped open. I turn to face the window that looks out over the narrow garden behind us, on the stone wall dividing our property from the next. I can just make out the streaks of graffiti that someone—I'm guessing some punks in their teens—sprayed within the last few days. The little bastards must have hopped the fence and done it during the night. I haven't had the time or energy to scrub it off yet, but it'll have to go before the next showing.

Our granddad and nanny would be rolling in their graves if they knew that someone had defaced their lovely garden. But I've taken it in stride, because I remember Aengus and me doing that exact same thing, back when we did everything together, good or bad.

Things have changed.

Aengus has changed.

But so have I.

"Jimmy will make sure he gets the message, and he knows exactly who he's messing with." Silence hangs between us. Finally, Aengus asks, "Eamon do that for ya?"

"Yeah."

Another pause. "So what now?"

"You idiot . . ." I mutter, hearing the meaning between his words. Can I be trusted not to say anything when the gardai come knocking on our door? Like I'd ever turn on my family. "Now I get up and go to work, just like every other day, and try to forget this." I pause, a pinch of disappointment in my chest. Four months ago, when I picked Aengus up at the prison gates to bring him back to the house we three brothers own—left to us by our nanny—I was hopeful that after losing six years behind bars, freedom would straighten out his priorities.

"There's an open house on Saturday. Make sure you're not here." The house is nothing fancy—a detached three-bedroom, one-bath home with dated décor, gardens in the front and rear, and a separate garage—but the mortgage had long since been paid off. It should fetch us at least 300,000 euro. Rowen and I will take our share and invest in some real estate together. Aengus will likely piss his away in a kip somewhere. "You're living on borrowed time, and I don't want to be around your poor choices. I don't want Rowen around them. And don't you fucking dare tell Jimmy that I was even at the Green that day."

For once, he doesn't argue with me.

FOUR

AMBER

"I know! It's crazy, right? I'm so glad I was out of the city that day." I wonder if he can hear my voice shaking from over four thousand miles away. My dad has a built-in lie detector, thanks to years of policing. The thing is, it's never been me doing the lying. I don't think he expects it. That's probably the only thing that's saving me now.

"How long are you in that country for, again?" Metal clangs in the background, telling me he's in the garage with Jesse, likely working on his retirement project—the green Mustang he bought after handing in his sheriff's badge last fall.

"In Ireland? Twelve days. I have nine left, now. I fly out next Sunday."

He mumbles something incoherent.

"Staying for free," I remind him. I made the mistake of admitting what this trip was going to cost me one night over dinner, before I left. The next morning there were real estate magazines on the kitchen table of our ranch house, with arrows and angry red numbers indicating what that kind of money could get me in the way of a down payment.

"Awfully nice of that teacher to arrange that for you," he finally admits.

"You mean Mary Coyne?" I smirk. Dad knows her name, so I don't know why he pretends that he doesn't remember her. I'm pretty sure he had a crush on her, back when she was thirty years old and teaching me freshman science. So did every other pubescent boy and half the male population of Sisters. She has always been a striking woman, her raven-black hair hanging in silky waves down her back, her skin porcelain smooth, and her soft Irish accent mesmerizing. She made me love science. She made me love Ireland without ever having been here. She's one of the reasons why I'm now on this trip.

I was her best and brightest student, and her favorite, she told me later. She wrote me a glowing letter of recommendation when I applied to college and we've kept in touch over the years, making time to meet for coffee at Poppa's Diner on Main Street at least twice a year. I loved listening to her regale me with her adventures from when she was a college student in Ireland, hopping all over Europe and Asia and eventually North America, where she met Arnold Coyne, the man who would later become her husband.

When I told her about taking this trip, and that Ireland would be one of the countries that I visited, she insisted on reaching out to her brother, a doctor in Dublin who spends several months a year lending his healing hands to Doctors Without Borders. It just so happened that he'd be away on one of his missions while I'm here, and his house would be vacant.

My gaze drifts over the master bedroom, an expansive room on the second floor with a glazed black fireplace and a spectacular view of a timeworn church tower from the window. "You should see this place, Dad." When the taxi dropped me off out front, I didn't think much of the semidetached house crammed into this quiet urban side street. From the outside, it looks just like any other building along the way—all brick and boxy, with tall, rectangular windows. By no means fancy and completely foreign, compared to the hundred acres of open fields and ranch-style house overlooking an Oregon mountain range that I call home.

I should have known better.

The moment I turned the key that Dr. Simon Hill left with the neighbor and stepped inside the three-story house, I began to appreciate just how much Mary must trust me. Every square inch has been gutted and remodeled into three floors of soothing whites and dove grays. The bathrooms have been finished in floor-to-ceiling marble and tile, the floors in rich honeyed wood planks, the final details opulent and old-world charming. I've never met her brother, but I can see that he has an appreciation for the finer things when he isn't helping the poor.

"So . . . What have you seen so far?"

"Umm . . . Wicklow Mountains, Trinity College, the Guinness factory . . ." I start rhyming off all the things I *should* have seen by now, had I not sequestered myself while recuperating, both mentally and physically. I lost track of how many times I bolted upright in bed the last two nights, after a loud thump or car backfiring on the streets below. "You know, stuff." I shove a piece of bacon into my mouth to avoid talking. The rest of my thrown-together breakfast stares back at me, growing cold. The fridge is full of food that I bought the evening that I arrived here, hoping to avoid eating out as much as possible. I've barely touched it.

"Stuff," he repeats, and I can almost see the weak smirk touching his lips. "Sounds like a once-in-a-lifetime opportunity alright." Gabe Welles never traveled in his youth, joining the Deschutes County Police Department fresh out of school. He and Mom didn't even leave Oregon for their honeymoon, a fishing trip in the wilderness. To say he doesn't understand my need to hop on planes and listen to foreign languages and see the world outside of Sisters, Oregon, would be accurate. He tried to dissuade me right up until the night before I left, grumbling about how I wasn't being responsible.

My dad sighs. "We miss you here. The Felixes are getting fat and lazy without you to ride them."

I smile at the mention of the horses next door. It's been almost four weeks since I left home with one turquoise suitcase and plans to make a lifetime's worth of memories. "Tell Jesse to give them a run."

A deep chuckle fills my ear. It's so rare to hear him laugh. "I'll be sure to suggest that to him."

My twin brother, Jesse, has avoided the stalls since a horse hip-checked him and he landed in a pile of manure that had yet to be mucked. We were eleven then and, if it weren't for Alex, I'm guessing he still wouldn't step inside that barn today, fourteen years later.

"Mom working tonight?" Dad was surprised to get my call at nine p.m. Oregon time. It's still yesterday back home. Here, it's five a.m. and I've already been up for an hour, unable to sleep.

"Of course. They need to hire more doctors. At least the new cardiologist they found to fill Aaron's spot is working out well."

My stomach clenches with that name.

After a moment of silence, Dad offers a quiet, "Sorry, hon."

"It's okay." I quietly push the painful reminder aside. "I'm sure Mom's heavier work schedule may also have something to do with a retired sheriff lingering around the house with too much time on his hands."

He grunts in response.

"Is Alex around?"

"Trying to get rid of said retired sheriff so soon?"

"Never." I smile. He's been driving my mom nuts, leaving the kitchen splattered with grease and filled with dishes in his attempts at making dinner each night for her.

"Listen, Amber . . ."

"Yes, Sheriff Welles?" I laugh, knowing that he just rolled his eyes. I only call him that to his face when I'm on the offensive. Particularly, an offensive to his coming lecture. Not that I'm never unreceptive to it. My dad may have been hard on us growing up but he was always fair, his staunch belief in right and wrong a thing to be admired. That doesn't mean I always agreed, or that sometimes I didn't wish he would just not share his opinion for once, but it's always been his voice in the back of my mind, helping me see through ambiguity to reason. My father is just one of those guys who can do no wrong, even when he makes mistakes, because his heart and his morals are always in the right place.

"Hearing about that bombing on the news, about an American girl with long brown hair, in her twenties . . . it scared us. The kind of people who are willing to do that sort of thing are dangerous, and you won't even be able to pick them out of a crowd."

The attempt to keep my identity out of the media was successful. All the newspapers could get was what the first witnesses could tell them, which wasn't much since I was fortunately too shocked to make the mistake of giving them my name. The reporters filled the rest of the articles with the description of the scene and comparisons to past bombings. Talk of the city's gang problem, extortion and retaliation shootings, the heroin and cocaine epidemic. The IRA. Or the RIRA. I don't understand the difference. I do understand the word *terrorists*, though, and the articles mentioned that more than once.

I push aside my guilt for lying to my dad, reminding myself that my reasons are valid. Between their careers and the past year with Jesse and Alex, my parents have dealt with enough stress to make them stronger than most. Still, I don't want them worrying about me more than necessary. "I'm perfectly fine."

"I'm glad you are. I'm glad this American girl is, too. I'm sure her parents just want her home now."

Oh, no doubt they would.

He pauses, and I can almost see him standing at the edge of the garage's concrete pad, peering out over the three mountain peaks that earned our town its name, his hand on his hip. "If it hadn't been for that man who knocked her down . . ."

"Thank God for good people," I whisper, my throat suddenly going dry.

I haven't forgotten about "that man." In fact, he's occupied my thoughts over the past two days more than anything else about that fateful morning.

Wondering why he ran, if Garda Duffy is right and he could be involved. And if O'Brien is right and he just saw me as a pretty face that needed to be saved.

But, mostly, just wondering if he's okay. On the drive home, O'Brien and Duffy reiterated how lucky I was. While the bomb was apparently small and not filled with nails and the usual stuff, the scattering of shrapnel from the pipe that they found was enough to seriously harm me, had I been caught upright in its crossfire. But that guy . . . the blood spots on his back tell me that he wasn't as lucky.

I'm remembering more now. Just bits of the puzzle, really.

A golden scruff coating his jaw.

Strong, solid-looking shoulders.

A stag on the front of a T-shirt the color of green clovers.

I've held Duffy's card in one hand, the phone in my other. But I haven't called him yet, haven't admitted to recalling more information. The memory of the guy's pleading eyes keeps stalling my fingers.

It's an odd feeling to have a complete stranger save your life and not be able to thank him. I know he's out there somewhere right now. Some nameless face I'll decide I need to search for one day, five or ten or twenty years down the road, whenever I'm back home and not fearing my father's reaction. I'll take out a random ad in search of him, or post a message on Facebook, or whatever social media tool will be most prevalent then, and I'll recount the day that an American girl was saved by an Irish boy in St. Stephen's Green.

And if I never find him? I'll probably still be thinking about him when I'm old and gray and lying on my deathbed, wishing that I had not hidden from the media, but had used them to express my gratitude. I guess I still could . . .

"One of the articles I read suggested that the guy was actually involved. What do you think?" I ask casually.

"Who knows. I've seen a lot of crazy things in my day." A moment of dead air hangs between us. "Okay, well . . ." Dad heaves another sigh. "Three more months, is it?"

"It could have been eleven, so count your blessings." When I started adding up costs, I realized that my original plan to travel for an entire year was too lofty. My only options were to either shorten my trip or downgrade to backpacker hostels, and, well . . . I shortened my trip. Four months abroad is still plenty of time.

"Have fun, Amber."

"I will."

"And watch out for thieves. Don't carry your passport with you. Store it somewhere safe."

I roll my eyes. "Dad, I'm not clueless."

There's a pause. "And get that Skype thing working so I can see your face next time."

My eyes flash to the dresser mirror facing me. To my purple-and-blue mottled shoulder and bicep where the guy's body collided with mine. I could have hidden it under a jacket or long-sleeved shirt, but the gash on my bottom lip is impossible to explain. Plus, he would have noticed my slow, stiff movements. When I woke up yesterday, I started to worry that something was broken. I couldn't turn my head without cringing.

"Sure thing, Dad. Love you."

I listen to the shuffle as the receiver is passed off, relieved that that conversation is over and that he didn't figure out what happened. It's better this way, for everyone involved.

"Hey." Alex's soft voice fills my ear and my heart. Of everyone back home, I think I miss her most, which is funny because she's not even my blood.

"Hey, Alex. How are things?"

There's a clatter in the background, followed by Jesse swearing. She chuckles. His normal broodiness doesn't seem to bother her. Probably because it vanishes the second he lays eyes on her. "You know."

"Anything . . . new?" I don't have to elaborate. She knows exactly what I mean. We've been through so much in the time since she arrived at the hospital that my mother and I work at, near death from a brutal attack, only to wake up with no idea what had happened or who she was. To be fair, I had no idea who she was either. Or more importantly, who she was to my brother. I should have known he'd be somehow involved.

More than a year later, she still doesn't remember everything, but I think that might be for the best.

"A few things." Her vague answer tells me that they're memories she isn't going to share with me. We have an odd relationship. I consider her my family—the sister I always wanted—and she probably outranks any of my childhood friends as my closest confidante. But the Alex I know comes with a do-not-pass door into her past, and what truly happened the night she should have died. She may not remember it all, but she carefully guards what she does remember.

At first I took it personally. I was with her through the months after the attack, caring for her in the hospital. I was with her the day she discovered what my brother had been hiding. If anyone, she should feel that she can trust me. That's what I assumed at first: that she didn't trust me. Finally, I decided to just go with it, figuring she'd tell me when she was ready.

Every once in a while, she'll mention something. It's always inconsequential, but for her, I'm beginning to think it's more a matter of safety. I don't know who her husband was, beyond the fact that he was a maniac with a psychotic temper. But I think silence is her way of protecting me. And Jesse. And, honestly, who knows who else.

So I just let her be, appreciating the present Alex in my life, because that girl is an inspiration.

"So? What's new? What's Ireland like?"

"It's beautiful," I answer honestly, at least the little bit that I've seen. My face was pressed to the glass in awe as the plane descended into rich, grassy hills speckled with tiny white and black sheep.

Gravel crunches on the receiver. I can picture Alex strolling along the driveway, her cornsilk-blond hair hanging free and natural. She's probably heading toward the barn. She spends a lot of time around the horses. "And the trip?"

I smile at my reflection, though the smile isn't as wide this time. I'm not sure if that's on account of my injured lip or my recently doused spirits. "Still worth it." No one believed I would get on that first plane. They thought that I'd find an excuse, a reason to not leave Sisters—my place of comfort, the town I came back to after college when many of my friends didn't.

I almost didn't. I've been saving for this trip since I landed my full-time nursing job right out of school. When Alex first met me, it was all I talked about, working extra shifts to earn more money. And then a thirty-three-year-old cardiologist by the name of Dr. Aaron Janakievski came into the picture and changed everything.

I had noticed Aaron around the hospital. Blond, attractive, rumored to be single . . . every nurse in the hospital had noticed him. The few single female doctors had, too. One day last June, Aaron turned around in the line at the cafeteria and asked if we could eat together. I held my breath and nodded, suddenly nervous that I'd say something stupid. I mean, the guy performs open-heart surgery!

I guess I didn't, because that one lunch in the cafeteria quickly became three, which escalated to dinners off-shift, and evenings at the movies . . . and nights at his condo in downtown Bend. By Christmas, we were tangled in sheets and talking about me moving in with him. It was fast, but he was charming and youthfully attractive and smart and . . . a doctor. Oddly enough, we had a lot more in common than I would ever have believed. Both of my parents had already given their approval, even with the eight-year age difference between us.

I was so sure that Aaron was it.

Just as quickly, though, our relationship crashed and burned. In late February, Aaron suddenly announced that he was moving to Boston, to work at one of the top cardiology hospitals in the country. He'd never even told me that he had applied, or that, during his trips out east to visit with his parents, he was also interviewing for the position. He told me over dinner at his place, and my mind's wheels immediately started churning, thinking about what life in Boston would be like. If I could get a job there, how much I'd miss Oregon and my family.

There was no need. Aaron ended things with me that same night.

He said that I was beautiful and funny but I was too young, and had lived an isolated existence. I couldn't possibly know what I wanted in a spouse yet. He was looking for someone with more life experience. What I heard was that I wasn't good enough for him, something no one had ever suggested to me before. It was a huge hit to my ego.

My plans to travel the world were back on with a vengeance, along with a promise to myself to never again divert my life for a guy.

"So . . . what happened in Halifax?" Alex asks, and I hear the smile in her voice. The last time we talked, I was sitting on a pier for lunch, overlooking the bay. Tables around me were filled—some with entire families, some with couples. One with a lone guy, quietly picking away at a lobster tail, his cappuccino-colored eyes mesmerizing.

It was my last day in Nova Scotia, and I debated simply walking over, filling the spare seat next to him, and striking up a conversation. Everyone knows a person who can do that. Gillian Flanders, a nurse at my hospital, is one of those people. She'll go to Cancún for a week alone and return with an album's worth of wild pictures and a dozen stories. I've always told her that she's crazy, but secretly I've envied her. I've never been that girl who can just walk up to random strangers and start talking, who can openly flirt with a guy, unafraid that I'll embarrass myself if he's not interested in me.

Back and forth, Alex and I texted that afternoon by the pier, with her encouraging me to just do it. What was the worst that could happen? By the time I had worked up enough courage, the handsome stranger was paying his check and I was still firmly planted within my small comfort zone.

"I ate lots of seafood."

She chuckles. "Yeah, I figured. Next time, maybe."

I smile. "Maybe."

"Oh! Before I forget . . . In case you want to see a friendly face, Ivy's in Dublin right now."

"Ivy?" That's not exactly what I'd call a friendly face. The last time I saw that girl, that fateful day a year ago when Alex was getting her tattoo, she looked ready to scrawl foul language across my forehead with her tattoo gun. Probably because I pretended not to recognize her. "I don't really know her."

"Yes, you do," Alex pushes. "You went to the same high school."

"Along with five hundred other kids . . ." I glare at my deep scowl in the mirror and then push the frown line between my brows smooth. "She was a year younger than me, anyway."

"Just a suggestion." A horse whinnies in the background, stirring a touch of homesickness inside me.

"What's she doing here?"

"Working. She's been there for a few months now, I think? She wanted a change from Oregon."

Well, I guess Ivy and I have one thing in common, then. Pretty much the only thing, aside from both being female. I was a Rodeo Queen and straight-A student in high school; Ivy was the resident graffiti artist. I've always embraced my feminine side, primping my long hair in fat curls or silky smooth and straight, and choosing the perfect outfit and jewelry. Ivy showed up to school one day in my senior year with all her hair shaved off. I'm a nurse, helping save people's lives. She leaves them with permanent scars all over their skin.

"I didn't realize you guys talked so much," I murmur, appraising my limp hair. I haven't showered since the detectives dropped me off two days ago.

"You should visit her. She works at her cousin's shop. The Fine Needle? Or something like that. Anyway, I'm sure you can find it easily."

"Sure, if I have time." Alex can probably hear the empty intentions in my voice. "Talk to you later."

"Have fun, Amber. And call me when you cross off number one on the list."

I hang up with a snort and then a laugh. One unusually mild night in March, Alex insisted on starting a list for me—Amber's travel "bucket list." I had just spent the entire day booking thousands of dollars' worth of flights and self-medicating my rejection by Aaron with a bottle of zinfandel. It was just the two of us out on the front porch, the creak of that old swing and our cackles disturbing the quiet, wrapped in blankets and warmed by the *chiminea* that Jesse had lit for us before he bolted, desperate to be free of female emotion.

The list actually started off as a complete joke, a way to get me excited about the trip. Wine made my suggestions bold, a few outright ridiculous. Guaranteed I'll return home with half of the lines untouched. And yet I find myself looking at the list almost daily, the opportunity to check something off giving me a small thrill.

Reaching into my small black travel wallet now, I pull out the folded paper that's tucked inside, reading Alex's neat, flowery handwriting with a smile.

1. Have a torrid affair with a foreigner. Country: TBD.

A torrid affair may be a little dramatic. It's definitely a few steps up from the common vacation hookup, another one of those things that I've secretly envied others for being able to do. Ever since my college roommate, Deirdre Carlino, came back from her backpacking trip with stories about this hot weeklong fling with a guy from France, I've wondered if I'd have the guts to do something like that. Shed my "Sheriff's daughter" cloak of integrity and common sense, and simply not care. Push aside all the real instances of unplanned pregnancies and STD cases that I've seen while working in the hospital and just embrace the experience.

A torrid affair could certainly help with the pang in my heart every time Aaron creeps into my thoughts.

Most of the items on this list are landmark-related and touristy: *float through the grottos, Capri, Italy; tour vineyards on a bicycle, Bordeaux, France*; *sleep on a beach, Phuket, Thailand*. That last one is a definite no. That's how you wake up mugged.

A few are just practical: *Take a picture of a Laundromat. Country: All.* With only one suitcase, I already have four snapshots for my collection.

Some of the items already have tidy little marks beside them. *Take a train through the Canadian Rockies*. Check. *Dress like a Bond Girl and play a round of poker at a casino.* Check. I groan with mortification at that memory, though in hindsight it's kind of funny. A young single woman in a flirty black dress and stiletto heels at a poker table in a Montreal casino . . . I guess I can see why the man who approached and offered me two thousand dollars for the night might mistake me for an escort. He was quite polite about the request, though, and extremely apologetic when my jaw dropped and he realized his terrible mistake. Of course I had to Google what the going rate is for paid escorts. Apparently, two thousand is considered high-end. At least I can claim that much out of the experience. Not that my dad—the man I begged for poker lessons before I left—would be too impressed with that story.

I scan the rest of the list for Ireland-specific lines.

9. Kiss the Blarney Stone: Cork, Ireland.

I'll be able to check that off soon. The keys to Simon's black VW Golf sit in a dish by the front door, at my disposal. I think it'll take me a few more days to work up the courage to drive it, though. I'm not sure I trust myself to stay on the wrong side of the road. And the roundabouts? They scare the hell out of me. I like my old dirt roads and quiet highways through the mountains.

Until then, there are a couple things I have listed for Dublin that I could mark off. That I could have already marked off, if my days here hadn't been derailed.

On impulse, I grab my pen and fill a new line with my own handwriting, almost as neat as Alex's.

42. Barely avoid mutilation and/or death by pipe bomb: Dublin, Ireland.

"Check," I murmur. Shaking my head at myself, I fold the paper back up and tuck it back into my wallet.

Falling into the bed, I stare at the thick crown molding that edges the walls and think about Alex. Most people could not bounce back from what she went through, amnesia or not. She can't even look in a mirror without the constant reminder of it in the form of a long, thin scar from temple to jaw. But she's not hiding in a room somewhere. She's living her life, grateful to have survived.

With a heavy sigh, I drag myself off the bed and wander over to the dresser to pick out a shirt that will cover the evidence.

I didn't come to Ireland to sit in this house, nice as it may be.

It's time to move on.

■ ■ ■

From my seat on the second-level balcony of this Asian tea shop, I feel like a queen, peering down over Grafton Street, a pedestrian-only street, jammed with tourists at eleven on a Friday morning.

Do they know that a bomb went off just a few blocks away from here? Because none of them seem worried. I sigh, closing my eyes and lifting my face to soak in the sun that promises another abnormally hot day for a country with a normally cool climate. I hope it can somehow restore my sense of adventure, too.

A part of me—the traumatized young woman who yelped at the sound of a car backfiring on her way here—wants to call my father back and tell him everything, let his concern wash over me in soothing words meant to comfort. Maybe have him or my mom book a flight to Dublin just so I can be wrapped within their arms by tomorrow.

But I can't do that.

I have no one to talk to, no one to take care of me. No one who even knows.

Except for the police, who aren't going to offer me hugs.

And the man who saved my life, who I can't find.

"Your Darjeeling tea, miss." The waiter winks at me as he sets it down next to a plump scone, his accent enchanting, yet odd. Not light, like my mystery man's. Not like Detective Garda Leprechaun Duffy's. Definitely not like the accent of the taxi driver; he had to repeat everything three times to me and I still couldn't quite understand him.

A hint of Irish mingles with something else, making it entirely foreign. "If you don't mind me asking, where are you from?"

"Sicily, originally. I moved to Dublin when I was fifteen."

"So, the two accents have combined? I didn't even know that could happen."

He chuckles. "Spend a few more days here and you'll hear many different accents in Dublin, especially in the bar industry." He throws me another wink and moves on to tend to another table, another tourist. I pick at my light lunch, turning my attention back to the street below. As commercial as this area is—retailer after retailer lined up and waiting to make money off an abundance of tourists—the old buildings that house these stores, the cobbled walkways that lead up to them, the street buskers who entertain outside, all blend together to energize and charm the atmosphere.

I lean over the rail to admire the flower stand to my left. Tiered rows of buckets burst with blooms in indigo and gold and crimson. It's tempting to buy a bunch of sunflowers and bring them back to add a splash of color to a lovely but somewhat sterile home. It's something my mom has done for as long as I can remember. Maybe I will, later.

To my right, a small crowd has formed around three men who are covered from head to toe in a thick matte charcoal paint and sitting statue-still. So still that I wouldn't believe them to be people, had I not read about this somewhere already. Farther down, the first strings of a guitar carry over the low buzz—a one-man band entertaining passersby, his hat awaiting a tip to keep him coming back.

I could forget about the Guinness tour and the old library at Trinity College that I've mentally committed myself to today, and simply sit here drinking tea and people-watching all afternoon. I just may, too, because up here in my perch, I'm not thinking about being blown up by another pipe bomb.

My waiter seats a young couple at the table next to me. The simple gold bands on their fingers tell me they're married. She mumbles something to him and I recognize it as French. Parisian

French, I'm quite sure. My time in Montreal taught me the difference, the Québécois dialect harsh by comparison.

The guy leans back in his chair, rubbing his chest slowly as he peers down on Grafton Street, just as I had a moment ago. The movement pulls my eyes to the logo on his clover-green T-shirt. It's a family crest of sorts.

The stag at the top makes my jaw drop open.

Could it be?

No. That's just too coincidental. There are probably dozens of family crests with stags on them. The Irish are all about pride for their heritage.

"*Excuse moi.*"

His sharp tone is what drags my gaze to his face. He's staring at me with an annoyed, arched brow. From what I've read, the stereotype that the French don't love Americans isn't so much a stereotype as fact, and for whatever reason, he's assumed I'm American. By now his young wife has turned around too, and her glare has teeth.

"I'm sorry. I didn't mean to stare." This is exactly how I *don't* want to strike up a conversation up with complete strangers. "Your shirt . . . Did you buy it here, in Ireland?" He glances down at it, a frown on his face, like he's trying to figure out why I'd care. "My boyfriend asked me to bring him a souvenir and he'd love something like that," I lie quickly.

Their expressions finally shift to something more friendly. "I won it. Last week, at this famous Irish pub," the guy admits with pride. "I bet the bartender that I could finish my beer before he could. He gave it to me right off his back. But I don't know if they sell them. It's their uniform."

My mind begins spinning frantically. Uniform? Does he mean a staff shirt? What are the chances . . .

"What's the bar called?"

He stretches the bottom out and I notice a name scrawled across the banner. "Delaney's?" he reads, as if in question. "Not far from here. But . . ." He smirks, his gaze scanning my face, my shirt, my bangles, dangling with sparkly charms. "I'm not so sure it is a place for you."

"Thank you." I dismiss his warning easily. If I have the chance to find this guy so I can thank him, then it's the perfect place for me.

FIVE

RIVER

"She keeps turning me down." Rowen tosses the bar rag over his shoulder, freeing his hands to lift the rack of dirty glasses going to the back for washing. "I don't know why."

"She must smell your desperation." A swift kick to the back of my knee has me cringing but laughing.

"Me? You're one to talk. I haven't seen a bird walk out of your room in months."

"You know damn well why." Since our brother was released. Six years locked up with a bunch of bastards meant Aengus has been humping anything he can fool into coming home with him. Plus, there's no way I want anyone I spend the night with to have the misfortune of running into him on their way to use the one toilet in our house. Aengus has no shame when it comes to ogling birds.

Growing up, Aengus and I were the ones attached at the hip, even though Rowen and I are only eleven months apart. I'd like to think that I was the buffer between the two of them, keeping Aengus from recruiting the youngest and most naïve Delaney boy to follow in his footsteps.

Fortunately, Rowen figured out that Aengus is a fuck-up all on his own.

"Hopefully we'll have the house sold soon. We can get a nice apartment in the IFSC and be done with him." When our nanny left the house to us, she said that we should live in it until we all went our separate ways. I think she meant marrying good Irish Catholic girls and fathering children.

He sighs. "I wish things were like the good ol' days."

I know the good ol' days he's referring to. The period was short. A summer, really. Aengus was twenty-two, I was eighteen, and Rowen seventeen—legally not allowed to pour pints, but he did a good job of hiding it. The three of us basically ran this place, giving Da a long-deserved break. Sure, Aengus had been helping Da for years already, but that had more troubles than merits. Aengus had a knack for weeding out the good servers from the bad with nothing more than a five-minute interview. His brute strength and affinity for manual labor meant Da rarely had to do anything besides pour pints and chat up customers. But a lot of what we do here involves keeping a smile on customers' faces and making them want to come back. Aengus was never good at that part. And he's as useless as tits on a bull when it comes to taking care of the books. He could hand out a paycheck, but figuring out how much we owed someone? Odds are half the staff would get paid too much and the other half would get ripped off.

None of that mattered, though, the day the cops slapped handcuffs on him. Da told him that as long as he was involved with any of these dissident groups, he didn't have a job here. In our father's eyes, having the likes of those madmen associated with Delaney's was like spitting on his family's graves.

I think Rowen was under the impression that Aengus would be reformed and slinging pints behind the pub with us again when they released him. But I'm the one who visited him the most while he was away, and while I had my own hopes, I knew better. Aengus has been out of the Delaney's picture for so long, I forget what it's even like to have him here.

Rowen's arm muscles strain as he disappears through the narrow solid door and into the back with the dirty glasses, only to reappear a moment later with another rack, this one steaming hot, fresh from the dishwasher.

"Have you seen Da lately?" I ask.

"He was supposed to come in yesterday but his leg was acting up again. Ma rang here, asking where you were."

"What'd you tell her?"

"That you were bucking some bird all night and she broke your cock."

There's no way he said that to Marion Delaney. The pint-sized woman would have appeared on our doorstep to drag me out by my ear and knock Rowen good across the cheek.

Before I can come up with a proper retort, a chirpy waitress—Selma, from Spain, who Aengus never would have hired—steps up to the computer by the bar, tray tucked under her arm. "Three Guinness and two Smithwick's please," she announces as she punches the order in, batting her eyelashes for Rowen. She used to do that to me, but I've given her so much flack about getting the pints of Guinness to customers as soon as they hit the counter that she avoids me now.

"Sure thing, love." Rowen grins. He waits until she moves on to another table of customers before muttering under his breath, "And she sure is . . ."

"And that's why Greta keeps telling you to fuck off." I grab a glass and start pouring. "I'll go see Ma and Da tomorrow morning, if you're good with opening. Unless you want to go instead?" While our da can't tend bar and lift things anymore on account of his bad leg, he still takes care of all the books.

"No bleeding way. Ma's still on my back about messing things up with Irene." Rowen's focus roves the bar as he pours the rich stout with the expertise of a man who's been doing it since he was fourteen, long before the law said he could. That's the thing about a pub like Delaney's.

We run our shit the way we want to run it.

For the most part, anyway. Delaney's has been a landmark in Dublin for far too long to take too much grief from anyone. Sure, we're not the oldest. A place down near the Jameson Distillery that's been pouring pints since 1198 has us beat. But almost two hundred years on this quiet street buys us a good amount of freedom.

The building's old. Some would say dingy. The exterior is stone and under a mason's watchful eye. The narrow windows covered by black iron gates cut most daylight out. The inside stinks of hops and smoke still lingers in the red-velvet cushions of the bench seats, six years after smoking was banned from all of Ireland's establishments.

But the charm is in the history, and this place has plenty of that. We use whiskey barrels for some tables, while others are made from the wood of run-down buildings in the countryside left abandoned during the Great Famine. The stools are worn but stable, and anyone who knows to look would see the names of infamous republican rebels and politicians carved into the underside, all patrons of Delaney's in their time.

Bronze statues of Michael Collins and Éamon de Valera stand proud. The walls are covered in framed plaques with stories of the many nationalists who fought for a free Ireland, including my father, my grandfather, and ancestors dating back many Delaney generations.

It's a pub rich in Irish heritage and familiarity, and I've always found comfort here.

I'm halfway through pouring the second pint of Smithwick's when the tap starts spurting air. "Shite. Can you flip a keg for me?"

Rowen's eyes flicker to my back. The wounds are starting to heal, but they still throb when I strain them too much. "Right. Finish this off for me."

I take over on the Guinness tap, keeping the glass at a nice 45-degree angle, and Rowen disappears into the back. My eyes wander. At least half the tables are full at any given time here. Mostly with locals, but when tourists get a clue and realize that the city's best watering hole is actually not in Temple Bar, we welcome them with open arms. It's near the end of a workday on a Friday, and I know we're about to get slammed with the after-work crowd.

"Testing . . . Testing . . ." A voice sounds over the stereo system, followed by a hard thumb tap. "It seems me instruments aren't working well today. Nothing a good, strong pint can't rectify. Right, River?"

I catch Collin's weathered smirk and throw him a thumbs-up. He's been playing his guitar and singing Irish lyrics at Delaney's since I could barely climb on the bar stools to watch, taking half his payment in beer. He won't start until he has a full pint sitting next to him.

I turn back to my task, prepared to grant him that wish as soon as I'm done with this other order. Nervous green eyes stare back at me from the other side of the tap.

The moment they capture me, the moment I see that face, I know it's her.

Fuck.

She found me.

How the hell did she find me?

"Your T-shirt," she says as if reading my mind, nodding to the fresh Delaney's shirt I slipped on this morning. The other one was shredded. She clears her throat and adds, in a nervous, soft voice, "I saw someone wearing it and I remembered the stag. I figured I'd come by."

We occasionally give our staff shirts away to customers. Usually it involves a bet that they can't drink their pints faster than us. Of course we lose intentionally, giving them more reason to wear the shirt in public. It's free advertising. I can't believe something as stupid as a T-shirt led her here. She was completely out of it and yet she noticed that?

Questions are spinning inside my head as I stare at that stunning face, panic rising in my gut. *How long are you in Dublin? Were you hurt? Why the hell would you track me down?*

What did you tell the gardai?

My eyes instinctively dart to the door. No uniforms from what I can see.

"Um . . ." She frowns, her attention dipping to the tap. I finally notice the Guinness spilling over the rim and pouring into the trough below.

It's the exact time that Rowen shows up to slam the tap off and stares at me, gob-smacked. "Wise up, River!"

"I'm sorry. I distracted him," she says. Rowen's gaze shifts between the two of us, settling on the scab over her bottom lip. It's bad, but not bad enough for stitches from what I can see. Purple-bruised skin peeks out from the sleeve of her flowery pink blouse. That's my fault. I hit her hard when I took her down. Not that I had much of a choice.

"Right." Rowen leaves for the other side of the bar so he doesn't have to watch me as I dump the entire pint and start over. I can't serve an imperfect Guinness pour to a customer. But few things piss him off and I know inside that head of his, he's screaming sacrilege. If there was anything our father taught us to believe in besides an independent Ireland, it's that wasting beer is downright blasphemous.

I grab another glass and start over, feeling her eyes on me the entire time.

"So . . . River." She has a soft voice. Her accent is a hundred times more charming than that of the American girls I usually meet. Maybe that's because they're usually drunk and yelling by the time I start talking to them.

And now she knows my name. *Bloody hell.* Won't take long for them to find me with that, should she share it.

"Yeah." I set the glass down on the counter to settle while I move on to another one, trying to quell the panic still burning inside. "My mother couldn't make it to the hospital in time and ended up having me in the backseat of the car, next to Castletown River." I've told the story of my unusual name so many times it rolls off my tongue.

"That's sweet."

"Right . . . sweet." I smirk despite everything. "Better than being named Castletown."

She smiles, pushing back a strand of her long hair—a pretty warm brown, like the cinnamon bark Ma likes to stick in her tea sometimes. I don't remember it being so long, but then again I don't remember much except her wild, green eyes—the color of a crisp cucumber's flesh—and how soft the skin on her legs was, when I slid my hands along them, checking for shrapnel wounds.

She's more beautiful than I remember.

Beautiful in that wholesome all-American girl way that the movies teach us about. Perfect, symmetrical features, smooth skin, straight, white teeth. Long, dark lashes that help trap my gaze. I can't even tell if she's wearing makeup. She's definitely not wearing too much.

Of course I've met enough American tourists to know that that's a Hollywood illusion, that they come in all shapes and sizes and degrees of brazenness, just like people around here. This girl, though . . .

She shouldn't be here. She's the only one, aside from Aengus, who can put me in the Green when the bomb went off.

"Well . . ." She takes a deep breath, as if gathering courage. "Hello, River." A dainty hand stretches out toward me and I'm compelled to take it, to hold it. "I'm Amber." She blinks several times, her eyes suddenly wet, tears brimming at the corners. "I needed to say thank you." The words she doesn't say out loud hang between us as a tear spills down her cheeks.

Bloody hell. I can't have this girl crying at the bar without raising questions. Maybe I should lead her to the back, where there's privacy. . . .

A few irritated plucks of a guitar announce that Collin is now impatiently waiting. He'll start getting obnoxious soon, and probably draw attention to the crying American bird in front of me.

So I do the only thing I can think to do. I reach out with my free hand and steal the tear with my thumb. "No need," I promise her, leaving her knuckles with a brief kiss before freeing myself from her grasp and settling it on the bar in front of her. "Selma!"

I pour Collin's pint while Amber tries to compose herself in my peripherals, carefully dabbing at the corners of her eyes with a napkin from the bar.

Selma swoops in with her tray not ten seconds later.

"That one's for Collin. Get it to him first so he'll shut up."

I can hear the small printer behind me churning, spitting out new drink orders from the other waitresses, but I ignore them for the moment to give all my attention to this creature in front of me, who's staring up at me like I'm some sort of knight in shining armor. She's composed herself again, at least. "How are you enjoying Ireland so far?" It's a stupid question to ask her, all things considered, but it's all I can think of.

A slight frown furrows her smooth skin, even as she smiles. "Good. Fine. Well, to be honest, I haven't really been anywhere since . . ." She swallows hard and averts her gaze around us. " . . . since I got here." She shrugs in a "you know" way.

Anger boils inside me. *Fucking Aengus.* This poor girl's holiday is probably ruined. She's forever going to remember Ireland for a pipe bomb. I'm surprised she hasn't hopped on a plane and gone home already.

"Listen . . ." I lean forward slightly, catching a whiff of spicy floral perfume. "What happened that day? That was one in a million. You should be more worried about our transit system."

Her lips break into a wide, gorgeous smile, deep dimples forming on each cheek. "I believe you. Those double-decker buses move fast."

I grab the drink orders from the printer and lay them out. She quietly watches me fill two pints and set them on the counter. "So, what can I get ya?"

"I actually—" She cuts herself off, hesitates, and then, looking around, makes a decision. Her voice drops and she leans in. "I have a few questions." She rushes to add, "Just for me. I just need to talk to someone about what happened. And you're the only one I can do that with."

Of course she has questions. What the hell am I going to say? If I were a dick, like Aengus, I'd either yell at her or throw out a few choice innuendos that would make most well-mannered birds cringe in disgust and run away. But I don't have the heart to do either. "I only have one question," I counter, stalling.

She waits, her eyes widening, worry mixing with curiosity.

"Will it be Guinness or Smithwick's?"

"Oh." She smiles, and then frowns, her nose wrinkling. "My friends made me try a Guinness before I left and I wasn't a big fan."

"You tried it in America?" I chuckle and grab a glass. "Take a seat then."

She does, perching herself on a stool, her gaze taking everything in. Collin tests a few notes on his harmonica, grabbing her attention. "Is he going to play real Irish music? I've heard places like this usually do."

Places like "this." I can't help but chuckle. She looks like a little doll, perched prim and proper in the middle of this kip. Completely out of her element. I'm sure the only bars she's heard about are the upscale ones in Temple Bar. They do play live Irish music. They also gouge the tourists' wallets. "I guess you'll have to stay and see, won't you?"

A sparkle of excitement twinkles in her eyes but she says nothing, her gaze drifting over my arms as I finish pouring and set the pint in front of her. I lean across the bar, resting on my elbows. "Do you trust me?" I ask, half in jest.

She bites the inside of her cheek and then nods.

Concern pricks my conscience. Yes, I may have dove in front of a bomb for her, but, really, she should be a bit more wary of me. Yet it's that trust, that admiration that radiates from her as she watches me, that's reeling me in tighter by the second, making me lean forward even closer, ignoring the printer that keeps churning with orders. "Go on, then . . . Try it. This one's on me."

A small bloom of red touches her cheeks and I wonder what that's about, as she brings the glass to her mouth to take the tiniest sip. A caramel froth mustache decorates her top lip when she pulls it away, smiling. When she catches me staring at it—at her lips—her cheeks brighten even more.

"Better than what you've had before, right?"

She nods, swiping at the foam with her thumb. Thoughts flicker across her face. "How did you know?"

"Because Guinness doesn't travel well. Everyone says it's better when poured at home."

She leans in, settling a shrewd gaze on me, her voice low and suddenly so serious. "That's not what I meant."

In the blink of an eye, we're back to the Green. I still don't know what to say, so I peel away from the counter and grab a few orders to stall. The bar's filling up quick. Soon I'll have customers banking either side of us and this conversation won't be able to continue. I could drag it out, let her walk out of here without any answers at all. I could let her form her own conclusions.

Likely they'd be bad.

Maybe they'd be right.

"I was jogging in the park," I finally say. "I saw a guy drop it in the grass before you came running."

"I didn't see anyone else." Her pretty brow pinches in thought. "Then again, I didn't see you either. I guess I was more focused on my map." A pause. "How did you know it was going to go off when it did?"

"I didn't," I lie. "I saw it and I saw you, and I ran as fast as I could." My gaze drifts over that creamy, perfect skin, that long neck, those slender arms. What would she have looked like, shredded by flying plastic?

"But why wouldn't you stay and tell the police? The . . . gardai." She tests that word out on her tongue with a cute scowl.

Selma slides in then to grab napkins and more drink orders, stalling the conversation. I wait until she's gone to lean over the bar again, this time closer. Close enough to avoid ears, close enough to catch the smell of spearmint on her breath. I remember it now. It's all coming back to me, the feel of her beneath me on that grass. The terror that stopped my heart as I ran for her, believing I wouldn't make it. The overwhelming relief I felt when I knew she'd be okay.

When I don't answer, she pushes. "You saw the guy who did it. You could identify him." She watches me and I can't help but think that this innocent-looking American bird is weighing my answers with the skill of someone who can see through bullshit.

So I decide on a skewed version of the truth. "What if I don't want that person knowing who I am, or that I could put him in prison?" I'm sure she's read the papers. They didn't waste time throwing out suspect groups. One, in particular. Pipe bombs are one of their signature methods, after all. She can't be so ignorant as to not understand the dangers associated with those three little letters that mean so much when combined. IRA.

She nods slowly. "You're scared of what he may do to you."

"And to my family." Now it's my turn to ask a question. "What did you tell the gardai about me?"

A flash of guilt fills her face. "They were asking me a lot of questions and inspecting my backpack. At first, I'm pretty sure they thought I set the bomb and was pretending to be a victim."

"You're joking." I definitely didn't see that coming, but I guess female bombers aren't unheard of. Especially young, innocent-looking ones.

"I wasn't hurt, right? Other than this gash on my lip." She touches it lightly with her fingertip, drawing my attention to it again. She's got a wide mouth and plump lips, the kind that can't handle a bright lipstick without looking clownish.

The kind that I like.

She shrugs. "So I told them that a man with an Irish accent saved my life. I said you knocked me down before the blast. But I told them I didn't remember anything else." Her gaze roams my face until her cheeks flush and she ducks away with a coy smile. If I didn't know better, I'd say she was flirting with me.

A string of notes finally catches my attention. Collin, beginning the first of many cheery Irish jigs. In the minutes while I was lost in conversation, regulars lined themselves up at the bar, perched on their stools, and waved for my attention. Delaney's regulars aren't patient when it comes to that first, cold after-work pint.

"River! You planning on working at all today?" Rowen hollers, glancing at Amber again with a knowing smirk.

"Go ahead." She dismisses me with a smile. "I don't want to keep you."

I stall, torn between my job and what I really want to do—get to know this American more. Even though I know that's a piss-poor idea. It's best that I let her walk out of here and never look back. Definitely best for me. But also best for her. She doesn't know me and I'm guessing, by the pretty little silver chains around her neck and the bangles on her wrist and the way she looks so put together, that if it hadn't been for what I'd done for her, she might not be peering at me in that awestruck way.

"I'm glad to see you're fine, Amber," I finally offer.

She bites her bottom lip, stirring my blood. "Same here. I mean, with you. That you're fine," she stumbles over her words. Is she always this shy?

"Make sure you see all of Ireland while you're here. It's a beautiful country." I take a deep breath. And then I turn my back on her, forcing myself to let the rush consume my attention as I dismiss Amber's presence. It's hard but not impossible to do, with the customers at the bar parched and hollering their needs at me. I lose track of time, working my half of the horseshoe-shaped bar with smiles and pours and quips to keep people laughing and drinking.

I get so good at avoiding her gaze that, at some point, she manages to duck out unnoticed, leaving nothing but an empty glass atop a napkin, with "thank you" scrawled across it.

It's for the best, I remind myself again, pushing aside the edge of disappointment.

SIX

AMBER

I stroll along the narrow streets, back the way I came, my heart both light and heavy. I wasn't lying when I told Garda Duffy that I couldn't remember what the guy who knocked me down looked like. And the bits that I've remembered since didn't prepare me for the guy I just sat and gaped at like a high school freshman for the past hour.

The second we locked eyes, I knew it was him. Those eyes, I don't think I'll ever forget them. Except they were deeper, greener than I remembered, like the lush highlands that decorate the Irish tourism magazines. Couple them with a wide, playful smile and an angular jaw hidden behind a few days' worth of golden scruff, and his face is a perfect blend of handsome features. And I had forgotten his voice—masculine yet melodious, his Irish accent obvious but not overbearing.

River . . . It's an odd name, and yet it seems to suit him.

I couldn't tell what he made of me in those first few moments, as a muscular arm held a glass up to the flowing tap, as his gaze landed on me and panic exploded within it. The panic I recognized instantly, and I immediately started second-guessing my brilliant plan to track him down, suddenly understanding that maybe he wants nothing to do with me or the bombing. Something I refused to admit earlier, when the GPS on my phone led me to this pub, my thoughts entirely focused on my need to see him again.

To be honest, I thought finding him was a desperate long shot to begin with. I was so convinced that I was grasping at straws that I killed four hours with touristy things before I could no longer ignore the magnetic pull to the address sitting open in my Google Maps app.

River seemed to get over the shock quickly enough, though, around the time that I lost my cool and started to cry. For the first time since the bombing, it was as if I could finally let my guard down. In that moment I was ready to clamber over the bar and wrap my arms around his neck. It threw me off when he wiped away my tears, and it thrilled me more than a little when he kissed my hand before letting go. I didn't think guys even did that anymore.

For a while after, I even thought he might be flirting with me—his dimples deep, his chuckles genuine, his gaze warm. It was a possibility that had me stumbling over my words. On top of the swell of emotions I was grappling with, the guy actually made me nervous!

But then he wished me well on my trip and that was that. Little prickles of disappointment and jealousy stung me as I watched him charm a dozen other customers from the safety of my stool, my face half-hidden behind my pint—which tasted nothing like the bitter tar that they serve at Roadside in Sisters, Oregon. I sat and I wondered how old he is, what his house is like, what his family is like, what he does when he's not working. Where did he go to college? Did he even go to college? What does he want to do with the rest of his life?

Does he have a girlfriend?

All the things you think about when you're attracted to someone.

And I'm definitely attracted to River.

Or am I? Is this warm swell in my chest merely because of what he did for me? Is that clouding my other senses?

I guess what I feel or don't feel doesn't really matter, though. I snagged his gaze just once more before I left, almost as if by accident. It was like he'd already forgotten about me. And that's when I reminded myself that he's an Irish bartender and flirting with customers is in his blood. A handsome, scruffy-faced bartender, serving beer in a dirty old Dublin pub to a bunch of middle-aged men who I'd bet money are here every single day after work, like any good alcoholic barfly.

He's a stranger, really.

And he probably has a girlfriend.

And I live over four thousand miles away.

Focusing on the bigger picture helps ground whatever deep-seated fantasies my subconscious has already started spinning.

After a little while, the place started getting crowded and hot and loud. I kept getting knocked and bumped by elbows and trays, each jolt reminding me how out-of-place I felt in that world. His world. Then a sweaty little man with a distorted French accent—sounding like he's been living in Ireland a while—dropped his arm around my shoulder to make small talk and I decided there was no point in me staying. The moment I stood, the crowd swallowed my spot up and pushed me out.

So I just left.

I didn't even think to leave a tip.

Now I meander through narrow old streets lined with shops and pubs, thrumming with people and Irish music, reminding myself that at least I got the chance to thank him. Something that, until this morning, I assumed I'd never be able to do.

But if I'm being honest with myself, I'm also searching for excuses to go back. Replaying the conversation over and over, chastising myself for the witty answers I didn't give, wishing I had asked a dozen other questions that have nothing to do with the day of the attack and everything to do with getting to know him.

Not that talking about the attack wasn't important—quite the opposite, in fact. Those few hushed moments, when River leaned in close, his undivided attention on me, allowing me the chance to speak out loud about it for the first time, were therapeutic. I feel a little bit lighter now.

A howl of laughter to my right pulls my attention to a group of friends in their early twenties. I can't tell if they're tourists or locals but they're definitely drunk, one of the guys nearly knocking over a floral planter as they spill out of a pub. Then again, this is the Temple Bar area and I've been told that no local with any common sense would come here, so . . . they must be travelers.

I sigh, wishing, as I have occasionally, that I weren't making this trip alone. None of my friends have the good fortune that I do, though, of being able to just leave their jobs for four months and have it waiting for them when they get back. I'd like to think that a lot of that leeway has come on account of my stellar performance at St. Charles Medical Center, but I'm sure having my mother, the highly respected Dr. Meredith Alwood, working there as well helps.

I move on, heading down the now familiar Grafton Street again, where a new round of performers demonstrate their talents—a guy throwing flaming knives, a bikini-clad woman juggling glassware, an older gentleman thumping on a bodhran. The lady manning the flower stand from this morning catches my eyes and I decide that I definitely need those sunflowers.

I fish through my purse as she wraps a bunch, my fingers deftly identifying and dismissing the bristles of my brush, a small umbrella, my tube of lipstick . . .

I frown, opening it up wide, peering inside.

My stomach drops as the realization hits me.

■ ■ ■

"Dublin sucks."

"So, you lost some money. You didn't get blown up by a bomb or anything." Jesse's cool, bored tone fills my ear and my heart with homesickness. I miss my brother right now. Even when he's making bad jokes.

"Three hundred euro. And my license. And my bank card." That's two strikes. I don't want to find out what the third may be. Ireland is officially a bust. I should just pack up and leave.

"But not your passport or your credit cards or any plane tickets or—"

"Since when did you become a ray of optimism?" He's right, though. Thank God I wrapped all my valuables, including my passport, in a plastic bag and stuck it into the fireplace. Because Sheriff Gabe Welles *always* knows best.

Metal clangs in the background, telling me that Jesse's in the garage, tinkering with one of his engines as usual. It's after two p.m. in Oregon, eight hours behind Dublin time, and five hours since I realized my wallet had been stolen. It took me that long to swallow my pride and call, hoping my dad would somehow be able to help me, even from thousands of miles away. "Where's the sheriff?"

"Just ran into town a little while ago." Jesse sighs. "He fucked up his brake job this morning, so he had to go for new parts."

I chuckle, despite everything. It's nice to see the two of them getting along well, after so many years when they didn't.

"Did you call the bank already?"

"Some 1-800 number, yeah. The card is canceled and I can use my credit card to pull money through my account. It's just . . ." I bite my lip.

"I know. You feel violated. But you're safe, and you don't have to go to the embassy and jump through hoops for a new passport."

"What about my license? Now I can't drive anywhere!"

"Well, you can. Just don't get caught."

I roll my eyes. Totally a Jesse thing to say. "No. Definitely not risking that in a foreign country." I don't need any more run-ins with gardai. Plus, I'm not even using my own car. I would never be that irresponsible with Simon's generosity.

"So then . . . whatever. You take trains, the bus, cabs. Don't let some dickwad ruin this trip for you."

I heave a shaky sigh, collecting the ball of used tissues from the kitchen counter, my cheeks finally dry of tears. "How do you think someone got it?"

"What do you mean, how? They stuck their hand into your

purse and they took it out. They probably bumped into you so you wouldn't feel the lift."

"Is that how you would have done it?" The question slips out before I can stop myself.

"If I stole wallets, sure." Irritation slides into his deep voice.

I sigh, not wanting to bicker. "I know you wouldn't do that, Jesse." Despite everything he has done—and the list is long—I know my brother's heart and he's not a lowlife.

There's a long pause and then Jesse finally asks, "So? Is this trip everything you hoped it would be?"

Aside from a few brief hi's and 'byes as he wanders past the camera during my Skype calls with Alex, I haven't really talked with my brother since I left. And the last time we spoke in person, a week before I hopped a plane to Vancouver, it ended in an epic fight. Jesse's friend Luke Boone had come by with another car for Jesse to fix up and flip. I told Jesse that I thought he was an idiot for still associating with that guy and he needed to cut him off. Luke may look like the perfect package—money, good looks, impeccable grooming—but by the bits of information I've been able to piece together, he's also one of the reasons Jesse got into that spectacular mess back in Portland. Of course, that's all a lot of speculation because no one will tell me shit.

Despite the wedge that's grown between me and my twin brother, I do care about him, which is why I said what I did. He didn't appreciate it, though, deciding it was the right time to lay my own faults and bad choices on the table. Apparently, I spend too much time worrying about what everyone else thinks, and maybe I should look at my own group of friends because they're all a bunch of stuck-up bitches and they've made me a judgmental snob. But that wasn't enough. He had to lay into this trip, too. I'm going to waste all this money to figure out there's no big miracle waiting for me out there, that I actually like my comfortable little town and my comfortable little life, and that I won't be happy being a tadpole in an ocean.

I stormed off then, with tears burning in my eyes. Not because he was so wrong, but because I was afraid he might be right.

"Yeah. It's been great." Maybe one day I'll tell Jesse the truth about my morning in St. Stephen's Green. Of anyone in my family, he'd be the only one who didn't care that I lied.

"Good." There's a long pause and, while I know I won't get an apology out of him over some of the things he said, I can feel it lingering there. "When'd you have your wallet last?"

I think back to my day. After the tea shop and the discovery of that T-shirt, I wandered around Dublin city center, deciding what I'd say if I saw the guy again. When I finally accepted that I had to try and find him, I hopped in a cab. So I know I had my wallet when I arrived at Delaney's because I paid for the ride, but I don't know if I left with it, seeing as I didn't pay for my beer.

"I was at a pub," I say, half-heartedly.

"Crowded?"

"Yeah." I lost count how many times I was bumped into.

"That's probably where someone lifted it. I'm sure you stuck out like a tourist who may have money."

I definitely stuck out . . .

"Call them. Forget about your cash. It's long gone. But the person probably ditched everything else. It's worth a shot."

"Good idea. Thanks, Jesse." I hang up. A bubble of nerves erupts in my stomach as I search for the number. It's ten at night and probably still busy. I don't expect anyone to answer.

That's why I'm surprised—and caught tongue-tied for a moment—when a man's voice fills the receiver with, "Delaney's."

Is it River? It sounds like him. "Hi . . . I was there a few hours ago and I lost my wallet."

"Lost it?" the guy repeats with his Irish brogue. Raucous music and clanking glassware compete in the background.

"Stolen, probably. I know it's not likely, but is there any chance someone turned it in to the bar?"

"They haven't. But I can keep an ear out. Where can we ring ya if it turns up?"

I give him my cell phone number. Thank God for my international plan and Simon's WiFi; otherwise this trip would be two months instead of four. "My name's Amber." I hesitate. "River knows me." Sort of.

"The pretty American bird who made my brother spill a pint, is that you?"

My face heats up, and I'm so glad that I'm alone in my kitchen and not in front of this guy. He must be the other bartender. I thought they looked related.

He chuckles, not waiting for my answer. "I'll let him know you rang."

I hang up the phone and exhale heavily.

Maybe they'll find it.

Maybe I'll have an excuse to see River again.

Nervous excitement grows inside me.

SEVEN

RIVER

"This can't wait?"

I ignore a hovering Rowen, my eyes glued to the computer monitor. And Amber, her slender back to the security camera as she sits perched on her stool, her long, shapely legs crossed at the ankles. Sipping the Guinness I handed her. I've already played back our entire exchange—the shock on my face when our eyes met was priceless. As was the tantrum Rowen just threw in our cramped office, watching the replay of me dumping the pint down the drain.

"I wish I hadn't said anything until closing," he finally mutters. "I need you out front."

"I'm glad you told me. If I find out one of our customers lifted that girl's wallet, and they're still here, they're going to wish they weren't," I mutter with cold determination, stewing in the anger that exploded earlier, when Rowen nudged me and told me that Amber had been robbed today. As if almost being blown up isn't bad enough.

"How do you know her, anyway?"

"I just do."

He sighs. He knows that he won't get answers out of me unless I want to give them. "I'll be at the bar, tending to the sheep."

I watch patiently as Amber sits and drinks, her head shifting from Collin to me and back again. Wishing she'd turn around so I could see her face again. Selma bumps into her with her tray and she flinches. Customers close in at her sides and she curls into herself. I wonder if she's always been like that or if it's because of what happened in the Green.

I'm about thirty-five minutes into the recording and I know she doesn't stay for much longer. I can see why. I did a bleeding good job of ignoring her. Too good a job. Part of me hopes this didn't happen here, because she's going to start tying all bad things about Ireland to me. But a bigger part hopes that it did happen here and I can catch the asshole who did it.

And have an excuse to see her again, because she's lingered in my mind ever since she left Delaney's a few hours ago.

My patience pays off when I see a patron bump into her from behind, and then apologize with a friendly arm stretched over her shoulder. The camera is angled in a way that shows his other hand slipping into her purse and retrieving a small black wallet.

"Fucking Benoit." I recognize him by his ponytail of wiry black hair. He's a regular here, a little Frenchman who comes in every weekday after his shift at the Guinness factory. Normally he's gone by seven, which is why I was surprised to see him staggering past the bar on my way to the office not long ago. I'm guessing he's getting drunk on her euro. Not a stealthy fella, if that's the case.

I grit my teeth against the urge to march out there right now and pummel him. Instead, I keep watching the video. Two minutes later, after I hand him his pint with a grin, he heads to the back of the pub, leaving her completely unaware.

A surge of adrenaline fills my limbs as I charge past the crowd and into the men's toilets. Yanking open the rubbish compartment, I dump its contents onto the dirty tile floor. It's mostly balls of paper towels, along with a used condom—I don't want to know—and a dirty needle.

But on top of all of that sits a small, black wallet.

I flip it open and find Amber's gorgeous smile shining out at me. I have an address for her, too—Sisters, Oregon. Wherever that is. I've never been to America. I've heard of places like New

York and Hollywood, and Florida, but it's hard to keep track of that massive country. She's twenty-five years old, which is what I would have pegged her at. The height and weight numbers mean nothing to me, but I don't need them because I already know she's the perfect size.

A few slips of paper sit tucked within but the cash is all gone, as I expected.

Back out front, I search the crowd of drunks, a few singing along with Collin, who's now on his fifth hour of music and as many pints, livening the place up as he does with quick banter and terrible jokes. It doesn't take long to find Benoit.

Ten steps before I wrap my hands around his scrawny neck, Rowen hops the bar and blocks my path. "River . . . you've got that look in your eye."

I hold up her wallet. "In our pub." I fucking hate thieves. So does Rowen.

"Just . . . don't get yourself into trouble," he warns, then shifts aside, knowing it's not the time to interfere. I'll admit it—the ripple of excitement that stirs inside me as I close in on an oblivious Benoit, that swells as I hold the wallet up and watch his eyes grow wide, that bursts when I grab him by the back of his collar and drag him out the front door, feels bloody grand.

■ ■ ■

"Ya going to call her?" Rowen sets the last of the washed beer-tap grates back. The pub is ready for a new day.

"Tomorrow." I flex my right hand, my knuckles sore after leaving Benoit with a few marks to remind him what will happen if he ever steps foot inside here again. Rowen's warning hung in the back of my mind, though, keeping me from going overboard. "It's one o'clock in the morning. She'll be sound asleep." I'm not entirely sure that's true, after what she's been through these past few days. I could have called her as soon as I found it, put her mind to rest.

Only, my mind was busying deciding how I want to use this opportunity. *If* I want to use this opportunity.

"I bet she'll be grateful. Even for an American princess." Rowen doesn't have to explain where he's going with this; the smirk on his face tells me. He assumes I've got plans to bang her, if I haven't already. Though he'd know if I had. For Christ's sake, we're practically attached at the hip. We live and work together, and when we're not at home or at the pub, we're usually texting or talking on the phone.

"It's not like that," I mutter, pulling out the various slips of paper tucked into the little pockets. Mostly receipts. A taxi from the airport, a large latte with extra sugar. A scone and tea from a place on Grafton Street earlier today. Not surprising, seeing as she's a tourist. Though there are better, less expensive places than that to go.

I unfold a sheet of lined paper, filled with feminine writing.

My eyebrows spike with the first line.

1. Have torrid affair with a foreigner. Country: TBD.

"What is it?" Rowen watches me from behind a sip of his closing-time pint.

"Nothing." It's something, alright. I'm guessing it involves getting laid. I need to look *torrid* up in the dictionary. I scan the piece of paper. It's some sort of "to-do" list. She must have a dozen different countries mentioned here.

14. Do NOT get eaten by a lion. The Serengeti, Tanzania.

"Liar," Rowen mutters when I start to chuckle. He leans forward and I shift farther back. I'm guessing this isn't something Amber wants anyone reading.

24. Spend a day on a nude beach. Athens, Greece.

Christ. Blood starts flowing to my cock with the mental image of those legs attached to a naked body, sprawled out in the sand. Maybe she isn't such a princess after all.

I quickly scan over the rest. A few of them are already marked with little checks, including the last one, clearly a recent addition, about the bomb in the Green. Yeah, I'll bet she never forgets that day as long as she lives.

I note that number one isn't marked off. That makes me smile. And wonder.

And hope.

Rowen hits the lights and throws me into darkness. "Come on, it's fucking late. I'm setting the alarm."

Downing the last of my own pint, I fold the page and stick it in my pocket.

Maybe all her memories involving me don't have to be bad.

EIGHT

AMBER

The shrill ring of my phone wakes me from a dead sleep. I simply stare at it lying on the nightstand for a long moment, trying to figure out who it could be, seeing as my family is eight hours behind and asleep. Do I even have the brainpower required to speak, after a night of tossing and turning with that sick burn in my stomach over my wallet?

In the end, I reach for it. A groggy "hello" escapes.

"Still sleeping, are ya?"

My eyes spring open at that deep male voice, laced with a light Irish accent, that I somehow can't mistake. "River? Is that you?"

"Yeah."

My heart begins racing. "Hey! How are you?" I sound way too eager.

"Tired. I didn't get to bed until close to three."

"What time is . . ." I glance at the clock to see that it's only ten a.m. "Why are you awake, then?"

"Too many things to do before work tonight." I can hear a smile in his voice. "Like tell you that I have your wallet."

My covers tumble away as I sit up, relief making me heave an obnoxious groan. "You're joking!"

"I wouldn't joke about something like that."

"But . . . how? Did someone turn it in?"

There's a short pause. "It was in with the rubbish."

Tossed. Just like Jesse said it would be. Whatever. It's found. Empty of cash, I'm sure. "Is my license there, at least?"

"It is, Miss Amber Mae Welles from Oregon."

My cheeks flush, knowing he's been looking at my information, my picture. "Great. I'll get dressed and come to the bar at noon, if you're open by then?"

"We are." There's a pause. "I have a better idea, though."

■ ■ ■

"Haunting, isn't it?"

My breath hitches with surprise as I spin around to find River standing behind me with two Starbucks cups in his hands, his smile reaching his eyes. "They're . . . incredible," I say.

His sneakers scrape against the cobblestones beneath us as he closes the distance, his threadbare navy T-shirt damp from the off-and-on drizzle falling, the strands of wet hair pushed back in a careless way.

He's even more attractive than I remember.

My heart skips a few beats when he thrusts a cup forward, the crisp white paper highlighting his red, scraped knuckles. They weren't like that yesterday. I know because I got a good look at his hands when I was checking for a wedding band.

"Latte, with sugar."

I frown.

"You keep your receipts."

"Right. I do that." I like to keep track of my spending. Heat climbs up my neck. That means he went through my entire wallet. And he must have seen that stupid list. While that doesn't make me feel as violated as having the asshole who stole my wallet see it, it still stirs a feeling of vulnerability. River may have saved my life, but I don't know anything about him. And now he knows me down to my home address and weight, and he probably thinks that I'm shopping for a movie-style fling on this trip.

Did he actually read it? What would have gone through his head when he saw number one?

I push the thought aside. "Thank you." I accept the cup and our fingertips graze, sending a warm current through me.

"Here." His hand dips into the back pocket of his jeans and reappears with my wallet.

A bubble of relief bursts as I reach for it, followed by another small thrill as his fingertips graze mine again. "God! Thank you! This is . . . you have no idea . . ." I expected it to be flimsy, the money all gone, but it has weight to it. When I open it and find the stack of colorful bills, I feel the deep furrow between my eyes form, the one that my mother warns me is going to leave a deep wrinkle by the time I'm thirty-five if I don't stop frowning. "But, how . . ."

"Our security cameras caught it all. The muppet was still in the pub, so I had words with him."

River said that he found it in the "rubbish"—their word for trash. "Muppet" or not, there's no way the thief threw it out with the cash, so . . . "He gave all my money back?"

"With his deepest apologies." River's right hand balls up into a fist before stretching out next to his thigh. And I suddenly understand why his knuckles are all bruised.

"You had words with him . . . Exactly how many 'words' did it take to drag out his remorse?"

That smirk reappears. "Are you angry with me?"

"No . . ." I'm not entirely sure what I am. I've never been a fan of violence, of guys pounding on each other. I see the ugly results of it at work all the time. At home, Alex's face is a constant reminder. But right now, it's making River all the more attractive to me. He must have watched the security tapes as soon as his brother told him—how did he have time for that?—and gone through the trash can to find it. "You could have kept the money—you know that, right? And just blamed the thief."

"But then that would make *me* a thief, wouldn't it?" A curious look flickers across his face that I can't read. "Is that what you think of me?"

"No, I didn't mean . . . A lot of regular people would have pocketed it."

"I guess I'm not regular people then."

You most certainly are not. I study his knuckles again—red and swollen. "You're not going to get into trouble, are you?"

"Trouble?" He frowns. "Trouble with who?"

"I don't know. With the police. With your boss?" I don't know how many times I've seen the cops in the parking lot outside Roadside after a fight broke out back home. All it takes is one call from the bartender.

But, in this case, that's River.

A soft chuckle escapes him. Nothing about his face or his stance says he's sorry for whatever he did. He's definitely not afraid. Is he afraid of anything?

Yes, he is, I remind myself. He's afraid of whoever set that bomb.

"Benoit isn't going to go to the gardai because he stole your wallet. And Ma and Da aren't gonna fire their son for giving someone what they were owed."

Ma and Da . . . "Your parents own the bar?"

"They do. Rowen and I keep it going for them."

Huh. "River Delaney?"

He nods. Somehow that piece of news makes him working as a bartender in a dive bar different. Like, if I were to tell my friends about him, and they asked what he did, my answer wouldn't be, "He's a bartender." It would be, "He runs his family's pub." It sounds better in my head. I know it would sound better to the sheriff's ears. Not a lot better, but still . . .

With a slow, calming exhale, I turn back to study the seven statues—six people and one dog—looming before me again, their faces gaunt, their lanky bronze forms in tattered, dirty clothes. It took half an hour for me to walk here from the house, but it was easy enough to find. "So you live nearby?"

"Ten-minute drive."

I frown. "Why'd you pick this place to meet, then?"

River takes a sip of his coffee and I inhale the clean, crisp smell of his soap with his movement. I'm guessing he jumped out of the shower, threw on some clothes, and came here. Such a difference between guys and girls—I primped for over an hour. Basically, since the second I knew I would see River today. I even curled my hair, something I only normally do now when I'm going out to a bar.

"A million Irish lives were lost to a great famine in the 1840s. It's one of the most critical events in our country's history, and this monument was erected to remind us of it. Do you know how many times I see a tourist walk past these statues, or stop to take a picture of themselves next to one, and I wish they had a bleeding idea what it stands for?"

Bleeding. That seems to be a popular word around here. My cab driver from the airport used it a lot. "Are you calling me an ignorant tourist?"

He smiles. "Ireland is about more than Temple Bar and kissing stones."

Ugh. That was on my list. He must have read it. "So you want to make sure I know what this monument stands for?" My gaze follows him as he strolls around each weathered statue, his shoulders broad and strong, his posture straight and proud.

He pauses to peer down at the homely dog, immortalized. "That. And I wanted to make sure you don't spend the rest of your trip in hiding, afraid of being blown up or robbed." He wanders back toward me with a soft smile, his gaze resting on my still-healing lip for a long moment before meeting my eyes again. "How are you?"

I shrug, trying to brush his worries off. "I'll have memories to bring home with me."

His gaze drifts over the River Liffey, which flows calmly next to us as he sips his coffee. I'm desperate to know what's going on inside that head of his. "How long are you here for?"

"Eight more days."

A drop catches his long lashes. It's going to start raining again any minute. "Staying with friends?"

"House-sitting for someone."

He nods slowly and silence hangs, prompting me to talk. "Now that I have my license back, I'm going to do a bunch of day trips, out to Cork and Galway. Maybe do some of those ignorant tourist tours." Unlike my trek across Canada, which was planned down to the day, with little downtime, I'm glad I decided to do Ireland differently. Mostly spur-of-the-moment and unplanned. Very unlike me.

He chuckles. "Sounds grand."

I hesitate bringing the bombing up, but since he kind of already did . . . "How are you?" He frowns slightly, as if confused, forcing me to elaborate. "I saw the blood on your back when you ran." I assume he didn't go to a hospital, since the police would have been scouring emergency rooms. Thanks to me warning them to.

Understanding flickers in his eyes. "Never been better." Downing the rest of his coffee, River wanders over to a nearby trash can to stuff the cup in. "I need to run now."

Already? He obviously made a special trip this way and he's been here all of five minutes, if that. I struggle to keep the disappointment from my face. Why not just let me come to the bar and pick my wallet up, then? Unless . . . maybe he didn't want me lingering there after all. I clear my throat to ensure my voice is light as I tease, "I thought you were here to teach me about Irish history?"

A playful smirk curls his lips. "I'm sorry, I can't. I have to see my parents today, before work. But we have fantastic museums, with tours for your kind."

Is this really it, then? Are we saying goodbye already? I open my mouth to thank him yet again, but falter, not sure that the simple words are enough anymore. Not for me, anyway. Taking a deep breath, I close the small gap between us and reach out, wrapping my arms around River's neck, coffee cup and all. Just tight enough to feel his chest against mine. His body stiffens under my touch for just a moment, and then his arms rope around my waist, squeezing me into a tight embrace, until I can feel his heartbeat and I'm resting my head against his shoulder like we've known each other for years. The lightest caress of his breath against my neck sends shivers through my body.

He holds me like this for five wonderful seconds and then his body goes lax, and he pulls away. With a deep exhale, he turns and begins walking away slowly, his feet dragging. Not uttering a single word.

"The famine was caused by a potato blight!" I blurt out after him. It's the first thing that comes to mind. I'm ready to say anything to make him stop.

And it works.

He turns and I flash him my smug smile. This American girl didn't come to Ireland completely unprepared.

"That's a good start, but there's much more to that story, Miss Amber Mae Welles," he smirks, emphasizing *Welles,* a well-known British surname. "You should check out the Collins Barracks Museum." He pauses, hesitating. "And stay out of any more trouble."

"But then you wouldn't be able to come and save me." *Superman.*

His head falls back with a burst of laughter that makes me both happy and sad. "You need saving, do you?"

I don't know what I need, but the way he just held me gave me a taste of what I definitely want. I hold up my wallet. "I could have just stopped by your bar to get it."

"You could have." He hesitates. "But then I might have missed seeing you again."

My heart flutters with excitement. *So he did want to see me again, too.*

"See ya, Amber." He winks. "Don't do anything . . . torrid."

Oh my God. He definitely read the list. I stare after him, red-faced, as he crosses the street and disappears from my sight.

See ya? He does realize that he actually won't, doesn't he? We live thousands of miles apart. It's virtually impossible that we'll ever cross paths in this life again. Unless . . .

I go to that pub again.

I thumb my wallet between my fingers, appreciating that it was just sitting in his back pocket not long ago. It was also in the trash can, but I'm not going to focus on that. Leafing through the little compartments, I find my license and bank card just as they were.

And all of my money, down to the last euro. The few receipts that I remember stuffing in there.

No travel bucket list.

The giddy smile that River put on my face slips off as I search through everything again. And frown. It's not there. How could it not be there? *Torrid* isn't a word most people use in their everyday vocabulary, which means River definitely saw it. So that means . . . he kept it? Why would he . . .

To give me an excuse to come to the bar, looking for it.

I feel the grin stretch across my face.

But showing up at that dingy bar again tonight, on a Saturday night, alone, so I can sit on the stool and watch him serve drinks and possibly be ignored . . . *Ugh.* I'll look desperate. Embarrassingly desperate. Budding stalker status, maybe.

So what, I hear Alex say in my head.

So what if I show up at that bar again and he knows I'm interested in him. And his brother knows I'm interested. And everyone in there knows. I'm a tourist. I can do whatever I want here and leave it all behind when I get on that plane. I am a tadpole in an ocean.

Plus, he took my damn list. As silly as the thing is, it's become somewhat of a guide for me.

I wander over to the rail and gaze out on the stretch of water that cuts through the heart of Dublin, watching the tiny ripples dance along the surface, and consider my next move. *This* is, after all, part of why I took this trip in the first place. To experience life while I'm young and unattached. To make memories that will last me a lifetime. To find out if the Amber I've known all these years—with an overprotective sheriff father and a practical surgeon mother looking over my shoulder—would make the same choices as the one who is free of scrutiny. Do I abide by the black-and-white limits I've set for myself because that's who I truly am or because that's who I am while being judged? And how far into that gray area might I venture before I go running back to my familiar boundaries?

Aaron was inside my familiar boundaries and look how that turned out. All of my previous boyfriends have been. If I want to test myself, River's definitely the one to do that with.

The problem is that my comfort zone absolutely abhors the idea of being so obvious. This would be so much easier to do if I had Bonnie or Tory here to help occupy my attention and time until he makes the first move. But I'm in Ireland, and all potential wingmen are thousands of miles away.

Well . . .

Maybe not.

I guess it just depends how desperate I am.

NINE

RIVER

"Have ya been sleeping?"

I flinch from my mother's rough grip of my face. "I'm fine. Just a long night at work."

She grabs my scuffed-up hand and then levels me with a stern look. "I see that, River. What happened?"

"I caught Benoit lifting a customer's wallet." I shrug. "So I told him not to."

"That slimy little bastard," Ma mutters. She brings Da in once a week, so she's there enough to know the regulars. She's always had a thing against Benoit that I didn't understand, said he gave her the creeps.

"Is he going to remember?" Da sits in his seat at the kitchen table, his favorite mug in one hand full of beer, a bowl of stew and the *Mirror* in front of him.

"I'm guessing so." Waking up with a black eye and a busted nose is always good for jogging the memory.

"And are the gardai going to be showing up at the doorstep for ya?"

I shake my head, though I can't ignore the voice in my head that admits, *Not for that.*

He nods with approval. My father never had a problem teaching someone a lesson if he deserved it.

"Here." I set the week's register readings and other paperwork down next to him.

He sighs like he always does, as if it's a great burden to count out how much money we've brought in. Delaney's has kept all of us quite comfortable over the years. "Good week?"

"Busy week." It's always busy at Delaney's. Through bad weather and bad times, we never lack drinking customers.

"Sit and eat." Ma drops a bowl of her lamb stew on the table, and then her sturdy hands land on my back to push me into a chair.

I hiss when her palm presses against one of my wounds.

"What's the matter, son?"

I shake my head, waiting for the pain to subside with gritted teeth. I've suddenly lost my appetite.

Marion Delaney isn't one to take a brush-off, though. "River Fintan Delaney! What is wrong with your back?" Her stubby little fingers fly to my shirt, tugging at the collar.

I swat her hand away. "Ma! Come on!"

"He's a grown man. Leave him be," Da mutters, but with a sternness that prompts her to listen. She turns on her heels and marches to the stove in a huff.

Da and I share a look. The fact that I'm twenty-four years old means nothing to that woman. If it were up to her, she'd still be washing my knickers. I do miss her cooking, though, I'll admit, as I shovel a spoonful of hearty stew into my mouth. No one makes it better. One day every year, on Delaney's anniversary, she sits at the bar with a vat of it, ladling it into bowls for customers, for free. It's the busiest day of the year for us, Rowen and me chasing away the greedy assholes who come back for a second helping.

"So, what's that about?" Da juts his chin toward my back.

"Nothing." I need to change the subject and fast. "How's your leg?"

He shifts and grimaces in his chair, as if I've just reminded him. "Uncomfortable. It's this bloody heat wave."

Heat waves, cold fronts, damp weather . . . all of it seems to bother his leg. Twenty-seven years after the bombing in Belfast that left him with severe nerve damage, there isn't a day when he doesn't suffer. I sure don't remember one, anyway. The doctors say there's nothing they can do. Not even surgery is going to fix it. I think he's been prescribed every painkiller under the sun.

"I'll come back midweek if you want, when Rowen's not in class. Saves you another trip in."

"That'd be grand. I don't want to go near Dublin right now with this sort of thing going on." He taps the newspaper headline, the article about St. Stephen's Green below it. "Tell me Aengus didn't have anything to do with this."

"Not that I know of." I keep my eyes on my bowl and feel his heavy stare size me up. He's no idiot. There's a reason Aengus didn't get out on license after just three years in Portlaoise, like his sentence offered. All he had to do was behave, but instead he fought and preached about the cause. The hearing committee denied his request, and he served out his entire sentence.

And then the day he got released, he skipped the supper that Ma had been preparing for two days and went to meet Jimmy. The metaphorical straw that broke our father's back and severed all ties. Ma will still call him occasionally and mail him a birthday card, like she did every year while he was behind bars, but she'll have to sign Da's name for him.

"Is he around the house much?"

"He isn't."

"Any prospective buyers?"

"Not yet, but it's only been on the market for two weeks. We should get an offer soon."

Da nods slowly, a mixture of resolution and sadness in his eyes. He grew up in that house. Even after he and Ma married and they moved to Dundalk in County Louth, he spent a lot of nights there, avoiding the commute home while running the pub with Granddad and Uncle Samuel, God rest their souls. "It's about time you and Rowen cut all ties to him. He'll never be anything but trouble to this family. I wish Ma never put his name on the deed. The bastard doesn't deserve any of me family's money."

It's unsettling, seeing the two of them so deeply at odds. It didn't used to be like that. Aengus is a mini Seamus Delaney in so many ways. They even share the same copper-top hair. When Da and granddad would sit around the woodstove and go off about all the years of persecution our people suffered at the hands of the English, how those bloody Protestants should have just packed up their things and left Ireland the hell alone, it was Aengus who'd sit cross-legged on the floor in front of them. Sure, Rowen and I were there, too, but Aengus lapped up every word. Da and Granddad had a way of telling a story that made you want to listen. By the age of ten, I knew more about our country's history than many grown people know today.

I wasn't even alive when my dad got hurt. Aengus was only two. Da figured he'd bring him to the funeral of the three IRA volunteers who died in what the media later dubbed the Gibraltar killings. Da had known one of them from childhood and wanted to pay his respects. When the Ulster Defense Association bomber showed up with grenades, Da managed to cover Aengus, protecting him from harm and taking the brunt of it. Sixty people were injured that day, and three died.

I can't say how much that experience impacted Aengus, if at all, given that he was so young. He certainly heard about it in later years, and just the knowledge that he was almost blown up by the UDA nurtured his resentment of all things English, Protestant, and police. Which is why I'm still shocked that he would have anything to do with what happened at the Green.

It sure put a fire in Da, though. Ma said that his hatred flared in the early days, likely fueled by the incessant pain in his leg. But that fire and the desire for vengeance that he spoke of dulled quickly. By the time the Provisional IRA declared a ceasefire in the late '90s, he fully supported the end of the violence. He'd been living with his injuries for almost a decade, running the pub when most days he'd rather drink until the pain went away. "The people of Northern Ireland have spoken," he had said. "It's what they want, so let them be."

The dissident republican groups that cropped up after the cease-fire? He abhors them, and lets it be known every chance he gets.

"This here? These so-called IRA?" He waves the paper and then tosses it. "Something needs to be done about this. These terrorists calling themselves republicans fighting for the good of Ireland! That's absolute shite! They don't even understand what those words mean. They're about extortion and drugs. They're tainting the memory of noble, strong men. They're tainting the name of what those men fought for. They don't know a bleeding thing about real suffering, and real purpose."

"Don't get all worked up, Seamus, or I'm going to stop bringing the papers home to you. It's not good for your blood pressure," Ma scolds. Aengus isn't good for his blood pressure, either. That's another reason I'm skirting the issue now. If he knew what really happened, he'd hunt Aengus down and beat him over the head with his cane. If he didn't die of a heart attack first.

Ma starts rambling, "Did you know I had to go to Limericks and drag your Da out by the ear yesterday when he didn't arrive for supper? All those old fellas going on about that mess down in Dublin."

I know exactly what she means. Dundalk, County Louth is known for an abundance of staunch Irish republican supporters, many of whom marched with the Provisional IRA back in its day. Now Da and his friends mainly sit around the pub with their pints, bitching about England and government and the policing system. Some of them have gotten into the political side of it, and occasionally they'll load up into a van and join a protest that the 32CSM is supporting. Not Da, though. He's had enough of all of that.

Mostly, they're devising plots to deliver righteous punishment to all these bleeding gangs who they blame the gardai for having allowed to thrive in recent years. Quick and justified punishment. Of course, it's all just chatter. But when that chatter turns to the splinter cells that have cropped up—terrorists and gangs using the notoriety and fear of the IRA name to extort money and deal drugs—the shouting starts.

"A bullet in the head, that's what these bastards need!" Da slams his fist on the table, rattling the dishes.

"Seamus," Ma warns, her voice sharp.

He takes a moment to calm down and then finally sighs. "At least no one got hurt."

A twinge of discomfort tugs at my back. I beg to differ.

Ma clasps her hand together and begins clucking like a hen. "And that poor American girl. Imagine visiting Dublin and almost dying over something so foolish!"

I wonder what Ma would say if she knew that American girl's last name is Welles? As a woman who lost many ancestors in the Great Famine, and whose own family was terrorized by the UDA as a Catholic girl visiting her relatives near Belfast, Ma has never had a lot of love or sympathy for anyone bearing ties to England, even though a few of her distant cousins now live in Bath. She'll die before she visits them there, on principle.

Probably nothing cruel. Ma may be singularly focused and a master at holding a grudge, but she's not hateful toward innocent people.

"That would have been bad," I agree, keeping my eyes on my bowl, still thinking about those few minutes with Amber today, by the memorial. She didn't notice me coming up from behind, as she peered so intently into the face of one of the statues. So I hung back, studying her for a good, long minute. Taking in those legs, bared in a pair of jean shorts that hugged her body just right. Her thighs are strong and sculpted like an athlete's, her skin tanned and smooth. She was wearing a simple white T-shirt today, but she filled it out with a perfect pair of tits. And that hair . . . I wanted to weave my fingers through it.

She's a smart one, her eyes zeroing in on the knuckles I used to get the money back from Benoit and putting the pieces together. I saw the recognition in them, and I was sure I saw disappointment follow. She glimpsed the true me, while I glimpsed how she felt about that.

And it bothered me. For a moment there I regretted my actions and wondered if maybe I shouldn't have pummeled him, especially after he emptied his wallet of all the money he stole. Not because I think he didn't deserve it.

But because the way she looked at me today, and yesterday at the bar, as if I can do no wrong . . . She obviously sees me in a better light than I actually warrant, and I like the feel of that light.

I was so surprised—and relieved—when she threw her arms around me. I lost a few breaths, just appreciating the feel and smell of her, in a way I definitely didn't in the Green. I almost kissed her. I was so close to her neck, so close to just turning in farther. But I held back because, while she may look at me like I'm some sort of angel, I don't want to assume that it's more. Worse, I don't want her to think I expect anything in exchange for what I did.

So I stopped myself. And I cursed myself for not growing a pair the entire drive here.

"Her family must be worried sick about her." Ma's prattling voice cuts into my thoughts.

"Probably." Good question. I never even asked. I was too busy trying not to stare at those legs of hers. She must know they're something to look at. She keeps wearing those little shorts.

"What's that smile about now?" Ma chirps, the heavy creases in her face folding with her frown.

"The stew. It's delicious," I lie, soaking a crust of bread in the gravy and taking a bite.

It was a split-second decision, as I was climbing out of my car to go meet her, to keep the list. And another split-second decision to hint to her that I've seen it. I figure it gives her an excuse to come back to Delaney's, if she wants one. And if she does, then she's definitely chasing me.

A prospect that has me beaming inside.

"You're such a good son, River." Ma musses my hair up. "When are you going to find a nice Irish Catholic girl to marry?"

I wonder if Amber's Protestant.

"When I'm thirty and she's old enough to work in the pub and get knocked up." I wink at Da and he roars with laughter. He and

Ma are twelve years apart in age. She applied for a waitressing job at Delaney's on her eighteenth birthday and he married her four months later. Aengus was born seven months after that.

"Six more years for grandbabies! Oh, River . . ." She clucks her disapproval.

I just grin wider at her and shrug my shoulders.

"These boys exasperate me some days."

TEN

AMBER

"Are you an art student?" an old man asks, parking his walker next to me, his white-knuckled grip of the handles telling me he'd fall flat without that support. The age spots all over his arms put him somewhere in his nineties, likely.

"No." I chuckle. "I finished school already. I'm just doing a little traveling and a friend told me I needed to come to the museums and experience some real Irish history."

"You're an American! Well, there's surely a lot to learn about here."

You're telling me. I just spent four hours investigating the Collins Barracks Museum and the National Museum of Ireland, my head swimming in information on the famine, the many rebellions and civil wars fought, the animosity between English and Irish, Protestant and Catholic. The Irish Republic Army. It's a lot to process, and all I really got out of it is that River was right and I am, indeed, an ignorant tourist.

"One of our most famous artists, Burton was," the old man muses, jutting his chin toward the painting. "But *The Meeting on the Turret Stairs* is arguably his best. Such a beautiful image of such an ill-fated couple."

I study the haunting watercolor painting that hangs before me in the long, narrow hallway of the National Gallery, and I immediately see what he means. The couple depicted is meeting secretly in a narrow stone staircase. The woman—royalty, in her vibrant blue dress, her long braid running down her back—both reaching for and pulling away from the knight who cradles her arm with a kiss. The description says that it's a story of a princess and her bodyguard, whom the king does not approve of and orders to be killed. This painting is of their final goodbye.

"It's tragically romantic," I agree. "I mean, why would the king kill a man whose sole job was to protect his daughter, and whom she obviously loved?"

He chuckles, a soft sound that reminds me of my grandpa. "I was on me knees on the cobblestone streets of Galway in the early thirties, shining shoes like I did every day, when I found me princess. She traipsed past me, on her way to school. It took me two years to work up the courage to talk to her and when I did," his face erupts into a mass of wrinkles as he smiles, "it was magic between us." The smile slides off. "Of course her da didn't think so. When I asked his permission to propose, he said he'd kill me with his bare hands if I didn't leave her be. No shoe shiner could ever be good enough for his daughter." He snorts. "How's that for a God-fearing Catholic."

Obviously the man didn't kill him. "So what happened?" I ask, intrigued. I'm a sucker for stories like this.

"Well, I broke it off." When he sees the disappointment settle on my face he quickly adds, "I liked me skin! But Darcy was stubborn and she refused to give me up. So we jumped on a boat headed for Scotland, settled in a small coastal village where I had friends, and eloped. Didn't come back for years, with three wee ones in tow. What was her father going to do? Kill her daughter's husband and the father of his grandchildren? Besides, I had me a good job by then. Could provide well for me family."

I smile at the man. "I'm glad that story has a happy ending."

"It does. God rest her soul, Darcy and I were together for sixty-four years before she left me," he says wistfully, his eye wandering over the many paintings that line the wall. "She used to love it here. Sometimes I can feel her still roaming the halls . . ."

I'm guessing he spends a lot of time here.

There's a long pause. "Why was I . . . oh, right! I was telling that story to prove a point. Her father was a doctor. He could have been a king, and he could have been a pauper, and he'd still be right about one thing: that I was never good enough for her. But luckily I was smart enough to realize that, and never stop trying to be the man she deserved." He lets go of his walker long enough to pat my shoulder gently. "Ya remember that, pretty lass. And maybe give the shoe shiner a second look."

I imagine what he must have been like, a young Irishman crouched on the streets so long ago, and what life was like back then. Even though times have changed, if I were to bring home a guy who shines shoes to meet my parents, I can't say they'd be thrilled either.

But what about if I were to bring home an Irish bartender . . .?

I stifle the eye roll that those thoughts deserve. Is there anything that won't make my mind segue into thoughts of River?

"Carpe diem, miss. Foolish youth is a strange and wondrous time that vanishes too quickly." He shuffles over to the next painting with slow, easy movements, sparking a conversation with a young couple.

Seize the day.

If I wasn't convinced before, that sweet old man surely helped sway me.

I'll take the bait.

I'll chase you, River.

■ ■ ■

I'm pretty desperate.

That's the only way I can explain why I'm standing in front of this funky canary-yellow door—edged with chunky white columns and a half-moon window above, an aged brass lion's-head knocker just begging to be used at eye level. I know I have the right place because the hand-painted sign above the door of this stone house on a narrow side street in northern Dublin says so. Still, it doesn't look like any tattoo parlor I've ever passed by.

With my purse squeezed tight between my arm and my rib cage, I push through the door and step into a reception area, cramped with paisley wing chairs to my left and a counter to my right. The lack of windows only adds to the dingy atmosphere. Even the lights from a multitude of tracks above seem to get swallowed up, creating dark corners wherever I look.

Low murmurs and that irritating buzz of a tattoo machine carry from a narrow hallway lined with sconces made to look like candles. "Hello?" I call out, distracting my own awkwardness by focusing on the colorful canvases decorating the exposed stone walls. Some are of artfully displayed tattoos. Others look like graffiti you find on the sides of buildings—a kaleidoscope of bubbly lines and chaotic images.

Alex did say that this was Ivy's cousin's shop. I guess they have more in common than just tattoos.

I hear the shuffle of feet along the sand-colored wood floors—the only modern element of this place besides the lighting, from what I can see. At least it's clean.

A guy with short jet-black hair styled in spikes appears, tattoos crawling up the back of his neck. "Sorry about that. Can I help you?" He reminds me of Ivy in that he's obviously a mixture of Asian and something else, his eyes bigger and rounder, his lips fuller, his nose more prominent.

I catch myself staring at him and blurt out, "I'm here to see Ivy."

He clicks the computer mouse a few times, checking the screen with a frown. "What time was your appointment?" He sounds American, but with hints of an Irish twang, suggesting he's been here a while.

"Oh, I'm not here for a tattoo." I've never had any desire to get one. I don't understand anyone who does. Another way in which Ivy and I are glaringly different. "I just wanted to stop in and say hi. I went to school with her, back in Oregon." That feels like a lie, even though it's not. I did go to school with her, but I'm making it sound like we were friends. Something we've never been.

He scratches the back of his head in thought. "Well . . . she'll be working on this guy for another couple hours."

"Hours?" I check my watch. It's close to five p.m. already. "Could you just tell her that Amber Welles is here?"

He shrugs and then nods, disappearing back down the hall. I take that time to flip through a binder sitting open on a claw-footed side table, full of pictures of tattoos on body parts, the skin pink and puffy. A hint of nerves touches me. Will dropping my name make Ivy more or less likely to come out here?

A few minutes later, the needle stops buzzing. Clunky footfalls sound in the hallway. I look up in time to see Ivy round the corner, surprise touching her almond-shaped black eyes before she hides it behind the cool mask of indifference that she wears so well. I haven't seen her since last summer, but there's been no miraculous transformation. Her long, arrow-straight raven hair has blue streaks running through it instead of pink. The full sleeve of ink up her slender right arm obviously hasn't disappeared. It's been added to, if anything. She's wearing a classic Ivy outfit—Doc Martens, black jeans, a tank top with a flannel shirt tied around her waist—only the boots reach up to her knees, the jeans are more like leggings, and the tank top is made of black lace and has *Diva* written across it in sequins. That's definitely something new.

"Alex told me you were in Dublin." She crosses her arms over her chest, as if hiding the fact that she's wearing something with a hint of femininity for once.

"Yeah, she gave me the name of this place, in case I wanted to come by." My gaze roams over it. "It's . . . not what I expected."

She just stares at me, as if waiting for me to get on with why I'm here and then leave. I can't tell if it's just Ivy being Ivy, or if, even after all these years, she still holds a grudge.

"So . . ." I busy my hands by flipping a page in the tattoo binder. "How come you're allowed to work in Ireland?"

"Why do you want to know? You gonna report me, Little Miss Sheriff?"

I roll my eyes at that.

She sighs and her tone changes to something less aggressive, but no more friendly. "I was born in Spain, so I can work anywhere in the EU."

"Really?" My eyes drift over her again. Maybe that explains her exotic face. I've never quite been able to place it. She definitely has Chinese—or some kind of Asian—in her, but her skin is darker, her hair thicker, her eyes bigger and rounder. I always thought she'd be so pretty if she actually made an effort to look normal. "I didn't know that."

"How would you?"

I shrug. "You're right. I wouldn't."

She frowns slightly, stepping forward. "What happened to your lip? And your arm?" She almost sounds concerned.

"Oh." *Shit.* "It's a long, boring story." The last thing I need is Ivy telling Alex about this. I pull my cardigan on as I stand. "Listen, I was wondering what you were doing tonight."

A second wave of surprise flashes across her face but she quickly covers it up. "Just working. I should be done by eight." A pause, then a doubtful, "Why?"

"Why don't we meet up somewhere after? I thought we could hang out. Get to know each other, seeing as you're such good friends with Alex."

She twists her mouth, as if debating her next words. "I guess, if you wanted to, you could come—"

"How about Delaney's," I blurt out, cutting her off.

"Delaney's?" She frowns. "Are you sure?"

"Yeah." I smile. "Meet me there at, say, nine?"

Another long moment and then she finally nods, easing a card from her back pocket with two fingers. "Here's my number, just in case you need to get hold of me."

I flip it within my fingers. *Ivy Lee, Artist.* "You actually have a business card?"

"I can read, too," she mutters dryly and then disappears back down the hall.

Okay. So Ivy Lee is going to be my wing-woman. As far as bad ideas go, this could be as disastrous as running through that park the day of the pipe bomb.

Even so . . . A giddy grin finds its way to my mouth.

I'm going to see River again.

ELEVEN

RIVER

"How's it been?" I slap Rowen's shoulder as I edge past him along the narrow bar corridor. Collin's in the middle of an upbeat jig that has the people cheering along.

"How do you think it's been?" Rowen swipes at his brow with his bicep while he pours. "This is my second shirt today. Why haven't we retrofitted this place with air conditioning yet?"

"Because it's a waste of money. Don't worry. They're calling for a break starting tomorrow. That's what Ma said. Besides," I grab an order from the printer, "hot customers mean thirsty customers. It'll be a good night for the pub."

"Let's hope that doesn't also mean a good night for a fight." Rowen nods toward my hand. "Benoit came by earlier to have a word."

I roll my eyes. The idiot doesn't know what to do with his evenings now.

"That's three tenners a week lost," he reminds me. "At least."

"He's a thief." I drop the pint on the counter a little too hard, splashing a bit on my hand. "We don't serve thieves."

"Fair enough, though we serve plenty of scoundrels."

"This place is run by scoundrels!" one of our regulars pipes up from his side of the bar, earning a round of chuckles and a few handclasps. A lot of these men have formed friendships over their years on our stools. I wouldn't necessarily call them healthy relationships, mind you—they depend on Delaney's being open and the beer flowing—but there's a sense of community here.

"Is this about the thief or the bird?" Rowen's not going to let up so easily.

"Both," I admit with a smirk, before grabbing another order coming in from the wait staff. It's going to be a long night. Saturdays always are, even in a city graced with a thousand pubs.

"River. You're here, finally." Nuala, a long-standing bartender and waitress at Delaney's, hip-checks me out of the way before bending down to pull a bottle of Budweiser from the cooler. "Which bird is your brother going on about?"

"An American damsel in distress," Rowen pipes in, stealing a glimpse of her round, ample arse over his shoulder. "Benoit stole her wallet last night and this guy dashed in on his steed to retrieve it for her."

"After an American. Really, River? Had enough of us pure Irish Catholic birds?" She bats her eyelashes at me. I can only laugh. Nuala and I have been friends for years now. Long enough to know that *pure* has never been the right word to describe her. "Do you still need me behind the bar or can I take tables now? I have me own Americans waiting." She raises her brow suggestively. "A whole lot of them."

"What's wrong, had enough of us strapping Irish fellas?" Rowen turns his lip down in an exaggerated frown.

She leans into him, resting her chin against his bicep, her hand rubbing suggestively over his back. "Stop pouting. It's unbecoming." It's impossible not to look at the wide gap in her front teeth as she flashes a broad grin. It's even harder to keep our eyes on her pretty, though average, face when she adjusts her tight-fitting work shirt over a pair of giant tits. Rowen and I, and the entire row of regulars by the bar, always fail.

With a loud bark of laughter, she grabs her service apron and rounds the bar. All the staff like it when Americans come in. It usually means a decent tip, unless they've bought into those tourist guide magazines that tell them not to bother.

Heaven forbid. It's not like we Irish need the extra money.

"Why'd you end that, again?" Rowen mutters, watching Nuala's curvy hips sway as she strolls toward her section.

"We never started." It wasn't anything, really, and it was a long time ago now. A few late nights alone together and a few too many pints after closing the pub. Things were bound to happen eventually.

He just shakes his head, his attention shifting from Nuala to Greta as the willowy blonde punches an order in, bobbing to the steady thrum of Collin's upbeat guitar rhythm.

I cuff him lightly upside the head. "It's too busy for daydreaming."

"Says the wanker who just strolled in," he throws back, but he's smiling. Rowen's by far the most relaxed of the three of us. He could man this bar alone on a Saturday night and make it out alive.

"Fair enough." I begin pouring drinks and collecting money while I flash the broad Delaney grin that's something of a trademark. Coupled with drink, it usually works to help slide the edge off anyone's shoulders, no matter how shitty their week has been. Working my way down to the end of the horseshoe bar, I find one of my favorite regulars sitting quietly, his face weathered, his gaze lost in the bottom of his pint. "Francis O'Reilly!" I slap the counter, snapping him out of his spell.

"River," he chuckles softly. "How has your day today been, fine sir?"

I pause to ponder that. Dragging myself out of bed was tough, but seeing Amber put me in a good mood. "Just grand. And you?"

"Yeah. Grand." His smile falls with his gaze and I know that he's lying.

I reach under the bar and grab a pack of smokes. Francis always gets his week's supply on Saturday night. "Nice and fresh, arrived from the Canaries last Wednesday." We have a steady stream of friends traveling to Spain and bringing back a suitcase worth for us to sell behind the bar, to the Irish folk who don't want to pay a tenner for a pack. Which is every person who walks into this pub. It's good side cash for us.

With a furtive glance around, he slides them into his pocket. "You should be careful, selling these here. You'll have gardai breathing down your neck."

"They're always breathing down our necks." I rest my elbows on the bar with ease, unperturbed. "So they'll confiscate the cases and I'll get a slap on the wrist and wait for the next delivery to come in." We've been selling packs under the bar for the last decade with only one incident. It cost us a bit in fines but in the end, it's still worth it.

He sighs and then nods.

"What's really going on, Francis?" I pause. This just isn't like him. We're normally three dirty jokes into the conversation by now. "Everything good with Cheryl and the kids? The grandkids?"

He nods, and for a brief moment his eyes gloss over.

"Business is good?" Francis and his family have run several popular fish-and-chip shops around Dublin for over forty years. I'd be surprised if it were to blame for his mood.

"It is. Too good, maybe, because it's attracting attention I don't want," he mutters, pouring back the rest of his beer. He slaps money down on the bar and stands to leave.

"Hey . . . what's that supposed to mean?"

He sighs, glancing around before leaning forward, his voice so low I can hardly hear him over the music. "Two fellas showed up at me store yesterday. They say they've taken care of a small debt I had with someone and now I'm to pay them. With interest."

Unease slips down my spine. I've heard of this happening before. "So tell them to fuck off."

"It's not so simple, River. They said they'd hurt me family if I didn't deliver a thousand euro every week to them." His jaw tightens. "They showed me the tattoos on their stomach."

I heave a sigh, but it doesn't relieve my growing anger. If I find out this is Jimmy's doing . . . "What do they look like?"

He shrugs. "I don't know. Like assholes. The one had this scar," he gestures at his forehead, "cutting into his hairline."

"I'm sorry this is happening to you, but you need to go to the gardai." As much as I hate saying that. But Francis is good people. They generally try to help good people. They didn't do much to help us the year some ballsy thugs broke into Delaney's at night and stole cash. It was a lot of cash, too. We usually make several deposits each week, always in the mornings. But on that particular day, I didn't have a chance and figured it would be fine locked in the safe for one more night. Gardai never figured out who did it; the two bastards who came to take my statement even suggested it might be a scam on my part.

"That's what Cheryl wants to do. But they said they'd break all our legs if any gardai show up at their doorstep with questions. What am I supposed to do?" His shoulders hang. "I can't believe it's come to this. See ya, River."

"Yeah. See ya." I watch him shuffle away with a deep frown on my forehead, my spirits dampened. Forget Jimmy . . . if Aengus has anything to do with this, I'll have him put back behind bars myself.

But even as I think that, I know I won't. Besides, Aengus doesn't have any republican tattoos on his stomach or scars across his forehead. And Francis knows Aengus. When we were little and visited our nanny on weekends, we'd sit on the front steps of Francis's nearby store, stuffing our faces with chips.

"River!" Rowen catches my attention and I think he's about to give me grief for slowing down. But he only juts his chin toward the other side of the bar.

To where the devil himself stands, filling a pint.

"Well, fuck," I mutter as I pass Rowen. I knew it was only a matter of time.

"Aengus."

He drains a third of his pint before setting it down and wiping his mouth with the back of his hand. "How's your back?"

The longtime regulars know enough about our family and the black sheep son to be watching closely. They're probably bracing for a brawl. No doubt it would be an ugly one, as most of ours tend to get these days. "Grand," I force through gritted teeth, grabbing an order for Nuala. "You know you're not supposed to be helping yourself to the taps."

He snorts. "What are you gonna do, throw me out?"

"Da didn't say you couldn't come in." Though if he knew what happened at the Green, I'm sure the ban would extend to Delaney's as a whole. "So why don't you grab a seat and I'll bring it to you."

He pulls his shoulders back and takes a step forward, until his chest is nearly butting against mine. "And what happens when Da's in the ground? You think you're gonna run things?"

The smell of beer on his breath tells me that Aengus has been sitting in a hole somewhere, drinking all day, and as much as I want to punch him in the face for talking about our dad being dead, or enlighten him to the fact that our parents had a will drawn up that specifically leaves the pub to me—against the Delaney tradition that the eldest gets proprietary rights—now's not the time to get ballsy with him. "We're just trying to work here. It's busy. Grab a stool. In fact, here . . ." I reach down and take the one and only stool tucked away behind the bar and bring it around to the side. "Look at that. One just became available."

After a long moment, Aengus relents, dropping onto the stool and pulling out his phone. "Don't push him. His fuse is short," I warn Rowen as we pass each other and get back to work, hoping that's the end of trouble with our big brother for the night.

But when Jimmy Conlon strolls through our front door, I know that isn't the case.

I watch with disdain as he weaves through the crowd with the arrogance of a guy unafraid of anything. Like there isn't a warrant out for his arrest and a hit on his head right now.

To any unsuspecting person, he's just a regular coming in for a pint. He's average looking, with a few more gray hairs peppering the black since the last time I saw him. His nose hasn't straightened out any. In fact I think it bends slightly more to the right now. I'm sure whoever hit him was left in worse-off shape. Jimmy may be short, but he's built like an ox.

What the fuck is he doing in here? Aengus knows better. I would think Jimmy does, too. I'm not the only one who recognizes Jimmy around here. Several wary eyes, keen on the city's politics and known criminals, trail him as he approaches Aengus. With a glance over his shoulder and a few quick words, Aengus climbs off his stool and rounds the bar, heading through the kitchen door that leads to the office without hesitation. Jimmy follows as if he owns the place, catching my glare and tossing a salute back.

A vice latches onto my forearm. "Why the fuck is he here?" Rowen mutters. He knows who Jimmy is.

"I don't know. Just keep pouring. And don't say a word to Da." This is exactly the kind of news that will give him another heart attack.

I last all of five minutes out front, and then my Irish blood is boiling in my ears and I decide I've given those assholes more than enough time back there. While I don't think Aengus would steal from us, I'm relieved that Rowen emptied the safe yesterday morning.

It takes everything in me to bang on the door three times by way of announcement before throwing it open. Jimmy sits in the office chair like he belongs there, while Aengus paces the cramped space like a caged bear.

"Bring a pint for Jimmy," Aengus demands.

I ignore him. "Time to go. You know this place gets watched. I figure you've got"—I glance at my watch—"twenty minutes before gardai start sniffing around."

"You sound like you're expecting them," Jimmy says in that calm, too soft voice that always sends chills down my spine.

I level a warning glare at Aengus. "Never can tell when someone will ring them."

Aengus isn't smart but he hears my threat—though empty—loud and clear. He kicks a box of coasters out of his way, reaching out to throttle me.

"Aengus, enough!" Jimmy snaps, and my brother freezes, though his stance stays rigid. "Have they come around in the last three days, River?"

He means, since the bombing happened. My eyes lock on my brother. Did he tell Jimmy I was there? That I know what happened? That I'm the Irish "jogger" who the gardai could connect to the crime, who could tie Aengus—and possibly, Jimmy—to it, should I want to avoid jail time? Because I wouldn't put it past a guy like Jimmy to put a bullet in my head, just to make sure I don't have a chance to talk. "No. They haven't."

"That's good." Jimmy twirls a pen between his fingers, his attention somewhere beyond the palpable tension in this cramped office. Scribbling a number down on a piece of paper, he pats it twice. "You'll ring me here if they do?"

"Aengus will be the first to know." And I'll burn that number the second this cocksucker is gone.

"Cheers, brothers." He exits the office quietly. I watch his back until it disappears through the door in the rear, and then I kick our office door shut and shove Aengus into the wall with all my strength.

Even though I'm ready for the blowback, I'm not strong enough to withstand it. Aengus sends me flying into the filing cabinet, the corner of it jamming perfectly against the wound in my lower back. I cry out as a sharp spasm of pain radiates, my knees weakening from the intensity, ready to puke up Ma's stew. That doesn't stop Aengus from pinning me with a forearm against my throat, his fist yanking at my shirt hard enough to rip the collar.

It takes a few deep breaths to see through the pain. "What the fuck are you doing, bringing him in here? You know there are always eyes on this place," I hiss.

"They can't prove anything."

"And if they do? What's Jimmy gonna do? He doesn't want to go back to jail."

"None of us do." Wild eyes that remind me of the color of pond scum right now bore into mine. "I didn't tell him you were there. All he thinks is that it was some muppet who knows better than to get involved with the gardai."

After a lengthy, wordless showdown, Aengus's arm finally relaxes. I let my head fall back against the nearby wall as a sharp ache throbs in my lower back.

When he speaks again, the fire in his voice is gone. He sounds tired. "I didn't know he'd show up here. Honest."

I don't believe him. Aengus lies so much, I don't think even he remembers what the truth is anymore. "What'd he want?"

Aengus releases a mouthful of booze-scented air and begins pacing. "Beznick's sister and her kids have gone to ground. Probably back to Romania."

And they're surprised? I could have told them that was going to happen. "So he got the message, I gather."

"He did." He pauses, twisting his mouth in disdain. "And just threatened retaliation on whoever was responsible. Tit-for-tat."

"What the fuck does that even mean . . ." I tug at the hem of my T-shirt until I can see the dark spot forming on the material. I must have torn a bloody stitch. "If anyone wants a tit, it should be me," I mutter.

"That Gypsy bastard thinks he can threaten us!" Aengus bellows. Now I know why he was pacing the room when I came in. He's spitting mad.

"And so you thought it'd be a good idea to meet with Jimmy here and talk about it?"

"Like I said, I didn't—"

"I don't want to hear it." I cut him off, yanking my T-shirt over my head. I reach for the medic kit. Being the pub that we are, it's well stocked. I dig out the roll of tape quickly. "How bad is it?"

"Two stitches. Here . . .You can't reach that." Aengus grabs the roll out of my hand and rips off a strip with his teeth. He's always been good at quick bandaging. He's had a lot of experience. I clench my jaw against the sting as he pulls the skin back together. "Pansy." In another second and with some gauze in his hand, he adds, "That should hold, if you stay out of any more fights tonight."

I toss the soiled and torn T-shirt into the rubbish can and rifle through the box of spare work shirts we have in the office. "You've got to be bloody kidding me . . ." The largest one I can find is medium. And women's. "Shite," I mutter, pulling out my old one to check over it again. There's no hiding that that's blood. And the tear . . . I can't be behind the bar with that, especially after a dozen witnesses watched Jimmy and Aengus come back here. That'll spark questions.

I have no choice. "For fuck sakes." I ease the new one on, tugging it over my torso.

Aengus doubles over in loud, raucous laughter. I haven't heard him laugh like that in years, and it releases some of the tension in the air.

"What's going on in here?" Rowen sticks his head in. His brow spikes with surprise. "You don't wear that as well as Nuala."

I jab a thumb toward the box. Rowen's the one who takes care of T-shirt inventory. "Are those the only shirts we have?"

His lips sit pressed together tightly, twitching. He's trying not to laugh. "They are. Told you to stop giving T-shirts away to customers because we were running low."

Fuck.

"We're getting slammed out front. I need you," he adds in a serious tone.

"And I need to get home before some arse reports me to the gardai for being seen with Jimmy," Aengus says through lingering chuckles, though the glint in his eye tells me he hasn't forgiven me for that one.

Shaking my head, I trail Rowen out.

Preparing my healthy male ego for the bashing that's about to come.

TWELVE

AMBER

I spot Ivy's slender figure leaning against the old stone wall of Delaney's as soon as the cab turns the corner. Those high lace-up boots crossed at the ankles are impossible to miss. She's exchanged her earlier Diva shirt and jeans for an asymmetrical gothic outfit, complete with black lace and burgundy satin. Her hair hangs smooth and shiny, framing a face that's been painted with a heavy hand of makeup.

I'd look trashy in that getup, but somehow Ivy can pull it off.

The customers passing her on their way into the raucous bar take a second look, not that she notices, her face glued to her phone.

In my short white shorts, flowing bubblegum-pink blouse—the single long sleeve ideal to cover the bruising on my right side—and silver jeweled sandals, we couldn't be more ill-suited to each other.

"Hey, Ivy."

Her inky-eyed once-over of me says she's thinking the same thing. "Are you really sure this is the kind of place you were looking for?"

"A local Irish pub? Of course. Why wouldn't I want to come here?"

Three middle-aged men stumble out the front door, laughing and slapping each other on the back as they pull cigarettes out of their pockets. Blithering drunken idiots by nine.

"Meet the locals," she murmurs, leading the way through the propped-open door and into a crowded, rowdy scene. The same guy who played yesterday plays again, only now he has a companion on a second guitar and they seem to be dueling. I shrink into myself as we move farther in. From what I can see, every last table is taken and the bar lineup is two deep. Whatever the fire code is in this country, I'm guessing this place isn't adhering to it.

"Wow. I didn't expect it to be so packed this early." It's just another pub, and if I've learned anything about Dublin in my wanderings, it's that they have a lot of pubs to choose from. "We're not going to find anywhere to sit, are we?"

"No one's leaving this place until the music stops playing and the beer stops pouring. Or they get kicked out."

I feel eyes on us as we carve our way through hot, sweaty bodies, avoiding the sloshing drinks. Having learned my lesson, I keep my small purse zipped up and tucked under my arm as we make our way to the far side to cram into an empty nook next to a bronze statue of a man.

"Are we allowed to just stand here?" I ask.

"Where else are we going to stand?" She shoots me a perturbed look, like this is my fault.

"Well . . ." I glance behind me. We're practically hovering over someone's table. I'll be getting a perturbed glare from them soon, too.

"I've had a long day, Welles." I bristle a little at the way she uses my last name, but I don't say anything. "There are plenty of places like this around Dublin. It's really nothing special. Or, worst case, we can go to Temple Bar. If you like loud drunks, you'll love it there."

She's wrong about Delaney's not being special. And I don't want to go anywhere else. Not if River is here. I stretch onto my tiptoes and search the horseshoe-shaped bar through the crowd, but can only make out the short, curvy blonde manning the taps. River said he'd be here tonight, didn't he? Unless that was just an excuse to get away from me? No, I have to stop thinking like that.

If that were the case, he wouldn't have left things as he did. "Can we just wait a bit, to see if something frees up?"

Ivy purses her wine-colored lips in answer, her dark eyes surveying the crowd with disdain. I'm guessing I have about five minutes before she simply walks out.

"Just stay for a bit. Please? I'll buy you a drink."

Her inky gaze, heavily lined with black shadow, settles on me.

"Two drinks?"

She sighs. That seems to win her over. "Well, we're not going to get served standing here. So—"

Hoots and hollers erupt near the bar, cutting her words off. First just a few, but soon everyone seems to be joining in on the fun. I lift to my tiptoes again, to peer over the crowd. Three heads—two golden brown with a hint of copper, and one clearly a redhead, only shaved—bob along.

The energetic singer stops mid-lyric and his laughter carries over the speakers to the tune of the strumming guitar. "Well, well . . . would you look at that strapping young Delaney fella! Did Marion shrink your laundry this week? Or did you lose a wager?"

A loud chorus of laughter erupts as more heads turn.

"Before you ask . . . that there fella is still looking for a Mrs. River Delaney. Perhaps if he didn't dress like a poof, he'd find her!"

A bubble of excitement jumps in my stomach at his name, as I watch the bar intently, waiting. I'm assuming the middle finger that flashes over the crowd is his. Finally, bodies shift.

His grinning face appears first, his cheeks just slightly flushed with embarrassment. A customer steps in, blocking my sight and earning my annoyance, but like a continuous wave, people shift again, and I finally see what the musician was referring to.

River's wearing a T-shirt that looks three sizes too small, the black cotton straining over every single one of his muscles, like one of those douchy gym pigs at the CrossFit where I belong. Worse, it's very clearly a woman's V-neck, the front dipping down just far enough to show a light patch of chest hair.

While I'll admit that River, with a body like that—all its ripples and hardened curves—has nothing he needs to hide, he looks ridiculous.

I can't help it.

I start giggling.

His bright green eyes drift over the crowd, past Ivy and me.

They dart back to lock on mine, a flash of surprise in them.

I purse my lips tight, trying to keep from laughing as heat burns my cheeks. He can surely guess why I'm here again . . . can't he?

What do I do now?

He dips his head, a sheepish smile touching his lips as he mouths something on his way past his brother. Customers poke and slap him as he rounds the bar and passes them.

I know that he's on his way toward me.

"So, of all the places you could go in Dublin, you're here . . . again." His gaze dips to my one bare shoulder for a second.

"I am." *God,* I don't think I've ever been this overt with a guy before. Sure, I've flirted plenty, but it's always after the guy has made his interest well known. I've never chased after anyone. They've always come to me. "The Great Famine began in 1845. Many accuse England of letting the Irish starve to death, robbing them of their oats and grains in the name of economy."

His brow quirks. "Not bad."

"I went to one of those museums for ignorant tourists that you recommended." I know I'm staring at him but I can't seem to help it, even as I see that sparkle of recognition that tells me he can see my thoughts plain as day.

He's just so beautiful.

An awkward pause hangs between us before I remember my manners. "This is my friend, Ivy."

His eyes dance with mine for just a moment longer before shifting to Ivy. He sticks out a hand. "Hello, Ivy. I'm River, and we appreciate your business."

She takes it, that tight smirk—like she's trying not to smile but can't completely hide it, which I'm coming to learn is her trademark—glancing over her lips. "We won't be staying long if we can't find a place to sit and relax."

I shoot a glare at her. Does she have to be a bitch to him, too?

Her brashness seems to slide off his back. "A place to sit and relax." He pauses, running his tongue over his bottom lip in thought as he searches the bar. "Come with me."

We follow him toward the back. The area doesn't have a prime view of the musicians but it does have a prime view of the bar, and I'll take that. He grabs a tray full of empty glasses from a small service table and hands it to a passing waitress. Dragging the table away from the wall, he orders with solemn eyes, "Don't leave this table, not for even a second." He disappears behind the bar and through the back door.

"Suddenly I'm seeing things so clearly . . ." Ivy muses.

"What do you mean?"

She rolls her eyes. "Right."

River reappears, his arm flexed with two wooden stools. Customers chirp at him about needing a seat as he passes but he only grins, making his way back over to set them on either side of the table for us. "Now you have a place to sit and relax, so I guess you're staying." His hand brushes against my shoulder on its way to settle along the back of a neighboring chair. "Now, what can I get you?"

Woman's V-neck or not, River's proximity and his charm is sending my nerves into a tailspin right now.

"A pint of Guinness?" I ask, more of a question.

"I knew you'd like that." His eyes dart to my bottom lip, where the injury is more of a dark purple splotch now.

"Double Jameson, neat," Ivy orders, tossing her purse and phone down on the table.

River's brow arches. "Good on you. Most people coming in here stick with beer. I'll have to dig our compulsory bottle out. It's probably coated in dust." He nods toward her arm. "And nice work, by the way."

The first soft, genuine smile that I've ever seen on Ivy's face takes over. "Thanks."

"Who did them for ya?"

"I designed them, but I have a few trusted friends who I let work on me." That edge to her voice when she talks to me has vanished. I'm not that surprised. River can probably charm the rude out of anyone.

"I'm looking to get another one done soon. The stag on our family crest."

My gaze starts searching his arms, looking for the one he already has. If it's there, it's hidden.

"I work at The Fine Needle if you're ever looking for someone. I'm awesome," she says so matter-of-factly. "My cousin, Ian, is pretty good, too. He just finished this one for me last week." She holds out her arm and taps the colorful Day of the Dead skull on the inside of her slender forearm.

River leans in closer to study it, his fingertip tracing the outer lines. Suddenly I'm wishing I had an armful of tattoos. Any excuse for him to touch me like that.

As if he can read my mind, he turns to me and asks, "You have any?"

Ivy bursts out in a cackle unnatural for her tiny body and her cool demeanor. "Miss Sheriff's Daughter marring her perfect skin? Are you kidding me?"

Now River's arched brow is reserved for me and it's much higher. "Sheriff's Daughter?"

"It's nothing." I shoot a glare Ivy's way but she only smiles back. A secret, vindictive smile.

"Oh, it's something, alright." He winks. "And you're going to tell me about it later. I'll be back with your drinks." He squeezes my bare shoulder on his way past, making me jump. I watch him go, catching more than a few glares from female customers lingering around the bar, likely waiting for seats to free up. Or maybe for River's attention.

I meet a flat gaze from across the table. "So this is why you showed up at my work today." Ivy's hard to read, with her dry tone, but I'm pretty sure she's upset. She hasn't even sat down yet. "You don't really want to get to know me. I'm your excuse for coming here . . . 'again.'" She air-quotes that word. "You were afraid to sit alone in a place like this."

I open my mouth to deny it but she cuts me off, shaking her head. "Save it. I should have known."

I sigh, suddenly feeling like a jerk. "You're right, okay? You're the only person I know in Dublin and I didn't want to come here alone to see River again. But . . . so what? We'll have a few drinks, get to know each other, I get to see him . . . What's the big deal?"

"I don't like being used." She tightens her jaw. "Alex emailed me to tell me you were in Ireland. She was afraid you might be lonely. She asked me to give you a chance, if you came by. I didn't think you actually would."

"I'm not lonely!" My cheeks flush. Sure, once in a while I get homesick, but lonely?

"Well, I wouldn't be surprised if you were. You could never survive so much as a library hour without your harem of girls fawning all over you."

"My *harem of girls* fawning all over me? Okay, first of all, I'm not a lesbian . . ."

Ivy's eyes narrow. "Funny you should mention that."

I bite the inside of my mouth. *Does this girl ever hold a grudge or what?* "So then . . . we're even. You didn't come here to get to know me either. You only showed up here tonight because Alex asked you to."

"Exactly. Because she's my friend."

I guess I should have expected all of this to come up. Just because Ivy obviously didn't tell Alex about what happened in high school doesn't mean she simply forgot. But it was a freaking decade ago. *Let it go!*

Two glasses land on our table, delivered by a waitress instead of River. A glance at the bar finds him laughing with a customer while pouring pints. I guess I shouldn't have expected him to be serving us, especially with waitresses to do that. Plus, he did go above and beyond already, getting us a table. Still, disappointment stirs inside me.

I sigh. "Listen. Can we please start over?"

"Until the second that bartender says he's done his shift and you ditch me, right?"

I roll my eyes. "I don't do that to my friends."

Her jaw clenches. "We were *never* friends."

"That's because we didn't really have much in common." I stare pointedly at her, but if she sees my meaning, she doesn't let on. "But we could be friends, now."

She snorts.

I bite my tongue before I agree with her, which I'm tempted to do. If this is the real Ivy—and not just a bitter exterior that she's saved for me—then I can't see myself lasting through this pint, hot bartender or not. "High school was a long time ago, Ivy. Maybe we can bury this hatchet you're intent on sticking in my back and actually get to know each other. Who knows . . . maybe you'll find out I'm not so bad."

After a long pause and a look around, she slides into her seat. Tipping her head back, she downs the entire shot of whiskey in one gulp. "I'm going to need a few more of these to find that out."

■ ■ ■

"I didn't have anything to do with starting those rumors. I swear!" The flat look on her face tells me she doesn't believe me. "Well, I know that Bonnie did, because I confronted her about it and she said that she had a highly reliable source who saw me discharged from the psych ward."

"And you thought my mother, a reputable surgeon, would tell me something like that, and I'd run off and tell Bonnie?" My mother didn't even tell me who Alex really was. Why would she divulge private information about a complete stranger who has no impact on my life at all?

Ivy slams back her whiskey and I follow, twisting my face up with disgust, the vile taste burning in my gut. It's taken four rounds for Ivy to break out of her spiky shell and tell me exactly how awful I apparently made high school for her. She must be feeling the alcohol because she's a lot louder and more animated than she was an hour ago.

"Three weeks into my sophomore year, in a new high school, in a town we had just moved to, and I was dubbed 'the crazy girl who might stab you.' Great reputation to have, right? I spent a lot of time at home, hanging out with my little brothers, that first year." She keeps her eyes on our empty shot glasses as she balances them on top of each other. "When those rumors started, Jesse gave me some lame excuse and broke it off. Just like that." She snaps her fingers, her short nails painted with black lacquer. "I know we'd only been seeing each other for a few weeks, but it still hurt . . ."

I groan out loud. Why does everything in my life somehow lead back to my brother? Of course Ivy's heart would fall casualty to his good looks and poor judgment calls. And, of course the blow-back would land on me. I sigh. "For what it's worth, I never knew you two were ever a thing in high school." Jesse had a lot of "things" with a lot of girls and got bored easily. I could never keep up, and by our junior year, I didn't want to. "And I can't make excuses for my brother except to say that he was an idiot back then."

"An idiot who didn't want a girlfriend that apparently sets houses on fire and tortures small animals. I don't blame him. I would have stayed away from me, too. I figured your dad demanded as much."

I snort. "Please! If my dad told him to not date you, he would have proposed." A quick replay of my words in my head makes me cringe, realizing that hearing that isn't going to help heal Ivy's deep wounds. "I'm sorry someone started saying those things about you. But it wasn't me."

Ivy's lips purse. "And are you gonna try and convince me that you didn't accuse me of spray-painting the side of Poppa's Diner?"

There it is. I knew this would come up. I knew that Ivy figured out I was the one who reported her to the sheriff. "No. That, I did do. Poppa showed up at our ranch in his El Camino in tears. Do you know how awful it is to see an old man cry?"

"Funny, because when your dad hauled me into the station for spray-painting the side of the diner, I *did* cry. Your dad scared the shit out of me."

"What did you expect? You can't cover walls with racial slurs and swastikas and get away with it."

She simply stares at me for a long moment, as if in shock that I would even suggest it. "I didn't do it, Amber. You did!"

My jaw hangs open as I stare into those accusing black eyes, looking for the joke in them. There isn't one. She's serious. "What?! You are insane!"

"Okay, fine . . . maybe you didn't actually paint the wall, but I know you were in on it. Don't sit here and lie to me, now, after all these years. You and your little posse of mean girls and dickhead boyfriends planned it all."

I roll my eyes and start laughing now. "Oh come on! Everyone in school knew you did it. You practically lived behind Decker's with that big box of spray paint."

"That's because Sue and Roger let me." The owners of the bowling alley were known to be really nice, fine with letting kids cover the massive brick wall in graffiti, as long as there was no profanity or gang symbols, or any sort of hate speech.

"Your tag was on the bottom right corner, Ivy. I know what your tag looks like because every new thing you added to Decker's wall had that little pink squiggly line." Her brow quirks sharply and I shrug. "What? So I admired your work. You're good."

She shakes her head in disbelief. "First of all, whoever did that to Poppa's was an idiot and a complete amateur. I'm better than that. I was better than that when I was seven years old. Second, do you really think I'd be stupid enough to vandalize a store and tag it?"

"Maybe you wanted people to know that you did it." I shrug. "You did seem kind of angry back then."

She throws her arms up in the air in a rare bout of melodrama.

"I *was* kind of angry back then! Because high school sucked! But it had nothing to do with the Jews or the Middle East. I was set up!"

I give a furtive glance around, hoping no one's paying too much attention to us. My gaze catches River's and a distracting blip of excitement flutters inside my stomach. He frowns and nods toward Ivy, then mouths, "Everything okay?"

With a quick nod, I turn back to her, not wanting her to accuse me of ignoring her for a guy. "Why on earth would I go to all the trouble to do that to you, Ivy? We weren't even in the same grade. We didn't have a single class together!"

She exhales heavily and her scowl softens. "Do you remember that big party in Piper's Mill Park in the spring? The one where Ashley Johnson tripped over a case of beer and broke her nose?"

"Yeah." I chuckle. She ended up needing two rounds of plastic surgery to fix it. I was at home, sick with the stomach flu that night.

"Well, Jesse and I had just started talking again, after breaking up the September before. He invited me to go, so I did. Anyways, that night we got really drunk and broke into the park office."

My eyes widen. "That was *you*? Man, my dad was pissed . . ."

"Yeah, well . . . young and stupid and drunk, right? Anyway, Bonnie barged in on us . . . *you know*."

I groan, seeing where this is going. At least she isn't trying to give me details, as Bonnie has tried to do on more than one occasion.

"She was pissed. Screamed at him for slumming with a psycho slut like me. Then, a week later . . . voilà! I get arrested for graffiti that I didn't do. By *your* father. I figured Bonnie told you and you got mad because you didn't want your brother with the 'psycho slut,' so you and her concocted that graffiti plan."

"Ugh . . . this sounds like the plot of a really bad teen movie. I hate drama!" But it's also shedding some new light on those years. "When did you say you and Jesse started dating for the first time?"

"The first day of my sophomore year, in art class." A soft smile touches her lips. "I was so nervous; I didn't know a single person. I spent most of the class with my head down, sketching tattoo designs on my notebook. I guess he looked over my shoulder and knew what I was doing because he asked me if I could design a tattoo of a '69 Plymouth Barracuda."

"The one on his back."

She nods.

I take a deep breath, because this is my best friend that I'm about to throw under the bus. Though, from the sounds of it, she may deserve it. "Did you know that Bonnie and Jesse dated for the summer between our sophomore and junior year?"

"I heard something about that. But she broke it off, right?"

I shake my head slowly. That's the story Bonnie told everyone, even though I knew it wasn't true. Jesse didn't care enough to correct it. "He ended it the second day into our junior year. She was devastated. She spent our entire junior year trying to get back with him. Secretly, of course. She'd never admit to being hung up on a guy to anyone."

She chews the inside of her mouth. "You think that's why she went after me?"

"She had a *huge* crush on Jesse."

"Huh." She leans back into her chair as realization takes over. "So she's probably the one who vandalized Poppa's Diner, isn't she?"

I shrug. "She never said anything to me about it. Probably because she knew I'd never be okay with it. But she was hanging around with Doug Bentley and those guys, too." *Complete shitheads.* "If I had to guess . . ." Bonnie has been my best friend since kindergarten, but she has her faults. One of them is being a jealous, competitive bitch, especially when it comes to guys.

"And you honestly didn't know about any of this?" Ivy's eyes remind me of an owl's—piercing—as she tries to read me.

"I knew that she didn't like you, but I didn't know why." And to be honest, I never really bothered to ask. I didn't care. "Bonnie and I had a rule about Jesse: she wasn't allowed to talk to me about him."

She chews the inside of her mouth, pondering that.

"If I wanted to keep you two apart, believe me, it would have been because I had *your* best interests at heart, not Jesse's or mine.

My brother was a major fuck-up. My father almost arrested him for stabbing Tommy," I remind her.

She rolls her eyes. "I knew Jesse would never do that. I can't believe your dad even considered it."

"He was just doing his job." And it nearly tore our family apart. "He let you off for the diner, though, right?"

She sighs, the steam fueling her anger before evaporating quickly. "Yeah, because he had no real proof. But my parents still made me paint the entire wall because they figured it was somehow my fault that it had happened in the first place. Plus Poppa banned me from the diner. For life."

"That old man has a long memory," I murmur.

She strums the tabletop with her fingers. "So she's probably the one who started that rumor about me making out with Liz DiPalma behind the portables too, then." My knowing stare answers her question. "What a fucking bitch!"

"Well, to be fair, you did shave your entire head out of the blue and start hanging out with the school's token lesbian student almost exclusively, so anyone could have started that rumor."

"Liz is a nice person."

"I'm sure she is. But that was high school, and teenagers can be jerks about that kind of stuff."

"What a bunch of assholes." Ivy flags the waitress down for another round.

I think I'm going to puke.

But I also feel somehow lighter with all that dirty laundry finally aired. "So you actually thought I was masterminding your systematic destruction?"

"Wouldn't you? I mean, no offense, but that group was like some single-minded neutron force and you were its leader. You all looked the same and acted the same and dressed the same." She snorts, twirling a strand of her hair between her fingers. "I remember when you started coming to school with those perfect, fat curls. Bonnie and all the others came to school with perfect, fat curls the very next day. It was pathetic."

"Curls? You hated me because of my hair?"

She rolls her eyes. "You know what I mean."

"All I know is that judging me for that would be like me judging you for your hairstyle choices." I stare pointedly at the shaved sides, hidden beneath that mass of long black hair.

"Maybe. But at least I didn't sit at that cafeteria table every day at lunch and gossip about everyone."

"Ivy . . . half the time I wasn't even listening to what anyone was saying," I answer truthfully. There were so many rumors milling around, I didn't even remember the one about Ivy being locked up in a mental institution until tonight, when she brought it up. All I really cared about was that I wouldn't be at the receiving end of one of the nastier ones.

But Ivy has clearly never forgotten, all these years later.

"That group was always talking about someone. Laughing at someone." She shakes her head. "High school sucked for me."

"Well, if it makes you feel any better, it wasn't so great for me either."

She tips her head back and throws out a huge, "Ha!"

"I'm serious, Ivy!"

"Most popular girl in school . . . perfect body . . . perfect face . . . valedictorian . . . sheriff's daughter . . . surgeon's daughter . . . freaking Rodeo Queen . . ." She bends each finger back on a hand, counting all the ways that my life sounds so wonderful on paper.

I start my own list, mimicking her finger-counting gesture. "Girl most talked about in school . . . girl who could never misbehave because her father was the sheriff . . . girl who most guys were afraid of dating because her father was the sheriff . . . girl who was never really sure who her true friends were . . . And how do you remember so much about me, anyway?"

She twirls her coaster. "Did you even notice that our lockers were four apart my first year there?"

"I saw you in the hallways sometimes." She had a tamer, almost mousy look to her back then. Less makeup, no tattoos. More plaid and loose-fitting blue jeans than lace and Goth. I remember thinking she could be pretty, with a little bit of work.

Her voice drops its edge, leaving vulnerability behind. "Then why didn't you ever say hi?"

I open my mouth to answer but nothing comes out, because I don't have an answer. Not a good one, anyway.

I'm saved from making something up by one of the men who stumbled out of the bar earlier, on our way in. He's drunker and comes to a standstill in front of our table, his red-tinged, glossy eyes boring into me.

"Can I help you?" I finally ask, sharing a glance with Ivy.

He drops to one knee in front of me. "I need me an American wife so they'll let me into America!" he professes in a slurred Irish accent, grabbing my hand and pulling it to his lips.

I tug but he holds on tight. I look to Ivy for help but she's laughing. No one around seems at all uncomfortable. Several are cheering and clapping, in fact.

"Go on now, Killian. Before I boot you out." River sets three shots on the table and then peels the guy's grasp from my fingers. I revel in the heat of his palm as he hangs onto my hand for three long seconds, giving it a light squeeze before finally letting go.

"Thanks . . ." *Superman.* That's now three times that he's come to my rescue.

The sly twist of his mouth is so subtle I almost miss it. "You're going to make me crack another bottle, if you keep this up. Locked yet?"

"What yet?" *What does that mean?*

"Ask us in another hour." Ivy lifts her glass. River does the same. I groan, lifting mine.

"Cheers." I watch him bring his to his mouth and pour it down like it's nothing. I'm tempted to plug my nose to handle this but I don't, seeing as he seemed impressed by Ivy's tough-girl choice of hard liquor over beer.

River sees my sickened face and just laughs, collecting the empty glasses and heading back to the bar.

"God, how can you stomach this?" I stick my tongue out with disgust.

She shrugs. "We can call it a night if you can't handle it."

"No!" That came out a little too eager.

She glances over to the bar and then back. "He's not your type."

"You don't know what my type is." She may be right, but making such a frank observation irritates me. She's judging me again.

"Well . . . let's see. There was Neil Allen, the preppy son of the mayor, who lived in a million-dollar house. Where is he now?"

"Harvard Law."

"Right." She drags that out with an obnoxious know-it-all voice. "You were with him for a long time."

"Most of my junior and senior year." Though I've known him all my life. I used to throw mud at him in the kindergarten playground. He was the captain of the ski and debate teams, honor roll; tall and blond and somewhat baby-faced, now that I think back to it. I don't think he even started shaving until college. He was considered the boyfriend to have in high school from any parent's point of view, and I had his eye for almost two years. I broke up with Neil before we both left for college, not willing to try a long-distance relationship while he was out East. That was the official excuse, anyway. I was ready to end it months before, but I didn't have the heart. He was such a nice guy, and we had such an easy, calm relationship. That was part of the problem. While my friends were partying in Portland and Seattle, we were sitting at home, watching movies. Even the sex was boring. What teenager has boring sex?

"And your boyfriend in college, what was he like?"

"Who says I had one?"

Her steady gaze is drenched in amusement, like the very idea that I'd suggest I wasn't tied down in college is preposterous.

"His name was Brody," I admit reluctantly, though I won't admit out loud that he reminded me of a slightly older version of Neil, in that he was tall, blond, and handsome in an average way. An intelligent guy, also from a small town.

"And he was in school for . . ."

"Philosophy major. He planned on doing his PhD and becoming a college professor." We were together for almost three years, until I realized that I liked the idea of him—the comfortable hum of routine he brought to my life in Portland, while I was in school—but I didn't love him. I made a clean break when I moved back to Sisters.

I don't know if Ivy can somehow read my silent acknowledgment in her eyes, but she's smirking like the Cheshire Cat. "Oh, and then there was a doctor, wasn't there? Alex told me about him. I'm guessing him and this guy, here, don't have a lot in common?" She must see the discomfort in my face because the smirk slips off and she offers a muttered, "Sorry."

My eyes roam the bar. I'll admit the pang in my chest now is nothing like it was before I met River. One date with this bartender and I may never think of "the surgeon" again. That tells me that maybe my pain over Aaron has less to do with missing him and more to do with missing the *idea* of him, and the humiliation of being dumped because, let's face it, if he *really* cared about me, my age wouldn't matter.

When I was with him, I felt like I wasn't far from a trip toward the altar with a well-respected, handsome doctor. I could see the pride in my parents' smiles, the envy in my friends' eyes. Which means I've now three times fallen for the concept of a relationship—and what that relationship looks like to the outside world—rather than the actual guy I'm with.

"So . . . Where'd you meet this guy?"

"At the park one day. He kind of . . . ran into me." I toy with a coaster to avoid her gaze.

"Sounds romantic."

"It was, in a way." If pipe bombs could be called romantic. He did save my life, though, and that's romantic, on steroids. *And* he brought my wallet back to me, cash and all, which tells me that he's honest, a quality I admire. "Whatever. I'm only here for another week anyway, so . . ." Next Sunday will come too soon.

"So don't waste time being so . . . you." She sticks her finger into her glass and spins it around. "What's his name again? River?" Before I can ask why, she's yelling it across the bar.

Green eyes flash our way and I hold my breath.

She holds up two fingers.

I exhale with relief as I watch him grab the freshly cracked bottle of Jameson from behind him and pour.

"Oh, and Amber's only here for another week, if you want a chance with her. She's a bit uptight, so you'll have to make the first move." Ivy points at me, in case any people in the immediate vicinity couldn't figure out that I'm Amber on their own.

The drunken patrons around us start spouting all kinds of encouragement. A dimpled grin fills River's face as he waves their words off with a dismissive hand.

"Why would you do that to me?" I push through barely moving lips, trying to keep my face expressionless as my cheeks burn.

The blond waitress with the gap in her teeth and giant boobs swoops by then, leaving two shots and a wink at our table.

"That's for being a snob in high school." As Ivy picks her drink up, her chest lifts and she sighs, as if in some monumental gesture. "Now . . . to new beginnings."

"You're such a bitch," I mumble. Lifting my shot, I clink her glass just hard enough to splash a little of it on her fingers. "To new beginnings." I inhale a nervous, shaky breath as I finally dare glance over at River. To see that his eyes are locked on me. A thrill courses through my spine. "And to an interesting week in Ireland."

THIRTEEN

RIVER

"Just gave her back her wallet, did ya?"

Rowen elbows me in the ribs but I ignore him, pouring pints and watching Amber giggle at something her friend said. And pretend she doesn't know I'm watching her. After five whiskeys, she's doing such a piss-poor job of it, I want to walk over there and tease her.

And kiss her.

Whatever good intentions I may have had have poured down the drain along with the tap runoff.

"So? Is that why you've been wearing that dopey look all night?" Rowen pushes.

"What are ya going on about, now?" I give the bar area a quick scan. Everyone's got their hands wrapped around a pint and the printer is staying quiet for the moment. Finally. I've been waiting for this break.

He leans in to ask, "What's her friend like?"

"Borderline hostile."

"Really . . ." Rowen's face lights up and I roll my eyes.

Pouring myself a Guinness, and a couple of tall glasses of ice water, I announce, "Taking five," and round the bar with my hands and my smile full. Amber jumps when I set the drinks down on the table.

"Drink these so your heads don't split tomorrow." Now that the first round of drunken fools have called it a night and staggered out of here, there are a few vacant stools around. I grab one nearby and drag it over. "Are you ladies enjoying yourselves tonight?"

They share a secret look that I don't understand. Then again, most women baffle me.

"I am," Amber says. "How about you, Ivy?"

"I'm having a great time, actually," her friend admits with a furrowed brow, as if she's surprised by that.

"How do you two know each other, anyway?" Both beautiful women in their own right, but they couldn't look more opposite if they tried. Amber's got that girl-next-door-who-bakes-cookies-in-high-heels look. Ivy looks like she could star in the next *Kill Bill* film.

"We actually just met today," Amber says, winking at Ivy, who, after a short delay, responds with a smirk.

"Making friends everywhere you go, are ya?" I lift my pint to my mouth at the same time that someone bumps me from behind, sloshing my beer up my nose. "Fuck!" I wave off his apology—after all, I'm the arse who's sitting in the middle of a throughway—and shift my stool closer to Amber.

"So, you said this is your family's pub?" Amber asks, twirling her hair between her fingertips as she stares at me with those translucent eyes, unabashed. The liquor must be giving her some courage.

"It is. Going on two hundred years now."

Both their mouths drop open.

I like that reaction, when I tell tourists. I've never been to America, but I've heard everything is new there, and one family owning the same pub for two hundred years is unheard of. With a smile, I move to take another sip, only to get bumped from behind again.

Another curse, another apology, another wipe across my face.

"Move out of the bleedin' way!" Rowen bellows from somewhere behind. I respond with a middle finger.

"Here." Amber makes an effort to shift her stool, but it's already as close to the wall as possible.

I drag myself over until my stool is butted against hers, resting my foot on the rung and the inside of my leg against her backside. *Bloody hell.* Just a bit closer and my cock will be pressing against her bare thigh.

I sigh as the cool, delicious beer slides down my throat, uninterrupted.

"Long night?" Amber asks.

"Yeah. And it's not over yet. I'm just taking a quick break." I check the far side, where a table of brazen Londoners holler and laugh, one of them ogling Nuala as she passes by with a tray. She warned me that they'd be a problem before the end of the night. There's always at least one here, every Saturday. We have a doorman for that reason, but sometimes Rowen and I end up giving someone a forceful hand out.

For now, though, I want to find out as much as I can about the American girl looking for a torrid affair. "So tell me, what brings both of you to my country?"

"*Your* country?" Amber mocks.

I grin. "My country."

"Well . . ." She rests her chin on her palm. "I'm actually on this big trip around the world. I just finished traveling across Canada, and Ireland is my first stop on this side of the ocean. I'm going to England and then Spain, France, Italy . . ." Her eyes search the ceiling as she recites all the countries I saw on the list now safely tucked into my wallet.

"Don't forget Greece," I add, struggling to keep my face deadpan.

She snaps her fingers. "Yes! Of course, Greece and—" She cuts off and her eyes narrow as they dart to me.

Naked on a beach. Oh yeah. I remember. I hide my smile behind a sip of my pint as her cheeks burn, waiting for her to ask about it. "That's a lot of traveling." And a shit ton of money. The girl must be rich. She certainly carries herself like she is.

"That's two years of cleaning vomit and sticking thermometers up rectums," Amber says, as if reading my mind.

I choke on my pint and she starts laughing. "I'm a nurse."

"Really . . ." Beautiful *and* caring. "I could have used you a few days ago . . ." I mutter under my breath. To mother me after Eamon tortured me on his dining table.

I guess I said it too loud. Recognition flashes across Amber's face, followed quickly by a wince.

I brush her worries off with a smile and, "I'm just kidding."

"So . . . what's with the lady's outfit?" Ivy asks, changing the topic, to my relief.

I smirk. "I accidently tore my shirt earlier and had to change. It was either this or shirtless."

"Shirtless. That would have been unfortunate. Right, Amber?" Ivy murmurs dryly.

Amber hides her answer behind a long sip of her water. Liquid courage or not, I still seem to make this bird nervous, and I don't want her to be. So I drape my arm loosely around her back, settling my hand on her bare shoulder. Her skin is so soft, her body so slender. "What are you implying? That I don't have the goods to pull this look off?"

Amber's smile stretches wide. *What's going on in that pretty little head of yours?*

Angry voices rise over Collin's melodic one somewhere in the bar, saving her from answering.

"River!" Rowen is already rounding the bar. Brennan, the hulk of a bouncer who guards our door on weekends, has his giant paw on one of the offenders' forearms, his other arm hanging over his shoulders like a trunk. Ready to drag him out by the neck if he doesn't go willingly, no doubt. Most times they're smart enough to leave. Sometimes they're not.

"I'll be back in a minute."

"Wait." Her hand lands on my thigh, gripping it tight. "You're not going to get into a fight, are you?" There's no missing the disapproval in her gaze.

"I'm going to stop one," I promise. A promise that I may have a hard time keeping.

She drops her eyes to where her hand rests, and they widen. At least she slides rather than yanks it away. I know she's attracted to me.

I head for the front, silently cursing myself. Really, this can't turn into anything because I don't think I can handle it tonight. My back is still killing me. Rowen and I cut past customers; the dueling guitars haven't stopped strumming. Collin has sat on that stool and watched this happen so many times over the years that it doesn't even faze him. In fact, he usually breaks into one of a few tunes he refers to as "fight songs."

"Have they paid the bill?" I ask Nuala on my way past her.

"Yeah. Right before the arse grabbed my tit," she snaps back. "If you don't hit him, I will." And she will, too. That's the difference between the birds I'm used to and a girl like Amber, who I can already tell wouldn't raise a hand to anyone, no matter how much that person may deserve it. She's so much more refined and even-tempered. I'm honestly not even sure that the two of us would mix well together. Amber flirts with those pretty eyes and smile, and blushing cheeks. But, plans for a torrid affair or not, I'm guessing she's never just gone home with a fella for a night and expected nothing the next day. She seems too proper for that.

She definitely isn't the kind of bird to hit the lights on the bar and then grab my cock through my jeans, announcing she's in the mood, which is exactly what Nuala did.

Rowen and I converge at the table and the telltale first notes of Collin's favorite brawling song fill the pub. Normally I'd be cracking my knuckles right now.

My brother pushes in front of me. He's always the more levelheaded of us two. "Thank you for your patronage, fellas. Let us help you on your way out."

Brennan's already guiding the loudmouth through the door. The rest of his friends climb to their feet, two of them swaying like they're five steps from doing face plants. "We were going anyway." The one to my right turns and spits on the floor.

Spits on the floor of my family's property.

I close my eyes and count to three. Normally, my fist would already be making contact with his nose. Normally, my back wouldn't be torn up by shrapnel.

Normally, I wouldn't have a girl watching me who I'd like to impress with my nonviolent ways.

Shoving aside my urge to clock him, I lock the spitter's arms behind his back and drag him out. The guy's bigger than me and drunk, twisting and turning and fighting me as we weave around tables and patrons. But I'm stronger and more hardened, and my growing anger only fuels me on when the struggle strains my muscles and my grip. I shove him free of me and watch the group stumble away.

Rowen's face is a mask of bewilderment. "What was that?"

I shrug. "You're always telling me to take it easy." I finally allow myself to flinch, the pain in my lower back searing.

"Your stitches again?"

I nod. I know without looking that the tape Aengus patched me together with has loosened.

"It's a good thing I stuck a few men's large shirts in the top left drawer of the desk," Rowen says casually.

I stop to glare at him. "You mean to tell me . . ."

He shrugs. "Oops. I forgot."

"You didn't," I mutter, shaking my head at my little brother as I chuckle all the way back toward Amber.

She's standing now, and I can't stop staring at her legs. I wonder how she keeps so fit. I wonder what they'd feel like wrapped around my hips.

My adrenaline is running too high after that little scuffle.

"Are you okay?" Her smile is tinged with worry. If she's upset, she doesn't let on.

"You should be proud of me. No fists, see?" I hold my hands up, the bruises from last night on display.

She rolls her eyes but she's smiling.

"Actually, I could use your help in the back." Where I'll get at least a few moments alone with her. "Do you mind if I borrow her for a minute?" I ask her friend.

Ivy dismisses us with a bored wave.

"Are you sure?" Amber asks her.

"With another shot of Jameson . . . sure." For such a tiny person, she should be falling off her stool by now. But she's not, so I assume she's a seasoned pro.

"My brother will gladly pour you one." I slip my hand into Amber's, so slight within my grasp. She lets me lead her back behind the bar and through the door without a word, following me past the dishwasher and storage closet and into the office. I kick the door shut behind her and throw open the lid of the medic kit, still sitting on the desk.

"Alright, nurse." With a wince, I peel my shirt up and over my head and toss it into the rubbish to settle on my other one. When I look over my shoulder, I find Amber with her hands covering her mouth and a look of horror in her eyes.

"It's nothing. Just a torn stitch." I pause, surprised by her reaction. "I thought this would be nothing for you?"

"No . . . I know . . . It's just . . ." She purses her lips tight. "Those are shrapnel wounds from the bomb, aren't they?"

"Just a few little ones that didn't get in too deep." I reach out to take her hand in mine. It's trembling. "I was lucky. Some of those things are loaded with nails. This was just a little, empty thing."

A frown furrows her brow. "How do you know that?"

Because my brother—the muppet who set it—told me. *Shit.* "Because then I would have had nails in my back, wouldn't I?"

"Right." She shudders. "I keep thinking about what would have happened if you weren't there. If I'd just been a few feet closer and that thing went off, I could have been—"

"But I was. And you weren't." I push her long hair back off of her face. "You can't think about that." I've thought about it plenty for her. She would have been dead. Or maimed. Her beautiful face riddled with plastic, one of these strong, smooth legs blown off. I've seen what my da's leg looks like beneath his jeans, the skin discolored and dimpled, his flesh permanently mangled. It's not pretty.

She nods, and then sets her jaw. "I need a sink to wash my hands. And fresh water."

"Just out there and to the left."

While she's doing that, I dig out a new shirt—*that bastard, Rowen*—and clear a corner on the desk so I can sit.

"Okay." She strolls back in with more confidence, pushing the door closed with her hip, her eyes skittering over my bare chest briefly before meeting my face. "I'm kind of drunk, so I can't promise that I won't hurt you."

I tense at the first touch of her cool fingers against my skin, sparking goose bumps. Slowly, she peels back the gauze. "This is taped." She pauses. "When did you tear these stitches?"

"A couple hours ago."

"In another fight?"

"You could say that."

She rifles through the medic kit quietly, and I can feel the disapproval radiating off her. Suddenly I feel like I need to defend myself. "I don't go looking for fights, Amber. It just comes with . . . this life." And not just the Dublin bar life. Life with Aengus. Life as a Delaney.

I hiss as she presses something cold against the wound.

"I need to stop the bleeding before I can clean and close it," she explains quietly.

"Right. Okay."

"I'm guessing you didn't get these done at a hospital?"

Clever bird.

"And you really didn't think you could have just explained what happened?"

"I know it doesn't make sense to a girl like you."

"You'd be surprised what makes sense to a girl like me," she murmurs. "Who stitched it for you?"

When I don't answer, her fingers slip around my side to give me a slight, almost hesitant, squeeze. A surge of blood starts flowing. "I won't tell anyone."

"A family friend. He's a doctor," I finally admit.

"I figured as much. They're well done. You may want to go back to him and get this fixed, if you're going to keep getting into fights before it fully heals."

I shudder with the memories of the pain on that table. "The fighting's done for now." Sundays and weekdays are tame around here. And Aengus usually spaces his fuck-ups apart by a few days, so we won't be bickering anytime soon. I glance over my shoulder at her. "I promise."

Her eyes skate over my face, slowing on my mouth for a moment before dropping to my back again. "If I had a needle and thread, I could stitch it for you."

"You know how to do that?"

She smiles. "I stay away from serious wounds, but this one's not too bad. My mom taught me. She's a surgeon."

"That's . . . impressive." I stare at the wall ahead as Amber's nimble fingers smooth a wet cloth around the cut, cleaning it. "Ma can darn socks and jeans. Not humans." What a different childhood I'm sure we've both had. Back in the day, when we were little, Ma worked here. She had to, after Da's injury. Rumor has it she was no stranger to getting into it with a customer if he misbehaved, giving him a good wallop before one of the men working here jumped in to "escort" the ornery patron out.

I'm guessing Amber gets her soft temper from her mother.

"Does she work?" she asks.

"No. Well, she does, if you count raising three of us and keeping my da fed and watered. Once in a while she'll help out here. She'd beat me with a plank of wood if she heard me say she doesn't work."

She giggles. "Three boys? So, you have another brother?"

"Yeah. Aengus." I can hear the lack of enthusiasm in my own voice.

"Does he work here too?"

"He doesn't."

I don't know if she can sense my hesitation in talking about the guy who almost blew her up, but she switches topics, to my relief. "Do you all still live at home?"

"No. My brothers and I own a house, here in Dublin. I moved there when I was eighteen. I love my parents, but . . ." I shake my head, chuckling. "I needed some peace. You?"

"Still at home. It's not too bad. We live in the mountains, near a small town. It's nice, quiet. Just my family and the horses on a lot of land." She tears apart packaging behind me. "Hold still. This butterfly bandage should keep it together nicely."

I wince as she pulls the skin together again. "Have you been out of Dublin at all yet?"

"No. I was booked for a day tour to Wicklow Mountains, the day of the bomb. So . . . that obviously didn't happen."

I peer over my shoulder at her face again, because I can't help myself. "You're here for another week, only? That's what your friend said?"

Her chest rises with a deep inhale, and her cheeks burn, her eyes flickering back and forth between my back and my face. She's likely replaying the rest of Ivy's words too. "Yeah."

Silence fills the tiny office. I don't have any interest in going back out to that loud, boisterous bar right now.

Another week.

Enough time for a torrid affair with a foreigner?

"What are you smiling about?" she asks, wariness in her gaze.

I clear my throat. "Nothing."

"Fine." She shoots me an exasperated look. "How about I clean these other ones." She peels the bandages back so gently that I barely feel it. "You should probably give them some air."

I watch her face, the lip she bites and then, as if realizing, releases. "How do they look?" I haven't even seen the wounds yet, though I imagine they can't be pretty. They've been itching, which is a good thing. Eamon warned me to keep an eye out for signs of infection. Maybe I should have been doing that.

Water trickles down my back as she cleans the areas. "They look like they must have hurt." Cool air dances over my skin, her breathing shallow and quick.

"It's nothing."

"Shrapnel wounds aren't nothing, River." Tentative fingers drag over my forearm, as if testing my response to the affection. "You have those because of me," she says so softly that I barely hear her, before fingers find their way up my arm to my jaw, to rub against the stubble on my cheek.

Dissolving whatever self-control I promised myself I'd have. I hook my finger around the belt loop of her shorts and tug her closer, until she's in front of me. Her eyes dip down over my chest, slowing on the tattoo over the left side—a black-and-red phoenix. I got it when I was eighteen, the same day Aengus got his.

If she knows what it stands for, she doesn't let on, her attention shifting to the finger I've curled under the top of her one sleeve, slipping the material down over her shoulder, until the spots of purple and green bruising appears. "This looks like it hurts, too."

"It's not so . . ." Her words falter as I lean in to kiss the ball of her slender shoulder, her skin carrying a hint of coconut. " . . . bad."

I shift my body closer to her, waiting for her to ask me to stop.

Instead, her mouth finds mine in a swoop, landing without any hesitation, and it's pretty obvious that I'm not the only one who's been thinking about this all night. Her lips are surprisingly fervent and her hands brave for a girl so seemingly nervous around me. Maybe it's only the Jameson, which I can taste with each swipe of her tongue, but I don't mind her fingers skimming over my neck, my shoulders, my chest . . . as if memorizing me. Torturing me.

The throb from my ripped stitches vanishes as another one forms in my groin. I pull her trim body in to fit between my thighs, while I gently coax her mouth closer with my fingers curled around the back of her neck. A slight moan from her lips promises me that she doesn't mind. The problem is I've never been shy or patient, and that little sound spurs me on. My hands find their way down to grip the backs of those thighs with a tight squeeze before sliding up under her shorts, getting palmfuls of that smooth, rock-hard arse I've been admiring.

She bumps against the corner of the desk as she tries to get closer, her arms wrapping around my head, enclosing our faces in our own little cocoon of hot breath. Not saying a word to slow me down.

"All good in—" Rowen barges in, his words cut off mid-sentence.

Amber breaks free, smoothing her hair back in place, her lips red and puffy, her breathing ragged.

His eyes dart between the two of us. "So you found the shirts?"

I spear him with a glare that promises retribution later.

"I should get back to Ivy." Amber steps back, creating some distance between us. "I promised I wouldn't ditch her tonight."

Her eyes skitter over my bare chest once more before ducking past Rowen. Mine trail her all the way to the door. "Hey, you said you had horses. Do you ride?"

Her curls bounce as she half-turns, her chin resting on her shoulder. "Two-time State Championship winner. Yeah, why?"

I smile. "No reason."

As soon as she's gone, I punch Rowen in the stomach.

FOURTEEN

AMBER

It's taken twenty-five years, a trip to Ireland, and six shots of whiskey to be able to say I'm ready to have a one-night stand with a man. If Rowen hadn't interrupted us back there, I'd likely be in the middle of that one-night stand right now.

And that's why I grab Ivy's arm and tell her we need to leave the second I emerge from the back, my hands trembling. I never would have let a guy I don't know slide his hands up my shorts within two minutes of our first kiss, and yet with River, it almost didn't seem fast enough.

I don't seem to have much control around him, and I like having control.

River and his brother push through the door almost immediately after, River fully dressed again in a properly fitted man's shirt, smoothing his hair back, his lips slightly swollen. Like I assume mine are too.

Ivy doesn't argue, hopping off her stool, tucking her credit card back into her purse, the little plastic holder with the bill in her hand. She slings her heavy black studded purse over her shoulder. "I figured you weren't coming back, so I asked that guy for the check."

"I told you I wouldn't ditch you!"

She shrugs. "I also figured you were lying."

I roll my eyes. "How much was it? I owe you half."

"Don't bother. You can get the bill next time. Right?"

The comment speaks volumes. She had fun tonight. She wants to hang out with me again. I smile. "Definitely. Just maybe less whiskey." I'm going to blame the whiskey for everything. Turning, I find River's green eyes glowing with a mixture of curiosity and disappointment, the memory of his mouth on mine and his hands on me still very clear and real and now making me blush. "You're leaving already?"

How do I explain this? That I'm just not that kind of girl, as much as I wish I could be tonight? And guys like River . . . they won't waste their time on a girl who's only here for a week and won't put out. So, we may as well avoid the awkward conversation altogether.

"It's my fault. I have a client tomorrow morning and if I don't get home now, her dragon is going to look more like a lizard," Ivy jumps in, saving me from having to make up a lie. She sets the receipt down on the counter in front of River. "Tonight was enlightening, bartender . . ." She waves a loose hand his way, dramatically, the only sign that she's been pounding back whiskey for the past couple hours. "Come by when you want that ink."

I'm not sure if River buys the story, but his focus shifts to the paid bill, then at Rowen. "What the bloody hell is this?"

His brother throws his hands up in the air. "She demanded the check. So I gave her the check!"

Shaking his head, I hear a mutter of "Just wait a minute . . ." as he punches a series of keys into the credit card machine. A paper churns out and he staples it to the other copy. Stepping out from behind the bar, he hands it back to Ivy. "Consider the whiskey payment for medical services rendered."

"Is that what the kids are calling it these days?" She throws a sly glance my way.

He chuckles and then calls out, "Be back in twenty."

His brother rolls his eyes, as if he doesn't believe him, but River looks like he couldn't care less. His arm finds its way around my lower back as he fishes his keys out of his pocket. And I realize what's going on.

"We can just take a cab," I argue. "It's not far."

"And let some bastard take two drunk girls in his backseat for a ride that'll cost them double? Is that a good idea, Rowen?"

"It's a terrible idea, River. Those taxi drivers mustn't be trusted." The excessive frown mocks my protest. I'm no idiot. I know exactly what's going on here.

"See?" River pinches my side softly. "Relax. You're safe with me."

Somehow I know that there's no point arguing with him.

And if I'm being honest, a part of me doesn't want to anyway.

■ ■ ■

"Whose house did you say this was?" River's eyes roam over the rooms much the same way mine did when I first stepped inside Simon's place.

"He's a friend's brother." It's the simplest explanation and, now that the whiskey is going head-to-head with my nerves, the most manageable.

"And where is he right now?"

"Africa, I think. He's a doctor." I trail River through the living room and into the kitchen, rambling, "It's nice, being in a home for a while, after jumping from hotel to hotel across Canada. Have you ever been?"

"I haven't. I hear that's a big country." He pushes a few buttons on the espresso coffeemaker before wandering past it to open the fridge. He pulls out a bag of green seedless grapes. "Healthy."

I smile. "I try. Especially since I'm traveling."

His gaze rakes over my body before he smiles and nods to himself.

"Are you hungry?"

He chuckles. "No." Throwing the grapes back in, he pushes the door shut. "Show me the rest of the place."

I take a deep breath, leading him upstairs, convincing myself that maybe this is completely innocent, that he's just curious about where I'm staying. That he appreciates good design.

Stupid Amber.

I never even invited him in. He just climbed out of the car, then trailed me past the gate and up the walkway. I figured he was walking me to the door. When his arm snaked around my waist and he stood there, waiting for me to turn the key, I knew that wasn't the case at all.

His impressed whistle echoes off the tiles in the bathroom of my en suite, and I silently thank God that I had the good sense to pick my panties up off the floor in there earlier. "It's nice, Amber. I'll give you that." When he reenters the master bedroom and sees me standing in the window, he stops dead. "Why are you so nervous around me?"

"I don't know," I answer honestly. "But right now you're in my bedroom. That may have something to do with it."

He walks toward me, his steps casual and slow, his hair slightly tousled, his eyes heated. "I am." His thumb grazes my bottom lip. "It's a little nicer than the pub office, wouldn't you agree?"

I open my mouth just slightly, allowing him a sliver of access. He takes it, his skin scraping against my bottom teeth. "I don't know. That office had a certain charm." My wavering voice makes my playful banter sound awkward.

He frowns, but he's smiling, moving his hands to grip either side of my hips. "Is it that calendar with the birds in bikinis that does it?"

I start to giggle, partly because I can't wrap my head around this term *birds* that it seems everyone in Ireland uses instead of *girl* or *woman*. He takes that opportunity to lean in farther, to lay a kiss along my jawline. "Or maybe Rowen's smelly runners dangling by the string beside the calendar."

"I did notice that," I admit. That office was the size of a walk-in closet, windowless and dimly lit, papers strewn all over the place as if two twenty-something-year-old brothers run the place.

In that office, I was the one who initiated the kiss. But here, in my house, in my bedroom, it's completely River, capturing my mouth with his, his strong hands beginning to confidently wander over my body, as if we've already become accustomed to each other, as if no part is off-limits, quickly finding the space between my panties and the inside of my shorts. He seems to really like that part of me, toned from years of horseback riding.

Before I know it, we've picked up exactly where we left off not long ago, in the place that made me temporarily lose control. Except now there isn't a busy bar behind us, or the possibility of a poorly timed interruption from his brother to stop us.

Instead, there's a neatly made bed with crisp white sheets and a plush blanket. It may as well have a red carpet to go along with it, because I know that if this continues, I'm going to forget who I am very soon.

And I'm not this girl.

Suddenly I'm more nervous than I should be. More nervous than I've ever been with a guy. A hundred times more nervous than the night I lost my virginity. That night wasn't even about nerves, really. Neil and I were at Tory Masters's seventeenth birthday party—an epic outdoor bash in the summer, the field behind her house scattered with tents and illuminated by a blazing bonfire. Neil and I had been dating about eight months by then, the progress to that final intimate step slow and steady. Slow enough that I was more than ready. I'd had enough time to consider my feelings, my motivations, and what the "after" might mean. I was confident that I'd spent enough time weighing everything out and that it wasn't a rash decision. Neil and I knew each other well enough that I didn't worry about being "good" at it. Neil wouldn't be comparing me to anyone else because it was new to him, too.

Then there was Brody, and the progress in the physical part of our relationship was reached in stages as well, though faster. Aaron and I had sex a month after that first impromptu cafeteria lunch date, after four dates and at least a dozen meals at work.

I've slept with three guys in my life and all of them were planned-out occurrences, decisions I made when I was sure that I would have no regrets. Spontaneity and I have never been fast friends, especially when it comes to big decisions like intimacy.

And yet, here I am, standing in a bedroom with a guy I met mere days ago, shared our first coherent words with a little more than twenty-four hours ago, and just kissed for the first time less than an hour ago. Whose hands are now dangerously close to finding out exactly how attracted I am to him.

"It's too fast. I can't do this," escapes me between kisses.

Just like that, as if he were waiting for the words, River breaks free, his hands leaving my skin cold as they slide up to settle on either side of my waist, an intimate but respectable touch. Giving me a light squeeze as his breath skates over my face through a tight smile.

And then his hands drop abruptly and he's moving past the door and down the stairs. "I need to get back to work. Rowen's had a long day. I shouldn't make him deal with closing alone."

"Oh, okay," I hear myself mumble, trying to process exactly what just happened. Thirty seconds ago, his brother and the pub seemed to be the farthest thing from his mind.

It's not that I don't want him. That's far from the case. My body is still wire-tight and humming from his touch. But does he understand that?

I reach the landing in a haze as he's tugging his shoes on, moving pretty quickly to get out. "So, how often do you get locked on Jameson?"

The unexpected question throws me off. "Uh . . . what does that even mean? Get 'locked'? You said that earlier."

He smiles, one hand on the doorknob. "It means get drunk."

"Oh . . ." Weird Irish slang. I can't wait to use that on my dad. "Never." I usually drink wine. Beer, on occasion. "And I'm not really drunk anymore."

"Either way, make sure you drink lots of water."

"River, it's not that I don't want to . . ." I convey with my eyes what I can't seem to do with words. I didn't ask him to drive me home. I didn't invite him in. I didn't lead him into my bedroom. If anything, I should be annoyed with him for running so abruptly. And yet all I'm worried about right now is if I'm going to see him again.

"I know," he says with a cute, crooked smile. "You're just not like that." He hesitates and then leans in to place a chaste peck on my cheek. I don't let him off with just that, though, my hand capturing the rough edge of his jaw to pull his mouth into mine. Afraid this may be the last chance I get. He complies, deepening it for three . . . four . . . five seconds before pulling back, my ears catching his hard swallow. "No more kissing tonight. That lip looks angry. And drink your water. Please." He turns to leave and my stomach clenches, the familiar sight of his back, the fear that this is goodbye, unpleasant and unwanted. "Hey, I keep meaning to ask you . . . did you by any chance take a piece of paper from my wallet the other day?"

"A piece of paper?" He pauses, a deep frown touching his brow. "No, I don't think so."

He's a good liar. I know for a fact that he did. "Are you sure?"

He smooths my hair back off my forehead, studying my entire face. "Why? Was it important?"

I play along. "No, not really. Just a list of things to do while I'm traveling."

"Things to do . . . huh." His expression reveals nothing.

"Yeah. My friend and I wrote it one night when we were drinking, as a joke."

"A joke." He bats those long lashes at me. "All of it?"

I stifle the smile threatening. "Not all of it."

"Well . . ." His scruff tickles my neck as he leans to whisper into my ear, "I hope you'll give proper consideration to some of them, at least."

He slides out the front door as my mouth drops open, as I watch him jog to his car. "Am I going to see you again?" I blurt out just before he ducks into the driver's side.

He grins back at me. "If you want to." Then he disappears into his car, the low rumble of the engine igniting into the night.

If I want to?

The problem is, I can't tell exactly what it is I want anymore.

FIFTEEN

RIVER

"What are you doing back here?" Rowen stares at me like I've sprouted two extra heads in front of him.

"Same thing I do every Saturday night."

"I don't remember ya being *that* quick," Nuala chirps from the customer side of the bar, sweetening the insult with a wink while she wipes down the computer.

I ignore the two of them, grabbing a rack of dirty glasses and carrying it to the dishwasher in the back. Reminding myself for the tenth time that I did the right thing by running when I did.

I didn't have to leave. Rowen wouldn't have cared if I didn't come back to the pub tonight.

But I *had* to leave.

Rowen trails behind me, undeterred. "So she realized that she was too good for you and kicked you out?"

"She hasn't. Yet," I mutter, adjusting glasses to make sure they don't crack in the cycle. "Have you called last call yet?" There were no more than ten people left out there. Even Collin had packed up his things and staggered home already.

Rowen glances at his watch. "We have another—"

"Just call it. I'm bloody tired." And I need to get away from Nuala before she grabs my cock, like she will when she notices the hard-on tucked into my jeans. It's been a while since I've had to deal with this situation.

"Fine. Fuck." He disappears back outside and I hear the telltale cowbell, followed by a chorus of grumbles and jeers. "Go home, ya muppets," I mutter. They've all had more than enough to drink and I'm in no mood to talk to anyone.

Leaving Amber tonight was hard. Painfully so. If I'm being honest, when I stepped into that house, into that bedroom, a part of me was hoping that I was completely wrong about her. But then I stepped out of her bathroom and saw her standing in that window, the streetlight shining over her face—her nervous face, her delicate hands clasping each other—and I knew that I wasn't.

And I'm glad.

But that still didn't stop me from giving it one last try for the night.

I kill a bit of time in the office, tidying up, before I venture back outside. All but three drunks have left, and Nuala's working on them.

"So?" Rowen asks, watching the printer run with the night's closing reports. "What happened?"

"Nothing. She was drunk."

"Drunk and she turned you down?"

"Not exactly." I know that if I stayed longer, kissed her more, eased her into it, her body would have ignored her doubts eventually. I could see it in her eyes, feel it in the way she instantly gravitated toward me when I touched her. But I don't want that. I don't want Amber waking up in the morning, her head throbbing from drink, her body sore from use, her stomach curling with countless screams of regret while I lie naked next to her, oblivious and sated. I don't want to be that memory for her.

"*You* turned *her* down because she was drunk?"

"Yes . . . No . . . Just shut up."

Nuala snorts from her spot across the bar. "That's not how she's goin' to see it." The bird's got ears like a bloody bat and opinions that she shouldn't share most times.

"She sees it just fine." We left things on a good note. She knows I like her.

"Did you make plans to see each other again?"

"I'll call her tomorrow."

Nuala drops the last tray of dirty glasses on the bar counter. "I'm only saying this for your own good, River. Because you can be a bit daft sometimes. The bird is smitten with ya. Why, I don't understand. I mean, you're a charmer, but you're not of her league. And yet she sat in this filthy kip all night, waiting for ya to bat an eyelash at her."

"So?"

"So, she's not going to spend her entire holiday here, especially if her pride's bruised. Tomorrow it could be another place, another Irish fella behind the bar; something to satisfy that itch she wants to scratch while she's here. I know. I've been on holiday too."

I level her with a look. "She's not like you." I'm sure Nuala's never taken a fella home and not fucked him senseless.

"She's got a cunt, doesn't she?" Nuala snips, strolling away to begin lifting stools and chairs so the floors can be washed, dropping them loudly onto tables. I know I've pissed her off. Nuala doesn't take too kindly to being compared to girls of Amber's pedigree, which is staggeringly higher. I'll bet Amber would never even use a word like that.

Still, Nuala's words linger in my mind. I think Amber understood why I left. I hope she did. What does she have going on for tomorrow? Will she come back here? Again? I did leave her hanging, a tease. Maybe she won't appreciate that. Maybe that'll piss her off. How long will a girl like that chase when she's only here for another week? That she's even chasing after me at all is a shock.

I consider calling her. Driving back there tonight and letting her know exactly how I feel, that I don't want her scratching any itches with anyone but me.

But when I leave Delaney's for the night and see the street up ahead, where I should turn left toward her place . . . I go straight instead, toward home.

SIXTEEN

AMBER

The shrill ring of my phone is ten times worse than normal.

"Hello?" My voice crackles in the receiver, my eyes squinting against the dull morning light streaming through the kitchen window as I watch rain splatter over the patio table out back. This is the kind of weather Mary Coyne warned was common in Ireland.

"You're up."

As happy—and relieved—as I am to hear River's voice, I can't manage more than a light moan in response.

"Did you drink water?"

"Three glasses and counting." I tip the tall glass—the only reason I crawled out of bed in the first place—to my lips, praying that the cool liquid will get rid of this dull ache. Clearly three hasn't been enough.

"Listen, I wanted to apologize for last night. I should never have come in like that." He pauses. "And I'm sorry I ran."

I smile. If he hadn't, there was only one way last night was going, and I honestly can't say how I'd feel about that this morning. As it was, my last thoughts before falling asleep were of him, and what he would feel like. My first thoughts this morning were of him, too.

In fact, all of my thoughts since I stepped into that pub two days ago have been of him.

"It's okay. Really."

"So, you're not pissed at me, then?"

I chuckle. "Why would I be 'pissed'?" If anything, the fact that he's so concerned makes my knees weak with the thought of him.

"Nuala made it sound like . . . never mind." A loud sigh fills my ear, making me wish he were here, in person. Just maybe not now, I accept as I steal a glance at the reflection in the hallway mirror. Smears of the residual black mascara that didn't wash off circle my eyes, and my smooth curls from last night are now a rat's nest.

"What are you doing today?"

"Probably sleeping this hangover off, as much as I hate wasting a day." I begin to climb the stairs.

The doorbell rings. I freeze mid-step and turn, my brow furrowed at the door ahead.

There's a long pause, and then, "Are you going to get that?"

"No. I'm not even dressed."

"I don't mind."

"What do you . . ." I scamper down and to the living room window, my eyes widening when I see River's forest-green MINI Cooper—a source of great surprise last night when he led me to it, seeing as I have a newer model, in red—parked next to Simon's car. "Are you outside?"

"It's really coming down now. Do you think you could let me in?"

This is not how I imagined our next meeting. But it's pouring out there. I can't leave him standing on my doorstep in the name of vanity. Spotting the long tunic sweater that I left draped across the chair yesterday, I quickly yank it on over my tank top. It just reaches past my underwear. It'll have to be enough.

"Amber?"

I glance at my reflection again, this time in the hallway mirror. And groan. And then I open the door.

River's eyes flash with surprise, grazing over me ever so quickly before lifting to settle on my face. He steps in, handing me a tall Starbucks cup on his way past, his T-shirt and track pants drenched, his hair plastered across his forehead. "I would have brought you a hearty Irish breakfast to go with those grapes but wasn't sure if you could handle it."

I take a step back, my breath likely as toxic as the taste swirling in my mouth right now. "And what's in an Irish breakfast?"

He shrugs. "Bangers and beans . . . potatoes . . . eggs . . ." He reaches out, brushes away a stray hair from my cheek. ". . . black pudding."

My stomach churns. "Maybe later." Bonnie warned me not to eat that. It has something to do with actual blood.

He chuckles, watching me closely.

"I just need ten minutes, if you don't mind." My bare feet are slipping one behind the other, in an attempt to escape up the stairs.

He grabs my hand, stopping me. "How about I give you an hour. I'm going to fit in a quick run, but I have a bit of time after that, if you wanted to go out."

My hangover is suddenly forgotten. "What'd you have in mind?"

He shrugs. "I figured I'd teach you how to drive on the right side of the road, maybe?" We share a chuckle. "Then maybe see an artist about some ink." A pause. "Unless you'd rather get that sleep."

"Yeah. No . . . I mean . . ." I stumble over my words with excitement. "That all sounds great." *Any time with you is good.* "When do you have to be at work?"

He glances at his watch. "In three hours. So I'll pick you up in an hour? Is that enough time?"

I nod, holding my breath as he leans in to kiss me on the cheek.

I watch his easy movements as he runs down my path. Much like he did last night. Only the dread I felt before is gone, replaced with anticipation.

I tear up my stairs toward the shower, peeling my clothes off as I go, the throb in my head forgotten.

■ ■ ■

My chest heaves with relief as I park.

"That wasn't so bad, right?" River sits in the passenger seat of his car, his legs splayed, his elbow resting on the armrest. The picture of calm. As if I didn't go the wrong way down a roundabout and almost crash his car and put us in the hospital.

"I'm actually a good driver," I promise, peeling my white-knuckled fingers off the steering wheel to open my driver's-side door and climb out. His car is just like my car at home, only backwards. And everything about driving these streets feels wrong. Except having River here, beside me.

"I believe you. It's not your fault." He meets me at the front of the car and entwines his fingers within mine, a sly smirk turning his lip. "You're just used to driving on the wrong side of the road."

I smile, his harmless teasing so much more appealing because of the way he says it. I've had to ask some of the locals I've met to repeat themselves, their accents are so thick. "What part of Ireland are you from?"

"Northern. We grew up in County Louth, just south of the border." He leads me past the heavy yellow door of The Fine Needle. "Why?"

"Because I can actually understand you. It's nice."

His laughter fills the quiet cave-like shop that I've now been in twice in twenty-four hours. Somehow it feels different this time.

Ivy is standing at the computer, her hair pulled back in a severe ponytail, highlighting the shaved sides of her head. Her gaze bores into the forehead of a heavyset woman with a dozen rings through her left ear—much like Ivy's piercings—who is busy scribbling her signature across the bottom of a sheet of paper. "First room on the left. I'll be there in five minutes," she instructs the woman with a light tone that I assume is reserved for clients. She even flashes a polite close-mouthed smile her way as she points in the direction. Urging the woman to move.

As soon as the customer is out of sight, Ivy tosses the clipboard with the signed waiver to the side, that professional smile replaced with a scowl.

"How are you feeling?" I ask.

She rounds the desk, her knee-high boots exchanged for low

ones and black leggings. The giant plum-colored shirt that reaches mid-thigh looks more like a potato sack than an article of clothing. "Like I want to stab myself in the eye with my needle," she says, deadpan. "Seriously, I probably should cancel my appointments for the day and just throw myself into a well."

"So you would recommend that I wait to get this done?" River grins, pulling a tucked sheet of paper out of his pocket and unfolding it for her. It's the same stag that's on the Delaney T-shirts.

"If you want me to do it, then yeah. That woman back there?" She drops her voice and thumbs back toward where her customer left. "She's so screwed. My cousin, Ian, could maybe do it for you today, though. If you don't want to wait."

"You said he's not as good as you, though."

"Not even close."

"I'll wait for you, then. If you think you can do a good job of this."

"Oh, I can do a *great* job of that."

River smiles, reaching out to pinch my elbow. "What about you? You want Ivy to mark that perfect skin of yours?"

"Are you kidding?" Now Ivy's brows spike. "I'm not putting a tattoo on Miss Sheriff's Daughter. She'll have something to hang over my head until the day I die. I'll never be able to go back to Oregon. Not that I'm missing much."

I glare at her.

"I take it you two didn't just meet yesterday."

"You actually believed that?" Ivy snorts. "Alright, I've got to get back there now, before I kill myself." She drags her feet as she turns to leave.

"So I guess you wouldn't be interested in going out with us tonight, then?" River asks.

And my heart rate skips a few beats. This is new.

Ivy stops and turns, that owl-like gaze of hers shuttering between the two of us. "The three of us?"

"Four. My brother, Rowen, will come out, too. You remember him from last night?"

"The grinning Irishman. Yeah."

I don't even have to ask to know that Rowen isn't her type, despite his being charming and hot. Her type is broody and dark. Basically, my brother.

"So you'll come? We'd love for you to come." He ropes an arm around my waist, pulling me to him. "Right, Amber?"

"Yeah, definitely. Just maybe no shots." I'd like to be in control of myself this time around.

Ivy's gaze hovers over River's arm. I'd pay to know what's going on inside that head of hers right now. "Sure. I'm in. If I'm not dead by then. Amber has my number."

The second she disappears, he pulls me into him, our chests pressed against each other. It's the first overt move on his part since he picked me up today. "You okay with spending tonight with me, Miss Sheriff's Daughter?"

I groan but then laugh. "Don't you start that now, too."

"That's the second time she's called you that. I'm guessing your father's a sheriff?"

I nod.

"And I take it Ivy doesn't like paying taxes?"

Taxes? I frown. "Uh . . . I don't know. It wouldn't surprise me, though." She seems like she could walk a fine line between right and wrong.

His one eye narrows in question. "Wait . . . What exactly does a sheriff do in America?"

"Arrests people? Keeps the peace?" Wreaks havoc on a teenage girl's love life? "My dad was the county sheriff. He ran the entire police department. But he's retired now."

"Oh." A strange look passes over his face that I can't read. "That's definitely different from sheriffs in Ireland. They just collect taxes from delinquents."

"Like the Sheriff of Nottingham?"

He chuckles softly. "Kind of." A pause. "So, what's your father like?"

My gaze scans the black ceiling above as I ponder that question. How do I describe Gabe Welles? "Serious, more than he's not. Difficult to please. A believer in the rule of law. Thrives on having control of the situation. Overprotective of his daughter." It took him a while to warm up to Neil as my boyfriend, even though he knew him as Neil, the kid who ate sand at the playground, for fifteen-odd years before that. Neil was about as innocuous as a teenage boy can get, and the sheriff still felt it was necessary to be cleaning his rifle on the front porch when the guy arrived to pick me up for our first date.

He was never a big fan of Brody, though he admitted the guy was decent as far as men go. And, even though my mom knew and could vouch for Aaron, I'm pretty sure my dad ran a background check on him before grunting his approval.

I don't even have to wonder what he'd think of River. He wouldn't like him at all, for the simple fact that he lives in Ireland.

"And what kind of daughter were you?" River plays with one of my gold hoop earrings. "The kind who listened to her serious, controlling, difficult-to-please father? Or the one who didn't?"

"What do you think?"

His eyes glance over my mouth. "I'm thinking you made him very proud."

Am I that obvious? By his suddenly serious expression, I'm beginning to think this is unpleasant news for River. "Is that a bad thing?"

"No." He chuckles. "Not at all. Believe me."

I smile. "I didn't really have a choice. I had to balance out my troublemaker brother."

"I know something about that." He sighs. "I should head to the pub now. Do you want me to drop you off at home?"

I'm guessing he's not talking about Rowen. It must be this mysterious older brother of his, who he mentioned the other day. The one whose very name made tension cord in his jaw and his back. "No. I can walk. It's sunny out now. Bizarre Irish weather."

"It's bipolar," he jokes. "Okay. I'll pick you up at your house around eight?"

"Sounds good." That's five hours from now. Enough time to hit up the overpriced stores on Grafton Street because, suddenly, I don't have anything in my suitcase suitable for a night out with River.

He simply smiles at me. Not moving closer. Not pulling away. Waiting for me to make the first move, I think.

I do, leaning in to steal a kiss and elicit a soft groan from him. His grip around me tightens, his fist clenching the back of my shirt as he pulls me into his body, his erection pressing against my stomach.

Really? He wants me that much? Knowing that excites me.

And then he breaks free suddenly. "See ya."

I grin, parroting him. "See ya."

SEVENTEEN

RIVER

"We're going out tonight."

Rowen peers up from the liquor inventory. "Can't. I need to catch up from the work I missed last Wednesday, when I covered for you."

"On our night off?" It's customary that we arrange for Nuala and another bartender to cover the bar for us on Sunday nights so we can take off at seven and have a few hours to relax. "No. You're coming out."

He groans. "With who?"

"Amber and her friend, Ivy."

That sparks his interest. "That hot, mean little one with all the ink?"

"That's the one. She asked about you." There was nothing about Ivy's face today that said she's interested in Rowen, but I still owe him for that gag with the work shirt yesterday.

"I'll think about it."

"Eight o'clock at Nosey Flynn's." I know he's in.

■ ■ ■

I'll never forget my first love. I was sixteen. Her name was Katie Byrne and she was a year younger than me. I'd known her and her family for years—they were members of the same small parish on the outskirts of Dundalk, and they lived about two minutes' drive away, in a small cottage with tomato-red framing and a thatched roof—but I only *really* noticed her that September, after she and her family returned from a summer in Edinburgh. Her body was suddenly full of curves, her face missing the baby fat, and her innocent hazel doe eyes were soulful enough to entrap most any boy.

I wasn't the only one to notice the changes. But she stayed unavailable to everyone, thanks to her father's strict rules about dating.

Her father was my rugby coach.

That November, I was riding my bike home after school one afternoon when I found Katie standing beneath a tall tree, her arms stretched high in the air, crying over the kitten that dangled from a limb, mewling. I climbed the tree—not an easy feat—and rescued her pet, earning myself plenty of scratches and nearly falling on the way down. But I also earned Katie's adoration, those doe eyes glued to me during mass the following Sunday.

I loved the way she looked at me, as if I could do no wrong. I would have rescued that mangy cat a hundred times over again if it meant she'd always look at me that way.

Her father's rules hadn't changed but something had for Katie, because she started seeking me out between classes and during lunch hour. We'd see each other in the library. I started walking her home from school. She'd hold my hand until we got closer to her house, in case either of her parents were home. It was months before she let me kiss her. The horny teenager that I was, I wanted more, but I held back, not wanting to risk chasing her away.

And then one day after class, biting her bottom lip nervously, her voice a low whisper, her pretty hazel gaze darting this way and that, making sure no one would hear her, she made plans to sneak out with me the coming Easter break.

I pulled up outside her house after dark in my father's Astra, my belly full from the Sunday dinner feast, after Ma had gone to bed and Da was passed out in the recliner from drink. Therapy for his pain, he'd always say. I waited for twenty minutes before a slight body slipped out from a window at the side of the house and rushed toward my car. She hugged her black knit sweater tight around her body, her pale white legs stark in the night. I remember thinking she'd be cold in that flowery dress.

It turns out that Katie Byrne had developed strong feelings for me and, having just passed her sixteenth birthday, she'd suddenly been bitten by the rebellious bug, a fact I discovered not long after we pulled up to the O'Hanlan farm—a property long since abandoned and left derelict. A great place for young people to get together and have some fun without responsible prying eyes watching over them.

I made to open the car door but Katie grabbed my hand and asked me to stay, waving a flask of whiskey that she'd magically produced. We sat for a good half hour—her taking three shots for every one that I downed—and shared idle, slightly awkward conversation, then a few kisses.

Then she boldly climbed into the backseat. Of course I followed, quickly finding a new appreciation for her choice of clothing. When she slipped her knickers off, her fingers trembling, I didn't balk. I was almost seventeen and quite happy to be rid of my virginity. I sure as hell didn't need any mental preparation.

We joined the party after. Rowen and a bunch of kids from school, and even Aengus—visiting for the holiday—were already tucked away between the house and the barn, keeping warm with a fire and beer. Katie kept drinking until she was tipping the flask upside down to get a drop into her mouth, her eyes half-shuttered, her words incoherent. I didn't know what to do with her.

Aengus is the one who helped me bring her back home, lifting her body through her bedroom window. He's the one who ventured into the Byrne house to find a large bowl to set beside her in case she vomited. And, when I wouldn't leave because I was afraid she'd choke to death, he's the one who banged on the front door until her father answered, telling him he had just dropped off a drunk Katie—who he had found stumbling along the side of the road—and he was worried. I watched from the shadows, terrified that her father might figure out what I'd done with his daughter. The age of consent was seventeen, and Coach Byrne was the kind of father to not only kick me off the rugby team but also press charges.

Now, it wouldn't be me they'd be blaming. It would be the twenty-one-year-old Delaney on their doorstep. Aengus would get into a boiling pot-full of trouble if the Byrnes decided to accuse him of something. The kind that could put him in prison.

Katie was admitted to the hospital for alcohol poisoning, and spent the rest of the break recovering. I spent the rest of the break waiting for a knock on the door, afraid she'd confess to what happened. Luckily, nothing came of it, her parents too mortified to say anything. She transferred to an all-girls secondary school, but I'd still see her in church on Sundays. That look in her eyes was gone. In fact, she wouldn't even meet my gaze after that. I never did find out if it was embarrassment over her drunkenness, fear of her father's wrath, anger that we'd ratted her out, or plain regret that she'd give something so valuable to me. The possibility of the last one bothered me most.

What I did know is that I would miss feeling like I could do no wrong.

I haven't thought about Katie Byrne or that night in years, but I'm remembering her now, as I watch Amber lock her front door and stroll down the concrete walkway, her hip pushing the gate closed behind her.

I've had plenty of birds after that, but not since Katie has one looked at me the way Amber does—like I'm some sort of hero. I don't want to do anything to fuck it up. Amber may be leaving soon, but for these next seven days, I want to live up to everything she thinks she sees when she looks at me with those adoring eyes.

I slip out in time to come around to her side. "I would have met you at your door."

"I don't mind. I was ready."

"You look nice."

She stretches the skirt of her flirty little dress out between her fingers. A white one with big, bold green flowers, too short to ever meet Ma's approval but it certainly meets mine, showing off those thighs. "You didn't tell me what we were doing. I hope this works." Her eyes skate over my dark jeans and black collared shirt. An upgrade from what I wear to work but by no means upscale.

"It does."

She flashes one brilliant white-toothed smile just before ducking into her seat. Her sexy green heels have my blood flowing already.

■ ■ ■

"How old is this place?" Amber asks, her fingers pressed against the rough stone wall to brace herself, taking each of the uneven steps down with caution.

"Old."

When we reach the bottom, she peers over my shoulder at the narrow staircase, just wide enough for one person to pass at a time. "That would never pass fire and safety codes in America."

I laugh. "Who thinks about things like that?"

Even in the poor lighting, I can see the flush of her cheeks, and I realize that I've embarrassed her. Reaching out to squeeze the side of her slender waist playfully, I add, "It's charming." I slip a hand in hers and lead her farther in, ducking slightly to get through the stone archway.

"Wow. This place is . . . medieval." Her words drift as her gaze takes in the low, stone-carved ceiling of the intimate cellar.

"Let me guess. This wouldn't pass code either."

Her lips twist into a smirk, and I can't help myself. I lean in and steal a quick kiss, surprising her. The sparkle in her eyes tells me it's a good surprise.

"Come on. Our seats are ready." I lead her to the rickety old table in the corner. Rowen's already there, pint in hand.

"My favorite American bird." He stands, rounds the table, and pulls out her chair before I can, winking at me.

She eases herself into it with a smile. "You Delaney boys sure are charming."

Not all of us.

"Where's your friend?"

"She said she's running late but will be here soon." Amber's not really paying attention to her own words, too busy studying the tapered candles burning from atop empty wine bottles that give this narrow, underground place the majority of its light. "What happens over there? Music?" She points to the corner, to the microphone sitting in a stand.

"Something like that." Rowen and I share a look. I warned him not to blow the surprise.

"It's been a while. How ya lads?" Kean, a middle-aged Galway fella and the latest generation to run Nosey Flynn's, drops four menus onto the table, dipping his head toward Amber in greeting.

"Grand."

Kean settles curious golden eyes on me. "Ya sure? I hear someone's wantin' to box the head off ya brother."

Christ. It doesn't surprise me at all that someone wants to beat the hell out of Aengus. Aengus could inspire violence in a priest. But now is *really* not the time to be rooting around our business, and Kean's known for doing that. Some say he's on payroll with the papers, feeding them bits of information from the streets. I shoot him a warning glare, thinly veiled behind a smile, for Amber's sake. "We're all grand."

"How long do we have to order?" Rowen runs his finger down the paper, as if there are a dozen options. There are only four. There have only ever been four: two types of stew, bacon and cabbage, and a vegetarian curry.

I don't know if it's a tactic to steer the conversation away from Aengus or if it's just Rowen's oversized appetite. Either way, I'm appreciative.

Kean gets the message. "I'll keep it open for another fifteen for ya. The usual?"

I squeeze Amber's shoulder. "Guinness?"

"And a water. Please."

Kean waves toward another table. "Rose'll be around."

"He seems nice," Amber muses, dropping her voice. "But I couldn't understand a word he was saying."

"Seriously? It was perfectly clear to me." I breathe a sigh of relief and curl my arm around the back of her chair. There's no need to spark conversations about Aengus.

"And here she comes . . ." Rowen belts out in a low, melodious voice, his curious eyes on a spot behind us. "My favorite American is here!"

Amber shakes her head at him, but she's smiling. Sandalwood and flowers catches my nose a second before Ivy appears, her dark eyes scanning the cave. "I would have happily crawled into this hole earlier today." She tosses the strap of her clunky purse over the edge of the only chair available, next to Rowen, a wary sideways glance at her "date." "Hello, Grinning Bartender."

"Hello, Hostile Patron." Rowen scans her outfit—a black tank top and a plaid miniskirt that's barely long enough to cover her arse—with interest. "You look pretty tonight."

I almost want to warn him not to try anything too bold on her. Almost.

But watching her eat him alive will be more entertaining.

"So, what *is* this place, exactly?" Amber asks again, stealing my attention.

"Just a local secret." I tap the menu. "Decide what you want to eat because Kean wasn't kidding. He'll close the kitchen on us."

■ ■ ■

"I'm Fergus, one of your *seanchaí* for the evening. Some know me. Some don't." The portly man strokes his graying beard as he scans the tables. There are fourteen of them—enough to seat fifty-six guests—and all are filled. That's common on nights like this. Most people here show signs of middle age, though there are two tables of younger couples, aside from us.

"But you're all here for the same thing—to eat good food, drink good beer, and have a good time."

"Shift a bit, ladies," Rose whispers, her arms laden with four dinner plates. "River, help me out, will ya?"

Asking a customer to take his plate would be considered terrible service standards anywhere, but Rose has known me since I sat on my granddad's lap. I carefully scoop up the plates, setting Amber's dish in front of her.

"Good boy." She pinches my cheek in thanks, just like she did twenty years back, when she was thin and free of the deep creases that now zag across her forehead. "And your pints are on their way." She disappears to another table.

"We ordered another round?" Amber whispers.

Rowen chuckles. "Rose won't stop bringing them until we ask her to."

"Can she switch mine to whiskey?" Ivy mutters, poking a chunk of stew with her fork.

Rowen settles an arm around her shoulders, his hand like a giant mitt over Ivy's slender shoulder. "Don't worry. It's dead."

Her sharp sideways glare at his fingers tracing lines over her skin makes me burst out in laughter.

"Ah, the Delaney boys." Fergus's deep voice ricochets through the cavern and numerous heads turn. "Might I introduce ya later?"

I simply wink at the old man, a longtime friend.

Amber leans in to whisper, "Why would he introduce you?"

I spear a chunk of creamy cabbage and bacon from her plate with my fork and hold it up to her mouth, waiting, avoiding her question.

With only a moment of hesitation and a shy smile, she parts her lips, allowing me enough room to slide the fork in. I feel the press of her teeth against the metal, the thrill of that sensation skittering from my fingertips through to the rest of my body.

Somewhere in the background, Fergus is talking again. But he's lost both of us for the moment, our eyes locked on each other. It isn't until he replaces that gruff, deep baritone voice with a slightly higher, more melodic one that he manages to steal Amber's attention.

"Storytelling!" Her eyes light up and she struggles to keep her voice low. "Mary told me about this!"

I have no idea who this Mary is but I just smile, because her excitement is palpable.

"She told me to find a place that did this, that it'd be an experience. I even put it on my list." I watch her face closely. The pause . . . the moment of recognition . . . the turn to stare at me, a mixture of amusement, annoyance, and something unreadable in her expression.

I hold my finger up to my mouth to signal silence. Fergus is known for lambasting people who talk through his performances. She presses her lips together, moving her gaze back to him, but reaching out to grab my hand that rests on my lap. Squeezing it once, tight.

I won't let it go, though, slipping my fingers through it and holding it against my thigh, forcing her to eat the rest of her dinner using her left hand. She doesn't seem to mind, her focus rapt on Fergus as he regales everyone with a tale about a fisherman and his son who followed the will-o'-the-wisp through the bogs of Munster, never to be found again. I've heard it at least five times before, but it's no less interesting, because Fergus is a masterful storyteller, his cadence musical, his movements elegant. He's an old *culchie*, spending most of his days tending to sheep, and listening to him reminds me a lot of nights around the woodstove with my granddad.

Even Ivy, who I was skeptical about bringing here, is turned completely in her chair to watch Fergus, making slow work of her supper.

Fergus monopolizes the stage for close to an hour—he's a verbose bastard—and wraps up just as Rose is collecting our empty plates and dropping another round of drinks off.

"This will be my last for tonight," Amber informs Rose sweetly. Ivy shoots her a skeptical look but Amber ignores it, smiling at me. "How much of his story is true? I mean, I know the whole will-o'-the-wisp thing isn't, but isn't there some truth to all of these stories?"

I shrug. "They could have been following fireflies or glow-worms, or little pranksters with lanterns. Who knows? These stories are passed on from generation to generation by word-of-mouth, so you can expect embellishments with each turn."

"Well . . . embellished or not, that was so great. I never would have found this place on my own." Her gaze darts to my mouth, and she bites her own lip with hesitation. "Thank you." She leans in and kisses me. It's more proper than last night in the office, but something tells me that simple move took a lot of guts for Amber.

Fergus's booming voice is back. "I'm sure you're all sick of me by now. Nosey Flynn's own Shannon O'Callahan will be up next, but I'd like to beg that strappin' young lad over there to share a story or two from his fine lineage."

Fergus's meaty paw gestures toward me and Amber's pretty mouth drops with her jaw. I can't help but laugh, giving her hand a kiss before I release it to take the makeshift little corner stage.

EIGHTEEN

AMBER

River is getting up there?

Butterflies churn in my stomach for him, because I don't know how anyone could ever stand in front of fifty-odd people and do improv of any kind. I'm sure these storytellers know their stories well before they get up there, practicing them out loud until they can say them in their sleep. But does River? No notes . . . no cues . . . and *everyone* is watching him.

River saunters over to the corner, an easy smile giving away nothing. No nerves with this guy. With a deft flick of his wrist, he steals the tweed newsboy cap off Fergus's head and settles it onto his own head, wisps of his golden-brown hair curling at the brim.

He perches himself on the stool and leans into the microphone. "All I wanted to do was enjoy a pint and a meal with me friends." A round of laughter erupts. I've noticed that sometimes when River speaks to others from Ireland, his accent thickens a little and his choice of words changes. I wonder if it's intentional.

"Well, that's okay. I brought a lovely American bird here tonight to experience the lost art of storytelling. Amber?" He holds out a hand, gesturing at me. "Come on, stand up. Give us a bow."

I feel my cheeks burst as all eyes suddenly shift to me. Contrary to what many think, I *don't* like being the center of attention, good or otherwise.

I shoot a glare at River, but he only nods toward me, waiting.

Oh, what the hell . . . With a deep breath, I slip off my chair and, tucking one ankle behind the other, I splay my skirt with my fingers and bend at the knee. A playful round of applause ensues.

"Right, of course. A curtsy. My American princess wouldn't bow." He winks at me and then, to my relief, takes the attention off of me. "My brothers and I had the pleasure of listening to two great men, Seamus and Fionn Delaney, regale us with fantastical lore throughout our childhood. We have an entire arsenal of stories passed down that I could choose from. Funnily enough, though, the tale I want to tell you tonight is not one of theirs. It comes from Marion Delaney. At least two or three times a week, I'd refuse bedtime until she'd tell it to me. Now, I'll apologize in advance because I'm not nearly as long-winded as that fat bastard over there," he sticks his thumb out at Fergus, who only laughs, "and it's not nearly as eloquent. But I was only seven when I learnt it, so you'll have to pardon me."

Another round of chuckles.

"I'm sure you've all heard of the Great Hunger, between the years of 1845 and 1852? A million men, women, and children lost their lives due to starvation and disease; another million left Ireland in hopes of a new life elsewhere. Terrible time for our country."

I can't help but frown, wondering what this children's bedtime story could be about.

"Well, the story goes something like this . . ."

I can feel the swing in the atmosphere instantly, that moment when River's entire presence shifts from casual banter to purpose, his gaze capturing the eyes of the audience.

"There was once a God-fearing man by the name of Seamus McNally," he begins, his voice suddenly deeper, calmer, more confident. "His wife gave birth to nine children in total: five girls and four boys. Not unusual back then to have such a large family, especially for farmers. Only, the boys never lived beyond the first year of life. Seamus and his wife kept trying, because they needed the boys to help run the farm. And when his wife died during childbirth with their fourth boy, who also passed on, Seamus was left to care for five little girls on his own. You can imagine what a terrifying prospect that is for any fella."

Despite the solemn introduction to this story, River's little quip has people snickering.

"Now, Seamus was actually a descendant of Brian Boru, High King of Ireland, and had the English not stripped his ancestors of their property in the centuries that followed, imposing ridiculous laws to persecute Catholics, Seamus might have been an estate owner, able to support his family in comfort. But it was not to be. For a few years he prospered as a tenant farmer, renting a four-hectare patch of land on the very property his ancestors once owned near Waterford.

"And then one day, almost overnight, a terrible potato blight swept through the country, turning the plant leaves black and potatoes rotten. All of Seamus's crops were destroyed, and when it came time to pay rent, he couldn't. The English landlord evicted him and his family and burned down his house, just like that." River snaps his fingers.

"Luckily, Seamus was a likeable, hardworking fella, and he secured a job as a laborer on another tenant farm quickly, helping harvest oats. In exchange for his services, he was given enough space to build a one-room mud hut for his family, their pig, and three chickens to share, and a tiny patch where he could grow potatoes for his family the following year, assuming the blight would be over.

"The family barely survived the winter but they all did, selling off their livestock and the few meager possessions they had. Seamus relied on Marion McNally, his eldest girl, to take care of her sisters while he worked the land from daybreak until nightfall, arriving home hunched over and aching. She was fourteen, and while they had no shillings to their name, she learned to become quite resourceful, taking the girls out to collect wood to burn for warmth, and nettle and seaweed and berries, both to eat and to barter with, for more clothes and necessities. They'd even collect sheep manure from neighboring farms, as it was considered rich in nutrients and good for growing crops. All she kept telling herself was that they needed to survive until the fall harvest, and then all would be grand again.

"But the following fall harvest saw virtually every last potato in all of Ireland again ravaged by this blight. Marion knew that her family could not survive another winter. Now, there was plenty of anger boiling in the Irish at this point, especially where the McNallys lived. Anyone who had been to the shorelines by Waterford could tell you that ships full of oats and grain were leaving the docks and heading for England. Entire families of Irish were starving—to death, in many cases—and yet the English landlords were forcing tenant farms to sell their crops in order to pay their rents. The land Seamus labored on was one such farm.

"Spurred by the sight of her little sisters' skeletal limbs, Marion decided she would face this English landlord of theirs, a wealthy man who visited his lands only once or twice a year and was rumored to have arrived a fortnight before. She knew Seamus would never approve, so she waited until he left for the day, and then, collecting a handful of berries to give her sustenance for the fifteen-kilometer walk west, she put the second eldest in charge and left their little hut. She had no idea what she would say as she marched through the fields, noting all the landmarks on her path toward this home—there was no road to guide her—but she figured she'd know by the time she arrived.

"You can only imagine what was going on in little Marion's mind as she crested a hill and caught her first glimpse of the landlord's home. This was a girl who, like many Irish farm families, had only ever seen the tiny, drafty cottages that her kind lived in. To see this huge stone building now . . ."

River sets his pint down on a side table, freeing his hands to animate his excitement. "Remember, I told you that Seamus's ancestors came from royalty, and so they didn't merely live in an estate home. They lived in a bloody castle! If you've been to Kilkenny, then you've seen something like what Marion saw that day—a beautiful home towering high above the ground, with turrets on the ends and half a dozen chimneys to help bring its occupants warmth. And real glass windows! Of course, it wasn't quite as grand as Kilkenny, but to Marion, it was worthy of a king. Which spurred her on even more, because that should have been her family's house. So she marched toward that castle, the massive wooden door in her sights . . . until a man's voice called out to her. 'Who are you?' She turned to see a young man atop a horse, trotting toward her. She guessed him to be maybe twenty, dressed in trousers and a woolen jacket, his waistcoat peeking out beneath. He was an ordinary-lookin' fella, but he was English and no doubt a Protestant, and therefore she despised him on sight.

"'What's it to ya?' she asked boldly, hugging her ratty shift dress close to her body. His horse circled around her once . . . twice . . . before he hopped off. 'This is my land and you're trespassing,' he said. *This* was her English landlord? She put on a brave face. 'Me name is Marion McNally and me family's starvin,' she announced. 'We're all starvin' and you're here, prancin' around with your fancy horse, wearin' your fancy clothes, livin' in your big castle. Don't ya know that people on your land are dying? That ya could feed them with what you send back to England to make your selfish countrymen fat and blissful?'"

I smile, listening to River mimic a much thicker, more pronounced Irish brogue to perfection.

"The young man simply stared at her, for so long she was beginning to think he might order her executed for treason. 'I'm sorry, miss . . . but we don't have much choice. If we don't collect rents and taxes from our farms, then we'll be forced to evict them from our land, or lose our land, altogether.'

"'It's not even your land. It's me family's land. You're a bunch of thieving bastards!' Marion exclaimed boldly, and then turned and ran as fast as her skinny legs could carry her, expecting to be run down at any moment. But she wasn't. And almost a fortnight later, when the weather had turned cold, a knock sounded on the wooden plank they used for a door to keep out the draft. They opened it to find two sacks of milled oats sitting outside, hidden beneath a few thick woolen blankets. The sound of horse hooves could be heard in the distance, galloping away.

"Seamus quickly hid the bags inside, because the situation for everyone had become desperate, and he was afraid they would be pillaged. There was just enough to keep his girls alive for the winter, he hoped. Now, it wasn't bad enough that the blight had stolen virtually all food for the farmers, but that year saw the harshest winter Ireland had seen in years. Cottages were buried to their rooftops in snow as storm after storm pounded the country. By the spring, bodies lay everywhere.

"But the McNally family survived yet again, hiding within their one-room home, keeping warm with the tiniest of fires and those woolen blankets and their body heat, rationing their oats for a daily helping of porridge, using melted snow to make it. Seamus knew he should eat more, let the kids go without so he could stay healthy and take care of them like many parents had to do in those long, dark days, but he couldn't bear listening to their hungry cries.

"And because of that, he fell ill. In the early spring, Seamus passed on, leaving Marion to care for her four sisters. The five of them, stronger than most laborers around because of the milled oats they lived off of through the winter, were able to keep their hut by working the fields as Seamus had, and planting more potatoes, in hopes that a third year of blight was impossible."

He pauses to nod a thanks to Rose as she drops off a fresh pint. The Irish really do love their Guinness. That's his fourth now, and there isn't even a hint—a slur, a lax face, a stray thought—that would suggest it's affected him in any way.

"When Marion heard rumors of the landlord arriving at the house again, she knew she had to visit him. To apologize. It was the right thing to do, especially after she had spoken to him in such a horrific way. She knew that it was that young man on a horse who dropped the milled oats and blankets at her door.

"So on the following Sunday, she again marched through the fields, along the stone wall, over the hill, her body weaker from hunger, her dress even more tattered and filthy. The man was not out on his horse this time. She found him standing before a two-hectare-sized garden patch, the soil freshly tilled, his arms folded over his chest, his brow furrowed.

"'What are you going to plant?' she asked by way of greeting. He looked at her for a long moment before saying, 'I don't know, Miss Marion. What do you think I should plant here?' She was surprised to know that he remembered her name but she pretended not to be and said, 'You're in Ireland, so potatoes, of course,' which made him burst out laughing. 'Perhaps,' he said, holding out his hand to show her the beans. 'But just in case of that pesky blight, I was thinking these, too. And some corn and cabbage.' She nodded her approval. Beans and corn were expensive to plant. He asked her how her family had fared over the winter, and she shared the news of her father. His father had died as well, over Christmas, he admitted. When Marion had met this man the fall before, he hadn't been the landlord, after all. His father had in fact owned the land.

"The young man's name was Charles Beasley, and he was happy to see Marion alive and well. She had been a pretty young ginger-haired thing the year before, the day she marched onto his family's property with fire in her eyes. She still was, though far too thin for his tastes. It had been a long winter for him, sitting in the comfort of his family's estate home near Bath, wondering if the bags of milled oats he'd dropped at her door that day would be enough to keep her alive. It was long enough to concoct a plan. He had already inquired about the McNally family in secret on the day he arrived in Ireland and knew what had happened to her father. He figured it was only a matter of time before that fiery little Irish girl would show up again.

"So when she did, he was ready. He told her that he planned on staying on his estate for the summer to ensure proper management of the land, and he needed servants to care for him, and workers for his crops. He asked if she and her sisters could move into the servants' quarters of his house and fulfill those roles.

"Even though he'd basically saved her and her sisters from certain death the winter before, Marion didn't trust this Englishman, or his intentions. But she also had no choice. The tenant farmer whose land they lived on hadn't paid his taxes and they'd all be evicted soon enough. The five McNally girls would be left to beg on the sides of the road. So she agreed.

"Despite the horrendous poverty that all of Ireland faced, life for Marion and her sisters improved drastically that summer. They had fresh water to drink and bathe in from the stream nearby; dry, warm beds to sleep in; cotton and wool for new clothes. For the first time in their lives, they knew what it felt like not to be hungry. They stayed within the castle's walls, as did Charles for the most part, not wanting to risk contracting the typhus or dysentery that was running rampant through Ireland during those years.

"Marion assumed it was only a matter of time before Charles expected other things—manly things—from one of the five girls. She hoped it would be only her that he targeted, given she was the oldest. And she assumed it would be her, given the looks he stole her way on a daily basis.

"But he never did. Charles Beasley stayed on in Ireland, not leaving for England in the winter, and not once in the five years that the McNally girls lived under that roof—their rightful roof, through their lineage—did Charles Beasley try anything untoward. He could have. Those girls would have given him what he asked for in exchange for their family's lives. While the entire country around them struggled through starvation and revolts against England for abandoning them in their time of need, valuing the market before Irish lives, somehow Charles held onto his land, giving the girls a home where they could grow into strong, independent Irishwomen."

River clears his voice, and when he begins again, it sounds huskier. "The same heart condition that ailed Charles's father took hold of Charles the winter of 1851. It was on his deathbed that he finally confessed his love for Marion. By then almost twenty, she had grown into a beautiful bird, and could have had any suitor she desired, had she put herself before her sisters. She finally admitted that she had grown to love him as well, and wished that things could have been different. 'But they can't,' Charles whispered through a weak smile." River's own smile mimics the emotion. "'You'll always be an Irish Catholic peasant girl and I'll always be an English Protestant lord.' Marion wasn't a woman who cried often, but she wiped her tears from her cheeks then, to say, 'If the likes of me was never going to be good enough for the likes of you, then why do all this?' With the last bit of strength left in Charles's body, he reached for her hand, grasped it tight. 'Oh, my dear Marion. It was the likes of me who would never be good enough for the likes of you.'"

A sharp ball forms in my throat as River suddenly grows silent. Nothing but a few sniffles and the odd clank of a dish from a kitchen behind the walls can be heard.

"Marion and her sisters left after Charles passed on and made their way to other parts of the country, met their husbands, and married. But Marion never stopped thinking about Charles Beasley, a man she was supposed to despise because of what he was, but a man she loved because of who he was."

With a slow, heavy sigh, River catches my eye for a moment, offering me a secretive smile before he leans into the microphone again. "And that, ladies and gentlemen, is why I cried myself to sleep a lot when I was a little boy."

A round of chuckles, followed by loud applause, ricochets off the stone walls as River clasps hands with Fergus, and the old man steals back his hat to cover his bald head.

"What is . . . hey, are you crying?" Rowen asks with sincere interest, peering down at Ivy, whose face is ducked in her lap, her compact mirror opened.

"No," she mutters, running her pinky finger along the bottom corner of her eye.

"You are!" Rowen claps his hands. "I don't believe it. You, I can see it," he throws a hand my way, "but I'd never have guessed that *this* one would be a romantic."

"It was a sad story!" she hisses, turning to glare at him as she throws a soft punch into his stomach.

River's return, his hands rubbing my shoulders affectionately as he squeezes around my chair to his, distracts me from the interesting spat across from me. "Your mother did *not* tell you that story when you were seven years old."

"She did! At least twice a week. You can ask, I begged her."

What would River and Rowen's mother be like? I push that curiosity aside—I'd love to meet her—and ask, "So that must make you a true romantic?"

That earns a smirk. "I guess I am." He pauses. "Is that bad?"

"No, not at all."

Tugging my chair closer to his, until our thighs press against each other, River quietly plays with my curly locks of hair as the next storyteller takes the stage.

I try to listen, but it's hard, my mind constantly wandering to a seemingly far-off place. A place where this thing with River isn't simply a vacation fling, the expiration date looming. A place where he kisses me and begs me to make it work. Where we lie in bed and make plans for future visits; where he sees the Oregon mountains and fields that I've grown up with; where he meets the sheriff for the first time; where I meet the Delaney family. Daily Skype and phone calls and texts that turn into talks of one of us moving. Could I actually move to Ireland? I guess I could . . . if we married. What would I do? Work in the bar? What would I need to do to be certified as a nurse here?

By the time Shannon O'Callahan has stepped off the stage to a round of applause—mine hollow because I didn't hear a word of her story—my imagination, inspired by a wish, has created an entire life for River and me.

■ ■ ■

"I'll make sure Ivy gets home safe," Rowen offers, holding the taxi door open.

With the slightest eye roll at me, she slides into the backseat. "Call me tomorrow night, if you want," she says through the open window just as they pull away.

"Why wouldn't your brother want a ride home?" I ask as River guides me toward his car, his arm roped around my waist.

"You want the truth or the gentleman's response?"

I answer him with a pointed look and he chuckles softly.

"He's hoping his night with Ivy hasn't ended yet."

The very idea makes me laugh. "What . . . him and Ivy? I thought she was going to stab him with her fork earlier tonight, when he started teasing her about getting emotional. Why on earth would he think she's interested?"

"Well . . ." River holds the passenger-side door open for me to climb in. "I *may* have led him to believe that with a few things that I said earlier."

I stare at him in disbelief. "Because you actually thought Ivy might be interested in Rowen?"

His green eyes are sparkling when he slides into the driver's seat. "Because I highly doubt she is."

I start giggling. "You realize that she may actually hurt him, right?"

He cranks the engine and entwines his fingers with mine, and we shift the car into first gear together. "I'm kind of hoping she does. Not too much," he quickly adds, a cute frown puckering his face. "Just a little bit. The bastard deserves it for the pranks he's played on me."

River weaves his car through the narrow streets, deftly avoiding bar revelers—really, there doesn't seem to be a night when the streets *aren't* filled with people enjoying Dublin's bar scene—whirling around the roundabouts, a comfortable silence settling into the car.

"How much of that story is true?"

River opens his mouth, then hesitates for a moment. "If it weren't for Marion McNally and Charles Beasley, I wouldn't be sitting here today, that much I do know. Marion and her sisters all went on to marry husbands and bear children. It was the youngest, Sally McNally, whose lineage I can be thankful for. In every single generation, the first-born girl carried Marion McNally's namesake.

Which is why my ma's name is Marion. And as fate would have it, she married a Seamus."

"That's just . . ." Tears well in my eyes. ". . . an incredibly tragic but uplifting story." I smile to myself. "That's why you wanted me to see that monument, isn't it?"

He pulls my hand to his mouth, kissing my fingers, before setting us back onto the gear to shift around a corner. As if telling me that he's so happy I understand the deeper meaning. Or, at least, that's what I want it to mean. "Ma never let us up from the dinner table until every last scrap of food was cleaned from our plates. While Da's side fared slightly better with the pub to support them, her family struggled greatly. The famine and starvation, the way the English government virtually abandoned us during those years . . . all of that is true, and I could tell you a hundred more stories about it. It's why Ireland was in a constant state of rebellion for a hundred and forty-odd years after. It's why the Irish Republican Army began in the first place. It's why we fought—" He cuts himself off, inhales deeply.

Irish Republican Army. "The IRA."

"Yeah."

"So, your family was a part of that?"

He glances at me once before refocusing on the road. "They were, up until the mid-seventies. My great-granddad and his brother fought in the Easter Uprising, back when violence seemed to be the only way that England would listen."

"I read about the uprising yesterday, at the museum. The British won that, didn't they?"

"They did. But they executed fifteen of the republican leaders and the Irish people hated them for it. That little uprising of two thousand Irishmen started the revolution. It's why we're free of England's rule today."

I can hear the pride in his voice.

"And then my granddad and his brothers fought in the civil war. He actually knew Éamon de Valera well. The Republic's third president," he adds for my benefit.

"And your dad?"

"Him, too . . . for a while." He clears his throat. "My uncle Thomas—Da's older brother—was killed in the Northern riots in '69, when he was eighteen. So, yeah . . . my granddad and dad were right pissed with anything British or Protestant. They fought with the IRA for a time."

I'm trying to keep an open mind here, even as I listen to River admit that he comes from a long line of men who fought in the name of the IRA. Does that mean that River's family members are . . . terrorists? I can't ask him something like that. Besides, he said that was forty years ago. And it's not River, I remind myself. It's kind of like Bonnie's family, who is German. Her great-grandfather was an actual Nazi soldier in the war—a secret that she's told only me. That's not her fault, or her parent's fault. I need to look at this the same way. "You said they stopped fighting? What changed for them?"

"Times changed. Violence—especially the kind that was happening then, with plenty of innocent casualties—wasn't the answer anymore."

"Huh. I bet you have a lot of stories."

"Some." He sighs, squeezing my hands. "For another night, maybe."

St. Stephen's Green stretches out to the left of us. I haven't gone back there yet. I haven't felt the need to, though it's probably something I should do, for a sense of closure. "The papers said that police suspected the IRA behind that. What do you think?" For a country I was so desperate to visit, I really had no clue about its history. My ignorance is embarrassing.

He stares hard out at the road, his jaw clenching. "Maybe. But if it is, it's nothing my family stands for."

I don't press the topic, leaning over to settle a soft kiss on his cheek instead. "Thank you for tonight. It's too bad I lost that bucket list of mine. I had this very item on it. Number thirty-two, I think."

"Huh . . . Imagine that." I catch his smile in the side mirror as he checks his blind spot and then changes lanes to turn down my street. In another minute, River's car is sitting next to Simon's, the quiet house looming before me as the car idles low.

"So?" His hands rest on his lap. He's making no move to turn off the engine, to step out of the car, to walk me to the door.

To climb into my bed.

"So . . ."

"So, I don't want to put the same kind of pressure on you that I unintentionally did last night, Amber. And I'm afraid that me coming inside will do just that." His gaze flickers to my legs before settling on the hedge out front. "We can say good night right here, and I can come meet you after work tomorrow night, and I'll be perfectly glad to do so. It's whatever you want."

I study his profile for a long moment—the way his Adam's apple bobs with a hard swallow, as if those words were difficult to say; the way that strong jaw clenches slightly; the way his right hand isn't really resting on his lap, but gripping it, as if keeping it at bay.

Twenty-four hours ago, I was torn by desire and indecision. Tonight, that same desire is raging, coupled with a newfound mass of emotions, unspoken thoughts, and compelling curiosities. But that indecision? That dissolved as if it had never existed. I don't believe I'd feel differently about River in three weeks than I do tonight. I'd only feel *more*.

I don't have the luxury of weeks or months or years with him. I have only days, and I don't want to regret how I use them.

"What do *you* want?" I ask softly.

A weak chuckle escapes him, his head falling back onto the headrest for a moment. "Do you really need to ask?"

Reaching over, I turn the key and the quiet rumble dies.

Heat flashes in his gaze as he turns to look at me, and then we both climb out of the car. Hand-in-hand, we walk toward the cherry-red door, the only sound my beautiful but painful heels clicking against the concrete.

"Thank God we're home." I groan, my fingers twisting the deadbolt shut once inside. "These shoes are killing me." They looked so perfect, sitting next to the dress at the boutique where I bought the outfit.

River steps in close and leans forward, peering down at them. "Those shoes?"

"Yes. They're pretty, but they—ah!" River suddenly slings me over his shoulder like a sack of potatoes. Gently, of course, one arm gripping my thighs. A breeze against my skin warns me that my dress is likely hiked far above any respectable level, but there's not much I can do about it at this point. Besides, it really doesn't matter. I'm sure I'll be losing it entirely soon enough, a prospect that leaves me with nervous flutters in my stomach. The good kind, this time.

"These *are* pretty," he agrees, carrying me up the stairs through my playful shrieks. He needs no directions to my bedroom, where he flicks on the muted bedside lamp. Strong hands somehow gracefully maneuver my body off his shoulder, setting me down on the bed. His fingers skim the length of my legs, from my thighs down to my ankles, hooking around the heels to flick them off. They thump against the hardwood. "But you're right. Completely impractical."

His eyes have changed color—from that lush, bright green to a much darker shade. A fact I realize as he stretches out on top of me, forcing me down onto my back. His gentleman's hesitation in the car earlier is gone, replaced with a confidence that provokes.

"So is this," I whisper, curling my fingers around his shirt, desperate to admire his muscular body again. He lifts his arms above his head, allowing me easy access to slide the material over his head, tossing it on the floor. Giving my hands access to his chest, his skin hot to the touch.

My heart races.

He simply watches my face as I roam his upper body, propped up on one elbow to allow for it. "What happened here?" I trace a long, thin line over his top rib.

"A scuffle between me, my brother, and a fence."

Of course. I shake my head. "Who won?"

"Some would say my brother, but I'd say the fence."

"Rowen?"

His fingers slide gently along the curve of my neck. "Aengus."

That elusive older brother that he doesn't like talking about. I continue my wanderings, to a scar on his collarbone. "And here?"

He gives me a sheepish smile. "A scuffle between, me, Aengus, and a hay wagon." His head dips, warm breath skating across my skin. "The wagon definitely won that one."

I start laughing—a deep belly laugh that cuts off with a light gasp the second his mouth finds my neck. I lose all interest in my investigation, happily roping my arms around his body.

He tenses, suddenly, as my nail catches a stitch.

"I'm sorry." I completely forgot. I can't believe I forgot.

"Doesn't hurt," he murmurs, grasping first my one hand, and then the other. Kissing my fingertips one at a time. "But you do have nails, so . . ." He threads his fingers between mine and pins both of my hands above my head. And he stares down at me, his erection pressing hard against my thigh. "I could just lie here like this all night."

I'm pretty sure that I can't, not with this intense ache between my legs. "Liar." I lift my head off the bed to skim my tongue over his lips in answer, teasing him. He groans, forcing my head back into the pillow as his tongue slides into my mouth with a deep, warm kiss and his body shifts to grind against me.

This connection between us is so much more intense than last night, now that I'm sure.

I'm so very sure that I want this, and him.

So sure that I curl my shoulder when his hand slips under my back to unzip my dress. So sure that I help him by tugging it up and over my head as he kneels, watching. So sure that when he slides my panties over my hips and all the way down my legs to my feet, his gaze taking in my body without shame, I reach for his belt buckle, his button, his zipper, slipping my hand into the front of his jeans to grasp him before he's had a chance to touch me so intimately.

I don't think I've ever taken the lead on that.

River seems to like it, though, helping by peeling the rest of his clothes off, giving me free access. Only he's not patient. With a gentle but aggressive move, I find myself lying on my back again, with his mouth and reverent hands wandering over every square inch of my body, inside my body, touching me with more skill than I've ever experienced before. In fact, every other experience I've had pales in comparison to the one I'm sharing now with River.

By the time I hear the tear of a foil wrapper, I feel like I've been waiting an eternity.

By the time he pushes into me—such a full, wonderful sensation—I feel like I've known him forever.

And by the time our raspy breaths slow, our limbs coiled around each other, our bodies sated and spent, I'm thinking of cancelling plane tickets and spending the next three months exactly like this, with River.

■ ■ ■

I open my eyes to catch a glimpse of River's bare and perfect backside a second before it disappears into his boxer briefs. The morning sun shines through the window beyond him. It's nine thirty and I knew he'd have to leave to get to work. But it leaves a hollow ache in my chest all the same.

I'm addicted to him. I certainly acted like it last night. And this morning. Twice.

The truth is, I've never felt even remotely like this about any guy before. That's kind of scary, seeing as I've had three long-term relationships and I had actually convinced myself that Aaron was it for me.

It scares me that he could have been. That I might not have ever known what *this* feels like.

"I can take those stitches out for you, when they're ready. If you want," I offer, my voice scratchy.

He peers over his shoulder at me, flashing a smile more devastating today than it was yesterday. "Better your hands than Rowen's."

"Did your doctor tell you when they could come out?"

He picks his jeans up off the ground, the curve and ripples of his stomach bringing back flashes to last night. I squeeze my thighs together with the memory. "A week or so."

"So . . . Wednesday. It's a date." That's two days from now. I hope I see him before then. I'd be quite happy to spend the next six days in this bed with him. I don't need to see any cliffs or quaint Irish towns while I'm here.

He stretches across the bed, leaning in until his face is only inches away from me, whispering, "That sounds like a very romantic date," before stealing a deep kiss, his tongue prodding. I give it access. Happily. I didn't even do that for Aaron, my fear of foul morning breath outweighing desire every time.

I trace the big tattoo—kind of like an eagle but not quite—on his chest with my fingertip. River's the first guy I've been with who's had any sort of tattoo. I'm not the kind of girl to swoon over them. But now . . . I'm attracted to anything and everything River-related. "Do you really have to go?" I hear myself murmur, my voice pleading and annoying and . . . I don't care.

Seizing my fingers and kissing them once before letting go, he stands again and pulls his jeans on. "I do. Rowen's got class on Mondays until one."

"Right." Rowen mentioned something about taking summer business classes at one of the universities. I hesitate. "What about you? And college, I mean."

"Me and college?" He sighs. "I've thought about it, but I don't know what I'd do. Plus, Delaney's will get passed on to me, to own and run. I have a responsibility to keep it alive."

I frown. "Really? Just you?" That hardly seems fair to his brothers.

"Tradition says it always goes to the eldest, to keep the feuds to a minimum. My uncle Thomas—the one killed in the riots—was supposed to inherit it, instead of Da. Their other brother—Uncle Samuel—would be helping run it, but he passed on when I was ten. Tumbled down a flight of stairs one night, drunk. That was the end of him."

I gasp. "That's . . . horrible!"

"Yeah, well, it happens," River says casually, as if he made peace with it long ago. "And he had no family of his own, so running Delaney's is all on Rowen and me now."

"But, you're not the oldest, are you?"

"No . . ." River's forehead puckers. "Aengus isn't interested."

There's something very wrong with this brother. I can feel it in the air every time River mentions him. But I don't like that feeling, so I change the topic back to us. "So, after Rowen finishes class . . ."

He yanks his shirt over his head with a smile. "Then we've got the after-work crowd."

"And after that?"

"After that . . ." He dives back down for another kiss. "I'm coming to get ya." His lips stretch into a smile, even pressed against mine.

"That's right. You are."

He breaks away, pressing his forehead against mine. "You're far too good for me, ya know that, right?"

"Like Charles Beasley and Marion McNally?"

He chuckles. "See? You're hooked. You're going to be begging me to tell you that story again."

"At least twice a week, at bedtime."

With a heavy sigh, he stands and stretches, peering down at me, a strange look on his face.

"What?"

"Nothing. Just . . ." He hesitates. "I wish you didn't live so far away."

"I know. I've been trying not to think about that," I admit, chasing away the sadness that comes with the reminder. I haven't completely dismissed the notion that came to me last night while resting against his body, to just stay in Ireland for the next three months. It is crazy, of course, and my conscience was quick to remind me that I promised myself not to abandon my plans for a man ever again. I'm trying to ignore that little voice for the time being. Besides, now that I'm out of the sex haze, I realize that it's not something I can decide today. Or even suggest to River. For all I know, this thing between us is so appealing to him—and to me—*because* I'm leaving on Sunday.

Still, knowing he's at least thinking the same thing brings me comfort.

"But, since I do live so far away . . ." I slowly push the sheets down, until the cool morning air skates against my exposed skin.

River's breath hitches. With the quickest glance at the clock on the nightstand, he peels his clothes off.

NINETEEN

RIVER

I can *always* count on Rowen to be on time.

Except today, it would seem.

"What the hell happened to you?" I glance at the old grandfather clock that ticks away on the wall across from me. Though it doesn't look like much—the wood dented, the glass casing scratched—it's a Delaney family heirloom. "You're an hour and a half late!"

"I needed a nap," he mumbles, giving his eyes a good rub.

"A nap?"

He grins at me. "A nap."

It finally clicks and I start chuckling. "I'm impressed." Ivy's obviously even harder to read than I ever suspected. "Her place or ours?"

He takes his time, stretching his arms over his head and releasing an exaggerated yawn. "Ours. Her cousin was home."

"I hope you at least straightened the place up. The real estate agent called. She has a showing this afternoon."

"Yeah. Did you warn Aengus? I haven't seen him in days."

"Left him a message." The guy never answers his phone.

"Right. Danny! You ready for the next one?" he calls out to a regular—a lonely old man who comes in every day from one until four and drinks exactly two pints of Guinness.

"I'm heading to the office for a bit," I announce on my way

past with a load of glasses for the dishwasher. The truth is, I'd kill for a nap right now. The last time I glanced at the bedside clock last night it was after four, and it was a long while after that that I drifted off, too enthralled with studying Amber's peaceful face.

If I inhale deeply enough, I can still smell her perfume.

Dropping into the desk chair with a groan, I power on the laptop, a luxury that Da fought for years, until Rowen and I gave up and fronted the cash. Once Da saw the value of it—how easily we could keep employee records, inventory lists, and the like—he reimbursed us.

Between the two of us, Rowen is the more computer literate. He's taken college-level computer courses. I've thought about enrolling a few times, but I've always had one excuse or another not to do it. I know enough to get by. I can use the internet, which I open up now, Googling "map of Oregon." The screen proves to me exactly how far Amber's life is from mine. Searching images of the area, I get a glimpse into her world. It's a beautiful one, full of mountains and farms that look very different from ours. Just for fun, I do a search of plane ticket prices. Seven hundred euro. Not too bad.

I heave a sigh. *Fuck.* Why does she have to be American?

And why am I even thinking about this right now!

Folding my arms over the desk, I lean forward and close my eyes, hoping a fifteen-minute nap will clear my mind of the ridiculous thoughts that have been churning inside my head since I kissed her goodbye at the door this morning.

Unfortunately, I don't manage to drift off before Rowen barrels into the office. The second I look up, the second I see his face filled with worry, I know.

"A garda's at the bar, asking for you."

"What exactly did he say?"

"He just asked when you'd be around."

I sigh, closing out the tabs open on the screen, but not before Rowen sees them and shoots me a questioning stare. I ignore it. He trails me down the hall to the door. I crack it just enough to see down to the end of the bar, where the garda is sipping on his coffee and reading his paper, before ducking back. "He hasn't said anything else?"

"No," Rowen says, adding in a voice too low for the busboy washing dishes behind us to hear, "that's the one with the hard-on for Aengus, isn't it?"

"His name's Duffy. Yeah."

"What's this about, River?"

"It's probably nothing, as usual." The gardai do this every once in a while, I remind myself. They think Delaney's is a hub for IRA information. It's not a big deal. I grab a rack of fresh glasses and push through the door, keeping my features relaxed and my eyes away from him as I make my way over to the counter.

"So you got the message?"

I look up, feigning surprise as the lanky-limbed man watches me from his seat, resting his elbows against the counter. "What message?"

His tight smile answers. "Have you talked to your brother lately?"

"A minute ago. He's takin' a piss but he'll be out soon, if you need him."

He scratches his temple, the only sign that he's irritated. "How about the other one?"

"Aengus?" I shrug. "He was here two nights ago."

"What for?"

The glasses clatter as I stack them noisily. "To have a pint."

Duffy slides his cup out without a word, signaling a top-up. As much as I'd like to tell him to fuck off, that would be a bad idea. So I grab the coffeepot and fill him up.

"Did he talk to anyone?"

"He talked to lots of people. You know Aengus, always so social." Rowen, stepping out from the back just now, hears me and snorts.

"Give me some examples of people he talked to, River."

"I can't recall. It was a Saturday night. You know what those are like around here." I carry the emptied dish tray over to its special spot, where we load it with the dirty glasses and send them back for washing. Hoping this guy takes the hint that I'm not going to snitch on my brother, no matter how big of a bastard he is. "But you should track him down and ask him yourself."

"I'm asking you." He wipes at the light sheen of sweat across his forehead with a cloth. "We got an anonymous tip that Aengus was meeting with Jimmy Conlon here."

"Really . . ."

"We have an arrest warrant out for Jimmy."

"Then it wouldn't make much sense for him to show up here, now would it? He'd likely go to ground."

"You would think. Especially seeing as we're not the only ones who want him. Word is Beznick's put a hit out on him."

"They must really want him dead then."

"What about you, Rowen?" Duffy shifts his questioning. "Did you see Jimmy Conlon in here on Saturday night?"

"Who?"

"Jimmy Conlon," Duffy repeats.

"Sorry. Never met the fella," Rowen offers. Smart kid. He's not lying. He has never officially met Jimmy.

Duffy's shrewd gaze lands on me. He's losing patience. Good. Maybe he'll leave us the fuck alone. "We got an anonymous tip that Aengus was behind the bomb in St. Stephen's Green."

I catch a flash in a mirror—Rowen's head whipping around—but I ignore it, leveling Duffy with an even stare. I have a pretty good poker face, even when my insides are about to explode. "That's a serious accusation." As much as I should be shocked that the gardai have heard, I'm not. Some of the guys around Jimmy, including Aengus, have too much arrogance and not enough intelligence. They get drunk in pubs and boast, and the wrong person's always listening.

"It is." He nods, watching me closely. "Carries a sentence of at least fifteen years if we can prove it. And I will prove it, if it's true." He delivers the warning with a light voice, though his mood is anything but light. I know Duffy's history. He lost his uncle and father to a bombing in Belfast in the '90s. He's been especially interested in dismantling all forms of IRA—both those who fight for a free Ireland and those who fight for the fight—since he put on a uniform.

"Well, you'll have to ask Aengus about that. I'm sure he'll tell ya the truth."

His upper lip twitches. "I was wondering if you know anything about it, seeing as you two are so close."

Of course it would appear that way. I visited him regularly, more than anyone else. "We haven't been close in years. And no, I don't. Sorry."

"That's good." He pauses, adjusting his cap. "Because if I find out you're lying about knowing something, I'll put ya behind bars with him." His stool scrapes against the floor as he stands. "Oh, and we also just heard that Beznick's men may be after Aengus now too. Pass the message along to your brother, will ya?"

"Wait. What?" Rowen snaps, no longer pretending not to listen. "What does that mean?"

"It means that Aengus has done something to piss off the wrong people."

"Ya need to do something to protect him, then. Isn't that what the gardai's for? Protecting people?"

"Didn't ya hear? Gardai won't be risking our lives for criminal organizations. We'll no longer provide protection for known offenders because of these street wars they get themselves into. We're only interested in protecting the innocent." His dull blue eyes land on mine again. "I'm just letting ya know so ya can be watchful. And perhaps share information with me, River. I gather ya don't want to be seeing the inside of Portlaoise anytime soon."

The arse saunters out the front door of Delaney's. I watch him, gritting my teeth. Coming into Delaney's, in broad daylight, and threatening me, trying to get me to turn on my own blood?

Rowen closes the distance in three quick steps. "This isn't nothing, River. What the hell has Aengus gotten himself into?"

I sigh. I'm so tired of this. And it's never going to end. "Check the kegs before the rush." There's no way Rowen is getting pulled into this mess.

I slide my phone out of my pocket and head to the back, where I can deliver the warning to Aengus in private.

Fear gripping my guts tight.

I can't go to prison.

Again.

TWENTY

AMBER

I brought my grandmother's diamond stud earrings for a special occasion. They've sat, nestled in their cushioned case and tucked away with my valuables, for a month now. Today, I'm putting them on.

Because every day between now and Sunday is special. And I'm already sure that I don't want to leave.

I check the clock. It's twenty minutes to six. A text from River said he was just showering and then would be over. I've basically been counting down the hours since this morning, killing time at the Glasnevin Cemetery and St. Patrick's Cathedral, my mind and emotions happily drowning in all thoughts River.

I've taken extra time getting myself ready. My hair is set in perfect curls, my mascara brushed on thick and smooth, my face contoured in just the right way. The canary-yellow halter dress I brought looks great against my tanned skin, even if it's not ideal for Dublin's crisp evening temperatures. My denim jacket will solve that problem, as well as the issue of my bruises, still visible on my right bicep and shoulder.

My cowboy boots—not a smart choice with limited space in my suitcase, but a requirement—finish the outfit perfectly.

I glance in the hallway mirror and smile. I want to steal his breath the second he sees me. I want River still thinking about me when I'm no longer here.

I want him to suggest that I stay.

The doorbell rings, and a rush of nerves and excitement erupts in my stomach.

I throw open the door.

The tall, lanky officer from the Green stands on my front porch, his smile polite and professional, but killing my excitement all the same. "Miss Welles. I'm Garda Duffy, if you remember."

"Of course. How are you?" *What are you doing here?* His vehicle sits in the street behind him, his partner in the driver's seat.

Duffy gestures inside, and it's then that I notice the tan folder tucked under his arm. "May I come in?"

I'm guessing that I don't have a choice here. "Of course." I step back to make room for him, hoping I can get this over with before River arrives. Not that it would matter. As far as Duffy is concerned, he's a friend I met at a bar.

"You certainly have some nice accommodations while you're here." He quietly takes inventory of the space, just like I've seen my dad do of any new place—his eyes drifting over the windows and doors and the empty couches. Identifying escape routes and potential threats, my dad would say, half in jest.

"I lucked out. The owner is away for the summer." I lead him in to the dining room table.

"Were ya on your way out?" Garda Duffy asks. "Ya look all . . ." His eyes drift over my dress and boots. When he catches me watching him, he quickly adjusts his focus to his folder.

"Yeah, I was two minutes from leaving, actually."

"This won't take long," he promises. Then pauses. "How have you been? Ya seem to be fine."

"I'm okay. The bruising is going away and my lip has almost healed." The dark spot left after the scab fell off will likely remain.

"Good. You haven't called, so I imagine ya still don't remember much about the man who fled the scene?"

"The man who saved my life?" I note his choice of words and I don't appreciate them. They're full of accusation. "No." I swallow hard. It's a lie, and I know it's a lie, and yet it's the only answer I want to give him.

"Right." The slightest frown shades his gaze. "We've been given some information and I was hoping you'd be willing to take a look at these." He lays a piece of paper out on the table. A mug shot. Duffy taps the face. "Does he look familiar to ya?"

The picture is of a tight-faced man with a mop of bright orange-red hair and a sneer. He looks every bit the part of a criminal—his eyes narrowed, his jaw square, his lips thin and hard, his expression not just unhappy with the circumstance, but generally unpleasant. "No, I've never seen him before," I answer truthfully. I would have remembered a head of hair like that.

"Okay." Duffy stuffs the photo into his folder and lays down another. "How about this one?"

River's eyes stare up at me.

I make a conscious effort to breathe, the shock a punch to my lungs. He looks to be a few years younger here, and clean-shaven. But there's no mistaking him in this photograph.

This mug shot.

River's been arrested before.

Even as nausea roils in my stomach, I remind myself that this could mean nothing. A fight that went wrong, a drunk-and-disorderly. River's not exactly a saint. Neither is my brother.

It's never come up in conversation, so it must not be a big deal, right?

Who did I just sleep with?

A guy who saved my life, who took shrapnel for me, I remind myself. Who has been nothing but kind and generous and sweet to me.

I feel Duffy's eyes on me. Waiting for my answer.

And I know what that answer should be. I may have lied a minute ago about what I remember—something I can easily get away with because they'll never see into my brain—but I *know* this man staring up at me from the picture. In some ways, very well. In too many ways, not at all.

And this is a police officer asking me.

"No." The lie escapes before I can stop it. I clear my throat, keeping my eyes on River's picture so Duffy can't see the guilt. "I'm sorry."

River's face disappears into the folder. "Worth a shot, right?" I don't miss the disappointment in Duffy's voice. He was hoping for a different answer. "Thank you for being so cooperative, though. I know ya probably want to just forget this happened and move on. Enjoy the rest of your time in Ireland. And here." He drops a business card on the table. I still have his other one in my purse. "Just in case you remember something. Even down the road."

I trail behind him as he walks briskly to the front door, my feet made of lead.

"Who are they?" I blurt out. "Those men you just showed me."

"Two brothers who got mixed up in some bad stuff."

Brothers. The redhead must be Aengus. "Bad stuff?" My voice is too shaky. I steady it. "What kind of bad stuff?"

"The IRA kind." He offers me a smile. "But don't worry. I've put them both in prison once. If they were behind this, I'll put them there again."

I grip the door for support as I watch him march down the path, closing the black gate behind him.

River said his family walked away from it all in the '70s because of the violence, so what does this mean?

Don't be stupid, Amber. It means he's lying to you.

So, everything I know about River up until now has been an act? I can feel tears threatening to spill over. How could I have been *so* wrong about him?

And what has he done? What does "the IRA kind" mean? Has he hurt people? *Killed* them? No, that's just not possible. I couldn't have misread him that much. But, then, what did he do that would put him in jail?

I glance at my watch. River is supposed to be here in five minutes.

Beyond the shock and hurt and an inkling of fear, a new sensation bursts.

Anger.

I do the only thing I can think to do.

I grab my purse and Simon's car keys, and I run.

TWENTY-ONE

RIVER

My car whips around the corner at a quarter past six. Trying to make up for lost time, late on account of the shower I squeezed in between work and here and the flowers I grabbed for Amber, a last-minute decision and something I've never actually done before.

I can't wait to see her.

An empty spot sits where the black Volkswagen normally sits out front. I don't think too much about it, though. Maybe a neighbor borrowed it. This doctor guy seems generous enough to allow for that. I park in the space beside it and make my way up the path, to ring the bell.

No answer.

Frowning, I check my phone. The last text from her was forty minutes ago, responding to mine that I'd be there soon. I quickly punch out a message to her, telling her I'm outside.

And then I wait for a reply. Maybe she's in the bathroom?

Another text and a phone call, and ten minutes later, she's still not answering. On impulse, I try the doorknob.

The door's unlocked.

"Amber?" My voice ricochets off three stories worth of walls.

No answer.

An edge of unease slides into me as I wander into the living room, the kitchen, the dining room, my footfalls slow and intentionally quiet. "Amber!"

She's obviously not here. So where the hell is she?

A card catches my eye on the dining room table. On impulse, I pick it up. When I see Garda Duffy's name printed on it, my blood turns cold. "Shit." This must just be a coincidence. He was probably the one at the scene of the bomb, the one who questioned her. A connection I hadn't made before.

But why is his card here?

And why is she now gone?

I dial Rowen's cell.

The low buzz of the steady Monday night fills the background. "What's the story?"

"Is Amber there?"

"Uh . . . nope. Isn't she supposed to be with you?"

"Ring me if she shows up there."

"Right. Is everything okay?"

"Not sure." I take the stairs two steps at a time, searching the bedrooms, my focus stalling on the bed I was in only hours ago, the sheets stretched out over the mattress, the pillows perfectly set. It doesn't surprise me. Amber seems like the kind of girl who wouldn't leave without making her bed every morning. I inhale, the scent of her perfume still lingering in the air. She was here not long ago.

But now she's not. We were supposed to meet, and there's a business card from the asshole garda who thinks I'm guilty of something sitting on her table. Her car is gone and the door was left unlocked.

I can't see Amber doing that on purpose. It's as if she was in a rush and forgot. Or a panic.

Fuck. What did he say to her? Did he come here? On the same day that he was questioning me about Aengus? This is too coincidental.

I search for a spare house key in the table by the door. Nothing. So I shut the door tight behind me, because I don't know what else I can do, and head back to my car, dread taking over. I don't want to leave the house open for her to come home to. This is central

Dublin. It's not a place you can leave your door unlocked, especially if someone knows the owner and thinks he's overseas.

I pull my phone out again, and I dial her number. It goes straight to voicemail.

"Amber . . . Ring me." I hesitate. "*Please.*"

TWENTY-TWO

AMBER

"I'm a disgrace to my heritage," Ivy admits, twirling her chow mein noodles around her fork.

"Just don't spill," Ian mutters, eyeing her lithe body that's wedged into the wing chair, one leg slung over the side. We both watched her douse the take-out with so much soy sauce that it pooled in the bottom of her bowl.

I'm not even hungry, but when Ivy said she was going to order Chinese, I numbly nodded. Now I simply shift the noodles around in their box. My eyes veering over to my phone. River has already left three texts and two voice messages.

"See anything ya like?" Ian asks me in that strange mock Dubliner's accent, pointing his chopsticks toward the big binder of tattoo photographs. I've been flipping through it for hours, listening to Ivy's needle buzz behind the walls.

"You did *all* of these?"

"It's my portfolio. Proof of my level of skill."

"He's alright," Ivy mumbles through a full mouth of food.

"Would you stop saying that to potential customers!" He throws an extra set of chopsticks at her, and they hit her boot.

"What's wrong, afraid of a little competition?"

He simply shakes his head at his cousin.

"I think you're very good," I offer, turning to the next page, and the next.

"See?" Ian smirks.

"She doesn't even know what to look for," Ivy mutters.

I ignore the little jibe—she's right, but there's no need to be so condescending about it—and keep looking through Ian's work. Until I come to a page with a black-and-red bird. It's large, taking up the client's entire bicep, the wings curling around on either side. And it's too similar to River's to be a coincidence. "Does this mean something?

Ian leans over. "That's the phoenix. It's represents the Irish Republican Army, back when they reestablished themselves after a series of riots in Northern Ireland, aimed at stopping the persecution of Catholics. If you visit Belfast, you'll see the phoenix on the gates into the Catholic memorial. It's quite something, really."

So, it's not an eagle. River has a tattoo that represents the IRA on his chest.

God, I'm so stupid.

Of course he'd never admit to being involved with something like that. But then, why would he have bothered telling me all that he did last night about his family? Why not just lie about that, too? I just can't make sense of his motivation.

"What do you know about the IRA?" I ask casually.

"Oh, man. Here we go . . ." Ivy groans. "You're asking a guy with a master's degree in political science, who wrote his thesis on the politics in Ireland, what he knows about the IRA? We could be here all night."

Ian rolls his eyes but smiles. "No we can't, because I have places I have to be." To me, he asks, "What do you want to know?"

"I don't know. I guess, just . . . how dangerous are they?"

"The guys who call themselves IRA today? They're pretty fanatical, and dangerous. The IRA today isn't what it was a hundred years ago, or even forty years ago. Most Irish, including those who once actively supported the fight for independence, are living their lives quite happily now. They've accepted the way the country has been divided and don't want any more violence. Sure, there are protest parades every July, up in Belfast, but even the Provisional

IRA—that's the organization who led much of the fight in Northern Ireland against the British and loyalist supporters; they're the ones this phoenix represents—they just want peace."

That coincides with what River said last night. So why has River also been to prison for his involvement with the IRA? He's only twenty-four—I snuck a peek at his driver's license this morning while he was using my bathroom; it only seemed fair, seeing as he's been through my wallet, too. If he's been to prison, it's been in the last six or seven years. So it can't be something as terrible as murder.

"The problem is this Real IRA that sprung up after the ceasefire. They're a much smaller organization—only a few hundred people in size—but they wreak havoc. The funny thing is that, aside from their army council—they're quite official in the way they're set up—not many of these rank-and-file 'soldiers' even know about what the IRA of the past fought for. They have no idea what you mean when you say 'sovereignty.' They just want to bloody fight."

His words are making my stomach curl. River does seem to fight a lot. "So that bombing in St. Stephen's Green . . ."

"Likely IRA, sending some sort of message. They've waged war with the city's drug gangs. They say they're fighting against the drugs and corruption in our country, but their methods are murder and extortion. In the end, it's all about making money. They're just another gang, hiding behind the fear and respect the name gives them." Ian frowns. "Though I don't quite understand that attack on the Green. Normally their messages are dead bodies or cutting off limbs, or blowing up places where there are actual people."

"Mmmm . . . yummy," Ivy mocks, her tone full of sarcasm as a forkful of noodles floats in front of her mouth.

"Right. Sorry." Ian gets up. "Make sure you bring the leftovers home and take the rubbish with you when you leave, okay? I don't want this place stinking of soy sauce in the morning."

Ivy sucks back a noodle in response, waving at her cousin as he disappears out the door, hitting the switch to the outside lights on his way out. A moment later, the lock sounds.

"You just made his day. He loves to geek out over Irish politics. You should listen to him when the IRA shows up in the news. He goes on these major verbal rampages. Not sure how we're related."

I wonder, too. I really know nothing about her. And right now, I could use the distraction of Ivy's entire life story, from birth until tonight.

"So, what exactly is your background anyway, Ivy? You said you were born in Spain?"

She nods through a mouthful. "Mom was born and raised in Barcelona. My dad is first-generation American, but his parents are both from just outside Shanghai. They moved to California before he was born. Ian's mom and my dad are brother and sister."

"That's where you moved to Sisters from?"

"San Francisco." She heaves a sigh, muttering, "I loved it there." Pointing the remote control at the stereo, she flips through the channels so fast that I don't know how her brain processes what's playing. "But my parents decided we needed to get away."

"Why?"

She shrugs.

I have a feeling she could say more, but I don't push it because my phone chirps, instantly stealing my attention.

Amber. Please answer me. I'm worried.

I can practically hear his deep accented voice coming through, making my guilt flare. What if this is all a huge misunderstanding? It has to be. I know River. *No, you don't, stupid Amber. Just because you've slept with him doesn't mean you know him*. I sigh. I can't ignore him anymore, fear or not. Hurt or not. Anger, or not.

I'm sorry, I can't make it tonight.

I power my phone off and toss it aside so I don't have to read his response.

Ivy's gaze bores into the side of my head. "This is the first time you've ever been stood up, isn't it?"

I showed up at The Fine Needle just after six. Ivy, just about to take a girl of maybe twenty back for her tattoo, said I stormed in like Freddy Krueger was chasing after me.

I forced a stiff laugh when she told me. No, not Freddy Krueger. I asked her if I could hang out and she simply shrugged. She never pushed me, never asked me why I was dressed like I was going out, why I would want to hang out in a dungeon instead.

Unlike Bonnie or Tory, who would have drilled me until I gave something up. She hasn't even mentioned River once. And I've appreciated it. It allowed me the chance to wrap my mind around what Duffy told me, and what I know of River, and how those two things just can't possibly align.

But I guess all things must come to an end; the better they are, the faster.

Tonight's the first time since I got on that plane out of Oregon that I've wanted to climb onto another one and go home. The sooner Sunday comes, the better.

"I wasn't stood up," I deny quietly.

By the flat gaze in her eyes, I don't think she believes me. I brace myself for some smart-ass comment, some glib joke about the Sheriff's Daughter or the Rodeo Queen or Miss Perfect not getting what she wants.

"I remember this one time I got stood up . . ." She sucks her Coke up through her straw. "I mean, I've been stood up a few times, but this one time stung especially bad. I was twenty-one and working at a shop in Portland. I had this super-hot customer and I was crazy about him. Anyway, Nine Inch Nails was coming to Portland and he had these special connections to get backstage. He knew they were my all-time favorite band. See?" She points to her shoulder, where a small "NIN" symbol fills one petal of a black iris. I can't stand them, or any heavy metal, preferring country and pop any day, but I keep my mouth shut and simply nod.

"So he invited me and of course I said yeah. We were supposed to meet at the gates at seven. I was there, in the cold rain. I stood there waiting for him until almost ten, until I could hear the Nails playing from inside the stadium." She snorts. "Of course I was worried, so I kept calling him. But it went straight to voicemail. I finally got a one-line text from him that said, 'Sorry, I fell asleep. Next time.'"

"Did you believe him?"

"Does it matter? Why kind of apology is that? But no, I didn't believe him. And I was pissed at myself for waiting so long. Then I found out through a friend that he was at the concert that night, but with some other girl."

Wow. "Did you ever talk to him again?"

"Sort of." She slides another mouthful of noodles into her mouth, so casually. "About three weeks later, he came into the shop with pictures of his shed that had been decorated with the *Pretty Hate Machine* album cover art on the side. He didn't appreciate it. I guess he wasn't as big a Nails fan as he claimed to be."

I burst out laughing.

"But I didn't tag it." She pokes the air with her fork. "See? I'm not stupid."

"Did you get in trouble?"

"He couldn't prove it. But my boss somehow figured out that I'd taken a photocopy of his driver's license and he fired me for that. So I moved back home and got a job with Beans at his shop in Bend. You remember him, right?"

I nod. The place where Alex got her work done. "You know a lot of tattoo artists."

"It's a close community, and having a female artist of my caliber working for you is always a bonus with the clients."

"Well . . . I wasn't stood up. But thanks for that story. For some reason it makes me feel less like an idiot right now." I toss my barely eaten food onto the side table, stuffing napkins into the container.

There's another long pause and then Ivy asks, "You know that first night, when you asked me how I remembered so much about you in high school?"

"Did I?"

She hesitates, as if she doesn't want to admit something. "It's because, for a long time, I wished I was you. My family and I moved to Sisters because my parents wanted to get far away from San Francisco. They decided a remote mountain town would be good. I didn't know a soul, and we didn't have a lot of money. I looked 'different' from other kids," her fingers air-quote that word. "You seemed to have everything going for you."

I don't know what to say to that. It's flattering, but sad, and probably not an easy thing for a girl like Ivy to admit. "Well, thank God you weren't—otherwise your relationship with my brother would have been *really* inappropriate."

For the first time, Ivy's head tips back and laughter bellows out of her, making me giggle. It feels good.

"Does Alex know about you and Jesse?"

"No . . . At least, I didn't tell her. Figured she wouldn't want to hear about it. So, let's keep that between us."

A secret between Ivy and me.

Climbing out of her chair, she collects my food carton and heads over to dump it into a trash can.

"For what it's worth . . . I'm sorry I never said hi to you in the hallway," I offer with complete sincerity.

Her hands slow for just a moment, and then they're tying a knot into the top of the bag, sealing the odors in. "So, are we going to sit here and be all depressed about whatever this asshole did? Or should we go do something?"

I take in her outfit—head-to-toe skulls and cheetah print. "Do you have something in mind?"

She loops her hands together and stretches her fingers. Loud cracks fill the silence.

She definitely does.

■ ■ ■

"Do you have something *else* in mind?" I ask, casting a furtive look to the left and the right of the narrow side street. Light streams on either side of the building, but where we stand next to this vast painted brick wall, we lurk in shadows, marginally visible by the lights shining from Ivy's Civic. Technically, Ian's. They share an apartment a block away from the shop, and she ran over to grab the keys.

"We're not doing anything wrong." She reaches into her trunk and pulls out a plastic bag. I immediately recognize the telltale sounds of spray cans banging against each other.

"Ivy!"

"Relax. It's just like the bowling alley back home. They allow it as a way to keep the graffiti centralized. And this wall . . ." She takes big steps backward across the quiet road, without looking. "Just look at it! Such a clean, white canvas."

"It smells freshly painted."

"Yeah, just this past weekend. They have to redo it every so often, when all that republican stuff takes over."

Five minutes. I've had five minutes to think about something else—namely, what kind of trouble Ivy is getting me into—before my thoughts returned to River.

My stomach tightens.

"What kind of stuff?"

She shrugs, pulling a can from the bag. "Flags . . . Gaelic words that I can't even read . . . black fists . . . I think a lot of it isn't even from people who understand the politics or have anything to do with the IRA. They're just kids trying to be rebellious." She tosses a can my way.

I fumble to catch it. "What am I supposed to do with this?"

She stares at me for a moment, as if she's trying to figure out if I'm kidding or not. "Leave your mark on Dublin."

"My mark?" I frown, staring at the dried pink lines running down the sides of my can. "But . . . look at me!" Diamond earrings, yellow dress, cowboy boots. Not exactly dressed for the occasion.

She rolls her eyes. Reaching into her trunk, she grabs and tosses something at me. "Put that on. It should fit."

I hold up the paint-spattered black material, identifying it as a smock. Pulling it over my head, it comes to mid-thigh. Ivy appraises me. "That works. And if not, they're only clothes."

Darting over to the driver's side, she leans in to turn the music on the radio up, her other hand shaking her can of black paint. And then she dismisses me, spraying the first curved lines of what no doubt will be a masterpiece, because Ivy is experienced, and an amazing artist.

And I've never done this before.

I simply watch her in her zone, an almost indiscernible sway to her hips with the beat of the music, her arms limber and expert with their strokes.

"You going to just stand there all night?" she finally says, never looking over her shoulder once.

I stare at the white wall in front of me, in shadows and yet somehow gleaming. "I don't know what to do."

She purses her lips, then steps away from her work to come over. In seconds, she's outlined a jagged blob. "Beginner lesson. Fill it in."

I smile. "I can do that." I test the nozzle, pushing it. A splash of pink hits the wall and I jump.

"Hold it like this," Ivy says with a laugh, adjusting the can to a vertical position. "And no closer than this." She demonstrates, her color smooth and controlled, perfectly within the line.

I try again, creating another blob. "I'm terrible at this."

"So what? Everyone's terrible at something. Even Amber Welles." She moves back to her artwork, leaving me to mine, and my thoughts. Her words remind me of something Mary Coyne said to me. It was at Poppa's Diner, weeks before finishing my last semester of college classes, when I told Mary I was taking the nursing job that was waiting for me at my mother's hospital. She quietly nodded and smiled, but there was a look in her eyes that I couldn't read, that bothered me for days. Finally I asked her to meet with me again, and I asked her about it.

She hesitated, but finally admitted that she was hoping I'd take time off and travel, open my eyes to more than the small-town bubble that I seemed so intent on coming back to so quickly. She said that she sees a lot of her younger self in me. The daughter of a teacher and a father who held rank in Ireland's police force, a girl firmly embracing the set of beliefs she was raised on and her comfort zone. A planner, a risk-avoider, someone who didn't understand much about people outside what she thought they should be doing. She even used Jesse as an example. I'd made enough comments about him over the years for her to see that I didn't approve of any of his life choices.

Mary said her years traveling changed her as a person. Made her wiser, more appreciative, more open-minded. She felt like she had "found" herself. She wouldn't be the person that she was today had she remained in her small town outside Dublin.

I adore Mary as a person—she's got a breezy, youthful personality, but she's also smart and intuitive. Her words resonated with me, slowly at first. I began wondering how much of the Amber I know would change outside of the world that I know. I began dreaming of different places around the world, researching them. Imagining myself on some adventure where no one knows me and I know no one.

I can certainly blame my travel bug on Mary. I can't wait to tell her about this. I wonder if she'll consider spray-painting the side of a Dublin building a valuable experience.

And what would she say about River? Will I ever tell her?

Will I tell anyone?

Maybe I should talk to Alex. She's the only person I know who might have something besides judgment to pass on. She knows firsthand what it's like to be involved with a guy whose past is shady, whose associations may be questionable. She's a good person, with strong morals and values. She's also a forgiving person. Has Jesse ever done anything outright illegal since he met her? Did he lie to her about it? I can't decide what I'm angrier about—that my heart-stopping foreign fling is a convicted felon or that he didn't warn me about that detail before he slept with me.

He obviously figured that a night like last night would never have happened had I known.

A heavy weight has settled on my chest. I struggle to remove it, and I fail, my thoughts constantly drifting to River while I leave my mark on Dublin. I'm sure it will be nothing like the mark Dublin has already left on me.

For the most part, we're left alone. One car turns down the street, slows on its way past, and my heart rate spikes as I glance over my shoulder, afraid that the people will think we're doing something illegal. But they keep going. Voices carry in the quiet night, late-night revelers leaving bars in the area. It doesn't matter what time of day or day of the week it is here—if the doors are open, the places are busy.

Soon enough, I've gotten the hang of this, though my fingers are a used paint palette of colors, my manicure ruined. I start envisioning what I can add to the Technicolor blob when I hear footfalls coming down the sidewalk. A lone figure approaches, his face hidden within the deep cowl of his sweatshirt. My panic automatically sets in.

"Ivy," I hiss, nodding behind her. She glances over but doesn't stop bobbing to the music, doesn't seem at all concerned as he heads directly for us.

I gasp as he leans into the open window of Ivy's car. I'm about to yell at him, yell at her, before this guy robs us.

The volume of the music spikes.

He was only turning up the radio.

Slapping hands with Ivy, he nods once to me as he passes, finding a spot farther down. He pulls a can out of his pocket and begins spraying the wall.

I smile at myself, at my own reaction. Legitimate, I tell myself, but also unnecessary in this odd community that Ivy belongs to. The three of us work away in the middle of the night, in a dark alleyway, respectful of each other. It's a world I don't understand, would never see myself venturing into. It's a world outside my comfort zone.

But so is Ivy.

It's almost two when I call it quits, stepping back to admire my own work. An obvious beginner's effort—the lines sporadic and splotchy—but still . . . it's my mark on Dublin for as long as it's here. "I think I'm ready for sleep, Ivy," I announce, peeling off the smock. My mind has worked itself in so many circles where River is concerned, it needs unconscious peace.

Our silent partner in crime left already, leaving a blue clown-like mask and his tag on the bottom right corner.

"I'm done, anyway." With one last stroke, she caps her can and tosses it into a plastic bag.

I was so busy with my own thing that I wasn't paying much attention to what she was doing. But now I see it in full. "Wow," I murmur, taking in the woman's face. Ivy's used colors to shadow the contours of her features and strands of hair in a way that I didn't know would be possible through a simple can of spray paint. "That's amazing." I commend her.

She looks over. "And that . . ."

I study my work next to hers, a mess of colors and indiscernible shapes, and I burst out laughing. "Looks like I'm taking my aggression out on the wall."

She snorts. "Well, I *definitely* know you didn't spray-paint Poppa's Diner now. Even that was better than this."

■ ■ ■

Simon's car comes to a squeaking halt in its parking spot. I'm actually impressed with myself for making it to and from Ivy's without crashing. And I owe that to River.

Having switched my phone back on, a message from Alex fills the screen, asking me how things are going. I'm hit with the sudden urge to call her and divulge my secret. Maybe she can help me make sense of everything I'm feeling right now. It's only dinnertime over there, so there's still plenty of time to connect with her tonight.

There's also a text response from River:

Okay.

That's all. Disappointment and hurt drag my body down as I unlock the front door and step into the house I fled from hours earlier. It's exactly as I left it in my hurry. Turning the deadbolt behind me, I kick off my boots, grab a glass of water from the kitchen, and climb the stairs, hoping a night's sleep will relieve me of the burn in my heart. This time last night, I was curled up in that bed with River, blissfully ignorant. Setting the glass and my phone down on the nightstand, I shed my dress and my bra, letting them fall to the ground in a heap that I don't bother to hang, as I normally would, exchanging it for a thin cotton tank top for sleep.

I don't see him there until I turn around.

Standing in the doorway, his hands tucked into his pockets, his eyes glued to me. Staring at me, his face—illuminated by the harsh streetlights that shine into the bedroom—easy to read. Apologetic, yes. But also filled with sadness, and frustration, and regret.

River's here.

In my house, in the middle of the night.

Waiting for me.

At least ten heartbeats pass into the silence before I manage to speak.

"Is it true?"

He sighs, and hangs his head.

TWENTY-THREE

RIVER

She knows.

I can feel her anger and her distrust radiating. The charade I've been starring in these past few days—the white knight, riding in to save her and sweep her off her feet—is effectively dead and buried.

She knows who I really am now, and she'll never look at me that way again.

"Amber . . ."

Her eyes flicker to the bathroom. She's planning to run from me. She could probably make it, too, though she's not going to get anywhere beyond that, the bathroom on the second floor, her phone on the nightstand. I guess she could always open the window and scream until a neighbor calls the gardai.

"You left the door unlocked when you went out earlier," I explain slowly, taking a step forward. "I was worried about you. I didn't want anyone breaking in, so I waited for you."

Her hard swallow cuts through the quiet room. "In my house. In the dark."

"I didn't know how you'd take to seeing lights on when you came home. So, yes, in the dark. I was in the living room when you came in, but you walked right past me." For hours I sat there, staring out the front window for her car, for any other cars, wondering when she might finally return, my leg twitching with anticipation over how she might react to finding me in her house, despite my best intentions. It didn't stop me from doing it, though.

When she finally did return, she moved past me in a blur, not noticing.

And I didn't say a word.

She shudders.

"I know this doesn't look good."

She stands there, rigid, like a doe about to bolt from a hunter. "Where's your car? It's not parked out front."

"I parked it down the street because, again, I didn't know how you'd take to seeing it." I was afraid she'd call the gardai and speed past.

"You just stood there and watched me change." This time her voice is softer, sounding almost embarrassed.

"I did," I admit. "I'm sorry. I know I shouldn't say this, but you look beautiful tonight." She had obviously made an effort for me. Until Duffy showed up, and ruined everything. I take another step. "I'm not going to hurt you, Amber."

"Why are you here then?"

"I just want to talk. That's all. I had to see you in person, explain everything."

Her jaw clenches as the tears begin to well in her eyes. She's fighting them. "Did you set the bomb in the park?"

"No. I would never do that. I swear. On my granddad's grave."

"But you know who did," she whispers. "You lied to me, that first day in the bar. You weren't just jogging in the park."

That, I can't deny. "It was for your safety. And mine. I figured it was best to leave you in the dark."

"I don't know how you could justify that with . . ." Her words trail off, her gaze flickering to the bed.

"I honestly didn't think this," I gesture between the two of us, "would happen. I mean, look at you."

"I can't believe I let it happen." She hugs her arms over her body, hiding her chest. Her words—her regret—cutting into me.

We simply stare at each other from either side of the bed. I don't know what to say, where to start. I don't know exactly what she knows. I don't know what she's told Duffy.

Finally, she takes a deep breath. "Are you a part of the IRA?"

"No." I make sure my eyes are level with hers.

"But you were?"

I hesitate. "Not in the way you think."

She swallows hard again. "And you've been to prison." She spits the word *prison* out like it's toxic, just like I expected her to.

I never wanted her finding any of this out. I wanted to be better than this. "Yes." I step forward, and she immediately takes steps away, until her back is against the wall.

"Amber, please trust me."

"The IRA, River? I may be some stupid, ignorant tourist, but I know enough to know that they're terrorists. *You* were a *terrorist*!" Her face twists up, as if she's going to vomit.

"It wasn't like that," I deny, though I know it's not a valid argument. "You're right. The IRA today is a bunch of terrorists." I slowly edge around the bed frame. "I have nothing to do with them anymore."

"But you did." She closes her eyes. "God, I'm so stupid."

"No, you're not."

A weak chuckle slips through her lips. "Innocent people don't run. You ran."

"I had to. With my history, they wouldn't have believed me. They would have arrested me."

"And I fell for your entire act: that smile, that charm, finding my wallet . . . Oh my God. Was that staged? Did you get that guy to steal my wallet so you could swoop in and be the hero again? Play me for an even bigger fool?" Tears slip out at the corners of her eyes and crawl down her cheeks at an agonizingly slow rate. I can't handle seeing her cry.

I use the moment with her eyes shut to close the distance between us. "It wasn't an act."

Her eyes spring open and she gasps slightly, hugging her body tighter.

"I won't hurt you," I say, realizing that beneath her anger, she's actually terrified. "For Christ's sake, I jumped in front of a bomb for you, and I didn't even know you back then. Now?"

Thick, combustible air hangs between us.

"This isn't me, River. I don't do one-night stands, and sleep with convicted felons, and—"

"I know. I knew it the day you showed up at the pub." I heave a sigh. "I should have put an end to it right then. I'm sorry. But I couldn't help myself. You were just so beautiful, so different from the girls I know, and . . ." I can't resist reaching out to run my knuckles along her slender bicep. "The way you looked at me." Then. Not now. Not ever again. "So you told Duffy I was at the Green?"

Wide eyes stare at me, panicked.

"I saw his business card downstairs, Amber. It's okay if you did. I don't want you getting in trouble for this. I'll deal with it." He hasn't shown up at the pub with handcuffs yet, but it's only a matter of time before he does. And I end up back in jail.

"I didn't."

It's so soft, I'm not sure I heard it. I lift my gaze to her eyes, to her lips, willing the words to repeat themselves.

"I didn't tell him. He came here with mug shots of both you and your brother, and asked if I recognized either of you. And I said that I didn't." She swallows. "I lied for you."

I shouldn't be relieved, because Amber could get into a lot of trouble, but I can't help it. "Why would you do that?"

Her head shakes before the words slip out. "I don't know." She wipes the tears from her face, her hands moving aggressively, as if she's angry at herself for crying. "Why does Duffy think you set that bomb?"

I let that question hang for what feels like an eternity, reminding myself of the promise I made to take my secret to the grave, of the danger of admitting it out loud.

"Because my brother did."

A fresh wave of tears spill out. "Why?"

There's just no way around this anymore. I reach out for her arms. They fall from their folded position easily, allowing me to slip my fingers through hers and pull her toward the bed. "I'll tell you everything you want to know."

■ ■ ■

"So, Aengus doesn't know that I found you?"

I peer over at Amber lying on her back in bed, her delicate hands resting against her stomach, her eyes glued to the ceiling. Her thoughts hidden in the darkness. She's been in that exact same position for almost an hour now, listening to me explain every last detail that I can remember about that day. And why.

Because my brother is IRA.

She looks like a frightened statue. Not frightened enough to run from me, though. I cling to that.

"No. And he didn't let on that I was in any way involved, either."

"Are you sure?"

"Yeah. Aengus is a lot of things, but he has always protected me when it counts. You and him are the only two who can ever say that I was there. Well, Eamon, too, I guess. The doctor," I add when she frowns.

"Then why was Duffy asking about you today?"

"Because he figures that I'm somehow involved, or that I know something. He came into the pub yesterday, fishing for information. Threatening me with prison. He's the one who put me in there the first time."

A long stretch of awkward silence floats between us, so long that I glance over to see if maybe she's fallen asleep. I've been doing most of the talking, with a question from her laced in here and there. Questions that I've answered with too much honesty, knowing it may burn me tomorrow, if she decides that what I have to say doesn't make up for the fact that I lied to her.

Her eyes are still open, though. "Why did you go to prison?"

I swallow, trying to decide how to explain this in a way that she—a foreigner, and a daughter of a police officer—might understand. "I told you about my family history already. I grew up in a household of staunch republican supporters, even if they weren't actively supporting the fighting. Generations of Delaney men fought for Ireland back when the fight was about freeing Ireland and protecting the right to be Catholic. They lived and breathed that fight with the strength of the army around them. Some of them died for it.

"It's what my brothers and I grew up hearing about. So for us, the IRA isn't about terrorism. It's about fighting for what we believe in. We'd still join the marches every year in Belfast, protesting for the rights of Irish Catholics, because that was our heritage. It's what we'd always done.

"When I was eighteen, I moved to Dublin, to the house that our nanny left us. Aengus was twenty-two and already living there, working in the bar. Rowen was still back home, finishing high school."

I feel her eyes on me now and turn to meet them, only to have her look away, her attention on the ceiling again.

"Aengus and I were close, despite the four-year age difference and him being so hot-headed. He told me that he'd met a group of guys who supported the cause just like our family did." I snort, remembering the conversation, how Aengus went on and on about Jimmy Conlon, who was second-in-command at the time, over pints and smokes, excitement flowing through his veins faster than the alcohol.

"He told me about this camp outside Dublin—just like the kind our da went to when he was a teenager. They taught you how to fight and load guns and stuff. I thought it'd be grand to know how to do that, because all Delaney men know how, right? I was eighteen and stupid and I thought we might be doing something important, following in some grand tradition. That maybe, if there was ever another uprising, we'd have our own stories to share with our kids, just like our da did with us." I had always been the smart one. How I let a fool lead me into that mess is still unfathomable. "So one weekend, I climbed into Aengus's car. We drove an hour, to this guy's property. There was a lot of land there, with targets set up to learn how to shoot. Aengus was one of the fellas training us. He'd been there plenty of times already, so he knew what he was doing. I never connected it with this RIRA group, and I never had any intention of hurting anyone.

"Anyway, the gardai had caught wind of this place—a bunker, they called it—and had been watching it for a while. They busted it that same weekend." I had an AR-15 in my hands when the shouts erupted and men emerged from the long grass surrounding us, the fluorescent garda name across their chests, barrels pointed at me. "We all pled guilty. The other fellas were sixteen and seventeen. They went to Oberstown, basically a juvenile detention center for boys. But because of my age, I got tried as an adult. And because of my family name, everyone assumed I was lying about not being involved with the IRA. I was really lucky, though. The gardai didn't have enough to make the paramilitary group charges stick—some technicality, I don't know—so I only got three years for firearms possession. Aengus got six for his part."

"You were in prison for *three years*?"

I roll onto my side to face her, to see the shock and horror in her face. I know what she's thinking right now. She's trying to imagine being locked up in a cell for that long. Three years of your life is a long time at any age. But at eighteen . . . it feels like an eternity. "I only had to do half of it, and then they let me out on license, for good behavior. I had a curfew, and had to report in twice a week to a license officer, but at least I was out, sleeping in my own bed." I used to be a heavy sleeper, but now I wake up at the slightest creaks in the house.

I study her as she processes that, her silhouette begging me to touch it, her chest heaving up and down with her breaths, the thin cotton tank top doing nothing to cover her tits, the two little sharp points that poke out thanks to the chill in the air. Or her fear. I had those nipples in my mouth just this morning. I'd do anything to have them again.

I stay on my side of the bed, though. I'm no idiot.

"What was it like?" she finally asks, tipping her head to face me. "Being behind bars for so long."

"Tough. Because of the circumstances, we were put in Portlaoise, a maximum security with murderers and rapists. A lot of really bad bastards." Men who had been in there as long as I'd been alive and wouldn't be getting out anytime soon. Men who'd become so acclimatized to prison life, they wouldn't survive outside of it. "It was a long eighteen months. I cried into my pillow the first night in my cell," I admit with a soft chuckle, adding, "I've never told anyone that." I wasn't the only one. The nights were quiet around there for the most part. Impossible not to hear the occasional sob, the regular piss. The too frequent grunts of a fella getting off, either on his own or with help.

"I spent most of it in my cell, reading books and working out. The guards treated me alright for the most part."

"Did you ever get hurt?"

I heave a sigh. "Once in a while I'd have some sick fuck sniffing around me. I guess I was considered a catch for the long-timers. I'll tell ya, I learned to shower really fast." Not quick enough to avoid witnessing what some inmates were willing to do to get their fixes. The first day home, I stood under that showerhead until the water ran cold. And then I called up an old girlfriend and fucked her for half the night.

A gasp escapes Amber's lips, drawing my eyes to them.

"Don't worry. Nothing like that ever happened to me. I promise." My smile slips off. "Aengus made sure that it didn't. He gave a few good beatings to make sure people knew not to mess with me. He has a scar that runs from here to here," I draw a fifteen-centimeter line just below my collarbone, "where this lifer—a serial rapist, a really mean one—tried to shank him after Aengus threatened him. My brother was too strong, though, too fast. Broke the guy's arm in three places." And was seconds away from killing him, but luckily the guards intervened. Amber doesn't need to know that part, though. "Aengus was my bodyguard in there. That's one of the main reasons he never made parole."

She sighs, understanding filling her somber face. "Is that why you're protecting him now?"

"He's my brother. My flesh and blood. He always had my back, growing up. He covered for me when I did stupid things, more than once." I'm not about to explain the Katie Byrne incident to her. "I was a scrawny kid until I hit puberty. Fellas would try to bully me, but Aengus would have none of that. He taught me how to play rugby, practiced with me like our da would have if he could. Went to every one of my games, cheered me on. I was pretty good, too. I earned a scholarship from Trinity College and had just started classes when everything happened."

"Wait . . ." She frowns, and I know she's thinking about our conversation the past morning. "So you *were* going to college?"

I nod. It's so long ago now. "Thought about trying to get back in, but with Aengus away, and Delaney's to run, there's just no time for school. Anyway, I'd die before I'd betray my brother. You have a brother. You understand that, right?"

"No . . . I don't." She sighs. "My brother has caused himself and others plenty of trouble. But I've never hesitated to tell my dad whenever I found out. I figured it'd help Jesse in the long run. Maybe keep him from making a bigger mess of his life."

Telling Da what Aengus is up to wouldn't really help Aengus. Da would never actually call the gardai on him; he trusts the likes of them less than we do. It would only raise Da's blood pressure and give him more reason to curse Aengus. "I guess the way your father handles issues is different from mine."

"I guess so." Her eyes start to close, the stress of the day no doubt finally catching up to her. I don't say anything more and, in less than a minute, she's drifting off.

I have no idea what's going to happen when those eyes flutter open. She'll likely tell me that she never wants to see me again. That I need to leave immediately. That's why I lean over, feel her shallow breaths cascade over my lips for a moment, and then steal a kiss. I settle back into my pillow and simply watch her sleep.

Clinging to the fact that she lied to Duffy for a reason.

TWENTY-FOUR

AMBER

In those first few seconds of consciousness, nothing concerns me beyond the stream of sunlight shining directly on my face. I forgot to draw the curtains last night, I realize.

Then I remember why, and the annoying light is forgotten.

I find River sleeping soundly on his back, fully dressed, one arm over his eyes, the other one stretched out, as if reaching for me. His lips, the ones I couldn't get enough of just yesterday morning, parted just slightly.

I don't know what to do.

I don't know what to think.

I don't know what I'm supposed to feel.

So I simply lie there, afraid to move, to stir him, and I let everything he admitted last night swirl in my head. Hoping it'll settle on its own and the answer will suddenly become clear.

He was arrested for attending a training camp intended to teach people how to kill and maim, to inspire terror. But it doesn't sound like that was his intention. I remember my dad arresting a group of teenage boys outside Bend, after they set up a target range in the mountains. A hiker called to complain about excessive gunfire. They had no explanation for him, besides it being something "fun" to do. Dad said that it was a fairly common thing among teenage boys. It didn't even faze them that they had no permits.

I guess I can understand how River might not think anything

of climbing into a car with his brother, to head to a place where he'd learn how to shoot guns.

But it doesn't sound like his brother was ever just in it for the target practice.

And here, I've always thought Jesse was a problem sibling. At least he never tried tangling me in his messes. Not that he'd ever be able to, anyway.

And yet River has.

I just lied to the police for him.

I've had a fling with an Irish bartender who spent eighteen months in a maximum security prison for weapons charges due to IRA affiliations, and I lied to protect him. River has somehow managed to push me off course, and I need to get back on. I need to feel like me again.

The problem is, as I lie here and stare at the guy lying beside me—not the convict, but the guy who saved my life and got injured in the process, who charmed me with his kindness and his smile, who swept me off my feet with his romantic storytelling, who proved to me exactly how quickly I could become deeply intimate with a man—I don't see how I can do that.

It's so hard not to judge River for what he's done, and how he's lied.

And yet it's hard to judge him after everything else he's done for me.

Maybe I should reserve judgment for the time being.

I just don't know.

And so I simply watch River sleep, until those thick lashes begin to flutter, and his strong limbs stretch.

And then those green eyes open to meet mine. Silently pleading for me to believe him, in the same way they did almost a week ago. He doesn't say anything, and neither do I. We simply stare at each other, trying to read what the other is thinking. I'm not afraid of him anymore. For those first five minutes last night, finding him in my house, I was absolutely terrified. I wanted to run, hide, scream.

I'm glad I didn't, though. I needed to hear what he had to say.

Our moment is interrupted by the sound of ringing.

He sighs in exasperation.

"What time do you have to be at work?" I ask.

He doesn't answer me. He slips the phone out and puts it to his ear, his morning voice extra deep and scratchy. "Yeah . . . No . . . Can you cover for me today? . . . Thanks, Rowen." He drops his phone on the nightstand beside him. "I don't. Not today."

"You're taking the day off?"

He reaches over, running the tips of his fingers over mine, still splattered with every color of spray paint I touched last night, which I didn't have a chance to wash off.

I could pull away. That voice in the back of my mind tells me I should.

But I don't.

"I think we could both use a day away from all this. Together." He slips his long fingers through mine. "What do ya say?"

I could say no. That voice in the back of my mind tells me I should.

"Okay."

His eyes roam my face, which I'm sure is streaked with mascara and dried tears, hovering over my lips. I see the question—and the wish—in his eyes, but he doesn't try anything.

■ ■ ■

I break off a piece of bacon. The plate of food and a coffee were waiting for me on my nightstand when I emerged from the bathroom. Which means River left and came back in the time that I had showered. While my appetite hasn't been fully restored, I'm hungry enough to pick away at this.

"Do you mind?"

I glance over my shoulder in time to see River yank his T-shirt off over his head. The sight of him still makes me catch my breath. Even with that phoenix, now that I know what it represents. "Go ahead."

"I won't be more than ten minutes."

I watch him disappear behind the door, the wounds on his back still red and wearing stitches. The rush of water sounds a moment later, and my mind begins to wander with memories of his jeans falling off him.

Jeez, Amber.

Shaking my head at myself, I open up the closet to peruse my clothing options. There aren't many; the pile of laundry in the corner grows every day. I'm normally so on top of things like that. Finally settling on a royal-blue summer dress, I throw it on quickly, hoping it's suitable for a trip into the mountains. The hemline sits high on my thighs. River loves my thighs; he's told me many times.

Subconsciously, that's probably why I've chosen it, I admit to myself. Even if our little fairy tale is dead.

How awkward is today going to be? Most guys would want nothing to do with a day like this, now that the chances of it ending in any kind of sex are long gone. So why does he still want to spend time with me?

A memory pokes its ugly head out. The memory of Alex being left in the mountains to die.

I push it away because I know River wouldn't do that. A guy who takes shrapnel for a stranger instead of running won't then kill the same person to protect his secret.

Right?

The shower's still running.

I quickly reach for my phone.

I'm heading to Wicklow Mountains with River today. If something should happen to me, find Detective Garda Garret Duffy. And don't ask questions. Please.

If there's one person who wouldn't freak out from a text like that, I'm guessing it's Ivy.

With that small safeguard out of the way, I finish getting ready.

■ ■ ■

River falls into step beside me as I head down the narrow, gravel path of the Glendalough Monastery, the tombstones flanking us covered with fine moss, the engravings mostly illegible, the corners rounded. The hour-long drive along the narrow country roads south of Dublin has been quiet but oddly peaceful. Neither of us attempted idle conversation, an unspoken understanding that we're not ready for that.

Now I take pictures of the ruins—what was once a church but is now only a grouping of stone walls; a tall, narrow Rapunzel tower where the monks apparently hid during attacks—and read the few legible markings, and eavesdrop on the various tour groups milling about. But my mind's not really here. I'm still trying to make sense of River.

I did ask for the truth.

Every once in a while, I'll look at him and wonder what he looked like in handcuffs, in an orange jumpsuit—or whatever prison inmates in Ireland wear. The thought makes me sad. This is a guy who yesterday I was actually considering changing all of my travel plans for.

The toe of my boot catches a large rock near a half wall of stone and I stumble. River's hands are there immediately to catch me, saving me from smashing into more stone.

Always saving me from something.

"Thanks," I offer with a small smile, inhaling the bit of cologne on his clothes, as his hands linger against my skin a touch longer than necessary before pulling away. Stirring my blood, despite my heavy thoughts. We continue on as if nothing happened, past the last of the ruins and toward the wooded trail that leads to the two glacial lakes. Must-sees, according to the tour guides I just overheard.

"I hate cemeteries," he finally says in a mumble.

"This one was beautiful, you have to admit."

"I spent plenty of time in old cemeteries, growing up." His eyes flash to me. "Ma likes to pay her respects to her relatives, and she's got a lot of them in the ground."

I hadn't really given much thought to his parents in all of this, until now. "How did your parents handle you and Aengus going away?"

"Da has always had high blood pressure. The night we were arrested, he had a heart attack." Knowing eyes flash to me. "So . . . not well. Our uncle Samuel had died some years before, and Da had nobody to help run the pub except Ma and Rowen. Rowen wasn't even out of high school yet and he was there every night and weekend. He was supposed to go straight to college, but he set that aside, practically living in Delaney's so my dad wouldn't have to work, on account of his health."

"Rowen's never been involved with any of that?"

"No. He's never even seen the inside of a prison cell, something no Delaney man for many generations can claim."

The trail splits off. Most visitors veer to the left. I'm not in the mood for crowds, so I head right, toward the lower of the two lakes, a trail lined with gnarly-rooted trees climbing a steep slope to the left and the lake to the right. Ahead are the soft green rolling mountains, nothing like the ones that loom from my window's view back home, rocky and jagged and capped with snow even in the summer months. "Your mountains are so different from mine."

"How so?"

"They're softer, warmer. Not quite so threatening."

"You should see the Cliffs of Moher. They're impressive."

"I've heard. I was planning on driving up there." I only have four full days left in Ireland. I probably should have gotten there already. My days here have disappeared, consumed first by the bombing, and then by River.

A clearing leads us down to the water's edge, to a crop of stones that reach into the water, their surfaces dry and bathing in sunlight. It's mid-afternoon now, and the sun is warm enough to cause a light sheen of sweat to gather along the back of my neck. I've always loved being near the water on a warm day. So I peel off my jacket and pick my way over the rocks until I've found a perch on a sizeable boulder off to the left, under the canopy of a leggy tree.

"I'll take you, if you want," River offers, his strong arm swinging with a practiced angle to send a small stone skipping along the water's surface. "To the Cliffs."

I don't answer him, using that moment to take an extra-long sip from the water bottle tucked in my purse.

Because I just don't know.

"Come on, Amber." I sense him closing in, his feet finding my boulder, which is perfect for me but too narrow for two people to sit on. Unless one sits behind the other, which is what River has figured out. He settles himself behind me, and a moment later his legs wrap the outsides of mine and his chest is pressed against my shoulders, and his hand is stealing the bottle of water right out of my hand to take a sip, a move that the charming Irish bartender I knew from just a day ago would do with ease. "I'm the same person I was when you met me."

I sigh. Is he? I desperately want him to be. Despite everything I now know about him, he still affects me. I know that I still affect him . . . I can feel exactly how much against my lower back.

"Please let me. You're only here for a few more days," he whispers, resting his chin on my shoulder, his fingertip slowly drawing a pattern on my bare thigh using a drop of spilled water.

And then I'm off to England, Spain, France, and Italy . . . and a bunch of other countries. Will I be thinking about him as I walk through the streets of each one? Wondering what he's doing?

Wishing I'd just accepted these days for what they are and enjoyed his company? This was always a fling. There was always an expiration date. Yet I think, subconsciously, I hoped that the fairy tale would prevail. That somehow this could turn into more. Some romantic whirlwind that would withstand distance and time. But it can't happen.

"I'm never going to see you again, am I? You can never come to America. They'll never let you in." A spikey lump forms in my throat, because I already know the answer.

His chest falls against mine with a heavy sigh, his breath skating against my bare shoulder before strong arms wrap around me, holding me tight.

■ ■ ■

In the country café of a quaint village just outside Dublin—complete with curving cobblestone streets and vibrantly colored storefronts—I finally ask the one question I haven't yet asked. "What are you going to do, River?" I dip my voice low enough to avoid the attention of the server puttering behind the counter. "Duffy already suspects your brother, maybe you. How is this ever going to end well?" I hear my dad's influence come through in my words—I've heard him say the same thing to Jesse more than once. Obviously under different circumstances, but the message was still the same: *Do the right thing.*

"It's not," he agrees, his finger tracing the bright red circles that smatter the vinyl tablecloth, a heavy weight settling onto his shoulders.

"What?"

He hesitates. "Duffy told me that they're after Aengus."

"*They?*"

"This gang that Aengus and his guys have picked a war with. The fella who runs it—Adrian Beznick—wants Aengus gone. It could be next week, or next year, but eventually someone's going to put a bullet in my brother's head. That's how these things work. Back and forth, like a backward game of chess, where each side takes turns going after the top. A new person rises, then, repeat. Just read the news. It's full of assassinations over the past few years, too many to count. Someone will get Jimmy. Someone will get Aengus. Eventually, someone will get Beznick, even while he's behind bars. And then people will just rise up into their places."

I just stare at River. I don't get this world, this kind of mentality, at all. I don't understand how people like this can actually exist. Had I not experienced the bombing, I might not have believed that they do. "So, what is your brother going to do about it?"

He shrugs. "I passed along the warning from Duffy. That's all I can do. He'll hide out, keep an eye over his shoulder. What else can he do?"

There's only one thing I know to do: go to my dad. He always knows how to fix situations. "You need to go to Garda Duffy. Tell him everything."

He chuckles. "That's not going to stop them from picking Aengus off. That'll make it easier for them to." He reaches out to take my hand, running his thumbs along the lines in my palm. "I'm never going to turn my own brother in, Amber."

"You think you're protecting him by staying quiet, but you're not." His unwavering loyalty to this asshole is beyond frustrating. "And what if you get hurt again because of something he does?"

"Aengus is keeping a low profile right now and he knows to stay the hell away from me. I'll be fine."

"I wish that made me feel better."

"What more can I do? Leave the country? I mean . . ." He smiles. "I guess I could wander around Europe with you for a while."

"Hide out in a grotto in Italy?" I murmur with a sad smile. Yesterday morning, I would have done anything to hear those words.

"On a beach, in Greece."

My cheeks flush. That's not the first time he's made a reference to Greece. What would that be like, hanging out in hotels all over Europe with a convicted felon?

Or just River.

"Could you?" I hear myself ask. Am I insane?

His mouth turns into a deep frown. "I don't even know if I can get a passport. Plus, I can't leave Rowen to handle the bar by himself again. As much as I would love to go with you." He pulls my knuckles to his mouth and I let him, reveling in the softness of his lips against them.

His phone starts ringing. "Speak of the devil."

I study him as he answers the phone, the hand that rests on mine never pulling away.

"What's the story?"

I smile. Ivy told me that's how a lot of Irish people say hello.

My smile slides off as a dark mask takes over River's face. "Don't go home. Keep driving . . . No . . . And if they mistake you for him?"

I squeeze his fingers and his eyes fall to mine. "Guys waiting outside our house," he whispers to me.

Guys? Does he mean . . .?

River's attention is back to his phone. "Amber . . . She knows . . . Everything. I told her everything."

I take a deep, shaky breath. Is it better that I know this? Had Duffy not shown up at my house yesterday, would I have made it until Sunday never finding out? Would I have climbed onto the plane with nothing more than ignorance and a broken heart?

"Where are you right now? . . . Okay. Listen. Go back to the pub and sit tight until I get there. I'll call Aengus. This is his mess. He can clean it up."

Wait. "How exactly is he going to clean it up?" I interrupt with a hiss.

Hesitation fills his eyes. "He'll probably go there to find them."

I grab his hand. "No. Call the police!"

He heaves a sigh full of frustration. "Gardai won't do anything, Amber. They've already said that they won't protect him."

"They will. Just . . ." I scramble to remember everything my dad has ever said to me. Little bits of random information, complaints about how television shows mess everything up. Anything that will convince River not to send his maniac bomber brother there. Finally, an idea comes to me. "Tell Rowen to call and report it. Tell him to say that he's pretty sure he saw a gun. Gardai will have to check it out."

He opens his mouth, looking ready to disagree, but I squeeze his hands tighter, pleading with my eyes. "Please. Tell him to do it. If they can catch them with guns, they'll arrest them. Then these guys can't do anything to Aengus."

"Yeah, but . . ." He sighs, saying into phone, "Did you hear that? . . . Do it. Then wait at the bar for me . . . I don't know! Sleep in the office."

I frown. There's nowhere to sleep in that tiny place, unless it's on the desk.

River sees my face and explains, "He was up all night finishing an assignment for school."

And then River asked him to cover for him today, so he could take me to Wicklow. I sigh as the guilt settles firmly on my shoulders. "Tell him to meet us at my place. He can sleep there."

"You sure?"

"Yeah." I've officially gone insane. It isn't even my house!

But I'm also going to feel better knowing Rowen and River are safe.

At least for tonight.

■ ■ ■

Rowen's sitting on my doorstep when River parks his car, his long legs stretched out on the walkway, his head resting against the cherry-red door, his eyes closed.

And Ivy is sitting beside him, arms folded over her chest, a scowl comfortably settled on her face.

Crap. This complicates things.

"She shouldn't be here," River mumbles at the same time that I think it.

This is why she texted me earlier, asking me what time I'd be home. She planned on staking out my place. I shouldn't be too surprised after the message I left her, but for some reason I still am.

I slowly make my way up the path to meet her flat, unimpressed gaze. "Hey, Ivy . . . what are you doing here?"

One perfectly shaped eyebrow spikes halfway up her forehead. "Really?"

"Look, can I give you a call later and—"

"Nope."

I give River a shrug, because I don't really know what to say, and unlock my front door to lead everyone in, kicking my boots off, my feet sweaty and sore and in need of a long soak in the tub that I'm not going to get.

"Drink, anyone?" Rowen pulls out a bottle of Jameson before tossing his canvas backpack to the floor. "Swung by the pub," he adds when River looks questioningly at him. "Figured I'd need it after I let that cab driver bend me over the backseat and rape me."

"He didn't really," River assures me, a gentle hand on my shoulder. "Rowen just has a thing with taxi drivers."

"Yeah. They're all thieving bastards! Who wants a drink? I know I need one. Ivy?" He passes her with a knowing smirk on his way to the kitchen. She merely watches him from her perch on the armchair, having somehow slinked past us all. Her lithe body looks ready to pounce.

And she's entirely unimpressed.

"I need to take a piss," River mutters, escaping her severe stare quickly.

It shifts, settling heavily on me. "What was that you said to me that first night? You 'hate drama'?" She air-quotes the words.

"I do."

"Huh. Really . . ." She hops off the chair, sauntering over, her eyes flickering in the direction of the bathroom. She drops her voice. "Because that message I got today? It was steeped in it. Seriously, what the hell is going on? Why would you be giving me the name of some detective garda to contact? Why would something happen to you?"

I try to shrug it off with a joke. "Were you worried about me?"

She rolls her eyes, but the wariness is still there. "Should I be?"

"No. I'll be fine." Physically, anyway. Although I'm not sure how much damage River will have done to my heart by the time Sunday rolls around.

"Okay." She nods slowly, checking over her shoulder to make sure Rowen is still occupied at the kitchen counter. "Are you going to tell me what's going on?"

"I can't, honestly. All I can say is that it's bad."

"Of course it is. You Welles kids, always getting into trouble."

I snort. "I can't believe it, but you're right. I can't just blame Jesse anymore." *Which reminds me* . . . "I need to talk to Alex. I should probably go and do that, seeing as that bottle of gasoline that Rowen's pouring over there is looking pretty good right about now."

"This must be really bad." Ivy nods toward the stairs. "Go ahead. I'll stay down here. I have nowhere I have to be."

"Do me a favor? Keep them downstairs." I'm not sure how this conversation is going to go, but I can't have River pressing his ear up against the door.

Ivy reclaims her perch. On guard. "I'll keep them occupied."

She really is a fantastic wing woman. Though I'm not sure I want to know what "keeping them occupied" means. Hopefully it doesn't involve spray paint.

Dismissing that worry, I run up the stairs.

■ ■ ■

Hey, Alex. How could you be with a criminal?

The second Alex's pretty russet-colored eyes find mine on her laptop screen, I bite down on my tongue. Though I know that her husband was a bad guy and likely involved in plenty of illegal activity beyond what he did to her, we've never really talked about it. Alex seems intent on putting that all behind her, and focusing on her wonderful new life with Jesse.

Who I know has broken the law on more than one occasion.

She frowns. "What happened to your lip? It looks a bit puffy and," she taps her own bottom lip exactly where the cut on mine used to be, "there's a dark spot right here."

"It's nothing. I tripped on my way to the bathroom at night, did a face plant into the wall," I lie, and then quickly try to push the conversation. "How are things back home? What have you been up to?"

"I'm fine. It's been fine . . . good . . ."

Now it's my turn to frown. She doesn't sound like her normal, chipper self.

With a heavy sigh, she asks, "You know Jesse's friend Luke, right?"

"Uh . . . yeah." Troublemaker or not, he's hard for anyone to forget. The first time I saw him walking into Roadside, with his gold watch and his expensive clothes and model-pretty face, he had my attention. I frown. "Why?" Alex and I have never really talked about Luke before.

"He was just here, checking up on the latest car. Brought a girl with him, who seems nice. But . . ." She rolls her eyes. "He was driving a brand-new Porsche."

"Oh yeah? Those are expensive. Did he win it or something?" I ask casually, the wheels in my mind churning.

"No, Amber . . . You know he didn't win anything." She shakes her head with some unspoken thought. "Luke's a good guy, with a good heart . . . who can be easily swayed by money. He doesn't always make the smartest decisions. I'm really worried about what his uncle may have gotten him into."

I know that the two of them have a close connection. Luke has popped in and out to the ranch a few times, shared a few beers with us, but he never stays long. It's like his city-boy style can't handle country for too long. But every time he's visited, he's never left without giving Alex a fierce hug.

Oddly enough, this conversation may help lead me in the direction I was hoping for when I dialed Alex's number. "Do you think Luke and his uncle are doing something illegal?"

"I *know* they are," she mutters, pushing her hair off her face, revealing the long, thin scar that normally hides behind a curtain of blond locks. "It has something to do with cars."

This instantly raises red flags for me, my tendency to be suspicious of my brother impossible to ignore. "Like the cars that Jesse's been fixing up for Luke, that he swore up and down were bought legitimately? Alex, he can't be bringing that sort of thing right to my parents' doorstep. It could—"

"Jesse's not involved in what Rust and Luke are doing, Amber. Trust me." She always defends my brother. Then again, if there's anyone who knows him, and whom he trusts to tell the absolute truth to, it's Alex. For a girl who's been through so much, you'd think she wouldn't want anything to do with a guy with his history, and yet it doesn't seem to bother her at all.

"That's not going to matter to the sheriff. If he finds out, he's going to ban Luke from setting foot on the property. You do realize that, right?"

Her mouth twists. "He already knows. Or suspects, at least."

My mouth drops open. My dad and Luke have actually stood in the garage together, drinking beer and laughing! "What are you saying? That he's turning a blind eye to it?" No, that's just not possible.

Alex shrugs. "He has a soft spot for Luke. We all do. Luke is one of the reasons I'm alive right now—you know that."

"I know a bit about that, but I don't know the specifics." Not enough to endear Luke to me as he obviously has endeared himself to others.

She bites the inside of her lip. "He put himself in a lot of danger to make sure Jesse found me."

"Wait a minute . . ." I frown. "I thought my dad found you."

She simply stares at me. I've seen that look before. It means she slipped and said something that she didn't mean to say.

"Alex . . ."

A burst of male laughter—Rowen's—suddenly carries up the stairs and through my closed bedroom door. I find myself wanting to go down there and see what they're laughing about. Somehow I've temporarily forgotten why they're hiding in my house in the first place.

Her brow spikes in surprise. She heard him. "So . . . how's Dublin?" Her voice, heavily laced with worry just a moment ago, suddenly lightens to an almost playful tone. She's using this as an excuse to steer the conversation away from my father.

As much as I want to steer it right back, badgering her isn't going to work. Maybe it's time I give her a reason to divulge her own secrets by sharing mine.

"It's definitely an experience," I begin. "I met up with Ivy."

Excitement fills her face. "Really? How did it go?"

"Strangely . . . good. She's alright." More than alright, in fact.

"I told you." A pause. "So what have you been up to? Made any friends?"

I fall back in my bed with a sigh. Where do I begin? I'm so conflicted right now. When I get off this call, I'm going to head downstairs and . . . what? Pretend that everything is okay? Pretend that none of this matters? Kick River out and tell him to stay away from me? None of those scenarios sits quite right.

Alex's voice floats into my bedroom. "Amber? Where did you go?"

I groan, reaching for my iPad, holding it above me. "I'm right here . . . confused. I don't know what to do."

Finally I see that patient, confident smile of hers. "Yes, you do. You always make smart decisions."

"Not this time, Alex." Our eyes meet and I know she sees my inner turmoil. "Where's Jesse?"

"In town."

I swallow. "I need to talk to you. Tell you stuff that you can't tell anyone else. Not even Jesse, Alex. I mean it."

"Okay."

"I mean it."

Her annoyed glare reassures me. "You know you can trust me."

I know I can. If anyone respects keeping a secret, it's Alex. Her entire life is one big secret.

Here I go . . . "So, you remember that bombing in the news recently? With the American girl who barely survived?"

Her jaw drops.

And she listens quietly, while I recount everything that's happened over the past seven days. Everything.

By the time I'm done, Alex is curled up in her desk chair, her legs pulled against her chest, her fingers weaving into the back of her hair in that worried way of hers. "Wow. That's . . . You've been busy," she finally murmurs. "Are you safe?"

"Yeah. I mean, I think so. River would never hurt me." This older brother of his, on the other hand . . . But he doesn't know me and I never saw him, so I can't imagine I'm much of a threat.

"This doesn't sound like a fling with a bartender."

I shrug. "I've known him for all of a week. And he lives in Ireland. And he's a convicted felon. It can't be anything else."

And yet my heart is telling me it's everything else.

Alex smiles softly, her eyes drifting off somewhere into the past. "Sometimes it can be."

"Not for me, Alex. I'm not that girl. I don't fall for a guy I just met, and I don't let my emotions make decisions for me that my head knows are bad. It's just . . . it's weak! I'm better than that."

She twists her mouth, hesitating for a moment before saying, "I fell for your brother the very first night I met him. I had an affair with him. A guy whom I should have stayed away from, but I didn't. I *couldn't* stay away from him. Our connection was so instantaneous, so deep. And Jesse was working for my husband, who happened to be a serious criminal. A man I was terrified of angering."

I stifle my gasp, because she'll think I'm judging her. I knew about the affair, but I had no idea that Jesse had been *working* for her husband. *Seriously, Jesse?*

"So, does that make me a bad person?" she asks softly. "Does that make me weak?"

"You're the strongest, kindest person I've ever met," I whisper truthfully. "But your circumstances were unique. They don't compare to this."

"I don't know, Amber . . . I'd say the circumstances surrounding you and this River guy sound pretty unique. And that other stuff is in his past."

"Not entirely. His brother is IRA."

"No one's without fault if you're judging them based on their connections. For God's sake, Jesse's best friend is a criminal!" Alex rarely raises her voice, so to hear it now is jarring. "You know that black car of Jesse's out there? Parked in front of the barn every day?"

Jesse's Barracuda. His child. I nod.

"It's stolen."

This time I do gasp. "What? He *stole* that car?" I remember joking about that once, but I never thought he'd actually stoop that low.

"No, he didn't. But it's not hard to figure out who did. Turning it in is more risky than it's worth, though, so your father told him to keep it."

My jaw hangs open for a long moment. "The sheriff knows about that, too?"

"There isn't anything that your dad doesn't know, Amber. Jesse doesn't keep secrets from him anymore. My point to all this is that nobody's without fault, and some of that fault can get pretty ugly. But you shouldn't hold it against someone if it's in his past. Jesse made his mistakes, but he learned from them. It sounds like this River guy did, too, if what he has told you is the truth."

It would seem like it. River talked nonstop last night, answering all of my questions, offering information without my pushing. And every time I stole a glance at his face, and his eyes, I saw only honesty there.

But none of that really matters, in the grand scheme of things. "What do I do, Alex? I need someone to tell me what to do."

"What do you see your options being?"

There aren't many. "I can either say goodbye to him today or say goodbye to him on Sunday. Either way, it's goodbye." He'll never hop on a plane and surprise me at the ranch. He'll never see what my world looks like.

"Would you consider turning him in to the police?"

"No," I admit, laughing bitterly. "And yet all I can keep hearing is my dad telling me to do exactly that. Even if it might get me into trouble."

"Yeah, that sounds like him," she begins. "Then again, your dad may surprise you."

"I doubt that. Not about this. You know him. It's black-and-white when it comes to the law."

"Not always, Amber. Your dad has gotten to know the gray area pretty well." A decision flashes in her eyes. "I think it's your turn to keep some secrets."

TWENTY-FIVE

RIVER

If I close my eyes to rest, I can't say for sure that she won't try to kill me.

At least, that's the vibe that Ivy's giving off from her little spot on the couch, her tiny all-in-black body coiled for an attack. Her dark, unforgiving eyes shifting back and forth between the TV, me, and Rowen, who's made himself comfortable on the couch with the bottle of whiskey and an annoying leg twitch.

Tap . . . Tap . . . Tap . . .

"Stop that!" Ivy finally snaps.

Rowen stills his leg.

"Why don't you get some sleep upstairs? I thought you were exhausted," I suggest.

"Like I could sleep now." With a groan, he pours himself another shot of whiskey. "This was the last bottle."

"Whatever. We don't go through much." I jut my chin toward Ivy. "Unless she's there, of course."

She merely glares at me in response. Everything about her drips with suspicion. If I didn't know any better, I'd think Amber had told her.

"Right. You want more?" Rowen doesn't wait for her answer, climbing out of his seat to top her glass up.

"Don't think I'm getting drunk again," she mutters, but she accepts the drink. She has yet to ask what's going on, why Rowen is here and wired. Why he pushed through the door like a man being chased. He's not, of course. If Beznick put a call out for Aengus's head, it's for Aengus's head. Even murderers don't like to add unnecessary body counts to their résumé. Not because they're particularly moral; it just makes things worse for them if they ever get caught.

But that doesn't mean Rowen or I wouldn't get caught in the crossfire. That happens often enough. A guy with a target on him, taking a walk down a street in midday with his buddies, starts taking gunfire from somewhere unseen. His friends are as likely to get hit by a stray bullet as the ones intended for their mark.

As long as we stay the hell away from Aengus—and don't get mistaken for him—we should be fine.

I think.

My gaze drifts to the stairs. Amber has been up there for a while now. Hiding. Talking to "home." What does "home" mean? Her parents? I've put her through a lot. Is it more than she can handle?

I can only imagine what this sheriff father of hers could convince her to do.

"Where are you going?" Ivy's cutting tone snaps me out of my thoughts, and I suddenly find myself standing at the bottom of the stairs.

"I'm just going to check on—"

"No you're not. She's talking to her sister-in-law, who has her own pile of shit to deal with. Leave them alone." She says it so simply. As if she could stop me from climbing those stairs if she had to. "Amber will be down when she's ready to come down. Don't be that guy."

"Ouch," Rowen mutters, but excitement dances in his eyes. He likes the sharp-tongued birds.

I didn't even know Amber had a sister-in-law, which I guess just proves that I should listen to Ivy. With another glance upstairs, I wander back to stare at the telly.

"You still want that ink?" She stares at me with her eyebrows raised in question.

"What. Now? Here?"

She shrugs. "I have my kit in the car."

Seriously? "You always travel with it?"

She darts past me, throwing an "of course I do, you idiot" look on her way by and out the door, before I can tell her no. I don't even have the sketch with me.

"Have you called Fern yet?" I ask.

Fern MacGrath is an eighty-nine-year-old woman and the resident neighborhood watch. She was our nanny's best friend. She despises Aengus, avoids me, and adores Rowen. The woman will sit in her front room with her knitting needles and her glasses on until after midnight each night, spying on all the comings and goings on the street.

"I tried once, but she didn't answer," Rowen murmurs, peeking past the curtain to watch Ivy. "You going to call Aengus?"

I thumb my phone in my hand, considering it. "Not yet. Hopefully the gardai do something useful." They should have been there by now. I'm halfway tempted to jump in the car and drive down the street, only for all I know these guys are waiting for a green MINI to show up. Aengus has borrowed it enough times. "I mean, if they see gardai round the corner and they take off, they'll just be back later, in a different car. Knowing Aengus, he'll camp out at our house, waiting to ambush them. And then he's got blood on his hands." I shouldn't have to spell it out. "We're protecting him by not telling him right away. If he doesn't know where the threat's coming from, he'll lay low. If we tell him, there are going to be two bodies outside our house." I shake my head. "Ma would collapse with that news."

He opens his mouth, but Ivy pushes through the door with a silver briefcase in her hand.

"You weren't kidding."

She sets it down on the coffee table, dialing the lock combination and popping it open. "Do I look like a kidder?"

"No, *you* don't," I mutter through a sigh. The girl's face might splinter with too wide a smile.

"Are we actually doing this, here?" Rowen reaches for the tattoo gun but she swats his hand away before he actually makes contact, earning his grin.

"If you stop drinking, I'll do you after I do him." I don't know if she meant it to sound like it does but there's usually only one way that Rowen will take something like that. Especially after Sunday night.

I roll my eyes. At least my little brother's easily distracted from more serious problems with her around. "Thanks for the offer, but don't you need to make a transfer of the sketch?" That's what they did for my other one.

"All I need is this." She jabs Rowen's chest with her finger, right over the stag on his pub shirt.

"Freehand?"

"Yup. And I'll do it better than any transfer." Deadpan. She's not even being arrogant. She believes it. "What's wrong. Scared?"

"No. Worried. Is this all clean and hygienic and stuff?"

"More than you probably are," I think I hear under her breath, but I can't be sure. I keep my mouth shut and down the rest of my drink as she sets her portable station up at the dining room table, complete with a blinding table lamp, aftercare tape and gauze, cleaners, gloves, and packaged needles.

"Seriously, why do you have all this stuff when you work in a shop?"

"Because I like to be prepared. So?" She kicks out the chair with her socked foot. "What else do you have to do while you're pretending not to be hiding from someone and in deep shit?"

Rowen and I share a quick glance.

"Fuck it." I crawl out of my seat and, grabbing the back of my T-shirt, I slide it over my head and toss it to the side.

Her eyes skate over the phoenix and then raise to meet my gaze in a knowing way, but otherwise she says nothing about it. "You sit here. You?" She snaps her finger at Rowen and then points at the chair beside her. "Here."

"I wouldn't be too demanding of him if I were you," I warn. "He likes it when birds boss him around."

"If there's one thing I can't stand about Ireland," she murmurs and I shudder, the stuff she sprays on the right side of my chest cool and sterile-smelling, "it's being called a 'bird.'"

"What's wrong with being called a bird?"

"Do you think I have feathers?"

"I *know* you don't have feathers." Rowen peers up at her face as she leans into his chest to study the stag on his T-shirt. "Though it's hard to tell either way, with that big tent covering you."

She ignores his comment on her choice of clothes—he's right, she's swimming in her shirt—and punches a few buttons into her phone. Music pumps out of the tiny portable speaker she brought.

"Okay. Ready?" Throwing her hair back into a ponytail and pushing her sleeves up, she slips on a pair of gloves and flicks the switch on.

I grit my teeth against the first burn of the needle. It hurts just about the same as the last one, which was a lot. And yet I forgot about it enough to do this again. My ma said it's the same way with childbirth—that had she ever remembered the pain that Aengus caused her, Rowen and I would never have been born. Apparently it was the angelic lock of bright red hair on top of Aengus's head that made her forget instantly.

Easing out an exhale, I let my head rest against the back of the chair, listening to Ivy's soft hum to the music.

"So this stag represents your family or something?"

"The Delaney family crest, going back a thousand years," Rowen explains.

"You Irish are awfully proud of your heritage."

"Aren't you?"

"I couldn't tell you the first thing about my heritage. Things just aren't like that over in America, by and large."

"That's sad." Rowen's eyes land on her legs, covered in black leggings.

"Maybe." A pause. "And this other tattoo. Does that have to do with your heritage, too?"

"It does," I answer for him. "A lot of Delaneys were nationalists."

"Is that a fancy way of saying IRA?"

Rowen shoots me a questioning glare.

"Relax, guys. I was hanging around my uncle's shop and watching him ink Hells Angels members when I was eleven. I'm not easily scared off."

"Hells Angels?" Rowen asks with a frown.

"Yeah, you know. One of the most notorious motorcycle gangs . . . Oh, forget it. Criminals, okay? How are you doing, River. You need a break?"

"Nope." I clench my jaw as the needle moves farther down, like a knife carving into my skin the closer it gets to my nipple.

"It's looking good," Rowen mutters, leaning over.

"You're blocking my light." She stops working on me to shove him back into his chair.

I watch the frown across her forehead as she concentrates, the only sound in the house the music and the buzz of the needle. She really is so different from Amber. "How long have you and Amber been friends?"

"Three days."

"No, seriously."

"Seriously. Three days."

"But I thought you guys know each other from back home?"

"We do. But we weren't friends. In fact, I pretty much hated her guts after she ratted me out to her dad for something stupid."

Panic instantly ignites in my gut. "She ratted you out to her dad?" *The sheriff?*

"Long story, but in case you haven't noticed, Amber's always been a stickler for the rules."

I glance up over my shoulder, to the stairs. *Fuck.* Is that what she's doing right now?

"I need to take five. Grab some water."

Ivy backs away. I stand and stretch my arms above me before wandering over to the kitchen to fill a glass. I take my time drinking it, staring out the back window at the terrace. It's simple but nice, with a dining table and latticed wall covered in vines. I wonder if I'll ever manage to have something like this. Delaney's is basically it for me, whether I love it or not. My options for other employment are severely limited by my criminal record. At least Delaney's does well enough. Rowen and I'll earn a healthy living, as long as we take care of it.

I'm basically living the life now that I will be in thirty years, minus the wife and kids. I know I'll find someone; an eighteen-month stint in prison isn't the worst thing for an Irish-born man. There are plenty of Nualas out there who wouldn't care. The thing is, I don't want another Nuala.

I want a girl like Amber.

I want Amber.

But she's leaving on Sunday and, unless I jump on a plane and go with her, that'll probably be the last time I ever see her. That thought did cross my mind earlier, during dinner, when she mentioned it. I doubt she was serious. But it did get me thinking that I should look into getting a passport. I never bothered applying for one before, figuring there was no reason to put myself through the hassle. I know I'll never set foot on American or Canadian soil, but I've heard that it's pretty easy to travel through the European Union without issue. Unless they've put me on some sort of watch list. It's not like they're going to tell me about that, so I guess there's only one way to find out: try to get on a plane. Of course, I wouldn't be trying that with Amber.

"Whatever you did, she's not going to call the cops on you."

I turn to find Ivy standing behind me. She would have seen the stitch work on my back.

"Like you said, you've been friends with her for three days. How do you know?"

"Because, if she were going to, she would have done it right away. And she definitely wouldn't have let you into this house."

I nod quietly, her words calming the worry simmering inside me.

"Can we finish that now, before your idiot brother drinks too much to get his matching ink?"

I glance over her head to see Rowen downing another shot.

■ ■ ■

The staircase creaks just as Ivy shuts off the tattoo gun, finished.

"See?" She whips out a mirror from her tool kit and holds it up to show me the fierce and proud stag now prominently sketched on my body. It holds my attention for about five seconds—she's right, her freehand is better than the original sketch I had—before my eyes dart to the landing, and a pale-faced Amber.

Looking like she just saw a ghost.

I'm on my feet in a second. "What's wrong?"

Her green eyes, full of disbelief, dart from me to my chest to Ivy, then finally to the floor, with the slightest head shake. "Nothing. I just . . ." Her words trail as she staggers into the kitchen, Ivy watching as closely as I am.

Ivy pokes me, then nods toward her. "Okay . . . Next up." She rolls her eyes at Rowen, who's already got his shirt off, revealing his bare canvas. "That's right. You're a virgin." She begins dismantling her machine to change out the needle and clean up. "I haven't had one of you in a while."

"Then you're in luck tonight."

I leave them to their banter and head over to the darkened kitchen, where Amber stares listlessly out the window, mimicking me from not long ago. "Everything okay?"

She sips from her tall glass of water, emptying half of it before setting the glass on the counter. "It looks good." Her eyes are on the stag, veering to the phoenix for a short moment. "Did it hurt?"

"Not at all." No man ever admits to the pain.

She drifts back to the window, but with a smirk now. "Liar."

At least she can smile. Sort of. "You should get one."

"Yeah? Where?"

I can't help myself. I step closer, drawing a circle on the back of her shoulder, over that blue dress that's been teasing me all day, so short. "Right here."

She shivers but doesn't pull away. "What would I get?"

"What do you want?"

"I don't know." She sighs. "I just don't know anymore. . . ."

Something tells me this isn't about a tattoo. "Is everything okay back home?"

"Yes. And no." A deep frown mars her forehead, and that line in between her eyes creases.

"Ivy said you had a sister-in-law?"

"You could say that. She and my brother aren't married, but they're forever."

"What's she like? Do you two get along?"

"Yeah. She's great." She smiles. "I think you'd like her." The smiles fall off. Because she's remembering that I won't ever meet her. Not unless it's here, in Ireland.

"Look, Amber—"

"She told me things about my dad," Amber interrupts me. "Things that he did, to protect my brother, and Alex. Illegal things that could have gotten him into so much trouble. I had no idea."

That's why she looks so shocked.

I tug on her shoulder until her lithe body turns to face me. I want more than anything to pull her into my chest, but Ivy's work won't allow that for that. Maybe Amber won't allow for that. I can't tell, the way she's peering up at my face. Has she forgiven me?

Ivy's snap of "Stop staring at me like that" pulls both our attention to the dining room table, where she's already working on Rowen, having positioned herself between his outstretched legs.

He winks at us. "I can't help it."

"It's creepy."

"Maybe *you're* creepy." He grits his teeth as if in pain, and I'm guessing he is based on how her little fingers are digging into his bicep. He quickly adds, "In a hot way. Hold on a sec, Ivy . . . I need to get this." He pulls his phone out of his pocket and checks the display screen. His eyes race to mine. "Hello, Fern. How are you?" His tone climbs five octaves to altar-boy status. "No way . . . Really?" He listens intently as the old woman talks. The longer it stretches, the more certain I am that this is about gardai showing up. "Thank you for letting me know, Fern . . . No, I'm good. Just at a friend's . . . I know. That Aengus, he's a problem . . . Okay, well, I'll stop by tomorrow to carry your rubbish out, just like always. See ya, Fern."

He hangs up and melts into his chair with a heavy groan, followed by a huge smile. "Gardai arrested two suspicious-looking fellas parked outside her house. She says it looks like they found guns on them, too."

My shoulders sag in relief.

"See? I told you!" Amber pinches my arm, her own beautiful face stretched into a satisfied smile. And, for a quick moment, everything is back to what it was before.

Fuck the new ink. I coil my arm around her waist and pull her into me, gritting against the sting of the touch as I rest my chin on the top of her head. It fits so perfectly in the crook of my neck. Her body tenses but then relaxes, sinking against me. I'll stand exactly like this for the rest of the night if it means keeping her here.

"I still need to dress that for you," Ivy reminds me over the buzz of her needle, back at her design on Rowen.

"I guess you can go home now," Amber murmurs, her breath skating against my bare collarbone, sending shivers down my back.

"I guess I can." I don't want to. I want to spend tonight with her, and tomorrow. I want to spend every second with Amber until she leaves.

I don't want her to leave.

Do I tell her that, though?

I don't let go of her and she doesn't pull away. I know she still has feelings for me. But are they enough? I need to find out. "Do you think you could take my stitches out for me?"

"Of course. Let me just get ready." She pulls away to dig a compact kit out of her purse, leaving me cold. Throwing the kettle on, she says, "Why don't you go wait for me in my bathroom upstairs. The lighting there's the best in the house."

"Okay." Her bathroom, attached to her bedroom. Where we can be alone and I can beg her to stay in Ireland. Perfect. Grabbing my T-shirt, I head for the stairs. "Let me know what I owe ya, Ivy."

I catch Ivy's penetrating gaze on me as I pass by. A warning, maybe? Or just curiosity. I can't tell.

Five minutes later, Amber finds me sitting on the edge of the toilet, my mind playing out a dozen possible ways for this conversation to go. "I'm going to leave the butterfly clip on, where you tore those stitches," she warns, scrubbing her hands with soap under the running tap. "That'll need a few more days to heal."

"I can peel that off easily enough." *If you're not here to do it for me.*

"Okay, hold still." I close my eyes, savoring the feel of her fingertips on my skin, even as she tugs the threads out of my flesh. "You really should have a doctor doing this."

"Aengus was always the one removing my stitches before. Trust me, this is a treat."

"Why him?"

"Because he's usually the reason why I needed them in the first place."

She's silent for another long moment. "You and Rowen could have been hurt tonight, because of him."

I sigh. "I know."

She's finished in minutes, sweeping the tiny bits of thread from her hand and into the rubbish. "I've only ever seen shrapnel wounds in textbooks, but they looked a lot worse than these. I think you'll heal nicely." She traces the scars with her fingertips, so lightly that it sends shivers through my body. Her voice thick with emotion, she whispers, "I haven't forgotten what you did for me, River. I'll never forget."

"I'd do it again. A thousand times over."

Suddenly her touch is gone and she's washing her hands again, her head bowed.

I stand and angle myself so I can see the reflection of my back in the mirror. The three lines are puffy and pink, but they're not too bad. "I was really lucky. You should see my da's leg. It's something else. He had pieces of metal coming out of it for years after."

She's quiet as she shuts the tap, then dries her hands. "What happened to him, exactly?"

"A bomber attacked at a funeral." I recount the story I've heard countless times.

"That's just . . . crazy." She turns around, leaning against the counter, the bottom of her dress hiking even higher, until I see more thigh than not. She peers up at me, not with that awestruck look that I loved so much, but with the beginnings of some new level of understanding. Or maybe just acceptance of what I am, I dare to hope. "I can't imagine things like that happening to anyone in my family."

"It's happened to mine. A lot." God knows my brother will be added to the death toll if he keeps this up. It might have happened tonight, had Amber not intervened, offering a smarter solution than the one I naturally reached. "Thank you."

"It's not a big deal. They needed to come out."

"Not about that." I step in until I can smell the floral scent of her hair, feel the wisp of air from her exhales and the warmth of her body. Until I can sense her heart rate begin to race, see her throat bob up and down in a hard swallow. I slide a finger beneath her chin and pull her face up to meet mine. "Please stay." It just slips out. I hadn't intended to say it so bluntly, but now that I've said it, I don't care. I want to be only completely honest with her. "Stay in Ireland. Stay with me. *Please*, stay."

Her eyes turn glassy. "I've known you for a week and you want me to just drop everything? Drop my entire life?"

"No, I just want you to . . ." I press my forehead against hers. What exactly do I want? Because when she says it like that, I feel stupid for even suggesting it. "I want you to look at me the way you used to. I want you to think that I'm good. I want you to still want me." I hesitate, suddenly feeling vulnerable. "Do you?"

A stream of tears slips down her cheeks. "We're so different, River. We don't make sense—this doesn't make sense to me."

"It doesn't have to." My insides clench with dread.

She hesitates for a long moment before admitting in a whisper, "I shouldn't. I can't. But I do. I still want you."

Relief overwhelms me. I feel like I've passed some monumental hurdle.

Until she shakes her head. "This can never go anywhere, River." She says it so convincingly. Is she trying to persuade me, or herself?

A painful spike settles into my throat. I know what I'm about to say is crazy, but I don't care. "It can. You can stay in Ireland, you could get a nursing job, live with me."

"Never bring you home with me, spend every holiday apart . . ." She's been thinking about it too, at least. "No, River. What you're saying . . ." Glossy eyes beg me to understand. "This isn't me. I know we've had an incredible connection but if I were back home, in my everyday life, this would never have happened. You and I would *never* have happened. Do you not see that?"

I curl my arms around her and pull her close to me, letting her face rest against my newly etched skin. The sting from that contact, the burn from the salt as she cries, is a welcome distraction from the deep throb inside my chest right now.

I've never regretted going to that bunker with Aengus more than I do right now.

Her cool fingers dance over my skin, contradicting her words, sending my own heartbeat into a frenzy. Dipping my head down, I coax her mouth with mine, tentatively at first to make sure it's okay. The smallest gasp from her, the way she trails her tongue along the seam of my lips, tells me it is. I can't help but groan in relief. But now it's like I'm in a race to see exactly how far I can get, how many kisses she'll give me, before she remembers herself and pushes me away.

She doesn't seem willing to do that just yet.

Amber's hands wander, grazing my cheeks, my throat, carefully bypassing the right side of my chest in their exploration. Slowly at first, but then more fervently, skating over my ridges, toying with my belt. I wrap my hands around her slender waist and hoist her onto the counter, fitting myself closely between her thighs. She squeezes them tight around me, pressing her hips into me.

I groan again. If she keeps doing that, I'll come right here, standing in the bathroom.

Her hands push against my chest, forcing our lips apart. She gazes up at me with heated eyes, her breathing ragged. And I wait for her to say that we're done, that this is over. That she "can't."

And then she pulls that tiny blue dress up and over her head, tossing it to the tile floor beside us. Her lacy white bra follows closely, leaving her in nothing but a pair of stringy knickers that, if I turned her around right now, would show off that incredible arse.

"You're just so . . ." My mouth finds hers again, and I can't keep my hands off her body anymore—her tits perfect handfuls, her nipples hard against my thumbs, the thin lace between her legs damp. She grinds herself against my fingers once, twice . . . and then her hands quickly find my belt buckle, unfastening it and reaching in to take a surprisingly firm grasp around me. As if she can't wait either. The very possibility sends my need for Amber into overdrive.

Grabbing my wallet out of my jeans, I slide one hand under her and lift her up, carrying her with her legs wrapped around my body to her bed, laying her down so gently, peeling the last of her clothing off. She reaches for me, grabs my hips, pulls me down with surprising strength. Tempting me to slide into her. I would. I know I'm clean, and don't doubt for a second that she is, too, and I'd do anything to feel her bare, just once.

But I also know Amber.

She nuzzles her face in the crook of my neck while I put a condom on, her tongue darting out to run along my skin, making my cock jump in my hand.

"Christ, Amber," I mutter, grabbing her by the back of one thigh, pushing it up and out.

I sink into her and she moans, the sound stealing my lungs.

"Stay. *Please*, stay."

She clasps either side of my face and holds it firm for a moment, peering up into my eyes, her mouth parted as if words hang at the tip of her tongue. But whatever it is she's thinking, she doesn't say. Finally, she reaches around and, seizing the back of my head firmly, she pulls my mouth down to hers.

TWENTY-SIX

AMBER

The sound of the door shutting downstairs wakes me. I assume it's either Rowen or Ivy who just left. A quick glance next to me finds River sprawled out on his back, his naked body tangled in the sheets, his face so boyish in sleep.

I'm not entirely sure what happened last night. I called Alex, looking for advice from her. Or maybe I just wanted her to give me an excuse for this jumble of feelings I still hold for River. But she left me in a cloud of confusion when we hung up.

Now that I've had time to process our conversation, a few things are clearer. For one, I truly understand why my father retired.

It's because he broke the law. He *was* the law, and he went against everything he has always stood for, has always preached. It wasn't simply one quick mistake—one quick, wrong yes-or-no answer. He made a series of choices, took several actions, told many lies, which would, if anyone ever discovered it, tarnish his exemplary reputation forever.

And he did it all to protect Jesse. And Alex, of course. But mainly, to protect Jesse. Because while my brother made some bad choices that led him into that mess, he also made some honorable ones to try to get Alex and himself out of it.

I walked away from that phone call in a haze, but also strangely comforted with the knowledge that my father, the man I always trusted to do the right thing, found himself going against the law he so adamantly supports—and that things worked out for the better because he did.

I walked away from that and into River's arms, unable to ignore the reality that I so desperately wish this could all work out for us, despite what he is. I know that it can't, but just accepting my feelings allowed me to give myself permission to enjoy the little time that I do have left with him.

I move carefully, so as to not wake River, and roll out of bed, throwing on my nightshirt before tiptoeing out. The smell of fresh-brewed coffee rises to greet me as I descend the stairs. Rowen sits at the table, shirtless and reading the newspaper. The creaking bottom step announces my presence.

"Good morning!" He takes a sip, his eyes casually skating over me.

"Anything interesting?" I nod toward the front pages. Would the story have made the paper's cutoff time for today?

He clears his throat dramatically. "'Gardai were called to a Crumlin area neighborhood after reports of a suspicious vehicle parked down the street from an address known to law enforcement officials for its affiliations to dissident republican activities. Two men with ties to organized crime have been arrested for weapons-related offenses. Gardai believe this is related to recent events in Dublin.'"

So they weren't surprised to find two potential hit men near Aengus's house. I wonder if Duffy was there. "That's all?"

He holds the paper up to show me the picture of a small white detached house sitting front and center in the dusk, the "For Sale" sign at the bottom right corner. "They made sure to get the known address included. I'm sure that'll get prospective buyers chomping at the bit."

I wander over to the coffeemaker to pour myself a cup. "Did Ivy just leave?"

"She had a client this morning. She wanted to get home to shower and change first."

Really . . . "Did something happen between you two?"

"A gentleman never tells." He folds the paper up with a smirk. "Don't you birds all talk about this kind of stuff?"

"Ivy and I are a little bit different."

"Well, Ivy's certainly different." He stands and stretches, giving me a good view of his chest and the bandage covering his tattoo. He's muscular like River, only much leaner. "I can't figure her out."

"Yeah, she's a tough one to read."

"But I do like her." Tipping his mug back to finish his coffee, he loads it into the dishwasher and then grabs his shirt. "Thank you for last night, Amber. I appreciate it. I know this isn't something you, or anyone, wants to get mixed up in."

"Glad I could help."

"When do ya leave, again?"

"Sunday morning." These last few days will go quickly.

He throws an arm around my neck and pulls me into his chest in a friendly way. "We better see you again before ya leave."

I smile. "You will."

A long pause. "River's a good guy. And he's mad about you. You know that, right?"

I flush. This is the first time I've ever had a remotely serious conversation with Rowen. "The feelings are mutual." Which makes this all that much harder.

"I've got to go open up the pub, but can ya make sure he gets there by one? I'm in class all afternoon and into the evening. I can't cover for him again."

"Got it."

Slinging his backpack over his shoulder, he disappears out the door.

It's ten fifteen now. That gives me less than three hours with River before he leaves. Pouring a coffee for him, I carry it upstairs to my room. He's just stirring as I set it on the nightstand beside him.

"What time is it?" he asks, his voice raspy and sexy.

I sit next to him, taking the opportunity to trace the ridges of his stomach muscles with my fingers. "After ten. You need to be at the pub by one."

"Right. It's Wednesday. Rowen has class." He rubs the sleep out of his eyes. "I've got a few errands to run before then. What do you have planned for today?"

I sigh. "Well, I was thinking that I haven't been to Cork or the Cliffs of Moher. I'm going to regret not seeing those places."

His hand settles onto my thigh. "You should definitely go. I don't want you to have any regrets from Ireland." The look in his eyes tells me he isn't just talking about the Cliffs.

"But both places are three hours away, so I'd probably need to stay overnight." Right now, I can't think of doing anything that doesn't involve having River in my bed again tonight. "I guess there's no chance you could come with me?"

He groans. "I'd love to, Amber. Honestly. But with Rowen's classes . . . and he has some sort of test tomorrow."

"It's okay. I get it."

"Tell you what. Go to Cork tonight and I'll get Nuala or someone to cover the bar with Rowen tomorrow night and Friday afternoon. Then we can go to the Cliffs."

Excitement stirs in my stomach. "Okay."

"Grand. So go . . . stay in Cork tonight." His hands find my waist and he pulls me onto him with surprising ease, tugging my leg over to straddle his, his morning erection pressing against me. My nightshirt comes off with quick, expert hands, leaving me in nothing but my panties. He pushes those aside. "But make sure you come back to me tomorrow."

TWENTY-SEVEN

RIVER

"Bloody perfect," I mutter, eyeing the towering steeple and stained-glass windows on my left as I ease my car into a parking spot, the gravel crackling beneath my wheels. Leave it to Aengus and Jimmy to be hiding out on holy property. Up ahead is the grand new building that serves as the parishioners' hall. Next to it is the old meeting place—a long, narrow ramshackle shed-like structure, no longer in use for anything but storage.

That's where Aengus told me to meet him.

I push through the heavy wooden door. It slams shut behind me, trapping me in the dank, dingy space.

"River." Aengus appears suddenly from around a stack of boxes as tall as me, a bottle of beer in hand. "What the bleeding hell happened? Jimmy just told me."

He and Jimmy seem to be getting tighter. "Exactly what the paper said happened."

"The old bird across the way called gardai?"

"That's likely." The lie is easier to deal with.

"Fuck," he hisses, turning to spit on the ground, his saliva joining the ranks of countless others on the gritty floor. "Has that cocksucker been back again?"

When I first called Aengus to deliver the warning from Duffy, he flew off the handle, a string of foul language that could strike a nun dead tumbling out of his mouth.

"No. And I think you should be a little grateful to him for the warning. If not for that, you could have been shot dead on our doorstep."

He twists his thin lips, not wanting to give me the satisfaction of being right, even though that pea-sized brain of his knows I am.

"Come on." He leads me around the bend and into a dim rectangle of a room, which houses a small table on the far side, with four men sitting at it. I try to ignore them, letting my eyes roam the drab brown panel walls, the stained brown carpet, the hard brown plastic cafeteria chairs.

Brown, brown, brown.

"Cozy." I want to leave now.

"I've had worse," he mutters, a wry smile curling his thin lips. "Besides, it's safe here." He takes another sip.

"It's noon on a Wednesday, Aengus." I flick the bottle. "Take a break."

He ignores me.

"Who do you think told Duffy about the Green anyway?"

"Probably one of Beznick's guy. Or Beznick, himself. That's the only person I can think of." His eyes search the floor as he combs his thoughts. "Though very few people know it was me. You, me. Jimmy, and he's not gonna say a thing."

Unless he's braggin', which he's been known to do.

"The security guard at the Green, but he's Jimmy's cousin. And Bobby made the device."

My eyes flicker over to the squat man, his face sallow, his balding head hiding beneath a cap. He went away the same time we did. I always thought that he knew far too much about explosives.

"That's it, I think." He pauses. "Other than the American."

"I told you, she was in shock. And she wouldn't have even seen ya."

"But she saw you."

"No way."

Aengus rubs his brow. "Well then I don't know."

The heavy door slams and a few moments later, Jimmy rounds

the corner with another guy who I've never seen before. Jimmy's eyes land on us immediately. With a wave to the other guy, he heads straight for us. "River. Good to see you. What do we owe this visit to?"

"Just checking in on my brother."

He takes a deep breath but otherwise shows no sign of deep concern. "Aengus told me that garda came to Delaney's. You handled it well."

I shrug. "I had nothing to tell them."

"Right. Why don't you come and sit. Have a beer."

"I've got to get to the pub. But thanks," I add begrudgingly.

"We'll keep an eye out, make sure he's safe. We won't let those bastards do anything to him." He pats my shoulder, like we're buddies and he'd be more than happy to help me out. That's how Jimmy works. You're a sparkle in his eye as long as he needs you for something, but he'll turn on you the second it pays to do so. I'll give Aengus one piece of credit—he's always been nothing but loyal.

"And Aengus . . . lay off the beer. You need to be alert." As much as my brother pisses me off, I don't want to be burying him anytime soon. "See ya." I pass the guy Jimmy came in with on my way out. He nods at me, giving me a good look at the line bisecting his black shaved hairline.

That's the guy that Francis O'Reilly—my favorite regular—was talking about.

And now I know.

Fucking Jimmy isn't just extorting Dublin's gangs. He's also going after innocent business owners. My feet slow to a stop in front of the man.

"Yeah?" he says in a deep, raspy voice, rolling his shoulders back.

There's no point in starting something here. Even simple accusations can get you killed with these kinds of fellas. But it makes me sick, just knowing that this piece of shit has threatened Francis, and his lovely wife, and their children.

Does Aengus truly not realize what's going on? If he does . . .

well then, he deserves whatever's coming to him. I just don't want to be dragged down with him.

I shove the heavy door open, my teeth gritted, promising myself that this is it.

No more visits.

No more warning calls.

I'm done protecting Aengus.

■ ■ ■

"It's so charming here," Amber purrs into my ear. It's just after eleven and we finally got the last customer out. I'm sure she's in bed.

"I know it is. I wish I were there with you."

"I kissed the Blarney Stone."

"Tourist," I accuse with a grin. "And how was that experience?"

"Kind of dirty. I wiped my lips right after." She giggles. "And the little inn that I'm staying in is adorable. The pathway up to the door is lined with rosebushes, and the lady who runs it serves scones in the morning. Everyone here sounds so different from you."

"That's because they're from the south. See? I told you it was a good idea."

"I know it was. It's just . . ." Silence hangs over the phone.

"I know. But we still have tomorrow, Friday, and Saturday." And if I let myself think I'm ever going to see her again after Sunday, once distance and time has woven its magic, I'm as big an idiot as the rest of them. But at least I got this much, which is more than I deserved. "Listen, you going to be up for a while? We're going to finish closing here. I should be home in an hour."

"Okay, I'll try to stay awake," she says through a yawn. "I'm exhausted from last night."

"So am I," I admit, unable to keep my wide grin from spreading. I can't wait for a repeat. Tomorrow. "Get some sleep. If I don't talk to ya again tonight, I will in the morning. First thing."

"Okay."

"'Night, Amber."

She makes a soft sound—a mix between a moan and a purr—that gets my blood stirring. "'Night."

"Is this what life is going to be like now?" Rowen mutters. "Me working while you whisper into your phone?"

"Shut up, dickhead." He came in to help me with the last hour, letting Nuala go home early. I snatch the end of the wet towel just before he manages to snap my thigh with it and yank it out of his hand, reversing the move. He tears around the bar to get away before I can make contact.

A sudden pounding against the door has us both frowning at each other.

"Open up!"

There's no mistaking Aengus's voice.

"Fuck. What is he doing here?" Rowen heads over to unlock the door and let him in.

Aengus stumbles through, slamming the door shut behind him. I guess he didn't lay off the beer, like I told him to. *Good job taking care of him, Jimmy.*

"You're supposed to be gone to ground!" I yell. "What the fuck are you doing in here? Did anyone see ya?"

"No one saw me," he slurs. "It's dark, and I'm stealthy as an alley cat."

Rowen snorts but says nothing, busying himself with the last remaining chairs needing stacking. Wanting to get away from him, I'll bet. Aengus is a mean drunk.

"And besides, those two fuckheads who were waiting for me on our street are in prison, so I guess Beznick's out of luck for now."

"Why are you even out? Where's Jimmy?"

"Ah . . ." He waves a dismissive hand. "Can't I come see me brothers? Hang out in me own pub? This place is rightfully mine and I'm not even allowed to come in for a pint? I have to sneak through dark alleys and beg you to let me in!"

Rowen shoots me a warning glance, not that it's needed. I'm not about to give Aengus a reality check about the future ownership of Delaney's.

"Grab a stool, Aengus." I sigh, holding a fresh glass up to the Smithwick's tap. At least we haven't cleaned it out for the night yet.

"Don't mind if I do." He kicks one over to sit opposite me.

"Rowen?"

"May as well," he mutters. Aengus can be the true sense of the term *barfly*. A fucking nuisance that's impossible to rid ourselves of once he's in.

I'm just setting a pint down in front of Aengus when the door flies open and a short fella steps in, his face covered from the nose down by a black handkerchief. I see the smile in his cold, narrow eyes. "Tit-for-tat, Delaneys." He rolls something onto the floor and disappears out the door as quickly as he came, slamming it shut behind him.

I have just enough time to see the long tube.

Just enough time to see the wick at the end, sizzling as it burns.

Just enough time to catch Rowen's eyes.

TWENTY-EIGHT

AMBER

"Amber."

"Hey, Ivy!" I'm surprised to hear from her, especially at eight in the morning. I got an early start to the day, wanting to explore a bit more before heading back to Dublin. River told me he'd come pick me up at the house by three. "Have you been to Cork before?"

"No."

"Ugh! You have to come. Even you would appreciate this place. It's so charming. I've never seen anything like it." My gaze absorbs a kaleidoscope of colors as I stroll down the narrow sidewalk. Each storefront is painted in vibrant hues—a bed-and-breakfast in gold and rust, a tea shop in peacock blue and brick, a woman's dress shop in canary yellow and indigo—and adorned with flowers and kitschy signs.

I sigh, sipping on the latte that Mrs. Harrington made for me before I left the quaint little inn. Such a sweet old lady. Her husband, too. They let me leave my car in their driveway for the morning.

"I guess you haven't seen the news yet?" There's something odd in her voice that I can't quite grasp.

I stop walking. "No . . . why?"

"You need to come back to Dublin. Like, right now."

■ ■ ■

I clocked well over two thousand hours in the hospital last year. Enough time that I've gotten used to the smells and the beeping sounds and eerie quiet. Enough time that I find comfort within those walls, able to navigate wings and signage without a second thought.

Today, though, after a white-knuckled three-hour drive home, turning onto the wrong side—or right side, in my opinion—of the road a dozen times, a frenzy of terrified thoughts distracting my focus, I'm finding no comfort within these Dublin hospital walls.

"Hey." Ivy's face so rarely shows any emotion that just the sight of her now—her brow pulled tight, a black mascara streak on her cheek—nearly unravels me.

"Have you heard anything?"

"Nothing."

I heave a sigh, but it brings no relief to the tightness in my chest. "Thank you. For calling, and for tracking them down." I passed out five minutes after talking to River last night. I figured he was still sleeping this morning when I texted him, though I was anxiously awaiting a response.

Now I know why I haven't gotten one yet.

She simply shrugs and then leads me down a hall toward the reception desk in the emergency room waiting area. A young, mousy nurse sits behind it, chewing on the end of a pen. Her badge says her name is Sally, and it makes me think of the McNally sisters.

"Hi, our friends were brought in this morning after an incident at their pub. I was hoping you could give us some information." I cross my fingers, having no idea how willing she'll be to share details with me, seeing as I'm not family.

"Names?" Sally's voice—deep and husky and laced with a heavy Dubliner accent—is a complete contradiction to her appearance.

"River and Rowen Delaney."

Her glasses shift with her frown. "Right. Terrible thing that happened."

My stomach clenches with her words, tears ready to flood my cheeks. This doesn't sound promising.

"You're American. You must be," she checks a sticky note, "Amber Welles?"

"Yes."

When she catches my curious frown, she explains, "River's been asking for you. Sent his mother here to make sure we let you in. Room 114—through that door and take a left." Her gaze shifts to Ivy.

"She's with me," I say.

She hesitates. "I'm not supposed to—"

"Look, I get it, Sally. I'm a nurse too, back home." I plead with her compassionate side, the one that may overlook policies. "She'll be in and out. She just needs to see Rowen. Even if it's for a minute."

The nurse's voice drops. "Go quickly, before the regular desk nurse comes back from break. She won't let you back there."

"Thank you." Tugging at Ivy's arm, I hurry her along as I follow the directions, my worry growing with each step. I hold my breath as I peek through the window of Room 114, unsure of what I'm about to see, fearing the worst.

"Oh, thank God," slips through my mouth with a heavy exhale as I immediately spot River sitting upright on the edge of the bed closest to the window, already dressed in jeans and a shirt. Aside from a few mild scratches on his cheek and a small bandage above his left eyebrow, he appears to be fine. The crushing weight that's been sitting on my chest all morning lifts. Not fully, though, because the bed next to River's is empty and stripped of all bedding.

Where is Rowen?

River's not alone. An older couple occupy the space between his bed and the window. His parents, no doubt. The squat woman paces, wringing her hands nervously, her sable-colored hair a frizzy mess pinned on top of her head. The man, with a full head of coppery hair, sits in a chair, his hands folded over the handle of a cane. He appears older than the woman.

They're people I never thought I'd meet. People I would never want to meet under circumstances such as these.

The man's gaze catches me in the tiny window and his mouth begins moving. River's on his feet immediately, a limp in his gait as he takes a few steps, then waves me in. "Amber!"

I push through the door. "Ivy called me. I came as fast as I could." I freeze midway, feeling his parents' eyes on me, unsure of what's appropriate here. I know what I *want* to do: attach myself to his chest, kiss him senseless, and never let go.

Fortunately, River answers my question for me, enfolding me in his arms and burying his face into my neck.

"How are you?"

"I'll be fine, aside from a concussion and a few bruises and cuts. I was behind the bar when it went off. We're just waiting for them to discharge me."

"Thank God." I glance over at the empty bed, and then at Ivy, who seems to be hiding in a corner. "And Rowen?"

He swallows hard, and I feel it right down into the depths of my stomach. "Still in surgery." Worry mars his handsome face. "It's been twelve hours. All we know so far is that he took a lot of shrapnel. Doctors are trying to save his leg. Twelve hours seems like a long time, doesn't it?"

Any surgery that lasts that long is serious, especially when it involves trauma like this. But he doesn't need to hear that now. "I've seen plenty of surgeries last that long and the patients turn out just fine." My own mother worked on Alex for over fourteen hours.

His slow, shaky exhale skates over my face, and then he finally nods. "Aengus is in critical care."

All three brothers were caught in that bombing. All three could have been killed. "Was this because of him?" I whisper.

He simply nods.

Behind us, someone clears a throat. River's arms fall, releasing me from their grip, enough that I can duck around him. "Hi, I'm Amber." I close the distance and offer my hand to his mom first, and then his dad. They each take it in turn, answering with "Marion" and "Seamus" and tight smiles. Not because of their displeasure with me; I understand that. I've spent enough time around worried families in hospitals to not take it personally.

"You're American?" River's father asks.

"Yes."

"Living in Ireland?"

"Just visiting."

His green eyes dart to River's, a quizzical look in them.

"She knows," is all he says, pulling me back into his side. I happily meld against him.

"How long are ya here for, Amber?" his mother asks, her accent so thick I have to process the words in my mind to interpret.

"Well, I was supposed to be leaving on Sunday for England, but . . ." I steal a glance River's way. "I'm going to make some changes to my flights." When Simon offered his house to me, he said I could have it for the entire month of June. I never thought I'd need it.

River's brow furrows. "Are you sure?"

"Yeah." I smile. "It's just another country. It'll still be there later." But River may not be, and I can't think of any place I'd rather be now than with him. This isn't about ditching my life plans for a guy. This is about doing what I truly want to do.

"And you?" Marion pokes her head around to take in Ivy, her shrewd eyes scrutinizing Ivy's boots and punkish dress.

"I'm friends with Amber." She hesitates. "And Rowen." After a moment, she darts forward awkwardly, extending her arm to offer a hand.

Marion's eyes widen slightly at the full sleeve of colorful ink covering Ivy's slender arm before taking it. I can only imagine what's going on in the woman's head. Not everyone can be like my mother—so open-minded and accepting.

"Ivy did the Delaney stag on my chest," River explains, adding, "on Rowen, too."

That seems to impress Seamus, his nod slow but approving.

"We should go see if there's any news on Rowen," Marion announces. "Come, Seamus."

"Right." He climbs out of his seat with a groan, wincing once before righting himself, setting his shoulders straight. As if defying the very real pain he feels. "Maybe we can track down that flighty bird who was supposed to release you by now," he mumbles to River on the way past.

The second the door shuts, River sits down on the bed with a grimace. "Fuck . . ."

"You said you were fine."

He sighs. "I lied. Ma will start yelling at the doctors to keep me here if she knows."

I shake my head with exasperation. "Maybe she's right and you need to stay!"

"Nah." He grabs my hands and pulls me onto his lap, carefully maneuvering me to, I imagine, avoid the injury on his leg. "I have my own private nurse. I don't need to stay in here."

I lay a kiss on his temple, aware of Ivy still in the room. "True."

The momentary silence hanging in the room is heavy with worry.

"How bad was it?" I finally ask.

"I don't really remember much. I came to with the paramedics. Bad, I think. I can't see the pub being opened again for a while." He curses under his breath. "They were watching, waiting for that idiot to come in. If he'd just stayed away like he was supposed to, this wouldn't have happened."

"How hurt is Rowen?" Ivy hugs her tiny frame.

"I didn't see him." River's voice turns husky with emotion. He clears his throat several times, his head dipped down. "The staff here is bloody horrible. I asked for a glass of ice water an hour ago."

"I'll get you some. Just stay put." I've done the same for countless patients before, but it's different now. I'll happily be at River's beck and call.

"I could use some, too," Ivy murmurs, trailing me. No matter how casual this thing is with Rowen, I can tell it's shaken her up. Passing through the door, I reach back to give her hand a slight squeeze and offer a smile.

When I turn to look ahead, I find myself face-to-face with Garda Duffy.

Two . . . three . . . four painfully long seconds pass, where my lungs simply don't work. Maybe he doesn't remember me. Maybe he won't recognize me.

Maybe he won't put two and two together.

I pray.

"Amber Welles." His gaze reads the number on the door, and then my face. There's no mistaking the shift from surprise to shock to recognition . . . to understanding.

I'm sure it's the same series of expressions that he sees passing over mine.

I'm in so much trouble.

TWENTY-NINE

RIVER

I shift and groan, the twenty stitches keeping the wound in my thigh closed tight and uncomfortable. That chunk of flying glass cut so deep into my muscle that I needed internal stitching as well. The doctors promised that this limp is only temporary, that it'll fade within a couple of weeks, as the tissue repairs itself.

I don't give a shit, truly. All I care about right now is knowing that Rowen will be okay.

Ma was with Aengus in his room this morning when he came to after surgery, groggy. Doctors said he should recover just fine, though with plenty more scars.

Until I get hold of him, that is. Because if Rowen doesn't pull through, I'll kill the bastard with my own bare hands.

My hospital room door suddenly swings open. Ivy rushes through, rare alarm in her eyes. "The gardai just arrested Amber. They're taking her to the station."

"*What?*" Any last bit of shock from the bombing vanishes instantly as panic sets in.

"I don't know why." She frowns. "But he knew her name."

Fuck. I should have known. Of course Duffy himself would be coming here to question me about last night.

And Amber lied to him.

"Shit, shit, shit . . ." What the hell is going to happen to her now?

"You need to fix this, River," Ivy insists through gritted teeth.

"I will," I promise. But how?

A knock against the glass pulls our attention up in time to see Duffy poke his head in.

"Call the shop when you have news about Rowen," she mutters, scurrying past him and out the door.

Duffy watches her with curiosity for a long moment, and then dismisses her, letting the door slip from his finger's grip to shut. He adjusts his hat. "River. Glad to see you up." He strolls forward, as if here to check on me, to see how I'm doing. As if he cares. I know that's not the case at all. "Terrible thing that happened. I hear you got a nasty bump on the head."

"Why did you just arrest Amber?" I blurt out.

He eyes me, flipping open his notepad. "She has some things to answer for. And I have a few questions for you, about last night."

I know how this works. It's a dance of information, back and forth, and he's not going to make the first move. He's still trying to pin the Green on me and he clearly has no evidence aside from some whispered rumors from his criminal informants. If I didn't care about Amber, I'd tell him to fuck off. The problem is, I *do* care about her. More than I've ever cared about any girl before.

And I think he's figured that out.

"What do you remember, exactly?"

All morning, I've been quietly piecing bits of memories together. "The pub was closed. Aengus showed up, pounding on the door."

"Was he running from someone? Afraid for his life?"

"No." I snort, recalling Aengus's arrogant attitude. "He was right pissed. Been drinking all day."

"So, you let him in."

"Of course."

"And did you lock the door behind him?"

"No." I've beaten myself up about that for a while this morning, but, really, there's no point. Beznick's fellas would have gotten in eventually. At least there weren't any customers.

"And then? What happened after that?"

"I poured a round of pints, because we still needed to finish up and Aengus wasn't going anywhere. Then suddenly a man showed up, tossed the bomb, and ran out the door."

Duffy's pen moves quickly, scratching down notes. "Did he say anything?"

"He did." I hesitate. "'Tit-for-tat, Delaneys.'"

His pen stops and his gaze levels with mine. "What do you suppose that meant?"

"He didn't care to elaborate."

"Right." Duffy's jaw shifts in thought. Deciding on whether to push me on it, I assume. "Did you see his face?"

"Half of it."

"Enough to identify him?"

"Possibly." If I don't kill him first. I saw a tattoo on his forearm—a giant scythe, or something like that. Between his eyes and that marking and his short stature, I might be able to pick him out of a lineup. That information would be of help to the gardai. Maybe they could lay charges. But I know that I could also pass this information on to Jimmy and guarantee that the guy is tracked down and punished, swiftly. Not because Jimmy necessarily cares what happened to me or Rowen, but because his right-hand man was nearly blown up and that's an affront to Jimmy's image.

"We don't have a lot of time to find the man who did this to your family, River," Duffy warns. The clever garda must be able to read the thoughts on my face.

"I know that." The bomber will go to ground as soon as he finds out that we lived.

He sighs. "They're releasing you soon, I gather?"

"Just waiting on paperwork."

"I'd like ya to come down to the station and look through some mug shots."

"Only if you let Amber go. She's completely innocent."

"Innocent of what?" he asks casually, his raptor gaze watching my every tic and twitch.

I swallow, not taking the bait. "Of whatever you're trying to drag her into."

"She lied to a garda. That's a serious offense."

Fuck. "If she did, it was to protect me."

"From what?"

I meet his question with silence. I can't let her take the fall for this, but I need to think this through before I talk.

"You must really like this bird." A heavy frown casts over his face. "Where do ya see this going, with you unable to step foot on American soil? Hoping she'll move here?" When I still don't speak, he goes on. "If she's found guilty of providing false information to an officer of the law during an investigation, she may never be allowed back in Ireland. Then where will that leave you two?" He flips his notebook shut. "Be smart, River."

Ma plows through the door, boring holes into Garda Duffy's back with her glare. "Not enough that ya disturb the son who's barely conscious, now you're here to bother another?"

I watch Duffy's eyes glaze over as he prepares himself for Ma's tongue-lashing.

"If you spent less time bothering us and more time chasing down Dublin's scum, maybe our entire livelihood wouldn't be lying in shambles now. And to think, ya knew someone was threatening me family and ya did nothing. I should bring charges to the lot of ya!"

Ma may seem the simple-minded *culchie* sometimes but she's not daft. She's already figured out this is Aengus's doing. Yet she'll defend her pride for her family until she's six feet in the ground.

"I'll be expecting you in later today, River." With one last pointed look my way, Duffy disappears out the door.

"That bastard!" Ma exclaims, glaring at the door.

"Any update on Rowen yet?"

Her bottom lip wavers with her firm head shake. "Your da's waiting for the doctor."

I collect my wallet and keys from the end table. I'm assuming my phone didn't make it out of the pub last night. "Tell them I discharged myself."

She frowns. "Where you goin'?"

"To talk to Aengus."

■ ■ ■

Aengus has always been a force to be reckoned with. Even now, bandaged like a mummy, cords dangling from his limbs, his eyes mere slivers as he watches me approach, I sense the fury radiating from him.

"Beznick's not goin' to get away with this," he mutters, his words slightly slurred from the heavy dose of pain medication. "I need you to go see Jimmy, tell him it was Jackie Hanegan."

"That's the guy's name? You sure?"

"Positive. I had words with the muppet a few weeks back. Tell Jimmy."

I sigh. "And then what?"

He pauses, and I can see him processing the question, not sure if he heard it right. "What the fuck do you mean, 'and then what'? Jimmy will take care of it."

"Yeah. He will. He'll put a few bullets in Jackie's back. Maybe blow up his house with his family in it, as a warning. And then Beznick will send someone after Jimmy, and maybe after you again. Open your eyes and look at what just happened! They're still trying to fix your baby brother in there. Don't you care?"

"Of course I care!" he spits back. I know he does, because Aengus is loyal to the Delaney name, to the beliefs that made us who we are today. The problem is he can't see how Jimmy's beliefs—and the actions of today's IRA—have diverged from what our family stands for.

The rhythmic beeping of his heart rate monitor increases and I pause for a moment, waiting for him to calm himself while I study the tiny, private room they've stuck him in. He won't be in critical care for much longer, I gather. Some poor fella will get stuck sharing a room with him soon enough. "Duffy was here to see you?"

"Tried, but Ma chased him away. I pretended I was asleep." He pauses. "You?"

"He came in."

"You told him to fuck off, right? We'll handle this ourselves. Garda's never done anything good for us."

"Neither have you."

He glares at me. "What the hell is that supposed to mean? Did you forget all the times I helped you out? I would've been out of prison years ago had I not been protecting you. Have you forgotten that so quickly?"

"I wouldn't have needed protection if it wasn't for you," I throw back. Though I don't truly blame Aengus. I made my own choices. "Everything that our family represents is now lying in a heap of rubble, my brother is lying on a surgeon's table, fighting to keep his leg, and that is all because of you." A glance over my shoulder finds a nurse peering in. I take a deep breath before I say what I resolved myself to on the way here. It's the only way out of this mess, and what I know Amber would tell me to do, if she were here. "I'm going down to the station now, to identify Jackie Hanegan's ugly mug, like a normal Irish citizen looking for justice. And then I'm going to try and help Ma and Da pick up the pieces of a life *you've* destroyed. And when Duffy shows up here and questions you, you are going to give him every last piece of information that he wants. Everything. Names and locations. He's going to connect this to the Green, and you're going to admit to it."

He chokes on his laughter, coughing and then grimacing against the pain. "Are you mad? Why the hell would I do that?"

"Because if you don't, I'll give Duffy what he wants myself."

Honest shock fills Aengus's face. "You're serious? You'd really do that? You'd turn on your own flesh and blood?"

"No. I'm *protecting* my flesh and blood. Ma and Da. And Rowen. I'm protecting them." And I'm protecting Amber.

He stares long and hard at me. "Do you even know what you're asking?" he finally whispers, realization dawning on him.

"That you pay for your sins."

"And put a nail in my own coffin?"

"Are you really too stupid to see that you've already done that?

It's only a matter of time before someone tries to pick you off again. I won't let you take the rest of us down with you."

The door flies open then, and our da storms in as quickly as his limp allows him to. The tears in his eyes are a swift punch to my chest. I've never seen Da cry, not even on his worst days of pain. "They couldn't save his leg. Your brother lost his leg because of you!" Da makes it all the way to the edge of the bed, his face the color of ripe tomatoes, too red for a man with his blood pressure issues. "And if that's not bad enough, there's also nerve damage to his other leg. He could be in pain for the rest of his life!"

If anyone understands what that's like, it's Da.

Ma sweeps in after him, her face wet from crying. "He's goin' to be just fine. Stop worrying, Seamus. You'll get yourself sick!"

Da's not even listening to her, though. "What did you do, Aengus!"

"Nothing," he grumbles like a sullen child who knows he's guilty but would rather take punishment than admit to it.

I guess the yelling caught the attention of the hospital staff because a nurse and doctor step in behind Ma. "You'll need to leave while we examine him," the doctor says, slipping a stethoscope around his neck. "You can come back a little later."

"I won't be comin' back," Da says, and his tone leaves no room for guesswork. It's a declaration. Aengus is dead to him. I don't think I've ever heard of such a thing happening in Delaney history.

My brother flinches, as if the words slapped him across the face.

With the doctor hovering, there's nothing left to do but leave.

"When Duffy comes, you tell him everything, Aengus," I warn him. "Because if *I* have to do it . . ." I let my words drift, the meaning clear. Going on the stand as a witness against the IRA sometimes doesn't end well for the witness. "And then that blood'll be on your hands, too."

THIRTY

AMBER

I'm guessing all interrogation rooms have a universal quality to them. The one in the Deschutes County station was like this—small, rectangular, with a simple table in the center and two hard chairs flanking either side, and a camera in the corner to record and monitor the interviews. My dad and I ate lunch in it one day, on a "Take Your Kids to Work" day.

I wish my dad were here right now.

I thought about calling him, but decided against it. For now, at least.

Garda Duffy shuts the door quietly behind him as he enters, a tan folder tucked under his arm, much like the one he brought to show me that day when I lied to him about knowing River. "Do you need anything? Water? Toilet break?"

"No." I clear the nervousness from my voice. "I'm fine. Thank you."

"Alright, then. Let's begin. Your rights have been read to you and you're aware that what you tell me today may be used against you in future."

"I am."

"And you're aware that you are entitled to legal representation."

"Yes, I'm aware." Maybe I should be pushing for that now. But I also know that I can ask for a lawyer at any time and that allows me some comfort, though it won't change the fact that I lied.

"Right. Okay, then." He goes through all the statements, introducing his full name and rank, identifying the dates and approximate time of the pipe bomb blast, and reading the verbal statements I provided to them. Pretty much a recap of our interactions thus far. He does it in a slow, monotonous voice, almost lulling.

"Three days ago, I visited the residence where you were staying, and I showed you this picture." He slides out the mug shot of Aengus. Now that I've met River's father, I can see the familial similarities, but I still find it hard to believe that this cold and calculating guy is related to River and Rowen. "You told me that you didn't recognize him."

"That's right."

He eyes me. "You're sure?"

I tap the picture. "I've never met this man. I've never even seen him."

"Okay." He slides out River's picture, and the bubble of panic in my stomach rises. "I also showed you this picture, and you confirmed that you didn't recognize him."

"I did say that."

"Was that true?"

I take a deep breath. "No."

"So you did recognize this man?"

"Yes."

"And how did you recognize him?"

"From St. Stephen's Green, the day of the bomb. He's the guy who pushed me down. He saved my life."

"And do you know his name?"

"River Delaney." It comes out scratchy. I can't believe I'm naming River like this. I just hope that telling the truth will help him more than the continued lies could hurt him. And I hope he doesn't hate me for it.

"When did you first meet River?"

"Two days after the bombing in St. Stephen's Green."

He frowns, confused. Or maybe doubtful, like he was expecting my answer to be different.

"Everything I told you about that day in St. Stephen's Green was true. I was just an American tourist at the wrong place at the wrong time. I told you all that I remembered of him. It wasn't until two days later when I was having lunch that something triggered my memory. A stag on a T-shirt, of all things." I chuckle, though nothing about being in this cold, sterile room is particularly funny.

"The Delaney crest," he murmurs, a small smile touching his mouth.

"Exactly." I go on to explain how I tracked River down to the pub, and everything after that, glossing over the private details. I think he can read between the lines just fine, my crimson cheeks likely enough evidence.

"So, when I showed up on Monday and asked you to identify his mug shot, you knew River Delaney quite well."

I swallow. "Yes. In some ways, I guess I did. And I panicked. It just didn't make sense. It couldn't be the same guy. I didn't believe it. I didn't *want* to believe it."

"Lying to a police officer is a serious offense, Amber."

I snort, the irony of this situation not lost on me. "Trust me, I'm well aware. My father is a retired sheriff."

That seems to give him pause, but not for too long. "You can be charged and convicted. You can have a criminal record because of it. If that happens, you won't be allowed back in Ireland again."

I squeeze my eyes shut, until I'm sure I've stalled the tears that threaten to fall. I hear what that threat really means. Never see River again.

Duffy regards me for a moment, chewing the corner of his lip in thought. "So, what happened next?"

"I ran. Avoided River while I processed."

"Because you were afraid?"

"Because I was angry." I settle my gaze on him, hoping he can see River through my eyes for just a moment. "He's made mistakes, but he's a good person."

Duffy watches me silently with that same steely look that my dad has, that tells me nothing. "And then?"

I know that I don't have to answer any of these questions. That giving this information may implicate me further. But they'll find out eventually. They'll pull phone records and see all the calls and text messages between us. They could pull Ivy in here and ask her, and I don't expect her to incriminate herself. In the end, I'll end up having to tell the truth anyway.

One of Sheriff Welles's many mantras: "Always cooperate with the police, and things will go a lot smoother for you." I wonder if those words were cycling through his head when he was helping Jesse cover up evidence of the murder attempt on Alex.

"And then I confronted him, and he told me everything."

"What is 'everything'?"

"His criminal record, his family's history."

"About his brother, Aengus?"

I nod.

"Did River tell you why he was in St. Stephen's Green the morning of the bombing?"

"Yes." If River isn't going to help clear their suspicions of him, I will. "He overheard his brother, Aengus, talking about delivering some sort of warning that morning. So he followed him, unnoticed, to the park, and witnessed Aengus set the pipe bomb in the field. He tried to stop him but he couldn't. Aengus ran and River was about to run himself, and then he saw me heading directly into the path. If not for River, I would have been hurt. Killed, perhaps."

"And that would have been quite a tragic end," he murmurs, tapping his pen against the desk in thought, though his gaze is still glued to mine.

I add, with hesitation, "But that's all hearsay, isn't it? What he told me, and what I just told you." I don't know how many times my dad would scold Bonnie and me for sharing "hearsay"—gossip—at our kitchen table. If we didn't personally witness it, it would never stand up in court, he'd say, and we shouldn't repeat it. I think he really just wanted to stop our incessant thirteen-year-old babble.

Duffy smiles gently, then tosses his pen aside, giving his forehead a firm rub with his palms. "I wish you had been honest with me on Monday. Maybe last night could have been avoided." He looks up in time to see my face fall—the blanket of guilt he just tossed over my shoulders weighing me down instantly—and quickly adds, "But probably not. What you're telling me only confirms what we already suspected and couldn't prove about Aengus. We still can't, beyond your words, which, as you say, are hearsay."

"So what are you going to do?"

He sighs. "Figure out how to get River to admit to it, and act as a witness. Given that he's as stubborn as he is proud, I don't see how I'm going to accomplish that."

"I can try," I mutter half-heartedly, because I know the answer already. River is never going to rat out his brother. He's already said so.

A knock sounds at the door, grabbing Duffy's attention. "Thank you for telling me the truth, Amber. I'll be back soon."

He leaves me alone in that small, cold rectangular room.

I rest my head on the table, wondering what his return will bring.

THIRTY-ONE

RIVER

"Any news on your brother?" Duffy asks, setting a steaming cup of coffee down on the table.

I don't have to ask which one. He wouldn't be asking about Aengus unless it was to gauge how long before he could throw cuffs on him. "They removed his spleen, and pulled some shrapnel from his lung and his liver."

"His leg?"

I grit my teeth. "Gone from below the knee."

Duffy shakes his head. "Such a tragedy for a young fella."

I can't tell if he actually cares or if he says it because it's the proper thing to say. "It is. He never did anything to deserve it."

"Did you?"

"No."

"Did Aengus?"

We stare at each other from across the table. "Look at us . . . two hard-headed bastards."

That earns a genuine smile from his end. The answer is right there for him. "If you can begin looking through this stack of photos . . ." He flips open the top of a thick binder, two more waiting next to it.

"A bit archaic, don't ya think?"

"Sometimes we like to do things the old-fashioned way," he murmurs.

I didn't miss the fact that I'm sitting in an interrogation room, instead of at a desk where we can peruse the mug shot database from a computer screen.

"Where's Amber?"

"A few rooms over. We just had a good, long chat." He lets his words hang in silence for a moment. "I don't take her for the criminal type."

"She's not. She's a good bird."

"I wouldn't want to see this all turn out badly for her. I don't think you would, either."

"You're right. Which is why I'd like you to get the information that you need."

"Uh . . . what do you . . ." He falters over his words, surprise splashing across his face. "Go on."

"I'll give you the name of the asshole who blew up my family's pub and I'll tell you who attacked the Green. But only if you let Amber go with absolutely no repercussions. The only thing she ever did wrong was give the likes of me a fair chance."

Duffy's fingers strum across the table, what I'm dangling in front of him too enticing to ignore. The chance to make arrests in two separate Dublin bombings? It's any officer's wet dream come true.

If I were bold—and stupid—I'd also tell him where Jimmy's hiding.

"I know Aengus is responsible for the Green, and that you were there to see it happen. Your girlfriend told me everything."

Hearing that doesn't make me angry in the least, I realize. Yes, Amber betrayed my confidence, but I know her well enough to know that she didn't do it to protect herself; she did it to protect me.

She did it because it's the right thing to do.

"Then I guess you know I'm useful."

"Are you saying you'd be a witness on the stand against your own brother?" There's doubt in Duffy's voice.

I take a deep breath. Never in a million years did I think these words would ever leave my mouth. "If he doesn't confess to it himself, then yes, I'm saying exactly that."

"Aengus, confess to the bombing?" He raises his eyebrows. "How hard did you get knocked in the head?"

"You're a persuasive bastard. Tell him he has no choice. Paint him a pretty picture about what could happen to me if he doesn't."

Duffy purses his lips together and then nods.

Honestly, I have no clue what Aengus is going to admit to. I know him well enough to know that he feels guilty and that he'll do anything to protect his family, but whether that's enough for him to do the right thing for once . . . ?

Duffy's fingers flip a page in the binder, then another. "You came in here to identify the man responsible for the bombing of your bar."

"Jackie Hanegan."

His fingers freeze. "You sure?" He quickly searches the pages.

"He's short and has squinty eyes. Has a tattoo right here." I draw on my forearm. "Heavy Cork accent."

Duffy spins the book around, and the familiar eyes stare up at me.

"Yeah, that's him."

"You said half his face was covered, though."

"It's him."

"Is he in any danger?"

"You can bet Jimmy'll be after him once he hears from Aengus."

"We'll pick him up, then. There's bound to be more evidence tied to him." Suddenly, Duffy is fumbling for his pen, his pad of paper, and his phone. "We'll need formal statements from you, about last night and the Green bombing."

"You'll get them as soon as you let Amber off."

"I'm not negotiating."

"Neither am I."

"Look . . ." He stops and sighs. "Even though she lied to me, and I'm well within my rights to charge Miss Welles, I'm not in the practice of punishing people who don't truly deserve it."

"You were already going to let her go?"

"I believe that the information she provided at the site, the day of the bombing, was truthful. Her only real mistake after that was falling in love with the likes of a Delaney."

I sigh with relief, his words filling my chest with warmth.

"So? Do we have a deal?"

"We do. But go and talk to Aengus first. I'll be more than happy to wait here and give my statement about the Green when you come back, if it's still necessary."

After a moment, he collects his notepad and stands. "I'm glad to say that I was wrong about you, River."

"Likewise." I guess maybe Duffy's not so bad, after all. His hand is on the door handle to leave when I remember. "I have an extortion case for you to look into, too. One of Jimmy's guys is involved." Let's see if Duffy can get them off of Francis O'Reilly's back.

He frowns. "You're just offering this information to me for nothing? Or is there something you want in return?"

"Let's just say I don't like seeing undeserving people punished either."

THIRTY-TWO

AMBER

Duffy holds the door open. And simply stands there.

I stare at him.

"You're free to go."

Is this a trick? I admitted to lying to him. I've been sitting in this room for hours, waiting for him to march in and tell me what's going to happen next to me, to River.

When I don't move right away, he adds, "Unless you prefer these accommodations to your other?"

My chair nearly topples, as quickly as I stand. "What about River?" Does he know that I told Duffy everything? Does he understand why?

Does he hate me now?

A secretive smile curls Duffy's lips. He finds that amusing somehow. I'm suddenly overcome with the urge to slap him.

"Relax, Amber." He points down the hallway and I peer past him, along the narrow corridor, to where River leans against the wall, his head tipped back as if resting. No handcuffs, no garda hovering.

What does that mean?

Duffy must see the confusion in my face. "I finally found something important enough to bend that stubborn Irish will of his."

Something important enough . . .

Me?

He chuckles softly. "Go on, now."

I don't wait another second. I tear down the hall and into River's waiting arms.

■ ■ ■

"We can still stay at your house tonight, if you'd rather be close to your parents." I flick the hallway light on. It feels like I haven't stepped inside here in weeks, even though I left for Cork just yesterday.

River drops the duffel bag of clothes he packed on the floor—he refused to let me carry it in—and struggles to kick his shoes off, his limp worse than it was earlier today. "Who knows what time they'll be back from the hospital. Besides, Ma would take issue with where you sleep."

"I don't mind sleeping on my own."

"*I* do." His chuckle is so weak. "I need my nurse in bed with me."

I smile, giving his back a rub. I haven't stopped touching him in some way since we left the garda station. "I'll be upstairs in just a minute."

He eases up the steps with great care. I still don't know what happened with Duffy. I asked but he shrugged it off, saying, "Later." I don't know what that means and, while I know he needs his rest, *I* need assurances that this is all going to work out for River. The only thing I do know is that he doesn't seem angry with me at all.

Opening his bottle of prescription painkillers, I fill a glass of water, throw together a few ham and cheese sandwiches—neither of us have eaten all day—and make my way upstairs to my bedroom.

River's already undressed and stretched out in bed. Gauze covers the phoenix over his chest. I didn't know he had an injury there as well. "Thank Christ. I'm starved," he mumbles, reaching for a sandwich.

"Does it still hurt?" I pull back the sheet to find more gauze bandaging wrapped around his left thigh.

He grunts in response, his mouth full.

I slide my hand over the curves of his healthy leg in a soothing manner. Such strong, thick muscles.

Rowen's leg was just as sturdy.

"What's going to happen now? With Aengus?" I watch him chew slowly, and I'm not sure if it's a deliberate tactic to stall.

"He confessed," he finally admits through a mouthful, his eyes downcast.

My jaw drops. "What? How? I mean . . ." I hadn't expected that answer. "What made him do it?"

Swallowing, he tosses the last bit of crust onto the plate and washes it down with water, chasing it with the pills I set out for him. "He didn't have much choice. Either he confessed to Duffy or I'd testify against him in court as an eyewitness."

"You said that you'd never do that."

"I know." He toys with the compass charm that dangles from my bracelet. "I never thought I would. But after what he's put my ma and da, and Rowen, through . . ." His fingers lace through mine. "Protecting him was going to further harm my family. Harm you. I couldn't live with myself if that happened and I could have done something to stop it. As it is, none of this would have happened if I'd spoken up sooner." His Adam's apple bobs with a hard swallow, and a sheen suddenly coats his eyes. "I'm already not sure how I'm going to forgive myself for that."

"Don't blame yourself. It's not your fault." I curl into his side, careful to avoid his injuries. "So Aengus would rather confess than have you put him in prison?"

"The IRA doesn't take too kindly to people testifying against them. Despite all the bad decisions that Aengus has made, he has always protected me when it's counted. I was counting on him to do it again."

There is a shred of good in that guy after all, I guess. "So, he's going to prison."

River nods.

"And you're safe?"

"I'm safe." He lifts my chin up until I can see his eyes. "And you're safe. No one's going to stop you from staying in Ireland for as long as you want to stay." Unspoken words linger between us.

How long does River want me to stay?

How long do *I* want to stay? Never in a million years would I ever have thought I'd actually be even considering questions like this. I've known River for a week. A week!

The single most memorable week of my entire life.

"Well, immigration might have a problem with me staying for too long," I joke, because I don't know what else to say.

So would my parents.

But what do *I* want?

THIRTY-THREE

RIVER

"It's all rubbish now." Ma lets go of the charred piece of paper, once a signed picture of Michael Collins, now worthless. It floats and lands on a tabletop by her feet. The table's body is elsewhere.

The inside of Delaney's is one giant heap of rubble. Pint glasses and liquor bottles shattered, splintered sticks where stools used to be, the fine dark wood blackened and punctured by nails and bits of metal. Two hundred years of our family history, which survived a famine, wars, and an entire revolution, destroyed within seconds.

And in the middle of it all stand my parents.

This may have been "tit-for-tat," but there's no mistaking that the bomb Beznick's men set in here was meant to kill.

"Have you called the insurance company yet?" I set down the box of receipts and other valuable paperwork that I just collected from the office. Close the door to the back and you'd never imagine that anything was wrong up front. Even Rowen's runners still hang from the laces on the wall.

I guess he won't be needing one of those anymore.

He also won't be running ever again.

Da leans against his cane, his stature bent. "They'll be in as soon as the gardai finish with it." He looks like he's aged ten years since yesterday. Ma says they didn't get to bed until well after midnight last night and were back at the hospital this morning, in time to see Rowen finally wake up.

"The back of the pub is fine, at least."

"I reckon, in a building this old, they're going to condemn it anyway and make us rebuild. It'll never be the same." He sighs. "Come on, we don't have long before they chase us out of here. We're lucky they let us in at all."

"It's our bloody pub!" Ma protests, never a fan of the police. Today, fueled by emotion, she's tenfold worse.

"It's for our own safety, Marion," Da mutters, nudging the remains of the grandfather clock with the end of his cane.

"Should we try to bring that with us?" Amber offers. "We may be able to get it fixed."

Da smiles at her, his tone softening instantly. "It's full of glass, lovey. I wouldn't want ya cutting those healing hands of yours."

She nods, that tiny frown line between her eyes appearing. "I really loved your pub. I'm so sorry this happened to you."

I reach over to pull her into me, her back to my chest, folding my arms around her.

Ma eyes us, pursing her lips tightly. I know what she's thinking—that I'm just going to get my heart broken. "We've survived worse. We'll survive this just fine."

Voices sound beyond the gaping hole where the door used to be. I don't know if it met its demise from the blast or the emergency crew who cut in here to rescue us.

"That's still a crime scene, sir! We haven't released it yet."

"But my daughter's in there," a gruff American voice answers.

Amber's body goes rigid within my arms.

THIRTY-FOUR

AMBER

"Dad?"

I blink several times, thinking my eyes are playing tricks on me, just like my ears may have a moment ago.

They're not.

Sheriff Gabe Welles, in his standard-issue blue jeans and plaid button-down—this one cotton and short-sleeved—is standing in the gaping hole where the door used to be, staring at me.

"Amber." I can't get a read on his tone—there's a hint of reproach, but more, I think it's just relief.

River's arms release me from their embrace, freeing me to scramble around the debris and fall against my father's chest, the knot that has suddenly sprung in my throat large and prickly. He pulls me into him tightly, the way I remember him doing years ago, when I was a little girl and he'd say that he'd had a really hard day. He smells the same now that he did back then—a mix of Irish Spring soap and Old Spice cologne.

I've missed him so much.

"Dad, what are you doing here?"

"Ivy called Alex and told her that you needed me right away. She said you were in some sort of trouble."

"*Ivy* did?"

"Yeah. That little graffiti artist I almost arrested once," he says, a smile barely touching his lips. "She even picked me up from the airport. I left her back there, behind the tape. I think she's hiding from you, actually."

I can't believe she called for my father. "What did she tell you?"

"Not much." His gaze scans the destruction. "Not nearly enough . . . clearly."

"But . . . I don't . . ." I'm stumbling over my words, still in shock. "You don't even have a passport!"

"You think I'd let you out of our country with no way of reaching you?" He smirks. "I applied for one the day after you booked all those flights. Just in case."

I shake my head at him. "Always two steps ahead."

His eyes settle on River. "Not always." I sense his demeanor shift, from loving father to suspicious law enforcement officer. I'm sure it's imperceptible to anyone else.

"Dad . . ." I warn, as River limps over.

"Sir. I'm River. Amber's told me a lot about ya."

"Has she, now . . . *River.*" I feel his sideways glare but I ignore it. Finally he shakes River's extended hand. "Gabe Welles."

"This is my mother, Marion."

Marion steps forward, wiping her hands against her blouse before taking Dad's hand. "Pleasure."

"And this is my father, Seamus."

Dad, seeing the cane, takes quick steps forward to reach Seamus.

"You have a lovely daughter. Ya must be very proud."

"We'll see," I hear my dad mutter under his breath, too low for anyone else to hear.

"Seamus, let me drive you back to the house so you can rest. There's nothing more we can do here for now." Marion hooks an arm through his and the two of them begin working their way around the rubble toward the entrance.

"You going to the hospital, Ma?" River asks.

"As soon as I drop your da off. They should have moved Rowen into a proper room by now." She doesn't mention a word about Aengus in front of Seamus, though we all know she'll take the opportunity away from River's dad to duck in to see his eldest, too. Which means she'll finally see the gardai stationed by the door, waiting until Aengus is well enough to be released into their custody.

She doesn't know that he confessed to the bombing yet.

River and I share a look. "I should be there for this," River whispers. "She's likely to take a swing at them."

"Of course. Dad, you're staying with me, right?"

"After what I just paid for a last-minute one-way ticket here? Yeah. I'm staying with you. I could use a meal and a nap soon. I feel like I haven't slept in days."

I smile. There was a time when his car would roll out the driveway before daybreak, and not roll back in until well after dark. His lifestyle has definitely changed since last fall. On a few occasions, I've caught him snoring on the couch in the afternoon. "Okay. I'll meet you outside in a minute."

Dad's gaze shifts from me to River and back. "Don't be long. I'm afraid that friend of yours is going to ditch my bags on the side of the street and take off."

I chuckle. "Ivy wouldn't do that. I think she's still afraid of you."

"Hmm." That seems to please him. I hear a mutter of "Maybe I've still got it" as he leaves.

River's arm ropes around my waist. "You seriously had no idea he was coming?"

"I can't believe she called him!" She must have done it the second they arrested me, which was just around the time the thought to call my father was going through my head. I smile. "She just did what I've always done. Call my dad. He always knows how to fix things."

"But you're in the clear, so what exactly are you going to tell him now? That she made a mistake?"

"I can't lie to him, River. He'll know."

"I know. I just . . ." He groans. "I'd like him to not hate me for at least a day."

I reach on my tiptoes to kiss him softly on the mouth. "How could he possibly hate you?"

"Now you're lying to me."

"You're right. I am." I chuckle. "Don't worry. I'll think of something."

■ ■ ■

"You certainly haven't been suffering," Dad mutters. Ivy and I hang back as he strolls through the main floor of Simon's house.

"I'm sorry," Ivy hisses, "but they arrested you! It looked bad and I didn't know what else to do. By the time you texted me last night, it was too late. He was already on his way."

"It's okay. I get why you called him. I'm not mad. But you didn't think to warn me?"

A rare, sheepish look passes over her face. "Yeah . . . I thought about it."

Dad nudges River's duffel bag in the living room with his boot—I meant to move that upstairs—and his brow tightens, but he says nothing.

"He said it was an open-ended ticket?" Ivy asks.

"Yeah. What exactly did you tell him?"

"I'm not deaf," he calls out, sizing up the bottle of Jameson that Rowen left here. "She didn't tell me a damn thing. Kept pleading the Fifth, despite my best interrogation tactics."

"And on that note . . ." Ivy slips out the door, leaving me to deal with Gabe Welles all on my own.

"So?" I wander toward the kitchen. "What do you want to eat? I have cold cuts and cheese, fruit . . ." I open the freezer. ". . .veggie burgers . . ." I don't have to turn around to know that he's rolling his eyes at that. "A lasagna?"

"Meat or vegetarian?"

Mom being a surgeon and a terrible cook, most of our meals growing up were frozen, pre-made grocery store finds. She'd buy a lot of vegetarian things, even though none of us were vegetarian. It drove Dad nuts, and he'd grumble about it, but in the end, he'd shut up and eat it. The first thing that changed when he retired was that he started doing all the grocery shopping. I haven't seen a vegetarian casserole in our house in the better part of a year.

"Meat . . . if saying that will make you eat it."

"You're too much like your mother in some ways."

"And too much like you in others," I retort, punching buttons until the oven preheat lights come on. "It's going to take an hour to bake. Can you make it that long, or should we go out to eat?"

"Nope." Flipping through three cupboards before finding the glassware, he pulls two glasses out and pours each to a third full with the amber liquid. He never drinks hard liquor. "Neither of us are leaving this kitchen until you explain why you were arrested."

My stomach drops. "How did you—"

"Told you, I'm not deaf. Besides, Ivy promised you weren't hurt, but you were in trouble. It wasn't hard to put two and two together." He sets both tumblers on the kitchen table, drags the chairs out, and sits. "Let's hear it, from the beginning. And I want to know exactly how this guy is involved, because I'm guessing he's at the center of it."

Crap. Dad's never been one for delays, so I shouldn't be at all surprised.

"So?"

I pour the whiskey back, grimacing at the unpleasant burn. It's not nearly as unpleasant as this conversation is going to be. "Remember that bombing last week?"

■ ■ ■

"It's not that bad, actually." I scoop a mouthful in. "A bit too much salt, but the sauce is good."

Dad twirls his fork in his hand absently. "The IRA, Amber. I ought to drag you to the airport right now."

"See? This is why I lied in the first place."

His answering glare is full of exasperation. "And now you're actually carrying on with this . . . *River*. What kind of name is that anyway? Doesn't sound Irish."

"I like it, actually. It suits him."

He snorts. "What's his middle name? Twigs? Bog?"

I roll my eyes. Dad's sarcastic side can be pretty predictable.

"He saved my life, Dad. If it hadn't been for River, you would have been flying here anyway, only it'd be to visit me in the hospital or collect my body."

The cords in his neck tense. "Because of his brother."

"Yes, *his brother*. Not River. He had nothing to do with it or with those people. Condemning him would be like condemning me for that mess with Jesse and Alex. You know . . . the one that cost you your job?"

"My choices are what cost me my job," he mumbles. "I can't blame Jesse for that."

"Yeah, so Alex told me . . . finally," I say softly. "I know what you did, Dad."

His gaze flashes to me. "I'm not proud of what I did but, to be clear, it was the best way to protect everyone under the circumstances."

"How do you know that?"

"I just do. And we're not talking about me here. We're talking about you, and what is going on here in Ireland. I know you're twenty-five years old and I can't dictate what you do anymore, but your mother and I raised you to be better than this. Just associating with this family is a bad idea, Amber. Look what's happened since that bombing. You've been arrested for lying to a police officer!"

"You lied to an entire police organization," I remind him. "And a judge. And Mom, for a while."

He purses his lips. I'm guessing Alex is going to get an earful when Dad makes it home. "Well, you're damn lucky that detective isn't pressing charges. I should go down there and kiss his ass. And do you realize that you could just as easily have been in that pub when it got bombed?"

"I know," I say quietly. Had I not decided to go to Cork, I likely would have. I would have met the infamous Aengus Delaney, looked the asshole right in the eye, perhaps shared a pint with him.

And then who knows? I could have ended up like Rowen. Or worse.

Dad pours himself another whiskey. "You know, since Jesse

finally settled down and started using his head, I thought I could finally relax. I thought our family was past this sort of thing. I never thought you'd do something so stup—" He cuts himself off, and then, in a slightly softer voice that screams of disappointment, he finishes off with, "so dangerous."

"Neither did I," I admit. His words burn, but not nearly as much as they might have in the past. "But it was the best way to protect everyone."

He heaves a sigh, shaking his head to himself. "How do you know?" He parrots me, just as I did to him.

I rest my chin on his shoulder. "I just do."

He chews his food in silence for a few moments, before asking, "So are you going to come home with me?"

I shake my head.

"I didn't think so," he grumbles. "Leaving here on Sunday?"

"I changed my flight this morning. I'm staying in Ireland for another week, at least."

"And then?"

"And then I don't know." I hope I find my answer soon, though. "I'm taking it one day at a time, like I have every day since I arrived here."

He stabs at his food with his fork. "This thing you have with him is doomed, Amber. You do realize that, right? That boy'll never *not* be a criminal."

"I do realize what he is."

"He'll never step foot in our home."

"I know that, too."

"And Dublin is 4,682 miles away from Sisters. I Googled it."

I smile, sadly. "I really care about him. 4,682 times more than I ever cared about Aaron, or Brody, or even Neil. In a different way. A deeper way."

I can see the frustration in his face as he mentally runs back through the obstacles to this relationship that he just presented. All of them are valid. That frustration is followed by a flash of realization, and then fear.

"You are *not* actually thinking of staying here. That's just . . . You can't do that, Amber! You have a career and a family in Oregon. A life! You can't just blow that off for some guy you've known for a minute!" Each word comes out faster, louder, laced with more panic. "That'd be just about the dumbest thing—"

"Dad!" I cut him off with a yell, but follow it up with a pat on his arm and a smile. "You're not saying anything to me that I haven't already thought about. You raised me well. Now you need to trust that I'll do the right thing for *me*." I have an envelope's worth of plane tickets to countries I've dreamed of visiting and yet I've been watching the clock on the wall, anxiously waiting for River to come back. Leaving Ireland doesn't sound at all appealing to me, and yet ditching all of my plans doesn't, either.

There has to be some other answer.

He heaves a sigh that turns into a monstrous yawn. He's exhausted, but too stubborn to turn in just yet. "Just do me a favor . . . please."

"What?" I ask with hesitation.

"Get on a plane and fly somewhere—anywhere away from here and *him*."

I open my mouth to protest but he cuts me off with a raised hand.

"No. Just listen to me. I get it, okay? You care about him, a lot. I'm not going to try to change how you feel. God knows I won't get anywhere with that. The boy did save your life after all. That's bound to create a strong connection. But, sometimes people need some time and space to think clearly. You're one of those people, Amber. Despite what you've been through and all these changes you may feel going on in your life right now, you're not suddenly going to become this spontaneous, fly-by-the-seat-of-her-pants girl who wanders through life 'one day at a time.'"

I hate it when he uses my own words against me.

"You've always thrived on thinking through your options, and that's not going to change. It's in your core, it's who you are, and there's absolutely nothing wrong with that, hon. I think you'll feel better with whatever decision you make *after* you've given yourself some time and space to weigh things out. I know *I'll* feel better about it."

He's right, of course. It's who Amber Welles is, at heart, no matter what's happened since coming here.

It's my current.

It's the only way I'll know what I want in the long run. It's the only way I won't wonder if I'm doing the right thing.

"You'll be happy with whatever decision I make?"

He snorts. "I did not say that. Just to be clear, I think that even having this conversation is insane. I'm not even sure who I'm talking to right now. But I'm hoping the level-headed daughter I raised will come back to me soon enough."

I plant a kiss on his cheek. "You know, that's not the worst idea you've ever had."

"I only have brilliant ideas. Like, right now, for example?" He stifles another yawn. "I have this brilliant idea to take a nap."

"A nap?"

He ruffles my hair. "A nap. We can talk some more in a few hours, if you want."

I smile, remembering how hard it was to adjust to the time zone difference. I watch him sling his duffel bag over his weary shoulders and head for the stairs. "See you tomorrow."

"Just a few hours! Which room is mine?"

"Take the one on the top floor." I'd rather not have my dad sleeping in the room directly beside us.

"I take it Stream will be staying here tonight?"

"*Dad* . . ."

Whatever he mutters under his breath, I can't understand it. Probably for the best.

THIRTY-FIVE

RIVER

The air is thicker in this little hospital room than elsewhere.

Or maybe it's that seeing my brother—his body basically mummified in gauze, with an IV drip full of morphine needed to numb his pain, and his usual perma-grin lost—is making it hard for me to breathe.

The chair legs scrape against the linoleum floor as I drag it closer.

Rowen's eyes open and shift to catch mine. "Have they arrested Ma yet?" he croaks.

I chuckle, despite everything. Breaking the news about Aengus and his looming incarceration to her wasn't easy but it was unavoidable, seeing as the second she saw the garda outside his door, she went off on him, accusing them of being "a little too late with the protection." "She's in the cafeteria, getting something to eat. She'll be back in a bit."

"I could hear her yelling."

"I don't doubt it." I pause to study the bandaged stump lying across the hospital bed. "What does it feel like?"

"Like I still have a leg." His listless eyes stare up at the ceiling. "Though I can't feel much with all these drugs, thank Christ. You should see the nurse that just popped her head in while you were gone." A lazy smirk lifts the right side of his mouth. "Do you think she'll give me a sponge bath if I ask?"

I shake my head. At least Rowen's spirit wasn't blown apart

with his body. He's always been one to make the best of any situation. I can't say I'd be making jokes right now, if I were in his place. And I deserve to be, more so than Rowen does. This shouldn't have happened to him. If I'd just listened to Amber in the first place and talked to Duffy, he'd still have his leg and Delaney's wouldn't be a pile of firewood.

That hard marble that lodged in my throat three hours ago, when Ma and I first walked in here, suddenly expands. I hang my head, unable to stop the tear that slips out from the corner of my eye. "I'm so sorry, Rowen."

Silence falls over the room.

Finally he sighs, and says in a rare somber voice, rank with emotion, "This is all on Aengus. Not you, not anyone else." When I look up, I find a matching drop rolling down his cheek. It only spurs on more of my own.

I wipe them away with my knuckles. He doesn't need me here, crying. Ma's done enough of that. "You're going to get better. We'll get you fitted with a leg. You'll be walking around and pouring pints again in no time." I hope the doctors are wrong about the nerve damage. I don't know if I can handle seeing Rowen in the kind of pain that our da has suffered all these years. "I'll talk to your school tomorrow."

"Was Ma being realistic about the pub being open again in a month or two?"

I sigh. And shake my head. "You know how slow insurance companies move."

"What are they going to do for money? How are they going to—"

"They'll be fine. Besides, that's not for you to worry about. You just worry about getting better and getting out of here. Ma will have your old room ready for ya."

He groans. "Bloody hell. She'll be trying to wipe me own arse, won't she?"

I start to laugh. Because he's right. "For a while. Then you'll be strong enough to come back to Dublin. At least we don't have to sell the house anymore." With Aengus heading to prison, the need to move away from him isn't there. By the time he gets out—if he makes it out of there alive—we'll likely be living elsewhere anyway.

"I heard you and Ma talking outside the door. Did he really confess to that bombing?" Aengus has never been one to own up to his mistakes, so I can understand the doubt in Rowen's voice.

"Yeah. I didn't give him much choice."

"What's going to happen to him?"

"Nothing that wouldn't have happened to him eventually." As much as I dread the day we get the phone call from Portlaoise informing us that we need to be planning for a funeral, at least we're not going to get caught in the line of fire again.

"I guess. I just . . ." Rowen's eyelids begin sticking together. He hasn't been conscious for more than half an hour at a time.

I ease out of my chair, gritting against the throb in my thigh. I have no right to moan about anything next to Rowen. "I'm heading back to Amber's now. I'll be here in the morning."

"Going to spend some quality time with your future father-in-law?"

Now it's my turn to groan. The second those sharp, near-black eyes of his settled on me earlier today, I knew he'd already made a decision, and it wouldn't be a favorable one for me. That was *before* Amber told him why he had to jump on a plane and fly across an ocean.

I'm actually dreading this. Part of me thinks I should just head home for the night. If I weren't so desperate to see Amber, I would.

"I'll save you a bed next to me. I'm sure you'll . . ." His words drift off.

"Get some rest, brother." I shut the door quietly behind me and head down the hall, around the corner. The garda standing outside Aengus's room recognizes me and nods once, his gaze darting behind me. Probably wondering if he'll need to restrain Marion Delaney again. I slow just long enough to peer through the window in the door, to see Aengus lying in his bed, his eyes closed. His wrist handcuffed to the bedrail.

"Have a good night," I offer to the garda.

And then I keep going.

■ ■ ■

"Hey . . ." Amber slips her arms around my waist, giving me a sleepy-eyed smile. The house smells like garlic and tomato sauce. Dirtied plates wait to be cleaned from the dining table, along with two glasses and the bottle of Jameson.

But there's no sheriff in sight.

"Relax. He went to bed already."

My entire body caves with relief. Amber starts laughing.

"Quiet!" I silence her with a deep kiss. "You'll wake him up."

"He's a deep sleeper." She reaches up to brush my hair off my face, the glimmer from a moment ago replaced with sadness. "How's Rowen?"

"He looks rough, but . . . he'll pull through."

She nods, blinking away the gloss that suddenly coats her eyes. "I want to go with you tomorrow to see him. Maybe I can get Ivy to come, too."

"I think he'd like that." Most fellas wouldn't want visitors right now, but Rowen isn't like most. "So? How was tonight? Has your da booked you a flight home for tomorrow?"

"He may have suggested it once or twice." A strange, somber look flashes across her face, but it dissolves with her smile. She slips her hands into mine and begins leading me in with backward steps. "It was fine. I mean, he's not happy about it all, but I didn't expect him to be. You hungry?"

"I could eat." Being in that hospital room with Rowen didn't inspire my appetite but now that I'm out, I'm famished.

She frowns at my limp. With everything else going on today, I forgot to bring my painkillers with me. "Go on upstairs. I want to take a look at that leg. I'll bring dinner to you."

I can't help the wary glance up at the landing.

"Oh, for God's sake. He's not waiting in a dark corner for you. Besides, he's on the third floor." She wanders over to the casserole sitting on top of the stove, grabbing a plate on her way.

"So, I'll be taking the spare room next to yours?"

Her exasperated sigh answers me. "I don't believe it. You spent eighteen months in prison with the worst criminals in Ireland and you're terrified of my father. Go on. I'll be up there in a minute." She shakes her head as she putters around the kitchen, grabbing my painkillers from the windowsill, filling a glass of water.

A little smirk on her face the entire time.

"Go on." She slaps my arse once as she passes me on the stairs and I watch her climb, wanting so desperately to return the favor. After the past two days, I could use the pure ecstasy that comes with being inside Amber. That's not going to happen tonight, though. For one thing, because I physically can't, and for another, because I'm sure, deep sleeper or not, that her sheriff father would finish the job that Jackie Hanegan failed to do, should he hear it.

I happily follow Amber's orders, undressing and lying in bed so she can tend to me. I watch her skilled hands go to work on my thigh, gently washing the area around the stitches and re-covering it with fresh bandages. She doesn't even flinch at the sight of it, and even I'll admit that it's grotesque. Enough that I can't touch my dinner while she's doing it.

"You're all set." She looks up to catch me looking down her tank top, the thin cotton leaving little to the imagination. Neither do my knickers, at the moment. A secretive smile flashes across her wide, full lips. And then those skillful hands of hers shift upward, to peel the waistband down and over my erection, so gently.

"You don't have to . . ." My words and all resolve are lost the second I feel her hot breath. I weave my fingers through her thick hair as I watch her, allowing myself a brief moment to forget everything else and just enjoy this time with her. To revel in the fact that this beautiful creature still wants me.

She just feels too good—better than any other girl has, and I've had my share of well-practiced ones—and I don't last long, covering my face with a pillow to smother the sounds of my release.

■ ■ ■

I haven't tiptoed down a set of stairs since I was eighteen and sneaking out of Marjorie Gilbert's bedroom with her parents sitting at the kitchen table, sipping on their morning coffee.

The difference is that Amber's father knows I'm here and it's three o'clock in the morning. I'm just hoping that I can fill my glass of water and limp my way back with him completely unaware.

My hopes are dashed when I hear the bottom step creak.

"River." Even in the unlit kitchen, I can clearly see his dark, annoyed eyes skate over me. In hindsight, I probably should have thrown some clothes on over my knickers.

"Hello . . .uh . . ."

"Gabe. Call me Gabe," he says smoothly.

I clear my throat. "Right. Gabe." Amber's right to laugh at me. I've faced murderers and rapists, and yet this calm, collected, honest man, with his clothes rumpled and his short hair standing on end, unnerves me far more than any of them ever did. I lay in bed next to her for a while tonight, trying to figure out exactly why. Finally, I think I found the answer. It's because I can tell that Amber values his opinion highly, and I'm guessing she makes most of her decisions based on what she thinks her father would approve of.

Whatever I'm imagining his opinion of me is, in reality, it's probably worse.

He walks over to open the refrigerator, his fingers strumming against the door as he surveys its contents. "How's the leg?"

"Sore, but I'll be fine."

He nods, pulling out some sliced ham and bread. "Amber mentioned your brother being in pretty bad shape."

"He'll pull through. He's strong."

"And your other brother?" There's no missing the contempt in his voice. The "other brother" who nearly killed his daughter.

"He'll have plenty of time to heal in prison."

"I gathered that."

I watch Gabe as he quietly fixes himself a sandwich, until I have to assume the conversation is over. "Have a good night."

His gruff voice stops my feet. "You know . . . my stomach was in knots the entire flight over. I didn't sleep at all, not since Alex woke me up yesterday to tell me that Amber was in trouble." He frowns. "Or was it the day before yesterday . . . ? Anyway, as exhausted as I was, I fell asleep as soon as my head hit the pillow tonight. But my mind didn't stop spinning. I saw Amber in handcuffs, in prison . . . lying in the debris at that bar of yours . . . all these horrible, awful things that *could* have happened to my daughter while she was here. With you."

I hold my breath, preparing myself for the condemnation. The "stay the hell away from Amber or I'll kill you" warning. I wonder if he'll give it to me straight up or veil it somehow, to sound more civilized.

"A week ago, when she ran through that park, she *would have* been hurt, or worse. Not *could have. Would have*, had it not been for you. I think my brain finally picked up on that critical part because suddenly I woke up." He stares out the kitchen window, simply holding the sandwich in one hand, not eating it. "Thank you. For what you did that day. I'll always owe you for that."

I nod. And then realize that he can't hear that, so I add, "I'm just glad I was there."

"So am I." He takes a bite of his sandwich. "Get some rest."

"You too." I make a move to head back upstairs.

"And River?"

"Yeah?"

Gabe finally turns and meets my eyes. "You'll never be good enough for my daughter."

I don't know if he's saying that to discourage me or to hurt me. Or challenge me. Or maybe he's just stating the obvious. He's right, though, and I'm glad he sees it, because it means he's good enough to be her father.

I smile. "But I'll never stop trying to be."

He pauses, something unreadable flickering across his face before it smooths over. "Good night."

THIRTY-SIX

AMBER

"You sure you don't want to stay a few more days?" I shut River's trunk—every time he calls it his boot, I giggle—and watch my dad sling his duffel bag over his shoulder.

"Your mother says she needs me back home."

"Is that what you heard? Because I swear I heard something *completely* different. How peaceful the house is and how clean the kitchen is . . ."

"Alright, alright." He hooks an arm around my neck and pulls me into his side. "Besides, the longer I stay here, the longer *you'll* stay here." His gaze drifts over to River, who's standing quietly by his car in the airport drop-off lane. He drops his voice. "Don't forget what I said, okay?"

I force my smile. *Get on a plane and leave River behind.* "I haven't forgotten, believe me."

"If it's meant to work out, then it will." He plants a kiss on my forehead. "Thanks for sacrificing a few days for your ol' dad. I had fun." Nothing about his tone suggests that's true, but that's just him. We spent more time together in the last four days than we have since Jesse and I were nine and we went camping for a week. Aside from the odd bickering—River can't believe how similar the two of us sound sometimes—I found myself laughing a lot more than I usually do with him. Something's changed between my father and me, a subtle shift in how I see him, and maybe in how he sees me. I'm guessing the last two weeks and the revelations they've brought has played a big role in that.

"Thanks for going easy on him." River gave us our space, spending most of his time with Rowen and his parents, but he did venture out for a few pints.

Dad grunts in response, though I can tell he's warmed up to River. Not to the idea of me and River, but . . .

"So, when will you be home, again? Beginning of September?"

The realistic answer to that would be "yes," but saying it now feels like I'm promising him that I will be. And I'm not entirely sure anymore. "Go on, you're going to miss your plane."

He sighs. "Right." Strolling over to River, they clasp hands. "Keep her out of any more trouble while she's here."

"Definitely," River promises somberly, standing tall. "It was a pleasure to meet you." Unless my dad finds himself back in Ireland, he's not likely to ever see River again.

Dad presses his lips together and then nods. "Take care of yourself, and your family. Tell your mother that she makes a mean stew."

River grins. "She'll be happy to hear that."

"Well, alright then." With one last nod my way, sparking a wave of emotion that brings tears to my eyes, my dad disappears into the Dublin airport.

River wraps his arms around my shoulders, pulling my back into his chest. I revel in his warmth. As much as I loved having my father here, it meant less time doing this with River. I've desperately missed it.

I don't know how I'm going to leave him, but I know that I'll have to at some point.

"So?" He rests his chin on top of my head. "What now?"

■ ■ ■

"Where did you say you found this place, again?" River's amazed gaze drifts first over the stone cottage, and then to the bay beyond, a sea of crisp blue waters as far as my eyes stretch.

"Online. One of those private home rental places. It had really good ratings and we lucked out because they had a cancellation." I haven't stopped grinning since River turned his car into the gravel driveway. He knew we were going to the Cliffs of Moher—like we had planned—but this was a surprise. "Apparently it was rebuilt about twenty-five years ago, using the stones from the original cottage, which was abandoned during the Great Famine in the mid–eighteen hundreds. Have you heard of it?"

He grins, sliding the bags from my grip and planting a kiss on my lips. "Look at you, Miss Know-It-All." I trail behind him as he limps past the thick border of brambly bushes and wildflowers and to a fuchsia door, the renter's key dangling from his fingertips.

Inside, the Irish seaside charm only multiplies, the expansive, open living space filled with oak and pine furniture and plenty of kitschy antiques. A massive, double-sided fireplace stands like a pillar in the center of the cottage, opening up to both a cozy sitting area and rustic dining room. Even the dated pastel blue floral couches and the pink cushions—décor that would belong in my late grandparents' homes—are something to be admired here. "This is perfect. Exactly what I wanted."

A quiet, peaceful place for just River and me after so much turmoil.

Upstairs, we wander through four bedrooms, each with two single beds sitting side-by-side. "The sleeping arrangements are the only weird thing," I murmur, dragging a nightstand out of the way, in a room that overlooks the Atlantic. That's the view I want to wake up to with River every day for the next four days. "But I figured we could just reorganize things . . ." I lean forward to push one of the beds over.

And find myself sprawled out on top, thanks to a playful push from River.

He chases my laughs away with a deep, all-consuming kiss.

■ ■ ■

"I think I could live here," I murmur absently, staring out over the purple-and-pink dusk sky and vast expanse of water from our grassy perch atop the cliffs, as we've done for the past four nights. River sits at my back, our bodies guarded against the crisp evening air by heavy wool blankets.

I feel him tense; I hear the hard swallow. Since that night when he begged me to stay in Ireland, before Delaney's was attacked, the topic of me leaving has sat in the middle of every room like a giant white elephant. It's our last night here. I don't think we can avoid talking about it much longer.

Before we left for this cottage, I had to make a choice. I'd already cancelled my trip to England, but there was another flight looming: the one that was supposed to carry me from London to Madrid in a week's time.

So I rearranged my ticket to fly me from Dublin to Spain's capital. The plane leaves tomorrow night. I know it's the right decision, I know that my father is right and I need to remove myself from this situation for a while to be sure I'm thinking clearly, but it pains me all the same.

River heard me on the phone with the airline, making the arrangements. He hid his disappointment behind a smile, but I saw it all the same.

I turn back to lay a soft kiss on his jawline. "So? What's your plan?"

He inhales deeply. "Rowen should be out in another week or two. I'll spend some time with him in Dundalk. Make sure Ma doesn't drive him mad. Then, I don't know. Perhaps take some classes."

"Really?" When we talked about college last time, he didn't sound at all interested in it. I'm glad to see that maybe he is.

A sheepish smile fills his handsome face. "When I went to talk to the college office about Rowen, I saw some flyers for part-time courses. Business and computers and whatnot. I figure that could be useful to me, for running the pub."

"Learning how to use basic technology? You're right, it could be." I giggle with the memory of trying to teach River how to use Skype on his Samsung. My amusement earns me a few sharp but ticklish pokes to my ribs. "What else are you going to keep yourself busy with?" It's going to be a while before he's slinging pints and charming customers again.

He scoops my hair back into a ponytail, pushing it off to the side, giving his mouth access to my neck, which he happily takes. "Figured I'd work on the house. Strip that peeling wallpaper, give the walls a fresh coat of paint. Maybe by then we can start looking at rebuilding the pub. Da thinks the insurance should come through sooner rather than later, seeing as they found enough evidence to arrest and charge that bastard who tried to kill us."

Just the suggestion in his words makes my stomach tighten. "Where do you think he'll end up?"

"Likely Portlaoise."

"And Aengus?"

"Same." He sighs, that perpetual cloud that comes with any mention of his older brother rolling in. "That should keep the guards busy."

I wonder what will become of Aengus. Whether he'll even survive, or if River is right and he's simply living on borrowed time. I don't really care, but I know it'll hurt River if something happens, and I can't bear the idea of that.

I weave my fingers through his. "Have you looked into a passport at all?"

"I did. We'll see what happens. It could take a while." He doesn't sound hopeful.

We sit in silence as the sun slowly descends along the horizon. I know that a mesmerizing blanket of stars waits in the wings for darkness. It reminds me of back home and years of lying across the hood of a car, taking in the vast night sky. A home that is not only thousands of miles away but now feels like light-years in the past. I don't know how I'm simply supposed to go back to it. And what? Pretend that this amazing thing didn't happen? That River doesn't exist? Or just chalk it up to a life experience? I may still be Amber Welles to my core, but my life has been irrevocably changed by this man and I can't pretend otherwise.

"So . . . what's the plan again? Spain, then France, and then Italy, is it?" he asks softly.

A lump forms deep in my throat. The last thing I want to be doing is talking about all the places where I'll be without River. "You'd better respond to my texts. Whenever I message you, you drop everything."

"So ya want me at your beck and call, basically?"

I nuzzle against his neck, the scruff from his chin scratching against my nose. "Not basically. Exactly."

He chuckles, but it's a heavy sound. "You could save yourself the hassle and just stay here. You can have me whenever you want, in the flesh."

There it is. I know he's not trying to make me feel guilty, but my tears begin streaming all the same. "It's just something I need to do. For me. I'm sorry."

"I know. You can't think straight when you're around me. It's the same way I am with you." His arms tighten around me. "But don't worry. You'll see that you're meant to be here soon enough."

I laugh, even as I cry. "You sound so sure."

"I *am* sure. Which reminds me . . ." River shifts behind me. There's just enough light to recognize Alex's handwriting on the creased piece of paper he holds out.

I snatch it from his grip, laughing as I scan over the lines again. How had I forgotten about this?

He produces a pen almost magically. "See anything you want to check off?"

"Number twelve, definitely. And thirty-two."

"Anything else?"

I stare at that first line and swallow.

1. Have a torrid affair with a foreigner. Country: TBD.

It was a joke when Alex wrote it down, a tease for River when he discovered it, and a secret wish for me in those first days with him. And yet now that I read it again—after what we've been through in such a short time—it feels wrong to think of what we had, or have, as nothing more than a torrid affair.

That makes it sound like it's already over.

"No."

"So . . . you're keeping that one open?"

The very idea of being with another guy makes me ill. I drag the tip of the pen through number one.

I shiver at the feel of his hot breath against my ear. "I took the liberty of adding a line. Hope you don't mind."

"Really?" I flip the page and see the new handwriting at the bottom.

My heart stutters.

THIRTY-SEVEN

AMBER

Sweat trickles down the nape of my neck as I climb the uneven stone steps, dragging my suitcase along behind me. I think the wheels may snap off at any moment, which will make the many days of travel ahead that much more difficult. It's been quite the production to get here as it is, two trains and six hours later.

It's worth it, though, I surmise, taking in the sand-colored caves ahead of me. It was a pure fluke that I stumbled upon this place over a year ago—an incorrect Google search that led me to a travel blog for the south of Italy. It was there that I found Sextantio le Grotte della Civita, a series of prehistoric caves that have been transformed into a boutique hotel just outside of Matera, not far from the Adriatic Sea. As soon as I saw the pictures of the candlelit rooms and the honeycombed walls, I knew I had to splurge, even if only for one night.

Still, I'm sweaty and tired and covered in a layer of travel dust. My hair is sticking to my skin. All I want right now is a long soak in my bathtub with the balcony doors kicked wide open.

The patient, smiling receptionist inside the rustic entryway—an almost ethereal woman with crystal-blue eyes and thick, shiny raven hair cascading down her back—checks me into my cave, one of only eighteen, which I reserved a year ago and thankfully didn't cancel, back when I was with Aaron and willing to give up this life-changing experience.

Finally, I step into my room. I push my battered suitcase to the side and toss my purse on the bed, relishing the temperature change in here as compared to the scorching midday sun outside. It's as picturesque as the hotel's website promised, the view of the mountains beyond the balcony even more so.

I sigh, soaking it all in.

Wishing, for the thousandth time, that River were here with me, just as I wished he were there with me to stand in awe of the majestic Sagrada Familia in Barcelona, and to smell the potent lavender fields in Provence, and to experience the countless wonders in between. All that I've done since he kissed me goodbye at the Dublin airport almost three weeks ago, I've done with every intention of enjoying. And I *have* enjoyed my time.

But River hasn't left my mind or my heart through all of it.

Each day I wonder if I've made the right decision by leaving Ireland. If I will one day regret not choosing him instead.

Maybe it's because I won't stop texting him—sending little messages and pictures—and he won't stop responding, within minutes of me reaching out. Maybe if I just cut him off, our time together could fade away into history. Maybe if I stopped pulling out that piece of paper and reading over the line he added, *he* could have the time and space he needs to realize that it's not true.

I don't see a good reason to let us fade, though. I don't want to give up on this yet.

But is this what my life with River will be like? A series of messages and pictures from thousands of miles away because he can't step off Irish soil? The thought makes me sick, so I push it away.

It's just after three o'clock here, which means it's two in Dublin. They have WiFi in the lobby, so I can touch base with him soon. While I don't want to lose exploring time, I need to clean myself up.

I'm just drawing water in the bath—a freestanding tub off to one corner—when a knock against the worn wooden door sounds. That must be the complimentary bottle of wine that the receptionist promised was coming.

I yank open the heavy door.

The sight of River standing there, a bag slung over his shoulder, steals my breath.

"We have caves in Ireland, too. You didn't have to make me come all the way out here," he murmurs in that light brogue that makes my heart pang. He steps into me, the familiar mix of soap and cologne stirring my senses, even though I'm still in shock.

"What are you . . . How . . ."

"You walked right past me in the lobby." He chuckles. "I've been sitting down there, waiting for you since noon. I figured I'd just follow you up here and let you drop your bags before I surprised you. Even the receptionist was in on it." A mock frown creases his forehead. "You know, you really should be more aware of your surroundings. It's gotten you into some trouble before. Have you forgotten already?"

That's why he wanted to know what time I was getting in. But, *how* is he here? A thought strikes me, along with a hint of panic. "You came here legally, right?"

He chuckles against my ear, sending shivers through my body. "My passport came through two days ago."

"Seriously? Why didn't you tell me!" I'm laughing, even as tears slide down my cheeks. Because I'm just so incredibly happy.

He tosses his bag to the rustic tile floor, and then, with his hands free, he ropes his arms full around my body. "I was afraid I'd have issues with customs once I landed, and I didn't want to have to explain that to you, if I was sent back. Duffy warned me that they rarely ask about a criminal record but, if they did, not to lie."

"*Detective* Duffy?"

"Yeah, I helped him out with some information on an extortion case for this fella who owns a few chips shops around Dublin, and he agreed to sign my application for me as a guarantor. Can you believe it?" He smiles sheepishly. "He's actually alright."

"So . . ." I can't help but simply stare up at his handsome face for a long moment. He's here, in the flesh, on my adventure with me. "I just can't believe that you're here. For how long?"

He shrugs. "As long as you're in the EU and I don't run into trouble. You still have Greece and the Czech Republic, right?"

"And Germany."

"Then I guess for a while. Assuming you're okay with that." His mouth seals over mine in a kiss. That uncontrollable physical craving for River comes alive again, as it always seems to when I'm around him, lighting a fire in my veins.

"So?" He releases me and wanders over to shut the running water off. "What are we going to see first? I passed a church in a cave not far from here. Thought you'd like that."

I look at the tub—now half-full of water—and at the bed. "You want to go sightseeing right *now*?" All thoughts of exploration disappeared the second I laid eyes on him.

"I do. Right now." He pulls me into his chest, the feel of him hard against my stomach contradicting his words. "And then I want to come back here, light all these candles . . ." He kisses me again. ". . . and tell you a story about a lowly Irish peasant bartender who falls in love with a beautiful American princess." He kisses me yet again, hard enough that I don't think we're going to get past the door at all today. "Do you want to hear that one?"

I do. I may not have all this figured out, but whatever time and space I've gained from leaving River hasn't changed what I've struggled to accept as possible until now. "Only if it ends with her falling in love with him and them living happily ever after."

Rich green pleading eyes stare down at me. "I truly hope it does."

EPILOGUE

AMBER

"Look at that! Me pint seems to be empty around the same time that me instrument cocks up. Now, how's that?" Collin chirps over his microphone.

I look across the bar to River, who's already holding a glass to the Smithwick's tap, shaking his head at their demanding musician. He's grinning, though. He's been grinning all day since the first customer walked through the doors of Delaney's at eleven this morning. A steady stream has followed since, old regulars and newcomers, curious to step foot into the "new and improved" Irish pub.

It's a zoo in here now.

Fourteen months after the bombing, with overwhelming support from the community to get the new building up and running, River and his family are once again pouring pints. They've done surprisingly well to replicate the look of the old place with antiques and mismatched tables that fit eclectically well.

"Would you mind passing this on to him so he'll start playing again?" River leans across the bar to chase the request with a kiss. He's also been doing that all day, and all day yesterday, since picking me up from the airport.

I weave through the crowd with the pint in hand, narrowly avoiding several elbows and backs.

"Oh . . . I must be special, to have this one serving me." Several whistles sound around the crowded bar and my cheeks burn at the attention. "Thanks, love." Collin winks at me once before sucking back a large gulp. He sets his glass down beside him and begins strumming his guitar again. "Would you look at that? Is there anything beer can't fix?"

A chorus of "no!" explodes.

"Amber!" Marion hollers from her makeshift station some fifteen feet away, stirring a cauldron's worth of stew that sits on a portable heating element. "Ya must be hungry!" River said she's been cooking for days, getting ready for the grand opening.

"I'm good, actually!" I yell back, because it's getting so loud in here.

"You're too skinny. Come here and take this now. Don't make me call your father and tell him ya turned your nose up at me stew."

Rowen passes between us with a tray full of drinks, his stride different from before but solid. If I didn't know better, I wouldn't know he relied on a prosthetic leg. Luckily the nerve damage that the doctors warned about is minimal. "She's trying to fatten you up so you can bear her grandchildren."

I laugh, though I'm sure he's right. I've traveled back and forth from Portland to Dublin nearly once a month for almost a year now, and I don't think I've left once without Marion or Seamus making a comment about a wedding or a baby. "River said you and your old girlfriend have been spending a lot of time together. Maybe you two can hurry it up then?"

He snorts. "Irene and I are just friends. She can't handle all these birds clamoring all over me, waiting to get a look at my stump."

"*Oh my God.*" I smack him playfully across the arm, but I'm laughing.

He grins. "By the way, have you seen Ivy lately?"

"No, but I talked to her. She's loving San Francisco." Ivy's a bit of a nomad, it would seem. She left Dublin last fall, ready for another change. I keep meaning to go down and visit her in California.

"Good. Well . . . tell her I said hi when you talk to her next."

"I will. She'll be happy to hear that." Whatever they were to each other, I'm glad Rowen and Ivy left things amicably.

"Amber!" Marion slops a spoonful into a Styrofoam cup and holds it out to me, her expression stern. Seamus sits beside her, watching with amusement.

"You had better take it before she tries to spoon-feed you," Rowen warns.

I make my way over and accept the cup with a smile, earning her nod of approval. "Grand turnout, isn't it?"

"It is! I'm so happy for you."

She lifts her pint in the air. "And for you. You've been a blessing to us all, lending your help, bringing such joy to River in these difficult times." Sadness flickers in her eyes as she takes a sip, and I know she's thinking about her oldest child. River told me that she visited him just last week, on his birthday, after months of no contact from anyone in the family. She's the only one who has. Apparently, he begged her to try and convince his brothers to see him.

I can't bring myself to persuade River to visit.

"Amber!" River waves me over to join him behind the bar. I've spent so much time in Delaney's in the last two months, helping get it ready, that it feels comfortable for me now. I even know how to pour a perfect pint of Guinness. Rowen and I have regular competitions.

River holds one arm out and I happily settle against his chest, willing to stay right here until my plane leaves for Oregon in five days. He nods toward someone. "Look who decided to visit us."

I turn and find myself face-to-face with Detective Garda Garret Duffy.

"He even ordered a beer. Can you believe it?" River jokes, setting a pint down in front of the lanky man.

Duffy dips his head. "Good to see ya, Amber."

I smile at the sound of his leprechaun accent. "You too. I hear you've been busy." I'm much more in tune with Ireland's happenings than I am of those of my own country now, especially since last October when Jimmy Conlon—the mastermind behind the St. Stephen's Green bombing and the head of the "IRA" gang that Aengus belongs to—was gunned down on a quiet side street at night. Three months after that, someone killed his rival—that Beznick guy—in prison. The prison that Aengus is serving his time in. They have yet to charge anyone with either murder.

"I have. Cheers." He lifts his glass and takes a sip. "So . . . River tells me you've been doing a lot of traveling. Must be tiring. And expensive."

"It is," I admit. I'm basically working at the hospital to pay for flights. I think my dad's going to have a coronary soon. "But it's worth it."

"Have ya given any thought to applying for a longer stay?"

"I have," I say warily.

"And?" Duffy's eyes twinkle as they flash to River's. "What's stoppin' ya?"

My suspicious nature tells me this isn't so much a curious bystander's question as something the two of them have orchestrated. Peering up at River's mock-innocent face, his jaw covered in a day's worth of stubble, I can't help but laugh. "First your mother, now the police. Do you have no shame?"

He grins. "I won't give up. Never. Not until you tell me to go to hell, and even then, I'll still be waiting."

I stretch onto my tiptoes to kiss him.

"Would you just say yes so the bastard will start pouring beer again?" Rowen yells from his side of the bar, earning a bunch of cheers.

"Alright, already. Quit your whining," River hollers back, kissing me once before pulling away to grab two empty glasses with skilled hands. "Maybe if you weren't so slow . . ."

Rowen throws his arms up. "Can ya believe this? Have some respect. I'm an amputee!"

I shake my head at the two of them as they get the crowd riled up with their banter.

"Amber." Duffy leans in. "In all seriousness, I have a few

connections which should make some of the approvals easier. Of course, you'd still need to meet all the requirements if you want to work, but I can help. *If* you're ready."

I smile.

And nod.

confluence:

A flowing together of two or more rivers or streams;

a coming together of people.

Amber's Travel Bucket List

1. ~~Have a torrid affair with a foreigner. Country: TBD.~~

✓ 2. Stay for a night in Le Grotte della Civita. Matera, Italy.

✓ 3. Go scuba diving in the Great Barrier Reef. Queensland, Australia.

✓ 4. Watch a burlesque show. Paris, France.

✓ 5. Toss a coin and make an epic wish at the Trevi Fountain. Rome, Italy.

✓ 6. Get a selfie with a guard at Buckingham Palace. London, England.

✓ 7. Go horseback riding in the mountains. Banff, Alberta, Canada.

✓ 8. Spend a day in the Grand Bazaar. Istanbul, Turkey.

✓ 9. Kiss the Blarney Stone. Cork, Ireland.

✓ 10. Tour vineyards on a bicycle. Bordeaux, France.

11. Sleep on a beach. Phuket, Thailand.

✓ 12. Take a picture of a Laundromat. Country: All.

✓ 13. Stare into Medusa's eyes in the Basilica Cistern. Istanbul, Turkey.

✓ 14. Do NOT get eaten by a lion. The Serengeti, Tanzania.

✓ 15. Take a train through the Canadian Rockies. British Columbia, Canada.

✓ 16. Dress like a Bond Girl and play a round of poker at a casino. Montreal, Quebec, Canada.

✓ 17. Make a wish on a floating lantern. Thailand.

✓ 18. Cuddle a koala at Currumbin Wildlife Sanctuary. Queensland, Australia.

✓ 19. Float through the grottos. Capri, Italy.

✓ 20. Pose with a stranger in front of the Eiffel Tower. Paris, France.

✓ 21. Buy Alex a bracelet. Country: All.

✓ 22. Pick sprigs of lavender from a lavender field. Provence, France.

23. Have afternoon tea in the real Downton Abbey. Newberry, England.

✓ 24. Spend a day on a nude beach. Athens, Greece.

✓ 25. Go to the opera. Prague, Czech Republic.

✓ 26. Skinny dip in the Rhine River. Cologne, Germany.

27. Take a selfie with sheep. Cotswolds, England.

✓ 28. Take a selfie in the Bone Church. Sedlec, Czech Republic.

✓ 29. Have a pint of beer in Dublin's oldest bar. Dublin, Ireland.

✓ 30. Take a picture from the tallest building. Country: All.

✓ 31. Climb Mount Fuji. Japan.

✓ 32. Listen to an Irish storyteller. Ireland.

✓ 33. Hike through the Bohemian Paradise. Czech Republic.

✓ 34. Take a selfie with the snow monkeys. Yamanouchi, Japan.

✓ 35. Find the penis. Pompeii, Italy.

✓36. Walk through the war tunnels. Ho Chi Minh, Vietnam.

✓37. Sail around Ha long Bay on a junk boat. Vietnam.

✓38. Stay overnight in a trulli. Alberobello, Italy.

✓39. Take a Tai Chi lesson at Hoan Kiem Lake. Hanoi, Vietnam.

✓40. Zip line over Eagle Canyon. Thunderbay, Ontario, Canada.

✓ 41. Rent a moped. Greece.

✓ 42. *Barely avoid mutilation and/or death by pipe bomb: Dublin, Ireland.*

✓43. MAKE A FOREIGNER FALL MADLY IN LOVE WITH ME. IRELAND.

ACKNOWLEDGMENTS

If you're reading this now, it is because you have made it to the end. I hope you made it here with a smile. I had so much fun writing this book and creating Amber and River's story. Perhaps it is because I was just in Ireland last year, and it sparked a great deal of nostalgia. Perhaps it is because of my weakness for all things Irish. Whatever the reason, I'm desperate to visit there again, this time armed with a great deal more knowledge of the country's rich history and its struggles.

Thank you to my readers, who continue along with me on this journey. Whether you buy a print copy at your local bookstore, order it online, or borrow from your library/sister/friend/mother, you are helping to give me the opportunity to write books.

A special thank you goes out to a few readers in particular:

To the bloggers who continue to share my book releases within their world.

To my followers on social media, who answer the random questions I put out there every once in a while, when I'm trying to gain insight that's not clear from my Google searches.

To the readers who helped me come up with ideas for "Amber's Travel Bucket List" at the end of this book. Of course, when they submitted entries into the contest, they didn't know exactly how I'd use those ideas. There were many great entries and it was a difficult process to select a handful. Thank you to Amanda Pedulla, Danielle Beckles, Kate Kirk, Amy Barnes Smith, Amanda Tse, Kaley Stewart, Jenny Doss, Peggy Ryan, and Maddalena Di Rienzo, for providing ideas that worked best for this story and for Amber.

To Stefanie Smith—my resident Irish "bird." I put out a request on Facebook a few months back, looking for a reader from Ireland who would be willing to answer random questions from me. Stefanie accepted that challenge and soon found herself being quizzed about all things Ireland, IRA, and the like. I'm not entirely sure that she didn't soon regret accepting the job, but she has tolerated me for over two months, providing answers and invaluable advice. Thank you so much, Stefanie (and Ray, the very knowledgeable chef!).

To my publicist, KP—for keeping the momentum going while I'm deep in my writing hole and for running to my aid when I come out in a panic.

To my agent, Stacey Donaghy—for your mutual love of all things Irish. Sometimes I think you are my own personal Superwoman, there to save me when I need it.

To my editor, Sarah Cantin—Every time I submit a first draft to you, I bite my nails in anticipation that you're going to come back and tell me that I just can't take it there. I swear, as I typed "IRA" into the first draft of this book, I was sure it would be this time. Thank you for, once again, letting me run with it.

To my publisher, Judith Curr, and the team at Atria Books: Suzanne Donahue, Ariele Fredman, Tory Lowy, Kimberly Goldstein, and Alysha Bullock—I get complimented all the time on what beautiful books I have, and I owe that to you.

To Lia and Sadie—You recently asked me why my books don't have pictures in them. I said that all the words put together make a picture. That sparked a round of "why" questions as well as some frowns. I can't wait until you're old enough to see that picture.

To Paul—your cooking, cleaning, and laundry skills are far better than mine.